THE REMARKABLE JOURNEY OF WEED CLAPPER

GWEN BANTA

For my family, whose love has never allowed for injustice.
And for Eric, who is sharing his Cheerios with Abraham,
Martin and John.

PROLOGUE

DEAR MURRAY,

I'm trying to write this on the bus, but the bumps are a challenge... not nearly as much of a challenge as the fumes are though. I'll be asphyxiated before I ever get to Indiana.

I'm sorry I got choked up at the station. It was really sad to see you and your folks waving good-bye. Thanks for saving the day by cracking me up with the straw-up-the-nose trick. That's always a crowd pleaser.

Tell your folks how much I appreciate them offering to take me in. I can't believe the Pennsylvania Gestapo for Hapless Kids thought it would be better for me to live with a relative I don't even know instead of with the family Goldberg. How many good-byes can a guy take?

I'm looking out the window at nothing but miles of flat land. These may be America's fruited plains, but there isn't a dang fruit in sight. It's the saddest expanse of nothingness I have ever seen. Even the Midwest cows look bored. Local farmers

1

would be wise to stay vigilant. A news alert of a Bovine Suicide Pact wouldn't surprise me in the least.

We hit a bump a while back and blew a tire, which was the only form of excitement we've had in hours. The bus driver stepped in cow crap, so now the whole bus reeks. I probably don't need to point out the obvious metaphor for my life. I suggested to the driver that they change the name of the bus line from Greyhound to Grave-bound, because this trip through the wasteland seems terminal.

Please don't forget to take flowers out to my folks on holidays, okay? There's a little bronze holder you can stick them in. And take Leland that stuffed animal I left him, but remember to put it in a plastic bag so the rain doesn't ruin it. He'll like that.

I'll finish this letter later. Right now I need to talk to the bus driver to find out where we are. I'm actually considering getting off the bus at the next stop. The one thing about being on your own is that you can disappear without too much fuss. Now that I think about it, I guess I've been doing that for a long time. Thanks for everything, Murd-man.

Your pal,

Weed Clapper
    August 23, 1960

CHAPTER ONE
SEPTEMBER 6, 1960

I THINK A GUY'S NAME MUST HAVE SOME BEARING ON HOW his life will turn out. Malcolm Clapper... now that's a peculiar name to be saddled with, huh? I suspect my mom was still sucking on the ether tube when she labeled me and my kid brother, Leland. Maybe she was hoping for a unicycle act. Anyway, as a result of my lean frame, I ended up with a good nickname, 'Weed.' Since Ginsberg and all the Beats smoke weed, I think my nickname gives me an air of sophistication. And it's a darn sight better than 'Peaches.'

Seeing as how I just moved to this hick town two weeks ago, my plan is to tell everyone here I got the name 'Weed' from smoking tons of dope with a real tough crowd back in Scranton. I figure a good addict story might scare off prairie thugs who have a hankering to mess with new kids like me. To ensure my safety, I might even hint that the dope habit has left me prone to violent outbursts. Insanity can be a good deterrent.

Being nearly eighteen, I should be a senior, but I was held back a grade for missing too much school last year. Thus, my prolonged high school career is NOT the result of an I.Q. depletion problem, as you might have concluded. Actually, the higher-learning authorities recently told me I'm a "near genius" in the I.Q. area. Seriously! Of course, they added way too quickly that I'm the most sorry-ass underachieving near-genius they've ever come across in their thrilling careers... which is kind of an achievement in itself, I'd say.

Frankly, I've decided I've had enough school. Even an under-achieving genius knows that much. But the authorities convinced me to live here on the prairie with my grandmother, who I hardly know, until I get an official diploma. I won't get my folks' life insurance money until this December when I turn eighteen, so it's not like I had a lot of other choices. So here I am stuck in the middle of the Indiana farm belt. It's dismal.

This place is a lot different than Scranton. The land in these parts is flat and dusty with acres of nothing but yellow. Ordinarily I don't mind yellow, but this is the loneliest yellow I've ever seen. It reminds me of old lady skin. And you wouldn't believe how sickening the air is. I heard there's a factory on the outskirts of town where they make corn products. When the corn is cooking, the air in town turns a dreary brown. You can *taste* the odor. It smells like infected feet. I'll never be able to face a bowl of corn flakes again without thinking of plantar warts.

Today I somehow tolerated the skin-coating stench long enough to make it through my first day at my new school. I was trapped in a hot classroom checking out the nearest escape routes when a vision by the name of Miss Saslow strutted through the door like Marilyn Monroe. I bolted upright in my seat faster than a launched Sputnik. Her skirt was wrapped around her hips so tight it was panting. (Well, okay, that was *me* doing the panting.) Anyway, she's beautiful and very young for a teacher. I wouldn't be surprised if she was sent by the Russians just to confuse America's youth.

Miss Saslow, who immediately became 'Sassy-Ass' in my lascivious mind, welcomed us to our junior year before going off on a tangent about how the teen years can be challenging. She suggested we seek support from others or even write about our emotions in a journal. I sensed she was implying that repressed feelings could harm a growing body. That sure got my attention because ever since my life turned to disaster last year, a lot of stuff has been festering inside me.

I was thinking it all over when Russell Kinney, the sap who was vegetating next to me in class, actually raised his hand and asked Sassy-Ass who a guy should talk to if he has "nobody who will listen." I was sure the collective groan for world-class rejects could be heard at the Pennsylvania Deaf School.

Before I could turn away to keep from staring at pathetic Russell, Sassy-Ass looked straight at *me* and urged us to come to see her if we ever "need a feel." (Well, perhaps she actually said, "need a friend," but my overactive imagination often affects my ability to hear.)

I was struggling to keep my manhood in check when Russell, obviously too dumb to let a chance to be even *dumber* pass him by, fell out of his chair. Yep, just up-and-fell. I'm serious. Sassy-Ass, who must have been totally alarmed to discover she had a full-blown freak loose in her classroom without arm restraints, covered it well... but I thought I'd soil my pants.

After her class, there seemed to be no reason to hang around the institution, but I forced myself to stay till lunch. Guys my age can't miss meals. The school feeds those of us with limited funds, so I'm "government subsidized." They've mistaken me for a crop of soybeans.

Even lunch was a trial. After the human boil sitting next to me dumped ketchup all over his spaghetti, I moved away to eat by myself. I saved my Jello for my brother Leland, which is a habit I can't seem to break even though Leland died last year. Eventually I offered it to a goofy little squirt with no front teeth, because all kids like Jello.

You might be wondering what a young boy was doing in the cafeteria. Well, this town is so small that elementary students are in the same building as us adult types. Frankly, I don't see how it can be good for innocent little kids with lunch pails to be surrounded by flying teenage sex hormones. Anyhow, when I spotted some more cute first-graders who reminded me of Leland, I felt a real sadness bearing down on me, so I ditched school and headed for town.

Along the way to the center of nowhere, I decided to stop by Searles Corner Sundry Store for a Coke. The store is actually a pharmacy that sells gift items, tobacco, books, and other stuff out of necessity because there are only a few stores in this booming two-street metropolis.

I have to admit, my mood lightened the minute I entered the place. An old tune called "Blue Moon" was playing. As I see it, that song is all about hope. I could really use some hope, so I took my time looking around. As I browsed through the books on a spinning rack, I found a Steinbeck I haven't read (*Sweet Thursday*) and a comic book Leland would've liked. Then I spotted a counter display of Old Spice Aftershave. As I took a whiff, I imagined my dad in the bathroom getting ready to go off to the Scranton Firehouse. It was a nice memory, but I had to let it go before the sadness could catch up.

What got my attention next was an old soda counter in the back of the place. Nearby there were four booths covered with bright red vinyl the color of candy apples. Miniature chrome jukebox machines were mounted to each tabletop, so the whole area felt pretty lively. I took a counter seat and was just opening my book when I heard a tone of voice I didn't take to too much.

"You planning on paying for that?"

No, I plan to rip out the pages, wipe my ass a few times, then make a big collage out of it. Well, that's what I wanted to fire back at the guy whose badge announced he was Mr. Searles. In my mind he instantly became '*Snarls.*'

"I'll be paying, and I'll have a vanilla Coke," I replied... but not too friendly myself. (Honestly, I'm a really nice guy in spite of how this sounds, but my nerves are a bit on edge these days.)

"Hmmm, all the other kids order cherry Cokes," Snarls sniffed, like he was the Betty Crocker of fountain drinks.

"Cherry Cokes taste like Smith Brothers' Cough Drops," I grunted, shooting my informed opinion right back at him.

"Harrrummmph."

No kidding, that's all he said. It was as if he'd been savoring a huge loogie in his throat for weeks before suddenly hacking it up to run around his pipes like a frenzied squirrel.

Snarls is a fascinating human. He's nearly bald, but in the middle of his sunburned crown there's a wild tuft of orange hair that seems to be shellacked into a permanent point. Imagine a baboon's ass holding the flag of Russia aloft and you'll get the idea. And his body is, well, oddly lumpy. I was still gawking at him when he served my soda.

"Wait a minute," he said, "are you Ollie's grandson?"

"Yes, sir," I mumbled as I took the drink.

"Ollie told me you were gonna live with her awhile," he nodded. I nodded back at him and forced my mouth into a respectful smile because my mom and dad raised me right.

The 'Ollie' he was referring to is Olivia, the grandmother I never knew until she agreed to take me in so I wouldn't be sent to some bleak home for sniveling orphans and orphanettes run by big-ass hairy

7

nuns in orthopedic shoes who alleviate their repressed anger on their snot-nosed prey...according to persistent rumors.

"Your grandmother told me you'd been badly injured, son," Snarls was saying. "But you look fit as a clam to me."

Not feeling good about where the conversation was going, I shot him a weak smile and made a note to ask Ollie to please zip her lip about me. Meanwhile, I opened my book and tried to ignore the sultan of sodas.

"Ollie sure is a good ol' girl. She's more fun than a barrel of fish," Snarls offered up in another effort at conversation.

What I wanted to tell Snarls was that he sure knew how to pummel a cliché, but I held my tongue so as not to make trouble for Ollie, who has been really nice to me. I tried to sit in silence, but Snarls was undeterred.

"I'm very sorry your family got killed, son."

Snarls's words crept up on me out of nowhere. They were so soft and gentle I wanted to stick a fork into his sad-looking eyeballs. It's hard for me to explain why. It's just that I've seen that look too many times these past months, and it always makes me feel drag-ass shitty and all jumbled up inside.

As I was thinking of a way to change the subject, I was distracted by the oddest guy I've ever seen...even stranger than Snarls. The guy, who looked only a few years older than me, was leaning on the counter staring at a pack of Luckies and bobbing his head. He had only one arm, and he kept grabbing for his missing arm. It was really unsettling.

When he turned to look at Snarls, I was shocked to see that the guy had only half a face. I swear to God. Part of his head looked melted. I tried not to stare, but I'm only human. His skull had a deep crevasse, as though his brain had been sucked out through his eye socket. He was wearing dirty camouflage clothes—the kind soldiers wear. And his one and only eye blinked nonstop like film stuck in a projector.

I was pretending not to notice him when suddenly he gasped and backed away from *me* as if *I* was the freak. (See, I have an injured leg. It's a painful subject, which is why I'm just now mentioning it. It goes into spasms when I'm tired. I admit, it was shaking, but jeez-Louise, by the guy's reaction, you'd think my damn leg was about to exit my pants on its own and dance on his broken face!) When his jittery attitude changed to a look of sympathy, I tried to act as nonchalant as possible just short of whistling "Zip-a-Dee-Doo-Dah." But I felt real uncomfortable about *him* feeling sorry for *me*.

"Hey, help yourself to some smokes, Andy," Snarls bellowed in my ear so loud I damn near sustained a concussion. Andy grabbed the Luckies and then limped out like a man with a rabid dog affixed to his ankle. His limp is even worse than mine.

"That's Andy," Snarls said as if giving a benediction. "He's shell-shocked. Got hurt bad in Korea and hasn't been normal since. Andy can't make sense of much. His brain is gone along with half his body. Can't talk... quiet as a cabbage. He has lived here since he was a kid, so we all look out for him when we can."

I was happy to hear that because Andy looked real lost. After I chugged my Coke, I gathered my stuff before any other village atrocities could drop by. I couldn't have felt more agitated if I had a case of the crabs. Unfortunately, when I stood to leave, I almost fell, which sometimes happens when my bad leg has been dangling too long.

"The Coke is on the house," Snarls announced after he caught my little sideshow, "and the book, too." It was a nice gesture, I admit, but the sympathy in his voice landed square on my chest.

"Thank you, sir," my voice barked, which it sometimes does when my words get caught in my throat. Just to assure Snarls I could take care of myself, I laid down a big fat tip.

I couldn't wait to get outside and breathe in the odor of rancid cornhusks. Anything is better than the stench of pity. I suppose a poor guy like Andy is lucky enough not to notice it. But I sure notice when the pity is being aimed at me.

———

By the time I hit the road to Ollie's, the smell of rotten corn had blended with the smell of fresh horse droppings, and I wondered if I could hold my breath until winter. I can't walk as far as I once could, so when I saw a battered red station wagon coming my way, I decided to thumb a ride.

As the car pulled over, I noticed the driver was an old Negro man. He's one of the few Negroes I've seen in these parts, although there are plenty of 'NO COLOREDS' signs. The guy had the whitest hair imaginable. When he saw me looking at it, he shot me a huge grin. "They call me 'Cotton,'" he said, "Cotton McKamey. An' it ain't jus cuz I used ta pick it. I ain't able to bend over no mo', but I stills got dis white top 'case I ever forgit who I is." Cotton's rolling chuckle came from so deep inside his chest you would have thought he started it yesterday.

"Pleased to meet you, Cotton." He seemed surprised as I offered my hand. When he pressed his skin against mine, his hand was warm and rough. I liked that. "I'm Weed Clapper," I announced.

"Weed Clapper? Now, thas a name dat bears listenin' to. Where ya headin' to, Mr. Weed Clapper?" he asked.

"Back toward Highway 40 is close enough, sir."

"Right this way." He gestured toward the road ahead as if he was leading a procession to Oz. "Hop in."

I was rounding the car to the other side when a blue De Soto that was coming down the road toward us slowed to a crawl. Two young guys were in the front seat of the De Soto, and they were wearing real dark expressions. I figured they were peeved at having to slow down to pass us on the narrow curve, so I made a show of hurrying. As I reached for the door handle, a terrified look glued itself to Cotton's face. Suddenly Cotton yelled, "Sorry, Mr. Weed!" He then floored the gas pedal and took off. I had to jump out of the way just to keep from being thrown off balance.

After I regained my footing, I turned to the De Soto. The burly driver cleared his throat and then spit a gob out the window, just missing my foot. "Watch yourself, boy," the creep hissed. "We don't put up with no nigger lovers 'round here." Before I could give him crap about his bad manners, he peeled out, pelting me with gravel. I was dumbfounded.

I stood there in the middle of the road for several minutes before deciding that walking was better for my health. It gave me a chance to ponder why a grown man like Cotton feared two mouthy twerps enough to speed off and leave me in a cloud of dust.

By the time I got back to Ollie's, I was pooped. After only one week, the old farmhouse still seems strange to me even though Ollie keeps saying, "It's your home now, darlins." Yep, I'm "darlins." There's only one of me, I'm happy to report, but Ollie sees things in the plural, which I suppose is a good trait if you need extra friends.

As I arrived, I heard her singing along to "Mr. Sandman," so I sat outside awhile. When my mom used to sing that song, my brother and I would join in on the "bum-bum-bum-bum" part. I lingered on the porch and tried to hear Mom's voice in my head, but I couldn't. The more difficulty I had remembering, the more frustrated I became, so I got mad at Ollie for singing. I know it makes no sense, but I was getting so stirred up I was thinking about setting fire to her records. Just a small fire of course. Then Ollie bounded out the door.

"Malcolm! I didn't hear you arrive," she gushed. (Ollie is a real gusher.) "How was your first day at your new school?"

Sometimes my mouth gets going faster than a hamster on a wheel. I can't explain what comes over me —nerves, I guess. Normally I try to contain myself, but I was quite agitated by the time she hit me with the school assessment question. "Oh, it's a *great* place, Ollie. Very welcoming. They have initiation rituals for new inmates like me where the evil education attendants shove a pick up your nostril and scramble your brain into Spam until you crap your drawers. It's a real party atmosphere."

"Well, that explains the bad air," she grinned. "And it's nice to know you're partaking in extracurricular activities."

I couldn't help but grin back and settle down some. "It was tolerable, Ollie," I shrugged. "The kids are mostly farmers' kids—a sad group." When I noticed Ollie's face cave with disappointment, I mustered up a fast lie. "I did meet a few neat ones though," I reassured her, displaying enough teeth to sell toothpaste. "I'll probably hang out with them." The last part was a bit extreme, even for me, but it did seem to cheer up the old gal.

"You resemble your father when he was a kid," she sighed as she lumbered to the green metal glider that is older than prostitution. The glider groaned right along with Ollie when she lowered her ample self into it. "I sure wish we hadn't lost touch. I ache down to my bones to think about him sometimes."

When I got the sinking feeling I was in for some ear-bending, I got up to go in. I didn't want to abuse my body by stirring up a bunch of psychic pain.

Unfortunately, my trick leg went one way while I went the other way, so I sat back down much harder than I wanted to.

"It'll take those injuries some time to heal," Ollie solemnly pronounced as if she were an orthopedic fortuneteller.

I knew then that it was time to detour the conversation before it got maudlin. "Tell me about the carnival days," I blurted out in a not-too-smooth segue that was way too obvious. But what the heck, it's not like I was at a cotillion. Ollie was "Queen of the Carnival" in her day. In fact, that's all I've heard since I got here. The photos on the walls are proof that she's no rat-faced liar either, although some folks might think her "royal" distinction was sort of tawdry. Ol' Ollie loves to re-live those days.

"Well, Malcolm, as you know, I couldn't take care of your daddy when I worked with the carnival, so he lived with my mama."

"Where was your husband?"

"Your grandfather was killed while conducting a train."

I was just testing her. She told me only four days ago that my grandfather was blown to bits in a mining explosion. And once she said he drowned in the tub. I figure that unless my grandfather crashed a train into a mineshaft laced with dynamite while scrubbing his hairy back, old Ollie is fibbing. My bet is that she got herself into some trouble and had no husband. No doubt her libido was as big as she is. I'm not judging though, 'cause she's a real nice lady.

"Well, as I told you," she was saying, "I was the best dancer that carnival ever had. I did French style numbers in gorgeous costumes, and I was billed as Bounteous Beauty, Queen of the Carnival. I could shimmy like a pair of mesh panties, darlins. And I got to travel all the time. That's likely how you got the travel bug in you. The carny life is in our genes."

I figure I inherited the tent pole part of the carny chromosome, which is why I keep getting these embarrassing boners. You can practically *hear* them explode. I could get a stiffie for a donut if it was wearing a skirt. I didn't dare let my thoughts drift to Sassy-Ass Saslow in *her* tight skirt. The last thing a guy wants to do is lasso his woody in front of his grandmother. "I plan to travel when I get my pilot's license," I blurted, forcing myself back into the conversation.

"A pilot, huh? But darlins, what about your physical problems?"

"For criminy sake, I'll be better by then!" My response came out pretty cranky, but I couldn't help myself.

"I'm sure you will get better, Weed, dear," she nodded. "I once had a carny friend with a bad leg who was billed as Monkey Boy because he was completely covered with hair, even his face. He resembled a big SOS pad. That lovely man became a great dancer, even with that bad leg... and in spite of a major sweating problem. I used to love to cut a rug with him. Isn't it lovely that friends come in all kinds of packages?"

It took me a minute to hoist my jaw off the porch. All I could imagine was a fat lady and a dancing yak. But I suppose when freaks are your friends, you learn to accept the differences in folks. That's reassuring, especially if you have a deformed head, or excess hair, or black skin like Cotton's... or a bad leg like me. I admire Ollie for not being the judgmental type. Our conversation made me feel much better about the decision of the Scranton Hospital authorities to send me here to live.

When our fantasy stroll through Igor's House of the Hideous ended, I thanked Ollie again for her recent hospitality and went upstairs to my room to write a letter to Murray, and maybe start a journal. I figure Kerouac writes, and it's a known fact that he's cool. Besides, it may help me deal with the loneliness factor now that I'm temporarily stuck here on the plains with some *very* odd people. I still have this nagging feeling that something isn't right here.

CHAPTER TWO
SEPTEMBER 7, 1960

THERE ARE SOME REALLY STRANGE THINGS GOING ON HERE. Last night I heard something that sounded like a water buffalo loose on our porch, and I don't mean Ollie. I got up a few times to check things out, but I couldn't see anyone. Although Ollie was up, she says she didn't hear a thing. An embalmed person would have heard the clatter, so it's all VERY suspicious if you ask me.

Despite the ruckus, I finally nodded off with my bedroom lamp on. Before I knew it, Jolly Ollie was hovering over me like the Hindenburg. She then sat down on my bed nearly catapulting my limp body to Peoria. I don't know why, but I pretended to be asleep. When she touched my hair and whispered my dad's name, I got a real aching feeling. As Ollie was trying to reach the lamp switch, her big ol' water balloon of an arm brushed against my face, reminding me of how squishy my brother Leland was when he was little. I'm sure that's what set off my recurring dream—the one about Leland.

See, one day when Leland was five, I told him I was going to become a pilot and fly to tons of exotic places. Suddenly he burst into tears and grabbed me by the leg begging me not to fly away and leave him. It was awful. That's when I hoisted him onto my back and began to fly him around the yard. I promised he could fly everywhere with me forever.

We flew faster and faster, which got Leland giggling like a freckle-faced hyena. As we were about to make a crash landing in backyard Bangkok, I felt something warm running down my back. When I glanced back at the poor little guy, I saw that his smile had melted, and his eyes were getting soupy because he had laughed so hard, he had wet his pants.

As fast as I could, I lifted off again with the roar of a jet engine. "You clever kid," I yelled, "how did you know we needed re-fueling? Your quick thinking saved everyone. Even the President! Even the Brooklyn Dodgers! Let's hear it for Leland, everyone!" I clapped and cheered as loud as I could. Leland finally laughed aloud, and I wanted to keep flying forever.

Except for the part of the dream where my brother cries, it's a good dream, but it leaves me all messed up inside because I feel like I don't have any connection to my old life anymore. There's nothing left to ground me to this planet. I couldn't sleep after that, so I stared into the darkness for a long time.

By the time I dragged my bones to the education institution in the morning, I was sure I'd sleep through my classes, especially excruciating American History, where the books are older than Death and have the same effect on the inmates' senses. But today Mr. Kennealy's class actually *interfered* with my sleep.

It all started with a heated political debate about Nixon and Kennedy. It seems the locals see Kennedy as a Satan-spawned Irish Catholic. Carol Beth Harper (many of these folks have two first names, just in case they misplace one of them, I presume) said her dad, the local minister, was convinced Kennedy would end up "taking orders from the Pope."

Before anyone could challenge Carol Beth, Cowpoke Russell detoured the debate with the astonishing, "Mr.

Kennealy, I've got to take a wicked squirt!" thereby
proving there's no depth to which a loser can't sink. I
swear that poor guy must have a hat with an arrow
through it in a closet somewhere.

During Russell's embarrassing exit, we all began
talking at once. Jimmy Dale ("JD"), who looks like he
popped out of one of those teen idol magazines,
suddenly turned to Carol Beth and evened the political
playing field. "If Nixon was an honest politician, he
wouldn't have accepted a dog named Checkers," he
proclaimed. "Nixon isn't supposed to accept political
favors—not even for his virginal daughters. The 'no
political favors rule' applies even to mutts!"

"Well, that's a dang rude thing to call Nixon's
daughters!" Carol Beth shot back at him, which sent us
all into fits of laughter.

"Well, he's better than Kennedy!" yelled a blockhead
in the back named Willard. Kennedy is nothin' but a
dirty, nigger-loving Mick."

Suddenly I could feel myself getting all worked up.
See, one of my best friends back home happens to be a
Negro. And I happen to know that Kenton is a good
guy, no matter what hue he is. And no idiot is going to
tell me any different.

Unfortunately, Willard's disrespect didn't end there.
Cowpoke Russell, who had returned from his squirt
break just in time to overhear Willard's racial slur,
offered the very brave and equally senseless, "that was
a pretty dumb remark, Willard."

To my shock (and everyone else's) Willard jumped
out of his seat, walked over to Russell, and smacked
him on the head so hard it sounded like a gun shot.
Russell was stunned. When he held up his hands to
ward off another assault, I could see he was trembling.
Willard, whose face resembles a salt lick, smacked
Russell again. Right about then, my stomach jumped to

my throat. I just can't handle that whip-the-wimp mentality.

Although Kennealy yelled at Willard to sit down, Willard decided to give Kennealy some lip. "You shouldn't defend nigger lovers—not if you know what's good for you!" Willard threatened. Then he actually shoved Kennealy out of his way. Kennealy fell over a desk but somehow managed to stay on his feet. It was an explosive moment unlike any classroom drama I've ever witnessed. It was a moment of such heavy silence I could hear my hair grow.

Without thinking (not something I recommend, but something I've perfected), I grabbed Willard and stood right up to him, which was like looking into the eyes of King Kong. I told him he'd better apologize to Russell and Kennealy if he knew what was good for him.

Willard pushed my hand off his arm and rose up to his full height. It took him about ten minutes. My hindquarters retracted so fast my trousers had to hold on for the ride. However, I did not back down. He did.

Willard slowly shot me the wickedest grin you could imagine. He sort of smoothed my shirt like a mom would do, and then he mumbled real soft-like, "We aren't done here, boy. I'm saving you for something REAL special." Then he sauntered out the door like Brando on the waterfront. After a brief period of very loud stillness, Kennealy stormed out after him.

As I sat back down in my chair, I was a little too shaken up to revel in my momentary victory, but I did see Janine Steele actually smile at me. When a kid with the dubious name of Sprocket had the mercy to speak to pathetic Russell in spite of Russell's humiliating squirt break and near-annihilation at the hands of Willard, I felt like the world was evening out again. But I still had a growing fear about what lay ahead for me.

When second period rolled around, I had a near-religious experience, mostly due to what Sassy-Ass was wearing. She had on a sheer blouse, and underneath was this lacy slip that formed a heart over her mounds. She's really young. I think she looks almost as young as me. And she's pure-looking...like a saint with sex parts. It was holy.

While Sassy-Ass was talking, I decided to concentrate on the view. I must have concentrated too hard, because the unspeakable happened. As Sassy-Ass was passing out books, she whispered in my ear, "Take me, Weed." By the time I figured out that she had really said, "Take one, Weed," I had lost all control. The boner of my career as a horndog sprang to life and hurled me back in my seat like some sort of spastic marionette.

When I looked up, Janine Steele was staring at my crotch with two bulging eyes glazed over in horror. As I lurched forward (not a recommended move for a guy so flustered he can't corral his body parts), I dropped a HUGE book right on my 'Mr. Happy.' I thought I'd pass out... and not fast enough! I couldn't even scream because screaming requires breath. It's a damn ironic day when *Great Expectations* almost wipes out a guy's entire future.

To make matters worse, when I got up to leave my leg quit working, so I fell. I was clinging to my desk like a human paint drip when Russell was suddenly on me like fur on a ferret. As he struggled to get me up, I mumbled something about an old track injury from when I was All-State back in Pennsylvania. It was the best cover I could come up with in a tortuous moment in order to avoid a bunch of embarrassing questions about my leg.

After squirting Russell got me to my feet, he accompanied me to my next class. It was a long, long walk. I mean a L-O-O-O-NG walk. It was my own private Bataan Death March. I considered drowning myself in the drinking fountain for harboring an overwhelming desire to ditch the kind-but-colossally-nerdy Russell. My guilt was as bad as my mortification... so I ditched school instead.

Just as I was making my way toward the side door, Willard and another thug suddenly appeared. I tried to keep walking, but Willard's punk friend thrust out an arm to stop me. On the guy's forearm was a huge tattoo of an eagle with letters underneath that announced his name was Dean. His breath was like a badger's.

"Welcome Wagon?" I quipped, trying not to show my fear.

"Smart ass, huh?" Dean sneered. "You need to fix your attitude, punk! We don't take much to nigger lovers 'round here."

"Hmmm...so much for Midwestern hospitality," I opined.

"I wasn't trying to be hospile...hospitally," Dean grunted.

I had to suppress a laugh. The guy is so stupid you can see daylight between his ears.

That's when Willard took over. He pushed right in my face and growled: "Yeah, we have our own way of dealing with coon lovers. In fact, we straightened out a confused out-of-towner just last night." Both of them seemed to think that was pretty funny. "Keep your mouth shut, or you're next, gimp," he warned.

Before I could muster up a retort, Willard kicked me in my bad leg. Even though it was excruciating, I tried to stand tall like my dad taught me. While I attempted to right myself, Dean's fist connected square with my gut. The next thing I knew, I was flat on the floor. I could hear them laughing as I struggled back to my knees.

Raising my head, I spotted Miss Saslow in the hall. I was relieved and humiliated all at the same time as she stormed up and helped me to my feet. I prayed Willard wouldn't touch Miss Saslow, because then I'd have to kill him, and I was just plain out of steam. She shoved Willard aside and then reached out to touch my face. Tears suddenly flooded my eyes as my cheek tried to dissolve into the softness of her hand. She pushed my hair back and waited for me to get my balance. "Are you okay?" she whispered. Even though her warm breath on my face was strangely comforting, I turned away.

I remember pushing Dean out of my way and mumbling something about being okay before bolting through the nearest exit. As I slowly made my way into town, I tried to focus on the memory of Miss Saslow's touch instead of the throbbing pain that was crawling up my leg.

By the time I got to the sundry store, I was still thinking about the methods Willard might use to dispose of my carcass. I must have been slumping when I entered, because Snarls greeted me with a Sunday kind of voice, the kind with no edges to it. "'You down in the gills, Weed?" he asked. I wondered how he knew my nickname but was too preoccupied to inquire.

"I'm fine," I lied.

"Good, then you'll try a Dusty Road. It's on the house."

I'd never heard of a Dusty Road, but I was too down in the chops to ask for an explanation. I just sat there and watched Snarls dish chocolate ice cream into a big sundae glass then drizzle marshmallow on the top. Over the marshmallow, he sprinkled a large spoon of dry malt, apparently that was the "dusty" part. He then added whipped cream, nuts, and a cherry. It did perk me up a little.

I thanked Snarls twice, and then just to show I can be social, I struck up a conversation as I ate. "Where does shell-shocked Andy live, Mr. Snar-, uh, Mr. Searles?"

22

"Oh, here and there," he answered. "He's usually on the streets now that half his brain is buried in Ko-rea." (He pronounced it that way: "Ko-rea.") "I'm told he's been sleeping in a tent out near the lake, which is not far down the old back road. Been there yet?"

"No, sir, but a lake sure sounds good to me." Actually, any place far from Willard sounded good to me. "I think I'll go check it out," I told him. My mood had improved, what with the sugar and Chuck Berry winding me up with "Johnny B. Goode," so after I finished my ice cream, I thanked Snarls again and headed out to see if I could find something more exciting than extensive bodily injury.

I was enjoying the signs of fall when I just happened to spot Andy coming out of Coonsie's Tavern. He seemed to be staggering, but it was hard to tell because of his awkward gait.

"Hey, Andy" I called, but he didn't answer. I got the impression he was trying to sneak away because I saw him look back at me several times. For the heck of it, I decided to follow him as he headed out of town along a scenic back road. My leg was still aching, but my curiosity made my feet forge ahead.

Eventually, Andy stopped in front of a neat old farmhouse. He stared at the house while he lit up a smoke, then he crumpled into a sitting position under the most colorful maple tree this side of Pennsylvania.

I didn't know whether Andy was staring at the bright potted mums or the Indian corn on the door, but something sure got him going. He began to pant and whimper like a lost dog. So as not to startle him into blowing the remaining half of his cranium, I hid behind an old stone wall and watched.

When I looked up again, I saw a vision. It was Sassy-Ass! I can't say where she came from, but she went right up the steps into the house. I was glad to see how such a nice solid home just sort of embraced her.

As the door shut behind her, the Indian corn turned red in the sun.

I stared at the door a moment, but then my attention abruptly jumped back to Andy because he was becoming more agitated. Suddenly he threw his cigarette on the ground, pulled himself upright, and slammed his crushed head against the tree. You could HEAR it connect! I cringed, but before I could do anything to help the poor guy, he shuffled off into the woods.

As he lumbered away, I walked over to the tree to make sure his cigarette was out. What I saw ruffled the hair on my neck. On the ground was a pile of cigarette butts—all Lucky Strikes, which told me Andy has been lurking around Miss Saslow's house a long time. But why would a guy with a damaged brain hang around to watch Miss Saslow, I wondered?

I looked around the area as much as I could while trying not to be visible in case Miss Saslow came out. When I noticed some butts and an old sock near a window on the side of her house, I got even more worried. It's obvious that Andy's got some real emotional problems, which makes me very uneasy about her safety.

All the way home, my mind kept churning. It seems this place isn't as nice as it looks on the picture postcards at the sundry store. My gut says something bad is going to happen. It's like biting into a piece of sweet pecan pie and getting a shell... it makes a guy afraid to swallow.

———

Ollie was waiting when I got home. I wanted to ask her about Andy and about the Negro situation here, but after I took one look at her, I knew something was up. She was sort of flapping in place like a bird that doesn't

THE REMARKABLE JOURNEY OF WEED CLAPPER

know which way is south. "Where have you been, Malcolm?" she asked in a voice laced with forced sternness. That "Malcolm" bit told me the ol' bird had suddenly found her direction.

"Just walking home, Ollie," I answered.

"I can *see* you walked home. But I also know you've been doing it since lunch. Oh, Weed, I can't be a good substitute parent if I let things like that slide, now can I? I'm not sure how to deal with this. Why did you cut school, darlins? Now tell me, dear."

I waited a moment before speaking because I wasn't sure if she was done. If there's one thing I know, it's never to step in front of a runaway bus. "Jeez, I don't know, Ollie," I replied, having lost all desire to defend myself, "I just needed to escape."

I must have been listing to one side, because a concerned look pushed the sternness right off her round face. "Were your legs bothering you, dear?" she asked.

"Somewhat," I nodded, wincing for emphasis.

"Okay, I understand," Ollie sympathized, "...but how do you think I should discipline you for this sort of thing, darlins?"

My brain couldn't believe my ears. Ollie must have consulted *Robert's Rules of Order* before taking me in. She was asking ME to decide my own sentence.

I don't know what came over me. I must have blown a circuit because my mouth took off on its own as usual. I was helpless in its wake. "I know I need to learn my lesson, Ollie," I sighed, "but I hope you don't make me sit out tomorrow... it being 'Club Day' and all."

"Club Day? I've never heard of that."

"Well, it's mostly social. There are no regular classes. It's all part of the homecoming festivities. There will be food. Maybe music. And door prizes. And dancing at lunch." I had to stop myself before I threw in whiskey and naked women.

"Well, maybe you should miss it, Weed. Or is that too severe?"

"Of course not. I understand, Ollie." I almost added, "I think I should go upstairs now to think about my bad behavior" just for the thrill of saying it.

I'm ashamed to admit it, but as I climbed the stairs to my room, I began to feel good again. I would never want to hurt my grandmother, and I sure didn't intend to tell her such a whopper. But somehow I felt like I once again had some control over all the darkness that's been coming my way as of late. Sometimes it takes only a small win to keep a guy going. At least for a while.

CHAPTER THREE
SEPTEMBER 11, 1960

I DRAGGED MYSELF TO CHURCH TODAY AS AN ANTIDOTE FOR my recent lying binge. My tendency to fudge the truth shifted into fifth gear last Friday when I had to miss school to go to the hospital in Greencastle for a check-up. I rode the public bus for the ten-mile trip because Ollie doesn't drive. To pass time, I entertained a little Negro girl named Martha Jane who I met at the bus depot. I could tell she was scared about traveling alone, probably because of the "No Coloreds" graffiti that was all over the damn bus.

Some folks scowled when I sat in the back of the bus with her, but I figured they could just kiss my keister. On the way to Greencastle, I wove some fat stories about me going to pick oranges in California. Although the orange-picking story was a bit of a stretch, it was a *necessary* fib in my book. Little kids need distractions sometimes.

When I arrived in Greencastle, I said good-bye to Martha Jane and walked around awhile. The town is built around a square with a neat old World War II buzz bomb in the center. And there's a nice college named DePauw University.

Eventually I made my way to the hospital, where the sadistic and humorless Men-In-Coats poked my bum

leg with cold instruments as my bare ass set sail from
the back of a hospital frock. Doctor Stab gave me more
pills, but I'll probably toss them away like I always do
because I'm not sick. Stab (whose real name is Stack and
who is overly dramatic) insisted that I come back every
week for "aggressive treatment." I said I would, which
of course was another fat lie.

That's why I've been mulling over this lying thing.
You know, I'm really not a bad sort. I was raised by
good folks. My dad was a brave and honest man. In
fact, he was the Audie Murphy of the Scranton Fire
Brigade.

One time he saved old man Knapp when Knapp's
flat caught fire. A newspaper photo showed my father,
"A LOCAL HERO," emerging from the blaze with
Knapp and his little mutt. Dad told the reporter: "What
kind of a hero would leave a puppy to die?" But for all
of Dad's heroic efforts, old Knapp croaked anyway, so
we got the dog.

Mom named the dog Fritz because the poor thing
was always on the fritz. When Fritz began bouncing off
walls with a lot of foam coming out of his barker, my
father took the dog for a ride to the veterinarian. After
Dad returned, he explained to Leland that Fritz couldn't
come home due to distemper. Leland didn't know what
that was, but he let out the saddest wail I ever heard
and plopped his head smack down on the table.

Dad pulled the little guy onto his lap and started
babbling about how Fritz was such a friendly little
pooch he had qualified to live at Fluffy Farm in Forever,
Florida, where the trees are padded with cotton candy
so the dogs can bounce off them at high speeds. Then
Dad suggested that if Leland would just stop crying,
maybe he could even find a photo of Florida in the
encyclopedia.

After Leland calmed down, I was all over my dad. "I
know what you did with Fritz," I said. "So why did you

lie? Huh, Dad, huh?" I really needed answers. After all, it only stood to reason that if he was a liar, he could also be an ex-con, or a Commie, maybe even a transvestite. (I was just a kid.)

"I don't know, son," was all he said. That stopped me cold. Fathers are *supposed* to know these things. Although my dad was a HERO, he was obviously a grade-A moron. Suddenly it dawned on me that maybe my father wasn't even brave. Maybe he had distemper like Fritz, and he just ran aimlessly into fires due to being mentally limited. And worse yet, I was probably doomed to inherit distemper! It made sense at the time.

I was silently contemplating a future of shock treatments when my dad put his arm around me and uttered so softly I almost didn't hear him: "Children need time to understand the world, Weed. They need to learn life is wonderful—if you only let it break your heart a little bit at a time." In that moment I learned my dad was a true hero and that sometimes even a good guy spins whoppers.

The lying thing still puzzles me. I get confused about when it's okay to fudge a bit. I don't know what's right or wrong anymore. Lying is supposed to be BAD, yet this nasty anti-Negro attitude, which seems much worse to me, is quite acceptable to the folks who live in these parts. And Ollie seems to be hiding something from me, so I don't completely trust her... but she is still the nicest person I know. My confusion is growing huge, and Dad's not around to help me out. That's why I agreed to go to church with Ollie today. I needed answers.

I was up early anyway because I didn't get much sleep last night due to more strange nocturnal sounds. In an effort to appear wide awake, I chose my blue shirt, which compliments my dark hair and blue eyes. My teeth are capped, so I get some nice comments about my smile. And my nose was fixed when it got creamed in the same accident that smashed my teeth, so I have a good honker, too. When I was ready, I thought I made a nice impression. That is, until Ollie swept onto the porch like a human car accident.

She was wearing a dress so white and billowy that it could have accommodated a revival meeting. Ollie's make-up was electrifying, and her purple hat was so small her head seemed to be sprouting a cupcake. Poor Ollie pirouetted for me like a fat glockenspiel. She looked at me with such expectation that I had no choice but to let out a wolf whistle. Then off we went.

As we walked into town, we turned down a shady street that I had somehow missed in my search for big city thrills. The street was very different from our neighborhood back in Scranton where there are rows of attached houses. We passed cozy homes with wide windows. They were the sort of homes where the kind folks who live there probably have big Christmas dinners for all the Tiny Tims and Poor Little Match Girls who are invited inside for roast beef and plum pudding instead of being made to stand in the cold with their runny noses pressed up against the window until they pass out in dirty, hungry little heaps. You get the idea.

At the end of the street was a church that could have been plucked off a Christmas card. The doors were open, and the organ music filled the autumn air. It all started with such promise that I was thinking today might be the day when I would end my confusion and finally find God, who, as far as I can tell, has been in a coma.

When we approached a group of church types, I thought it odd that EVERYONE was white. And no one shook hands or even welcomed us. Snarls was there, and I'll at least credit him for flashing a smile. "Good morning!" he called. But his smile died when his bony wife abruptly yanked him in the direction of salvation.

When I heard someone snicker, I got all worked up. I couldn't help but be embarrassed by Ollie, who could have passed for a parade float. But at the same time, I was tormented over being so ashamed of such a kind person. My guts were in such an uproar I would have killed myself with my penknife, but it is rusted shut.

Then I saw a beak-nosed lady in a fancy hat raise her eyebrows as she appraised Ollie's cupcake hat. When I guided my grandmother past the arrogant woman, another tight-ass lady deliberately snubbed Ollie. In a split-second, my attitude changed. I suddenly became very protective of Ollie. I swore to myself that if anyone messed with Ollie, they'd end up with so much of Weed's Religion-of-the-Mighty-Fist shoved up their holy asses they'd be crapping communion wafers until the Second Coming. I grabbed Ollie's arm as if she were Jackie Kennedy and ushered her big-as-you-please into that House of the Godless.

I heard very little of the sermon, as I was thinking about how confusing all this God stuff is in the first place. We Protestants (a label which has been inaccurately attached to my person) are supposed to believe in the Trinity—God, Jesus, and the Holy Ghost all in one. That strikes me as being a crock. First, they tell you not to believe in ghosts, yet if it's the old Holy Ghost they're referring to, you have to make an exception. God is supposed to be almighty, but he has three personalities, and that can get you the ol' Frances Farmer loony bin treatment if you're a human.

It's no wonder kids get screwed up. When I was a kid, I thought Dad was God, and not just because Dad was a hero. Mom taught me a prayer which I thought went: "Our Father, alert in Heaven, Harold be Thy name..." My dad's name was Harold, so my conclusion wasn't as dopey as it sounds. But my friend Kenton informed me that if my dad was God, then he was a big wart. After we went a few rounds, Kenton recited the Lord's Prayer: "Our Father, a *wart* in Heaven..." I had to concede that Kenton had a point. That's when I set out to find out who *really* had the score on God. I had no choice in the matter.

When I discussed it with my other pal, Murray Goldberg, he told me the Jews are still waiting for the Son of God, "and we don't plan to kill Him like you did." I then turned my religious search toward Catholicism because they seem to have all the answers.

When I asked Mom about Catholicism, she explained how the Catholics have wooden closets where they can go to get instant forgiveness for their sins. To me, the Catholics seemed to be quite clever until Murray's cousin swore the Catholics were heathens who would burn in Hell for worshiping idols. We all sneaked into a Catholic church and, sure enough, there were idols of some questionable saints everywhere, so the whole question of which God is the *real* God remained.

When Murray and I were ten, he came over to my house crying one day because Liam-Bearer-of-Unbearably-Bad-Tidings-O'Gara had proclaimed that the "Jews had lost their way and were destined to wander the earth forever without so much as a place to hang a hat." Dad assured Murray it was obvious Liam was a pickle-brain because Murray had obviously found his way to our house, and he was welcome to hang his hat in our closet anytime he wanted. He also assured us that the purest religion of all is Love.

What my dad said made sense to us, but Murray and I still felt gypped because even blockheads like Liam O'Gara had the whole Catholic confession thing going for them. That's when Murray and I decided to confess to each other in my dad's tool shed. We even swiped some pop beads from Murray's mother to ensure proper procedure. Unfortunately, there are certain nocturnal habits a guy can't even confess to his best friend, if you get my drift. As a result, somehow that spring the sex and God thing got mingled. I suspect that happens to lots of us mortals.

Then one day Murray told me how an older kid on the block, Tommy Demetrius, told him about queers, which he said were guys who prefer "same-sex." Murray reckoned that "same-sex" must refer to when a guy rubs himself for his own perverted pleasure. I knew then I was doomed. And, according to Tommy, all queers became dancers in pink tutus and tiaras. That killed me. I had always planned to be a pilot, and I was sure there were rules against flying in a puffy dress. As a same-sexer, I was destined for failure.

I started praying every night, promising God I'd stop touching myself if He wouldn't make me wear a tutu. Somehow, that got me even more obsessed with my tooter. I couldn't keep my hands off it.

I decided to talk to my dad about becoming a Catholic so I could get pure over a string of pearls. I confessed how sometimes a guy could try his hardest and still have a devil of a time resisting sin, especially under the covers. Dad cleared his throat of everything except his tonsils and suggested that I just do something nice for someone else if I felt I needed forgiveness.

That night, the need to sin came on me worse than the measles, probably because I was in a weakened state from all my worry. After I same-sexed myself, I sneaked outside to do one of the things I hate most in life, reasoning that a deplorable task would help me accumulate points in my suffering for mankind. I dragged out the mower and cut the grass in the moonlight. I fell asleep on the lawn, wondering if I would have to move to Hollywood, which I had heard was a haven for the same-sex depraved.

The next morning I woke up as my father was carrying me into our house. I was covered with enough grass to start my own park. Mom's flowers were confetti, and there were big gouge marks in the lawn.

Dad took me aside and insisted I could rub myself anywhere I damn well pleased, and no stinking ghost-- holy or otherwise--would ever make me wear a tutu unless I damn well chose to. Not on *his* shift! In that moment, I knew that although my dad wasn't God, he was the closest thing, because I had finally found the only guy on earth who really could tell a kid the score.

Since Dad died, I haven't had any answers on the religious stuff. But when I was in church today with old Ollie, Reverend Harper told the congregation-of-the-confused that if we pray *in His name*, our prayers would be granted. Harper was so darn sure of himself for a puny weasel in white-tipped shoes that I took note. And I discovered what I had missed previously: the *IN HIS NAME* business.

I was mulling it over when the preacher added, "Of course, sometimes God refuses because He has something better planned for us." That sounded like a big rationale for God's erratic behavior to me. It was an excuse for God and all His personalities to let us down whenever he was feeling sadistic or hadn't taken His medication.

I wanted to stand up and shout out, "You're a stupid fool, and I'm going to yank out my tooter right now and same-sex-myself all over the place just to prove it!" However, I just didn't have the heart for it. There were some little kids in choir robes drawing on their hands, and I didn't want to ruin their innocence with a tooter caper.

At that instant I realized the preacher was looking right at ME. There was no mistake. His eyes were drilling into me so hard my backbone was welded to the pew. "Faith," he told me, "...you can never lose faith." I think he even muttered "Weed Clapper" under his breath because EVERYONE in Indiana was looking at me.

But the 'faith' word got to me. I remembered what

my mom often said: "Faith is believing that good still exists, even when all hope is gone."I suddenly realized that's really why I was in that church. I've been trying to find faith because my hope is in short supply right now, and I haven't seen any good in life since everything went wrong last year. I'm just a guy trying to find a reason to go on.

So today, right there in the pew-of-the-pitiful, I decided to give faith another shot. I asked for something. It was something small. I didn't ask for my mom and dad to come back because I didn't want to be selfish. But God never should have taken a little guy like Leland who never even got to ride his new bike or taste a Dusty Road or fly around the world with me. I knew God wouldn't make Leland rise up from the dead, but I just wanted to hug him and tell him he was safe, and that I never cared that he peed down my back. That's all. Just one lousy hug was all I wanted.

I just knew something was on the line here. If God failed me on this one, then I just wouldn't have any hope left to hang on to. But I asked anyway. *In His name.*

I was so worked up that it took me a moment to notice that the congregation was rising. I wiped my brow and jumped up so fast I dropped my hymnal. Then I banged my head trying to retrieve it.

In my flustered state, I almost didn't notice Janine Steele smiling at me from across the aisle. But I couldn't miss her. Not in that tight sweater. Not even in a house of God.

After church, Janine approached me. I was afraid she might want to spit on me because of the boner incident at school, but she was very nice. She told me there was a pep rally at the field house at seven o'clock and invited me to join her and Patty Lynn Stevens.

Before I could answer, Ollie suddenly blurted out, "What a good idea, especially after missing Club Day!" While Janine was flipping through her mental calendar of school events for Club Day, I promised I'd meet her at the pep rally, and then I dragged Ollie away from there as fast as she could waddle.

As we hustled off, I spotted Miss Saslow in the distance. She was talking to another teacher, but she saw me. When she waved, her smile was so dazzling I lost my hearing for a moment. I really did. She confuses all my senses.

———————

When I showed up at school for the rally, I had that fear of being in a room full of strangers and discovering toilet paper hanging out of my pants. As I arrived, I was surprised to see some Negro kids sitting together off to one side. I then glanced around to make sure there was no sign of Willard and Dean. They weren't there, but I did spot Janine, who signaled for me to join her on the bleachers.

The pep rally was peppy all right. I felt like a phony pretending to be full of school spirit like the rest of the frothing crowd. The truth is, I was more interested in what was going on five rows down. A guy who looked like a young William Holden was being very chummy with his date, despite her frequent reprimands. When he suddenly syringed her ear with one big, rude, energetic tongue, I realized that his date was Sassy-Ass. I didn't like that much at all.

After we moved outside for a big bonfire, I had a chance to drill Janine on the details of life in this bump on the map. She informed me that Sassy-Ass has been dating Rick Bills, a professor at DePauw, for a long time. According to Janine, Rick is "dreamy." I didn't let on that I think Rick has barely passable looks and should keep his sticky mitts off Sassy-Ass.

I decided to talk about my trip instead. When I was telling Janine about going to Greencastle, home of

DePauw and dreamy Rick Bills, I mentioned the little girl, Martha Jane Williams, who was on the bus. Janine sniffed, like she smelled a bad odor, and told me Martha lives on the edge of town with "the other coloreds."

I found her attitude pretty stupid. A lot of Negroes live back in Scranton where I'm from and we had a lot of fun together. When I told Janine about it, she informed me that "their kind" was certainly welcome here "as long as they behaved themselves." According to Janine, behaving means not mixing with white people. She added that it didn't mean white people couldn't reward "those folks" for their services. As proof, she related how her family had employed Cotton McKamey as a handyman, and they had even let his son eat on the porch. I sarcastically assured her it was such a congenial act that she might even get a trip to the White House out of it.

When I related the incident with Cotton, she said he should have known better than to stop to pick up a white man. That irritated me so much I announced that I planned to invite Martha Williams to sample one of Snarls's Dusty Roads over at the sundry store. Janine rolled her eyes the way she always does in class when she's frustrated by the malignant ignorance of others. "Negroes don't belong in *our places*," she sniffed, "and you shouldn't stir things up just to be contrary—it could be dangerous!" (Apparently, she hadn't gotten word yet of my scuffle at school with the Hitler twins.)

That got me going. It's my nature. Before I knew it, I was spouting off about how Negroes have been staging sit-ins in the South to force desegregation of lunch counters at Woolworth's and other places. "You know, we could change things here if we tried, Janine," I said. "Didn't you hear John Kennedy speak at the Democratic convention? Don't you want to be one of the 'new pioneers on the new frontier'?" Just saying those words got me fired up. My heart was pounding, and I wanted to call for a spontaneous Pledge of Allegiance. I might even have been eyeing a megaphone one of the cheerleaders had.

"The National Guard is probably already pin-pointing this place on a map and maybe even gearing up for an uprising of mythic proportions!" I further insisted. I was about to advise her to get herself a gas mask when she cut me off. And rather abruptly, I thought.

Janine scowled. "You are messing with something dangerous by mixing," she warned. "We've been having trouble around here. And you don't know as much as you think because you're not from this area."

"No, I'm from Planet Suck-My-Sausage," I almost said. Honestly, I was trying to be polite, yet I briefly thought about tossing her into the bonfire because she was so annoying.

"What trouble?" I pressed.

After a sufficient number of pregnant sighs, she patiently explained to me how Negro men just have to look at white women to get sex ideas, and so I shouldn't be so hell-bent on stirring things up.

"Well," I concluded, "then I must be a Negro because I can't look at too many women without having sex ideas myself." I figured Janine was extremely naive not to know these things. I can't be the only guy in this town who would make out with a less-than-attractive field turnip if it was doused in Chantilly perfume.

Just as I scored my point, I had to shut up while the coach introduced the football team, a puny looking bunch. Meanwhile, I wondered what I was doing at a rally full of hyper-enthusiastic and very narrow-minded strangers. I was trying to swallow a real sad feeling when Janine asked me to walk her home. I said yes because it beat being alone.

When she added that I could hold her hand if I

wanted, I decided that an effort toward peace was reason enough to initiate physical contact.

We got all the way to her house before I got up the nerve to kiss her. When I finally made a move, she opened her mouth and unwound a tongue that could win blue ribbons on the rodeo circuit. Janine should give her tongue a name and buy it a saddle. I was so impressed I almost didn't notice that I wasn't aroused. When I *did* notice, I feared I had same-sexed myself to tiara land. Then it dawned on me that Janine smelled delicious—like peanut butter, and I last smelled peanut butter when I was wrestling with Leland on his eighth birthday. He was wearing my old coonskin hat, which kept falling over his eyes causing him to bounce off the furniture the way Fritz did. My brother had just eaten peanut butter, so he had a sticky face and bread in his teeth. I laughed every time he opened his mouth.

So, there I was with Janine in my arms, but I felt as though I was hugging Leland. It was too real to describe. Suddenly it occurred to me that maybe that's how God answers prayers--in an obtuse way through others... although you'd think He would have better communication skills. I'm willing to consider the possibility of it all. But I need someone to help me get clear on all this.

I've decided to talk with Miss Saslow about all these recent events. Maybe she can help me understand what's right in this very wrong world. And things like why I'm alive even though the rest of my family got slaughtered. And I plan to talk to little Martha Jane and Cotton, too. I want to know what they're both so afraid of. Janine's warning against "stirring things up" doesn't mean a hoot to me. I'm not afraid, not even of dying; it's the 'living' part that I'm not so sure I can handle.

CHAPTER FOUR

SEPTEMBER 12, 1960

LAST NIGHT'S GLORY WAS MORE SHORT-LIVED THAN I expected, but for a while, I was James Dean. At school, Janine was hanging on me like an extra sleeve. She said the girls all think I'm "handsome and mature," and the guys say I'm cool because I dress hip, being from a big city and all. I was feeling great until she turned to me like I was a carnival sideshow attraction and asked how long I'd limp the way I do.

I had no choice but to make up some story about how my old track injury was getting better until a lady on the bus to Greencastle dropped her four-ton suitcase on my leg. I don't know why I lied that way, but I think Janine had it coming.

When Janine mentioned she had heard some speculation about polio, I told her it was a damn crock. "Even if a person did have polio, it wouldn't make them a twisted cripple," I snapped. "Look how fast Wilma Rudolph ran in the Rome Olympics, and she couldn't even walk till she was four due to polio. And if I had polio, then how did I win the East Coast Division of Track and Field where I set records and won buckets of money, which I plan to spend on a jazzy new Thunderbird, huh? Answer me that, Janine!"

That shut her up fast. Still, I didn't have the heart to

hang around after that, so I decided to ditch and go somewhere to read my new book. Steinbeck makes me believe there are real Joes out there who accept a guy for whatever he is. No one cares about physical anomalies in Monterey. It's a democratic environment.

I was walking through town when I heard about as much commotion as you can find among the barely living. After I got to the scene of the action, I learned that an old lady named Mrs. Byrd had rammed her car straight into the war monument which sits, if-you-please, smack dab in the middle of the only intersection in town. It occurred to me that perhaps the old gal intended the ramming as a social comment.

You can't miss the monument, even if you're unconscious. It's bigger than the town, and it's a MacArthur-on-a-horse-of-course. The horse's ass alone could double as a bomb shelter. The town forefathers had the bright idea to point the horse North, so cars have to pass under his sphincter to make a left turn. It's a symbol of how life craps on your head when you least expect it.

Back to the old lady: She was propped up in the seat, and her hair was suspended a foot above her skull. At first, I thought she had been scalped by a curtain rod she was transporting. It seemed oddly exciting, I'm ashamed to say. It turns out she'd just lost her wig in the collision with MacArthur's horse's ass.

I felt sorry for Mrs. Byrd. She was so embarrassed to be without her wig. Baldness will do that to a person. She tried to put a Kleenex on her shriveled head, which was as effective as a Band-Aid on a tuna. The old gal was crying because she didn't want to be seen. I couldn't take it. Old people kill me.

I rushed over and threw my jacket over her head to give her some privacy. At that point, some moron started yelling at me to stop smothering the frail thing and to "back off, Jack."

Suddenly my protective instincts took over, and we both began to tug at Mrs. Byrd as if she was a prehistoric wishbone. I finally let go when the moron screamed, "I'm with the ambulance crew! Give her air, you damn fool!" (I think I did hear the old girl gasping.)

I did what he ordered, but only after I shoved Mrs. Byrd's wig back on her skull. Although she resembled one of the Marx brothers when I was done, I suspect she appreciated the effort.

I wanted to keep an eye on the action, so I walked over to Coonsie's Tavern to stand with a group of spectators who had gathered by the door. I was there only a moment when I noticed shell-shocked Andy sitting on the sidewalk. He was leaning against the brick building with a Lucky dangling from his half-mouth while he checked me out with that one eye of his. I walked closer and nodded out of respect. Snarls had said the guy couldn't talk, so when Andy spoke, he startled the stuffing out of me.

His voice was raw, as if it had been scraped out of a furnace. "Joey?" Andy croaked. I thought I was hearing things until he struggled to his feet and repeated, "Joey?" The right side of his body—the side with the missing arm—was flailing like an impaled marlin. And he seemed really excited.

"Joey?" he said again. I couldn't be sure if he was calling me Joey or asking for someone named Joey. He looked so lost that I suddenly felt as if the world was being shoved down my throat with a fist attached to it. "'Member me from the Army?" he rasped.

I was so flabbergasted I didn't know how to handle it. I didn't want to hurt his feelings, so I let on as though I remembered him. "Hey, Andy," I said. "How are ya doing, buddy?"

"Okay," he managed to say. "Okay."

"Do you need something, Andy?"

"Joey."

"Joey who?"

"Joey's waiting."

"Well, then I'd better go," I said, seeing my escape.

Andy shook his mangled head back and forth. "Those bastards crippled you, too, huh?" he whined. The sound of his torn voice made my back shrink, and the way he was looking at me was humiliating. I knew I had to get away from there, but suddenly Andy grabbed my arm with an iron grip.

"Let go," I cried. I tried to free myself, but his one hand was so powerful I couldn't get away. I started to panic. Andy sized up my leg, and then he stared at my right foot which has been rolling to the side lately. I tried to put pressure on it to flatten it, but it was just hanging there like a block of old cheese. "Stop looking at me like I'm a freak!" I yelled.

"Awww, pal," he moaned, shaking his head sympathetically.

The longer he stared at me with such pity, the more worked up I got. I was mortified. All I could feel was rage toward this monster head who was all over me worse than a stinking crotch disease.

Before I could stop myself, I shoved Andy up against the building and yelled right into his pile of a face: "Screw you! And screw Joey! Screw this town and all the half-brains who live here! Don't you ever look at me with pity, you freak, or I'll beat the rest of the life out of you!" Then I ran as far away from him as my burning leg would take me.

After I cooled off a bit, I felt so ashamed at my outburst I just wandered aimlessly. I was thinking about running away from Cowville when I realized I had wandered into an area of town I'd never seen before.

There is a short row of houses on the eastside of town. They are built along a dry creek bed that winds its way to the lake. The road is gravel in some parts, and dirt everywhere else where rain and snow have washed away the surface. Most of the houses are quite neat, although some yards are littered with the remains of old washing machines and battered cars. I spotted Cotton's old station wagon.

As I rounded the bend, there was music coming from a blue house. I was really surprised to see Martha Williams, the young colored girl I met on the bus to Greencastle, playing on her front steps. She was singing a tune from *The Music Man*: "'Oh we've got trouble! Right here in River City! With a capital 'T,' and that rhymes with 'P,' and that stands for POOL!'"

Martha looked up when I made a convincing trombone sound, then she jumped down off the porch and came at me like a runaway bowling ball. "Did you bring any oranges?" she yelled.

"I haven't gone to California yet," I grinned.

"Martha Jane," I heard a voice call from just behind the screen door, "who are you talking to out there?"

When I looked up, a vision stepped out from behind the screen door. No kidding. She had on a pale gray skirt and a matching sweater. Her hair was pulled back with a scarf that was more of a lavender color, but it sure worked with her outfit. It was her eyes that got to me. She has the biggest brown eyes a face could hold. And her skin is one of those warm colors that make you crave gingerbread. You should see her. She's beautiful.

"Denise," Martha was saying, "This is the boy I met on the bus when I was going to the dentist... the one who made me laugh."

"Hi," Denise smiled. "I'm Martha's sister."

"Hi," I said back as I watched her smile spread. "I'm Weed Clapper."

"What a great name!"

That was a good sign as far as I could tell. "Where do you go to school?" I inquired.

"I graduated last year. I'm going to business school in Crawfordsville now. What grade are you in?"

44

"Well, I'm a junior, although I *should* be a senior. Don't think I'm a dunce though... I just missed too much school last year, so I had to repeat a grade, but I get good grades even though I cut school a lot, which doesn't mean I'm reform school material or anything like that, because I always try to stay within the boundaries of the law..." By the time I wrestled my flapping tongue to the floor of my mouth, I was relieved to see she was still smiling.

"Well, do you want to come in for a Coke?" Denise offered.

I was moving even before Martha took my hand. We followed Denise into the kitchen like she was the Star of the East. Denise poured some milk for Martha and got us some Cokes, and then we all sat down at the big Formica table to chew the fat.

I found out Martha goes to school in the next town because the school is more mixed. Their father lives in Detroit, so they live with their mother, who works for a family in Spencer, which is a town just down the road. Denise stays with their aunt in Crawfordsville while attending business school, but she comes home often for visits.

We talked a long time. And we laughed about silly stuff such as Snarls's hair and Martha's friend who got so much gum in her hair she didn't know she had a Don Larsen Trading Card stuck to her head. I was so wound up that right out of the blue I whipped into, "Oh we've got trouble, right here in River City—" Martha and Denise joined right in, and we all started pounding on the table until the plastic fruit in the center bounced out of the bowl.

By the time Mrs. Williams came home, we were pretty raucous. She was very nice, even though she was too pooped to care what kind of trouble was brewing in River City, so Denise offered to take Martha and me to the drive-in burger stand while her mother got some

45

rest. Naturally, we both said yes, because even a cow couldn't turn down a good burger. We all piled into Denise's old '51 maroon Studebaker and took off for the Roundabout.

As we pulled into the hamburger stand and parked, I was surprised to see Janine sitting across from us in this cool Ford Fairlane her friend Patty Lynn drives. I waved, but she didn't seem to notice me. I admit, I was hoping she'd see how pretty Denise is and maybe realize how lucky she was to have had me in a lip-lock last night. In fact, if Janine hadn't made that comment about my leg at school, I might have been with her instead of with Denise. I wanted Janine to think about that.

After the carhop took our order, I got out and went over to say hello to Janine and Patty Lynn. When I walked up, Janine had a snide look on her face. I thought her arrogance was out of line, especially considering the big blob of mayonnaise that was clinging to her lip like a buzzard dropping.

"How long have you known *her*?" she asked me. That's what she said—no 'hello' or nothing.

"Who... Denise? I just met her. She's real nice. Her little sister Martha is with us. Should I call them over to say hello?"

"No, thanks," they sang in unison, like two-thirds of the Andrews sisters.

"You're with them?" Janine asked. "It's not real classy."

That's not a good thing to say to us distemperoid-types. I felt some stupid, unexplainable need to defend myself, and I didn't even know what for! She really set me off.

"Well, back home my buddies and I used to hang out with Dizzy Gillespie, and we ate everywhere you please," I snapped. "Folks do that in big cities, Janine. And just so you know, Ray Charles is my friend

Kenton's cousin, so we've even sung a few tunes with Ray right at Kenton's kitchen table! And you know Ella Fitzgerald, well—" If Janine hadn't cut me off, I'd have been playing strip poker with Ella Fitzgerald and Etta James.

"Well don't have a cow," Janine grunted as she looked over at Denise. "I'll see you in school tomorrow, okay?" she winked. That sort of threw me. Just as I was working up a good hate toward her, she had to do something cute. Girls are that way.

"Okay," I mumbled, although I wasn't really sure how I felt about it. On my way back to the car, I suppose I was holding my shoulders higher than necessary. When I saw Denise's smile, I was happy to get back inside the Studebaker where I could just be me.

———

After we ate, I had Denise drop me at Miss Saslow's house. I was still mulling over the hugging-Leland incident, and I was also feeling guilty about telling whoppers about Dizzy Gillespie. It seemed ironic that Janine was responsible for both my brief joy AND my present turmoil. I guess that's what women do to a guy. I just knew I had to get someone else's viewpoint.

After Denise drove off, I sat on the stone wall awhile, planning what I wanted to say to Miss Saslow. I was just getting up the nerve to knock on her door when I saw Andy Johnson limping up the road. I ducked behind the wall before he could see me.

Andy paused near Miss Saslow's yard. He looked around to make sure he was alone, then he sneaked behind a huge oleander alongside the house and stared in her window like a regular peeping Tom. I didn't know what to do, so I stayed put. After ten minutes, Andy finally shuffled off, but I was sure he'd be back. I also knew I had no choice but to warn Sassy-Ass that

Andy was lurking around her house like Lee Marvin in that old movie, *Shack Out On 101*. So that's what I did.

My heart made more noise than her doorbell. I was so involved in forcing moisture back into my mouth that I jumped when she opened the door. She was wearing a pink blouse and Capri pants. I never saw her look so gorgeous, or so young. When I remembered that Russell told me (during our Bataan Death March) that she's only twenty-four, my nerves suddenly got worse.

"Come in," she said softly. She didn't even seem surprised to see me. After she led me to her living room, we sat down on a dark red couch. I was too paralyzed to talk, even though she really tried to make me feel right at home. She asked me some questions, which I think I answered, although my main focus was on my noisy intestinal tract. I heard a gurgle, so I didn't dare move in case a gas cloud was forming. I just nodded a lot as though my head was loose.

It was hard to concentrate on what Sassy-Ass was saying because she was stroking her leg with her hand. I was so fixated on her fingers gliding up and down her leg that my lips dried up. It's hard to talk when your lips are stuck to your teeth.

Then she derailed me with: "Is there something on your mind, Weed?"

My throat seized up and I coughed long enough to convince a deaf person I had tuberculosis. Finally, I got up the guts to speak the truth. "I do have some things on my mind," I confessed, "but I don't know many people I can talk to."

"I don't either."

That struck me as strange when she said it. So naturally I replied: "I'm from Scranton." You could hear the thud. What a stupid thing to say. Stupid, stupid. I am the KING of Stupid!

"I know," she nodded. "I saw your records. That's

48

how I learned that you prefer to be called 'Weed.' Is your leg bothering you, Weed?"

When I looked down, I saw my leg twitching worse than a dog with fleas. "I'm just nervous," I said. "It's my personality."

Sassy-Ass smiled when I said that, and then she got up and disappeared. I was sure she'd gone off to have a good laugh by herself because I'm such a fool. I could just picture her in the kitchen bending over and holding her sides as she laughed, with a pot holder stuffed in her mouth to stifle her loud guffaws.

A quick exit seemed like a damn good idea to me until Sassy-Ass returned with a pot of coffee. I was grateful she didn't fix me chocolate milk or Ovaltine, like I was some goofy little kid.

"Thanks, Miss Sassy--"

She laughed and pronounced, "Saslow," while I watched her lips move. I was glad she laughed because I was sweating out loud.

"What's troubling you, Weed?" she pressed.

"Well one thing I'm worried about concerns you," I answered. "Do you know that guy who got shell-shocked in the Korean War?" I sensed she was surprised by my question.

"Yes, I know Andy Johnson."

"Well, I thought you should know that on several occasions, I've noticed him hanging around here."

"Andy's harmless, Weed. I've seen him out by the oak tree, or on the wall where you were sitting. I'm sure he just doesn't know where else to go."

I was mortified when I realized she'd seen me out there, too. I didn't want her to get the wrong idea. And I sure didn't want her to lump me in with the likes of Andy. I leaned forward to make my point. "Andy was peeping in the window at you," I explained.

She set down her coffee and just stared out the window for a minute. "Are you sure, Weed?" When I nodded, she grew still, and her blue eyes took on a really sad expression. I sensed I had said something wrong, but I sure had no idea what in the heck it was.

"I just wanted to warn you to be careful," I explained apologetically.

"Thank you. I'll be careful. But let's not talk about Andy now. Tell me about you. How do you like our exciting city?"

I started with my more astute observations, and then all of a sudden, my tongue launched into a wild jig about my meeting with Janine and Patty Lynn. I lost all control and even confessed my whopper of a lie about Dizzy Gillespie. My mouth didn't stop until it was perfectly clear that she was aiding and abetting a lying pus-sack.

Sassy-Ass was quiet for a moment, as if she was in the presence of a lobotomy survivor. Finally, she suggested perhaps I'd been aiming for a metaphor with the whole Dizzy Gillespie tale in order to defend Negroes. She also suggested I cut down on the metaphors because some people, especially bigots like Janine, are too shallow to understand them. That was her word, "shallow." But I was in complete agreement. I've had trouble in the past with shallow people not always getting my most colorful metaphors.

The sun was going down when she asked me if I wanted to stay for supper. I said that would be "cool-as-a-moose," just to let her know I was getting into the local jargon. Of course, as soon as I said it, I felt as ridiculous as a turd hat. But by then I was feeling at home enough not to hurl myself through a window. I followed her to the kitchen where we made meat loaf sandwiches and baked apples. I never expected to have such a great time.

I was thinking about my mom's baked apples when Sassy-Ass asked me if I enjoy poetry. I told her if she tied me to a rack, I'd have to confess I like Frost's "The

Road Not Taken," so she insisted I borrow Frost's *A Witness Tree*. Of course, I didn't confess that I don't like poetry *that* much, because now I have an excuse to return.

It was a great evening. The only mishap was when I got up from the table to help clear the dishes. My foot was asleep or something, so I stumbled across the floor, wiping out two plates and a glass along the way. While I was on my knees cleaning up the mess, I told her about my track injury. I must have overdone it with the metaphors because when I looked up, she was smiling sadly.

She reached down and touched my face so gently I was sure I'd never breathe again. But suddenly I thought I saw a look of pity, as if I had a hump on my back the size of a buffalo head. My guts went haywire, and I knew I had to get out of there fast.

"Thanks, Miss Saslow," I mumbled. "I gotta go."

"Thank *you*, Weed," I was surprised to hear her say. "I know I'm your teacher," she continued, "but I'd also like to be friends. When no one is around, why don't you call me Laura?"

Laura. That's her name. I didn't actually say it, and I don't remember saying good-bye. I was too busy holding the word 'Laura' in my mouth.

———

By the time I arrived home, Ollie had returned from having her hair destroyed at Dora's Doll House. (Dora must have a thing for Elsa Lanchester in her *Bride of Frankenstein* period.) Nonetheless, I told Ollie her hair looked classy. She was so thrilled I thought she was going to cry, which made me want to hug her. I almost did. We were having Chef Boyardee spaghetti when I finally grilled Ollie about the rotten attitude the locals have toward Negroes.

"Do you have any Negro friends here?" I inquired.

"No, Weed. I used to see more coloreds—that's what we called them then—when I traveled through the South with the show. My two best pals were coloreds. They taught me how to swallow swords. That made me a real hit with the fellas," she added devilishly.

(That's NOT an image a guy wants of his grandmother.)

"Were they treated as bad as I read about?" I asked, trying to get her back on the subject before I upchucked.

"Oh yes, darlins, and much worse. I was with my friend Caleb one time in a cafe in Louisville where they wouldn't even feed him a slice of bread. Me being white and all, I got up the nerve to insist they serve us. They finally sent out two ham sandwiches, but I knew by the smell that the cook had peed all over them."

"That's gross! What did you and Caleb do?"

"I was about to give 'em what-for, but Caleb stopped me. 'Time,' he whispered, '…in God's time, Olivia,' was all he said." Ollie shook her head sadly.

"So why aren't there many Negroes around here?" I inquired.

"Probably because of the Ku Klux Klan."

When I heard that, I choked on my spaghetti. I certainly know about the Klan, but I was sure they were more of a Southern presence. The idea of the K.K.K. here in Sleepy Hollow astonished me. (Remember, I'm a failure as a genius.)

I remember first hearing about the Klan when I was seven. It all started when Murray was rehashing the "Hansel and Gretel" story. That's when it dawned on him that if the old lady in the story baked kids in an oven, then she must be a Nazi. Murray began having nightmares, especially after Liam-Doom-Monger-O'Gara said some Nazis had escaped to our area after the war. (I'm getting to my point here.)

When Murray came whimpering over to our house

THE REMARKABLE JOURNEY OF WEED CLAPPER

to ask my dad about the Nazis, my father set him straight. He said, "Murray, Murray, you don't have to worry about Nazis coming to Scranton, son. Know why? Because every yellow Nazi out there is scared to death of Harold Clapper. I'm a bona fide, Nazi-stomping, purple-heart-wearing, no-crying INTERNATIONAL HERO! I've got photos to prove it!

"Even Tokyo Rose warned those bile-spewing cowards about Harold-the-Horrible, only she pronounced it: 'Harood-da-Howable.' Those Nazis are so petrified of me they have secret Harold Clapper Air Raids where they cry and scurry underground like the dirty rats they are. Nowadays, all Nazis have to swear on the heads of their mutant mustachioed mothers to STAY THE HELL OUT OF PENNSYLVANIA!"

Murray felt so much better he fell asleep on my dad's lap. The next day I told Murray, no offense, but I was glad I wasn't a Jew because of all the Nazi stuff, not to mention that he had to attend Hebrew school to learn to speak like Moses. Murray agreed that being a Jew was a burden, but he insisted that I had my own serious problems "with the Ku Klux Klan, a *branch* of the Nazi machine."

Murray went on to describe the unspeakable things the K.K.K. do to Negroes and Jews, and to *friends* of Negroes and Jews. He warned me that seeing as how Kenton Smith and I had become blood brothers, and Kenton's a Negro, and I had a genuine Jew right there in my house, that I was probably going to find a cross burning in my yard one day...But then again, maybe not, because this was Pennsylvania, the home of Harold-the-Horrible.

So you see, I learned about Klan activities at an early age, but I never suspected they could be in Indiana. Not in 1960. "Jeez," I exclaimed to Ollie, "I always thought the K.K.K. were down South!"

"I don't know how organized they are these days,

but they're still around, darlins. World War II stirred up a lot of feelings again. There's a silent understanding that the races shouldn't mix."

"It's not all that silent."

"I guess not. That's why Caleb didn't stay long when he came to visit me after the show closed. He moved on to Binghamton, New York, to his sister's place. Do you want to hear something really ironic? He was in Binghamton only a short time before he was shot in the head for touching a white woman in a 'familiar' manner in public."

I didn't know what to say to that. And I could tell Ollie was upset thinking about Caleb, so I knew it wasn't the time to press her for the morbid details.

After Ollie went up to bed, I did a lot of thinking. This K.K.K. thing makes me nervous. I don't want to be anywhere near the likes of those thugs. Good sense says it's time to hit the road.

But I need to talk to Laura once more before I go. I don't want to stir up my emotions too much because being numb is safe. Still, I'll take my chances just to see her one more time.

CHAPTER FIVE
SEPTEMBER 27, 1960

TODAY LAURA'S CLASS WAS AS FANTASTIC AS THE FORMAL educational process will allow. She said ALOUD that my interpretation of Lady Anne's soliloquy in *Richard III* was more "insightful" than most she has heard. I think everyone was impressed. After class, Laura smiled and suggested I drop by her house again for drinks and sex (maybe it was "drinks and a snack.") Either way, I was all for it.

Because I was still disappointed with Janine, I was feeling vindicated when she smiled at me today as if I was the captain of the basketball team. (That's actually handsome hole-in-the-head-Jimmy Dale. He most likely thinks Richard III is the third Nixon daughter.) Janine caught up with me in the hall and asked me to come over to her house after school. I admit, the thought of her energetic tongue influenced my decision to see her again.

Things were going so well that I decided to hang around for my afternoon classes for a change. I don't mind metal shop, but they also make you take an agricultural class to study crop rotation. Then there's Latin. That ought to come in handy when we take on the Commies in a ferocious pharmacy war.

You can understand my surprise when fourth period turned out to be a blast for once. Someone had a transistor radio, and just before class, the DJ played "The Twist," a hit song by Chubby Checker. A few of the kids were dancing, which is against the rules of the institution, when Janine and I bopped up. Being the "insightful" person I am, I thought, what the heck, why not show these farmers how to cut a rug? I threw down my books and started grooving. The Twist is easy on my bum leg because I can keep it in one place and just let the rest of me go to town.

Out of nowhere, Russell-Up-Some-Grub, the legendary "I've-gotta-take-a-squirt" geek, shocked us all by jumping into the groove-fest. I was prepared to be so embarrassed for Russell that I'd end up in a fight with someone for humiliating him in a Darwinian feeding frenzy that would no doubt leave him in a quivering heap. I can't stand by and watch such painful stuff.

Well, 'squirting Russell' was a regular Fred Astaire, only much hipper. He and I took over, and then Janine jumped in with some slick moves of her own. I have to say, we made an impression. By the time Mr. Perry arrived, everyone was getting into it. Needless to say, we were all really wound up by the time he herded us into algebra.

I usually sit in the back row next to Russell and Patty Lynn Stevens. I've had algebra before, so I know my way around a square root. Thus, I've been reading *Sweet Thursday* during the few times I've attended class. Today I saw Russell poring over some unassigned reading material of his own.

When I asked what he was reading, he claimed it was a book about plowing. That was a bunch of crap because he was flipping through drawings of couples doing sexual gymnastics you can't imagine. They were in positions a human body could never achieve without permanent injury. The book was *Kamasutra*.

I just grinned and asked, "If that's plowing, can I come over and drive my plow through your sister's pumpkin patch?" Well, that got him laughing, and I split a gut, too. Soon Patty Lynn began giggling because Russell and I were laughing ourselves senseless. When old Perry gave all three of us a warning, it was the finishing blow to our self-control.

At that point, Russell let go of a stream of snot which landed on the back of Bill Linder's chair. Patty Lynn squealed, and I thought I was going to piss myself. The constipated Mr. Perry, fed up with the commotion, threw all three of us out of class. To the other math-tortured captives, we were instant heroes.

Russell, Patty Lynn, and I were trying to beat it out of there when Russell dropped his books in the aisle. As he was scrambling to cover up his extra-curricular reading materials, someone yelled, "Look, naked broads!" That immediately sent Russell up the "cool cat" scale by about fifty points. It also sent us into spasms.

After the three of us pulled a Stooges stunt where we all tried to exit at the same time, we went flying out into the hallway and continued howling until we were limp. Then we all decided to bail out of there. Patty Lynn wanted to wait outside of school for her friends, so Russell and I said good-bye and took off. That's how ol' Russell-Up-Some-Grub and I ended up having a good talk.

"You got yourself into the revered Horndog Hall of Fame with those naked ladies photos," I told him, "and I think some of the girls thought you were cool with your Twist moves."

"Yeah? They never noticed me before."

"Well, if you don't mind my saying so, I bet it's that hangdog haircut. It's gotta go, man." (Most guys around here have crew cuts, although I heard from Janine that they admire my sleek Elvis look. Unfortunately, Russell's hair looks like someone stuck a pot on his head then chewed off the fringe.)

"Who cuts your hair?" I asked, suspecting it was a one-armed blind person with a drinking problem.

"I get it cut at Dora's," he blushed. Before I could retort, he held up a hand. "Dora's my aunt," he winced, "I have no choice."

"Well, no offense," I said, "but your aunt's not up on what's cool. I've seen her workmanship on Ollie. She must've trained under the Spanish Inquisition. Com'on," I said, "we're going there right now to have her copy my haircut."

"Okay, you're on. What else do you think I can do to get the girls to notice me, Weed?"

"Practicing all the positions in your 'plowing' book ought to help. And here," I added as I rolled up the short sleeves of his shirt two turns, "keep these rolled up, and keep your top button open so you look more relaxed. You'll look less like a Sunday school teacher. That's it. Now, we're going to pick up some smokes for you to carry in your sleeve. It'll make you look real hip."

"I don't smoke."

"Neither do I, Russell. I've been carrying this pack of Camels around with me since I could tie my shoes. They're so stale it's like smoking termite droppings. You only have to light up in an emergency, like when you're with a girl and can't think of anything clever to say. It keeps the ball rolling."

"I'd gag."

"You don't have to inhale the dang thing. You say something about being in training for a sport. Any sport. Then you explain how the coach has ordered you to break your pack-and-a-half-a-day habit. That's when you snuff out the cig and complain about how demanding life is for an athlete."

"So I should lie about smoking?'

"It's not exactly a lie. It's a metaphor."

"A metaphor."

"That's right. A necessary fabrication. Harmless color. It's all about making a point."

"I wish I'd been raised in a big city," he smirked as we entered Dora's.

The odor in Dora's place was a lethal mixture of permanent wave solution and old ladies' perfume. But Dora is a friendly sort, so she really got into the reinvention-of-Russell business. Her dentures danced faster than a chorus line of Rockettes with every snip of the scissors, but she did a darn good job for an old gal with cataracts and the shakes.

When Dora was done, I showed Russell how to take a gob of Vitalis, mix it with some pomade, then smear it through his hair. I helped him smooth back the sides into a modified ducktail and coax a hunk of hair out over his forehead. The pomade even made his hair look less mousy, so it was quite a physical transformation.

On the way out of Dora's, I informed Russell that his name had to go. "From now on, you're just Russ,'" I told him, "cause it's much cooler."

When I promised him he'd be beating off the women instead of himself for a change, he flashed me a shit-eating grin. "What do you think my chances are of dating Patty Lynn Stevens?" he asked.

I waited for the appropriate dramatic moment before I answered, "About as good as your chances of dating Amelia Earhart!"

We were both laughing when we split up. Then I headed for Janine's house. If I'd known what was going to happen next, I gladly would have stayed with randy ol' Russ.

To tell the truth, I was wishing I was on my way to see Denise instead of Janine. Denise is much more mature and a lot less judgmental. However, I won't see Denise until Thanksgiving because she went back to business school in Crawfordsville.

Nonetheless, Janine acted very friendly when I arrived. Her parents were down at the fire station setting up for tomorrow night's Lion's Club Fish Fry, so Janine and I were all alone. She laughed at everything I said, even the serious stuff. I know I'm not bad looking, but her attention seemed a little forced.

"When are you going to get your Thunderbird?" she asked me out of the blue. She was listening so hard I thought she was going to take notes in case I gave her a pop quiz later on.

"I'm not exactly sure. I want to take my time selecting." I figured that's the truth. Well, if you get technical.

"I can't wait to see your new car," she oozed. "I hope you'll let me be the first to ride in it. Did you know everyone's saying I'll probably be class queen this year?"

"Yeah, I've heard that. That's neat." I was just going along with her patter. Frankly, I hadn't heard anything of the sort. For all I know, Mamie Eisenhower will be named class queen. I was hoping Janine would settle down and turn on the TV so we could watch "The Many Loves of Dobie Gillis," but she kept right on blabbering. Girls sure love to talk at the wrong time.

"You're planning to buy a class ring, aren't you?" she asked.

I got the impression I definitely would be, whether I wanted to or not. "Well, I don't know, Janine. I just got to town, so I don't even have a city map yet." The irony of a map for this two-street whistle stop flew over her head higher than a lunar probe.

"Well, I was just thinking I might want to wear your ring."

That flabbergasted me, but I should have seen it coming. The girls here flip out over rings. When they get a guy's ring, they wrap angora around it, then brush the angora until it fluffs up like angel hair on a Christmas tree. I admit, it's a very feminine look.

"Well, I'd have to think about the ring thing," I muttered, still miffed about her attitude toward Denise and Martha.

"I just wanted you to have someone you could feel close to, being an orphan and all," she smiled sadly.

The word orphan set my butt on fire. Janine had a look of such sticky compassion on her face that I expected her to fetch me a moldy old crust of bread and a cup for collecting loose change. "Who told you about me being an orphan? Do I look like Little Nell to you?" I sputtered in her face.

"Oh, you have a sister?"

I should have known a reference to Dickens would throw her almost as much as an Aqua Net shortage. "Did you see the debate on TV last night?" I blurted. (I've never been one to hold back on an abrupt transition when I want someone to drop the subject before I remove their liver.)

"No, but I heard my parents talking about the debate. They said Nixon was great."

"No way! Nixon? Nixon? He was very antagonistic, Janine. And he sweats more than Monkey Boy."

"Who?"

"Forget it. I'm just saying that Kennedy was very confident, and I bet he'll change this country if he gets a chance. For God's sake, he was a hero in the Pacific! And Nixon almost started his own war! What kind of a nut would poke Khrushchev in the chest in the middle of a Cold War? We could have been bombed because of the Kitchen Debate!"

"Don't exaggerate, Weed. And why should it matter what Nixon does in the privacy of his own kitchen?"

That left me speechless. Yeah, imagine me with no comeback. I had to reach way down past my scowl just to come up with a few civil words. "Janine," I finally said in my most patient, approach-with-caution voice, "the argument between Nixon and Khrushchev took place in a model kitchen at a technology show."

"Oh, who cares? Besides, my dad says if Richard Nixon's good enough for Ike, then he's good enough for the whole dang country."

I was about to mouth off about Ike wanting to dump Nixon from the ticket when Janine put on some records and asked me if I wanted to make out on the couch. When she licked her lips, I settled down fast. Making out seemed a lot more exciting than politics. I took one look at her mouth and decided I could love her, at least for an hour, despite the fact that I didn't like her much at all.

That leads me to one of the most eventful moments in all my mature years. But first, I want to make it perfectly clear that I'm NOT inexperienced. I had a girl back home named Annie Peterson. She sure loved to kiss. We never completed the sex act, although that doesn't mean we didn't come sinfully close. But she was more the virginal type.

So you can imagine my shock when Janine and I were making out and she unzipped my pants. That zipper was so noisy I was sure it startled the residents of Peking. But the loudness of my zipper turned out to be the least of my problems.

There I was, exposed in front of all six eyes of the Trinity. All that was missing was a spotlight and one of those revolving mirrored balls. Janine displayed remarkable skill. You'd think she'd had as much practice as I've had. She may have even said, "Wow!" Someone sure did.

I believe we were kissing. I don't honestly recollect because all my brain cells had headed south. I was trying to hold back, which was torture beyond description, when Satan arrived to take his due. Janine abruptly detoured with her energetic tongue and began to lick my ear. I was a goner. I started firing like Jesse James on a drunken spree. I was just shy of a groan when suddenly I heard someone scream, "Fly!"

I opened up my eyes to see a little kid in his jammies. As my oxygen-deprived brain tried to absorb the phenomenon of my zipper literally awakening some neighbor's kid, the boy jumped around as if he had a fish in his farter. "Fly!" he screamed again. My logic told me to close my fly, but it's not easy to wrangle a bronco.

"Com'on, Weed, we have to help my brother Timmy," Janine yelled. At least that explained who the kid was. Having a little brother is a detail Janine had never even bothered to mention.

I took off after them, all the while trying to stuff myself back into my jeans. When we got to Timmy's room, Janine grabbed the most godawful, nose-assaulting, tongue-coating insect killer and sprayed half a can while Timmy hid under a sheet. But the odd thing was, there weren't any flies! Ten minutes later, the kid finally fell asleep. Either that, or he was asphyxiated.

Afterward, Janine and I went out on the porch where she explained that Timmy is terrified of flies. Believe it or not, when he was three, a fly flew into his ear. Nobody knew it until he started acting strange, which would be a behavior hard to detect in that family. Timmy began batting his ear to "make the airplanes go away."

When they took Timmy to the doctor, they discovered the fly had laid eggs, but the doctor said he couldn't get all the eggs out without damaging Timmy's eardrum. He instructed Janine's mom to hold a flashlight up to Timmy's ear after dark. When the maggots crawled out, she had to swab them with alcohol till they were gone.

Janine swears it honestly happened. And I can swear one thing, too—when Janine was done telling the story, I didn't have my boner problem anymore.

But now I have a problem with Janine. She wants to go steady. I've gotten myself in so deep I wish I could just erase the entire event. Except for maybe the sex parts. I'm only human.

————

When I returned to Ollie's, I was pretty spent. As I was climbing the porch steps, I heard a scuffling noise out back. I glanced to my left then froze in my tracks. In the dim light, I was able to make out a bloody pile of flesh on the front porch. I crept a bit closer, and then I gasped. On the floor in front of the glider was a decapitated chicken! My first impulse was to run around back to see who was there, but just at that moment, Ollie came out.

I threw my jacket over the carnage so she wouldn't see it, but it was too late. The look on Ollie's face was awful. I was praying she wouldn't collapse, because I knew I'd never get her up without a crane. After I assured her that it was just some yokel's damn pathetic idea of a prank, I sent her inside and discarded the carcass (the chicken's, not Ollie's).

She left the door ajar, so I was able to hear the old gal talking to somebody as she crept up the stairs, which is not easy for a mastodon to do in the first place. I went inside and glanced up the stairs, but no one was around. I thought I heard nervous whispers just before I heard her bedroom door lock. However, I was distracted by the sound of laughter in the woods out back, so I put the subject of Ollie's clandestine activity aside while I checked all the locks.

My most pressing concern is not Ollie's phantom guest, but the UNINVITED guest who is sick enough to kill livestock as an unspoken threat. I don't even know if the warning is for me or for my grandmother, but it sure is coming in loud and clear.

CHAPTER SIX
OCTOBER 8, 1960

NOT LONG AFTER THE DEAD CHICKEN INCIDENT, I WAS packing my suitcases so I could head for greener pastures when Ollie knocked on my door and asked me to escort her to the town Fish Fry. I was already feeling guilty about leaving, so I decided it wouldn't hurt me to stick around long enough to accompany her to some hokey town event. Besides, I've suddenly developed this strange desire to protect her.

When Ollie and I got to the fire station where the fish fry was being held, the first thing we did was load up on hot dogs, corn, slaw, and some amazing fire-roasted corn. No fish for me, I told her, as I always make it a point to avoid anything that poops in its own bath water.

While we were eating, I checked out the games they had set up for the kids. I was looking for Denise's little sister Martha when I saw Cotton drive by in his old car. He slowed down to look at the festivities, but then he kept going. That's when it dawned on me that there wasn't one Negro there.

Another thing I noticed was that people were intentionally avoiding our table. Ollie was acting so bubbly I knew she was faking, like those synchronized swimmers who dance under water for half an hour then emerge smiling, even though they're half-dead and delirious from chlorine poisoning. I couldn't help but wonder what a nice lady like Ollie could have done to offend the locals.

Then it occurred to me that perhaps the hungry masses were afraid my gimp leg would spoil their appetites if they sat too close to me. I get self-conscious about those things. But before I could get myself too overwrought, Russ and his parents came over and sat down with us. To my relief, Russ's dad, Roy Kinney, flashed Ollie a big grin, so I knew he must be as nice as Russ is.

At first things were going well because we were talking about the two monkeys, Abel and Baker, who went into space. Roy said if we ever try for the moon, we should name the spaceship Alice because Jackie Gleason always said, "To the moon, Alice!" Ollie got a kick out of that. She batted her eyes at Roy and told him he was "a hoot-and-a-half."

Right at the 'hoot' point in the conversation, Laura Sassy-Ass Saslow walked over like an ambulatory cream-filled pastry and asked if she could join our happy little group of fish fryers. That would have been swell... if she wasn't dragging along her hotshot professor boyfriend, Rick Drop-Your-Panties-Girls Bills.

Unfortunately, I was not able to disguise my irritation. I harrumphed at the wrong time and sucked a kernel of corn up my left nostril. It was HUGE. It felt as if I had inhaled my shoe. As I tried to snort the damn thing back out into my hand, which was not too appealing as dining events go, I imagined my obituary:

According to reports, a fist-sized kernel of corn was extracted from the victim's brain. The lack of oxygen affected the part of the brain that controls social behavior, thus explaining why the rude corn-snorter ripped off his clothes and shoved pickles up his orifices before spinning around on his butt in the center of the table at the Lion's Club Fish Fry.

It is presumed that Weed Clapper expired believing he was a rotating condiment tray.

I can laugh now, but it wasn't too funny at the time. As subtly as possible, I tried to suck the kernel back down my throat, but the more I tried to free it, the more wedged it became. I coughed enough to expectorate brain matter. All the snorting and gurgling did nothing but garner the attention of everyone there... and maybe some people who weren't even there yet. I was mortified. I'm sure parents were hiding their children from me. Everyone stopped talking. Fish stopped frying. Even the slaw stopped slawing. If I could have talked, I would have requested a noose.

Finally Rick whacked me on the back so hard that the corn shot right out onto the table like a fulminating chancre sore. The entire Midwest waited in expectation until I came to my senses long enough to reach out and sweep the offensive kernel away.

After an epoch of excruciating silence, Laura saved the day. "So that's what headcheese looks like!" she giggled. The crowd erupted. Ollie squealed, and Roy Kinney gagged on a wiener. Soon the corndog clan was laughing hysterically, so I didn't have to kill myself.

Laura sat down next to me, so eventually I started to enjoy myself again—until I saw Rick do something very disrespectful to Laura. He winked at Patty Lynn's older sister, JoAnn, who was languishing like a wet noodle near the drink stand. JoAnn gave him a look that was so seductive she would have been arrested in most states. When I glanced back at Laura to make sure she hadn't noticed, she smiled at me like the actress Kim Novak, all pure and sexy at the same time. I was so messed up inside I wanted to pummel Rick for acting like a dog in heat. Fortunately, the three-piece combo struck up some music, so Rick and Laura got up to dance. I couldn't help but notice how he was holding her real close.

While the band went on break, Rick went for drinks

and Laura returned to our table. A barbershop quartet took over with a sleeper called "Back Home Again in Indiana," and the Hoosiers, which is how Indiana folks refer to themselves, all sang along. A corpse parade would have been livelier. But then the quartet suddenly whipped into "A Teenager in Love" originally recorded by Dion and the Belmonts (before Dion deserted to become a heroin shooter). That doo-wop tune sure resuscitated us, and by the time the quartet ripped into "I Wonder Why," that place was shaking.

Naturally, I was surprised when Rick abruptly announced that he had to head home to grade papers. He looked around as if he expected applause. For a moment, I thought he might pose for photos. After he and Laura walked off holding hands, he stood real close to her as he opened the door to his fancy green Chevy BelAir. If he'd pressed up against her any tighter, she would have suffered skin abrasions and contusions. I also noticed how Rick eyeballed JoAnn again before sliming his way into his car. When Laura left, the fish fry was over for me.

———

I couldn't stop thinking about Laura all night. The next day, I was supposed to go to Greencastle to get my leg examined because my limp is getting worse. I took the bus there, got off, and then caught one back ten minutes later.

Somehow, I ended up on Laura's porch, probably because I needed to be around something familiar. I had been there awhile when she and Rick pulled up in Rick's BelAir. As I turned to make a fast exit, Laura kissed Rick good-bye, and then she called out, "Hi Weed!" It was her smile that convinced me not to flee.

Laura and I went inside, and we talked some while I helped her make a pie. We had only been peeling apples for five minutes before I abruptly asked her if she planned to marry Rick, which, I admit, was as subtle as a heart attack.

"Rick wants to wait awhile," Laura answered quietly.

It seemed to me that Rick must be daft not to seal the deal with a woman like Laura as fast as he could. "What the heck is he waiting for?" I asked.

"I don't know, Weed," she shrugged, "I suspect maybe I'm too small-town for him."

Man, did that throw me, because Laura is as big as Christmas to me. "It's not the size of a hometown that determines how big a person is," I protested. I'm sure that sounded corny, especially coming from a dope like me.

Laura smiled as if she really appreciated what I said, then she asked if I had read the Frost book she had lent me. "Not yet, but I did write a poem," I offered, hoping to impress her with my literary leanings. When I noticed her face light up, I quickly qualified myself. "On the bus to Greencastle, I saw a Korean woman and her crippled GI husband. I could tell the woman was very sad," I said as I pulled the paper out of my pocket. Of course, Laura insisted on reading the dang thing.

SON OF SEOUL

Child presses sweet head to her,
While mother holds fast to him
Man busses forehead, soft lips tight
'Gainst acorn-colored skin.

From ashes G.I. soldiers rose
To souls of Seoul set free.
Much taller than the rest, one stood
'Bove war-torched Calvary.

But drifting now to streets of home
And bird-song tones of voice,
Her heart aches for freedom sounds.
Her sentence, Life, was choice.

Hiding loneliness in a treasure chest
Her soldier man won't find,
She forever bleeds for Seoul's sweet spice
to free her captured mind.

This child on her lap had been
Her altar-offering hope
That life could rupture forth again
Through scourge of blood and smoke.

But images of her home dissolve
As Soldier-shell draws in
And presses tight dead lips against
Her acorn-colored skin.

After Laura finished reading, a deafening silence swallowed the room. She seemed very unsettled. I feared she was going to demand I drop her class and move to Idaho. I know I'm not the Merlin of iambic pentameter, but I couldn't believe she hadn't heard worse poems come out of a high school student before.

"You wrote that, Weed?" she asked.

"I was VERY tired at the time," I stammered apologetically.

She turned away so I couldn't see her, and I was so beside myself that I wasn't sure what to do next. "Laura?" I whispered, using her name for the first time. Then my mouth took off as usual, filling the silence with useless information. "It's just something I scribbled down on the spur of the moment," I said. "There was a silence so loud between those folks on the bus it needed its own bus seat. I felt sorry for the Korean lady because she's far away from home, and I know how it feels to be alone in a strange place. Laura, it was a bad poem, I know. I'm a moron. If I upset your delicate system in any way, I'm sorry. And I—"

"Shhh," she said to slow me down. "Weed, your poem was beautiful. It touched me. I'm truly sorry you and the woman on the bus feel homesick. Sometimes I get real homesick myself." That confused me even more than I already was because this is Laura's home.

"There are different kinds of homesick," she said softly. "I think we're all looking for home."

"I know what you mean. It's like when you hear Bing Crosby sing "I'll Be Home for Christmas." Even though you may be home when you hear it, you can still feel very lost. Every time I hear him sing it, I long for the things that are missing in my own life...the things I can't put words to."

Laura looked up at me as though she was seeing me for the first time. "Yes, Weed," she said, "that's it exactly, but I've never been able to vocalize it as well as you do. It seems we all want to live inside a Currier and Ives drawing. But life has too many dimensions!"

I knew her outburst had nothing to do with my amateur poetry OR Currier and Ives. I can recognize a feeling of loss when I see it because I live with it all the time.

"You know the 'soldier-shell' you referred to in your poem?" she asked. "I really felt bad for him. He's back, but he'll never be 'home' again. War took that away from him."

As Laura was looking out the window at a maple tree that was ablaze with color, I finally got the drift of things. My poem had made her think of Andy. I suddenly realized that when I wrote it, I was thinking about Andy, too.

Laura and I peeled apples in silence awhile before we spoke again. "Has Andy ever told anyone what happened over there?" I asked.

"No, Weed. Andy can no longer talk."

"Sure, he can, Laura."

Laura didn't look up, she just stopped moving. "Weed, Andy has never talked to anyone since he returned," she insisted.

"He talked to me."

"You mean the moaning sound he makes?"

"No, I mean like real words. Just the way you and I are talking now, only he was very confused when he spoke to me. I don't think anyone else heard him."

Laura dropped into a chair. "When did he talk? What did he say?" she demanded as she grabbed my hand. "I know his parents, Weed. Please give me something I can tell them."

I tried to repeat exactly what Andy said because it seemed so important to her. "He said: 'Those bastards crippled you, too, didn't they?'" I replied. "I don't know why he said it, Laura. Maybe it's because my foot was asleep, and I was limping. He asked if they hurt me. He was very confused. He called me Joey."

"'Joey'? You're sure he said Joey, Weed?"

"Yes. He told me, 'Joey's waiting.'"

Laura sat motionless for a long time. Finally, she stood up and said she had a terrible headache. She apologized for being rude and asked if I could please come back tomorrow for some pie. She looked so small and sad.

I was heading toward the door when she placed her hand on my shoulder, then she pressed her face against my back. For a moment, all the split parts of me came together. Her embrace lasted only a few seconds, then she let go. Somehow I managed to catch my breath, then my senses told me the appropriate thing was to keep walking. So I did. My back was still hot when I heard the door close behind me.

I left there determined to find out more details about Andy. Even though I'm still upset about my encounter with him, perhaps I can learn something that will give Laura hope. That's why I can't leave town yet. Because of Laura.

CHAPTER SEVEN
OCTOBER 15, 1960

AFTER I GOT UP THIS MORNING, I SAT ON THE PORCH FOR some time just to gaze at the trees because they're spectacular right now. Someone was burning leaves. That was a pleasant change from the smell of rancid corn and horse pucks.

I was going inside for more coffee when Ollie flew downstairs like an inflated macaw in her lemon-yellow blouse and turquoise skirt. (I've concluded that Ollie's "color" is an attempt to be noticed. I guess even a large person can get lost in a small town.)

While we were chewing the fat, I subtly mentioned I had heard strange noises again last night, and that it wasn't the first time. Ollie suggested maybe the raccoons were after her lettuce again. I figured that's likely only if she's growing lettuce in her bedroom. But I kept my trap shut.

Ollie changed the subject by announcing I had received mail, which got me all keyed up. She handed me two letters with such a look of expectancy on her round face that I decided to share them with her.

The first was a note from Denise Williams, who I wrote to last week because she seems like a sensible person to talk to. Denise says I'm welcome to visit her and her aunt in Crawfordsville anytime. Her aunt

Hattie owns a little boarding house with an antique shop in the front, which Ollie said she'd love to see, so I'm thinking it might be nice for Ollie and me to take a little trip up there sometime.

The second letter was from my friend Murray back in Scranton. I've been waiting to hear from him. As I read aloud, I demonstrated for Ollie how Murray moves his long, skinny fingers when he talks. You have to picture it—it's as if he's pulling taffy. We both got a kick out of Murray's letter.

October 10, 1960

Howdy, Stink-Weed! Yippee-tie-ie-ay!

What's that dull humming, that rumble, that explosion!? It's me, Mighty Murray, surfacing like a super-powered shit slick from beneath a mountain of homework and miscellaneous crap.

That place you're being held captive in sounds like a ghost town. And no Hebrew types??? Too bad, because us Jews are a fun bunch. It's the Shriners you have to watch out for. Those hats are pathetic.

Hey, I got accepted to U. of Penn., but I'll need to get a scholarship, so I've been working my butt off at school. I wish you were going to Penn with me. You'd have no trouble getting in. Remember how my dad always said you were quite the thinker, except you "thunk" too much? (The senior Goldberg is such a wit.)

Guess who I'm dating now? Michelle Stahl. That's right-- Miss 'breast-assured' herself. Her personality is even nicer than her rack, which is amazing. Whoooew (that's me

*whistling innocently). So, Weedster, have you and Janine
done the deed yet? Give me DETAILS, man!*

*And speaking of dames, I saw Annie Peterson last week. She's
still on my shit list for dumping you while you were lying in
that hospital bed. I hope her melons fall off.*

*The Family Goldberg sends their love. They say they miss you
and your peculiar sense of humor HUGELY. Even so, I don't
think they've ever forgiven you for dressing up as a bleeding
Jesus and collapsing on our porch that one Easter. (But I'd
give it a '99'!) Give my regards to Custer.*

I'll spring you soon, pal.

Your Murrayness

*P.S. Liam-the-Load warned me I'll end up in San Quentin
because I just sent you Lady Chatterley's Lover, which, he says, is
banned from the U.S. Mail. That turdbrain WOULD know that!*

After I read the letter to Ollie (omitting the sex parts), I
told her all about Murray and Kenton (a, gulp, Negro!) and
and my other friends back home. I even told her about
annoying Liam O'Gara so she would understand
Murray's assessment that Liam is a turdbrain.

See, Liam is a killjoy know-it-all who sees doom
lurking around every corner. He's the one who told
Murray to get himself some good shoes because Jews
are destined to wander the earth forever. And there
were other equally morbid theories he tortured us with.
Whenever Murray and Kenton and I crossed our eyes,
Liam would tell us our eyes were about to pass each
other on the orbital plane. He said they'd freeze on the

wrong side of our heads and then we'd end up looking over our shoulders for the rest of our miserable lives. Liam, hungry for power, went on to describe the legions of the visually befuddled who never knew where they were because they could only see where they'd already been.

Liam even progressed to THEOREMS to prove his forecasts of doom. When we all went to see a horror movie about a tarantula that eats a potion that makes things grow bigger than Texas, Kenton (who's younger and has a wild imagination) was so petrified he got hiccups and spewed Jujubes all over his shoes. He was squealing like a rusty radiator until some kid yelled, "Tell that whiny girl to shut the hell up!"

I assured Kenton that we had no reason to worry about a tarantula eating us. "A real scientist would feed the growth formula to a frog," I reasoned, "then the airport-sized frog would eat the tarantula, and the whole thing would be settled."

Out of the blue, Liam steamed over us in THE LIAM DOOM TRAIN: "Major premise: Gigantic frog eats huge tarantula!" he yelled. "Minor premise: Now the world is left with a nauseous, pissed-off mutant frog! Conclusion: The putrid creature would stare us down with bulging eyes the size of an alien spaceship. Then suddenly, SPLA-A-A-T! That thing would hop on top of you and crush you to a bloody pulp right in your bed. Blood would squirt all over the walls, and your head would rupture like a grape. THE PAIN WOULD BE SO INTENSE IT WOULD KILL YOUR MOLDY, DECEASED FOREFATHERS, AND THEN YOU'D SHIT YOUR PANTS JUST LIKE THE DEAD KID YOU'D ALREADY BE!" (We eventually had to peel Kenton off Liam, but only after we let him land a few solid blows.)

Ollie said she agreed that Liam is a turdbrain. And I was really pleased when she added that she would love to meet Murray and Kenton and that they could wander to this end of the U.S. anytime they pleased. But after our discussion, I was feeling homesick for my old life. I decided to give Russ a call to see if he wanted to meet me at Searles' Store. It seemed like a positive thing to do to beat the blues. I took my letter with me just in case he wanted to hear it, too.

While I waited for Russ, I pumped Snarls for information about Andy Johnson. Snarls, who is a walking historical record of these parts, told me Andy graduated in 1950 and went overseas soon after. "Andy used to come 'round with his girlfriend, Jeannie Beth Price," Snarls reminisced. "She was cute as a cucumber. And everybody loved Andy. He was a real whippersnapper, so Jeannie Beth never let him out of her sight. Andy was good at everything. 'Loved to swim and fish out at the lake. After he returned from the war, his parents did everything they could to get him help, but he ran off. He wouldn't let anyone near him. His folks didn't have the heart to commit him, so they finally gave up. They moved one town over because it was all too painful to face every day. And Jeannie Beth married someone else and moved East somewhere," he shrugged.

"That's pretty sad. Did Miss Saslow ever come in here?"

My personal interest must have been obvious, because Snarls grinned and raised his brows. "Yep. She's younger than Andy, but she was a looker even back then. Y'know, we used to have lots of fun in here. There was even a time when we had a little dance floor over there where the booths are. Every so often, the kids would talk me into dancing a bit myself. Those were good times."

"What kind of dancing? Jitterbug?"

"Sure, and swing. And my specialty, which is tap."

I got a kick out of picturing the Mr. Pickwick of the

pharmacy world in tap shoes. "You're kidding! You can tap?" I prodded.

Snarls winked at me, and then he started humming "Singin' in the Rain." Before I knew it, he was singing and dancing behind the counter like a regular Gene Kelly while I whistled and hooted.

"That's great, Mr. Searles!" I told him. "You ought to perform in the church charity show."

"That fish won't fly. The wife says tap dancing is for women or coloreds, not old pharmacists," he frowned. "Please, don't tell anyone you saw me." He did a quick turn then stopped. "She won't let me play my accordion either," he complained. "She says it makes her think of her father, who was German and nastier than a sinus infection."

I remembered how Snarls's troll of a wife snubbed Ollie at church. "Is your wife a Nazi?" I inquired with mock innocence.

Snarls laughed and shook his head. "In her own way. But we've been married forty years, so I guess she has her good points."

I had to restrain my tongue. I was trying to coax Snarls into dancing again when I glanced out the window and saw Cotton McKamey pull up in his station wagon. A woman got out of his car and walked to the back door of the store, but she waited outside.

"Excuse me," Snarls said. "I have to take an order outside."

"It's Cotton! I'll go tell them to come in and join us," I said as I spun around on my stool.

"Don't bother, Weed. The coloreds stay outside, even though I've told 'em they're welcome to come in and shoot the breeze anytime."

It made me uncomfortable to see Cotton waiting out there by the door like a beggar. I was about to go say hello when Russ lumbered in the front door and sat down on the stool next to me.

When Snarls came back in, he nodded to Russ and brought us a pile of old yearbooks. "I keep 'em all," he smiled. "I thought you might want to look up Laura Saslow," he said with a wink before going back to work.

Russ yanked a yearbook out from under my nose. "Saslow?" he prodded, shooting me one of his jack-o-lantern grins.

"Yes, Saslow. Find Andy Johnson, too," I directed.

It didn't take us long to find Andy's senior photo. He was the class king of 1951, and back then he resembled the actor Gary Cooper. To be blunt, it was strange to see Andy with two eyes and a complete skull. His photo had some interesting comments printed below it:

Senior Class King. Boys' State. Class V.P. Honors. Best Smile. 4-H. Letters-Baseball & Track. Pizza, Luckies & Jeannie, Jeannie, Jeannie! Off to the U.S.M.C. Semper Fidelis.

Russ then discovered another provocative tidbit of information. At the end of the yearbook was a list of miscellaneous questions fired at the seniors. Andy 'A.J.' Johnson was asked:

Q: Who knows your deepest secret?
A: Joey

The name Joey leaped off the page at me. I had to know who this 'Joey' guy was that Andy had confused me with. "Let's look up every Joey in the senior class, Russ," I urged.

"There can't be many," he nodded. "Each class only has about thirty students."

He was right. We found only two Joeys.

"I remember 'em both," Snarls volunteered. "Joey Larkin was only around here two years. His family

moved on. The other one, Joey Burris, was Andy's pal.
He joined the Marines after graduation. As I recollect,
him and Andy went overseas 'bout the same time. Joey
fell on a land mine. Poor kid never made it home."

We read the info on Joey Burris, a guy with a
friendly grin and a small chip in his front tooth:

**Class Treasurer. Track and Field. College?
Science Project Finalist-State. Debater.
Latin Club. Loves Horses. Crazy for Corn
Dogs. Just Plain Crazy. Likes Laura Lots.**

Russ and I looked at each other. I know he was
wondering the same thing I was—could Laura Saslow
have been Joey's girlfriend? I couldn't picture them
together. Joey had zits the size of marshmallows.
Although Joey sounded nice enough, I was hoping
Andy hadn't mistaken me for his friend based on the
skin factor. I get paranoid about stuff like that.

Russ found Laura in the Class of '53. She looked so
sexy I had to think about gross things like foot odor, just
so I wouldn't do anything lewd to make the town
newspaper. I bet Russ was picturing her nude, too.
(He's pretty canine himself.) Russ read the information
under her photo aloud:

**Sophomore Princess. Honors. Senior
Homecoming Queen. Loves Literature. The Poet
Princess. Plans to Teach. Loves Frank Sinatra &
Pink Roses. Girls Softball. Off to Ball State.**

"Nothing about Joey," Russ said. "Are you gonna
tell me why you're looking up this stuff?"

I couldn't think of a convenient metaphor, so I told

him the truth, except for the part where Andy called me crippled. "I'm just curious," I explained. "I've seen Andy hanging around Miss Saslow's house. She's concerned about his welfare, but I'm not so sure he's as harmless as she believes. I think he could go crazy and do something stupid."

"Listen, Andy's half-gone... and Joey's dead," he said. "And Miss Saslow can take care of herself. Maybe that's what you need to start doing, too, buddy," he added with a transition that was almost as neck-breaking as one of mine.

I wasn't sure what Russ meant until I saw him looking at my bad leg, which was shaking like a runaway belt sander. I guess Russ meant well, but I suddenly felt like I was naked in a cell full of convicts. After another ten minutes, I made my polite good-byes and headed back to the house. I wish I had known then what was about to happen, 'cause I would have stayed put.

As I was limping back, I was thinking about Andy and Joey and about Russ's comment. I was so preoccupied that at first, I didn't notice the De Soto on the road next to me. Finally, I realized that the two genetic mistakes who had scared Cotton had surfaced again. I recognized the car immediately. A Spencer Gun Club bumper sticker leered at me from its prominent spot on the chrome bumper.

The driver slowed the car and followed alongside me as I walked along in silence. After a few minutes of their game, the guy who was riding shotgun squinted his pink eyes and asked me if I had committed any carnal acts with any Negroes lately. Only he used worse language than that.

I can't repeat what I retorted, but it didn't shed good light on his fornicating father, or sheep, or his recreational patterns with his mother.

They hurled some ugly threats at me, but I just kept

83

on walking because my leg was in no shape to run. After the thugs got bored, they finally burned rubber leaving me in a hailstorm of gravel. I suspect they were just trying to scare me, but, as much as I hate to admit it, it worked, especially when they said they're gunning for me. I should have left here sooner, because now I seriously wonder if I'm going to get out of here alive.

CHAPTER EIGHT

OCTOBER 23, 1960

OLLIE FELT LIKE SKIPPING CHURCH TODAY BECAUSE THE autumn leaves are so beautiful, she preferred to enjoy the outdoors. I suspected she wanted me to go for a walk with her, but my leg was not cooperating with the rest of my body. I've noticed my toenails are rotting, and my foot is a pasty color. (I've made a mental note to get some new socks.)

'Anyhows' (that's Hoosier), I came up with a great plan to thank Ollie for all she has done for me. I suggested we jump on a bus and go visit Denise up in Crawfordsville. It's about an hour's ride away. After I got on the phone and squared it all away with Denise and her Aunt Hattie, Ollie was dizzy with excitement.

She got all jazzed up in a red dress, a black hat, and her white gloves. I was praying we'd get out of the house with a bit of color control, but at the last minute, she grabbed a yellow flower for her hat and matching beads with a huge bumble-bee clasp. I had to admit, she was cheerful to look at... as if a person had a choice.

On the bus we got talking about the past, which I've learned is something old folks love to do. Ollie has some good stories though. She told me about the time the carnival was in Louisville, and she and Caleb got soused and climbed in a bathroom window of a club to see Fats Waller. She said, "I'd walk barefoot through a field of steaming cow paddies to see a guy like him or Muddy Waters perform!"

Then Ollie started to hum a medley. At first it was soft and pleasant, but then her gears started grinding. Suddenly Ollie let loose with "I've Got My Mojo Working" right there on the bus. "Com'on, hon, snap your fingers!" she urged as I was checking to see if I could fit under the seat.

Ollie has a good voice, but EVERYONE on the bus was looking at us as if we were a two-bit act from Appalachia. The more Ollie got her mojo working, the more her hat wobbled and rotated on her head. All I could picture was a dog looking for a place to squat. She nearly did me in when she yelled, "Everyone join in." By the time we pulled into Greencastle, I was wondering if her garter belt would fit around her larynx.

After we changed buses in Greencastle, she settled down long enough to tell me an interesting story about her trip on a river boat when the carnival was playing Shreveport. It seems Ollie and her friends took a dinner cruise one warm summer night when, according to Ollie, the crickets were so noisy they "must have had microphones." Ollie told the story as if it was a dream.

"When that old paddle wheel started turning, you could smell the lazy river," she said. "It was like rain on a dusty sidewalk. Friends were shouting from the dock. In the background, I could see Shreveport sparkling brighter than the Milky Way. When we went into dinner, the captain came 'round and introduced himself. He even pulled out my chair. After eating a magnificent supper with a slab of meat THIS big, we moved into a gambling salon where a man in a flowered vest was playing a mean piano."

Slowly Ollie started tapping her foot and singing "Alexander's Ragtime Band." Soon she was on a roll again. And when Ollie moved, the entire bus moved. I thought we'd be thrown off into a cornfield if she didn't settle down. I was eyeing the exit door and imagining kissing the pavement at forty miles per hour when Ollie closed in on another rousing chorus.

"Was your friend Caleb with you?" I suddenly interrupted, being the quick thinker I am during moments of unparalleled horror.

"No, coloreds weren't allowed aboard except as deck hands. Caleb and Samuel dropped us off then waved to us from shore. I felt real bad, but that's how it was in the early 1920's. It wasn't long after the release of that D.W. Griffith movie, *The Birth of a Nation*, which was about a group of K.K.K. 'heroes' who ride into town to save the women from all the sex-hungry Negro men. It was an ugly depiction of coloreds, but many whites believed it. Even Woodrow Wilson said it was a true portrayal. Those were bad times."

"Didn't any whites defend the Negroes?"

"Some tried. Unfortunately, the Klan was real strong then. We ran into them wherever we traveled, but the South was the worst. Caleb was flogged when we were in Natchez, Mississippi, for falling into a white man's swimming pool. They said he contaminated it, so they nearly killed him. We were scared all the time."

"Didn't the police help?"

"Oh, no, darlins. Many people in law enforcement and politics were tied to the Klan. Even Hugo Black had to renounce his K.K.K. membership to become a Supreme Court judge!"

"That's unbelievable!"

"It's true, Weed."

"Why didn't you just come back here?"

"It was bad here, too. A monster named David C. Stephenson ran the K.K.K. in Indiana in the '20s. I get sick down to my boots just to think about him. He raped a young gal up in Hammond, and then he chewed her like an animal! She died a terrible death."

I was flabbergasted. "Didn't anyone do anything to stop the K.K.K.?" I asked.

Ollie sighed and looked out the window. "Many of us were just plain afraid, I guess. We had all seen people get hurt real bad for fighting back. If we weren't scared to death for ourselves, we were scared for the people we loved. Everyone said it just was the way things were and that you couldn't change the world. But I wouldn't accept it if I came face to face with it now, Weed. Never again."

I mulled that over as we waited for two men to board the bus. I wondered if I would have had the courage to fight for Ollie's friends back then. I can't say. I guess a person doesn't really know how much courage he has until he's forced to dig deep for it.

When I glanced at Ollie, she seemed to be in some sad place in her head, so I tried to get her talking again. "Did my dad ever go with you on your travels, Ols?" I asked. (I call her Ols a lot.)

"No," she said quietly, "I wasn't even allowed to visit him. You see, darlins, I disgraced my mama. I wanted to be a dancer in fancy costumes, and I didn't think I'd ever get a chance if I stayed around here. So I became a carny--and then Mama shunned me. She did take in your daddy when I needed help though, Weed, but I was forbidden to come visit. She was a bitter woman, but at least she provided a home for Harold. I always planned to take back your daddy once he got his education. The sad thing was, when I reached the point that I was finally able to support him, he hardly remembered me.

"By the time word got to me that Mama died and I could finally come home, your daddy was grown and on his own. When he was in the war, I was traveling down South, but I came back here to live so he could always find me. I didn't see him much after we reconnected, but I sure was proud of him." Suddenly Ollie's face crumpled. She seemed very small for such a big lady.

"He must have loved you, Ollie," I consoled her. "Otherwise, he never would have tried to find you."

"I suppose. I talk to him all the time in my head, Weed. I hope he wasn't ashamed of me," she said softly.

"How could he be? Besides, you're fantastic. You were the only one who would take me in, and that would have made Dad real happy. Now how 'bout another song?" I said enthusiastically. (That last part just sort of slipped out because I wanted her to smile again. But it worked.) By the time we hit Crawfordsville, we were singing "Hard-Hearted Hannah," and I was feeling darn good.

Denise was waiting for us at the bus stop. She was dressed all in blue and smiling like a White Westinghouse model. She seemed so pleased to meet Ollie that Ols glowed like Times Square.

We rode in Denise's Studebaker for a brief tour of scenic Crawfordsville, which has a quaint town square. (When the Hoosiers find a good building plan, they go nuts.) We passed a lot of neat old Victorian houses, and trees that were glowing with such bright oranges and reds you'd think a sunset had melted all over them.

When we got to the small boarding house Denise's aunt owns, we all piled out like a bunch of rowdy sports fans. Denise's aunt is her mother's sister. Aunt Hattie is the friendly type—just like her eight-room establishment, which is a real old and comfortable place with lots of nooks and crannies.

While Hattie and Ollie sat down for a cup of coffee, I asked Denise to take a walk. I was excited to see the rotary jail I read about where all the cells rotate around a central axis operated by a hand crank. When Denise told me they don't allow visitors who aren't related to the inmates, I was pretty disappointed not to have a convict uncle because I wanted to give the ol' cellblock a spin.

"Sorry," Denise said, "but you don't look as though you feel too much like walking anyway. Let's take the car."

I was relieved, I admit, but as we climbed into the car, I had to say what was on my mind. There are some uncomfortable matters which a person has to bring up before the subject becomes as heavy as a silent fart. I took a breath then asked Denise, "So how come you haven't asked me about my leg?"

"I don't know," she shrugged. "I just assumed you would tell me what happened if you wanted me to know."

"I'm glad you didn't ask," I confessed, "because I might have made up something, and I wouldn't want to lie to you."

"I see. What do you tell the people who are rude enough to ask?"

Somehow, I didn't mind discussing my penchant for metaphors with Denise because I knew she wouldn't judge me. "Well, I can be quite inventive," I admitted. "On the bus ride out here from Scranton, I told a guy I was shot in the leg while running numbers for Tony 'the Meat Hook' Mancini. I figured no one would want to mess with an apprentice to the mob."

Denise laughed, which made me happy and still inside for a change. "I fell, Denise," I admitted. "That's how I creamed both legs, smashed my nose, crushed my right foot, and knocked out a lot of my teeth. That was about a year ago, but I'm almost okay now. That's all I want to say about it, if you don't mind."

"I'm sorry for all your pain," she said softly.

Suddenly she pulled the car to the curb, and I feared she was about to shove me into the nearest gimp-pick-up bin, but then she gestured for me to look over my shoulder at a neat group of old brick buildings. As you might have guessed, they were built around a square. The walls were covered with ivy, and the trees were fat and colorful. A stone sign identified the place as Wabash College.

"Isn't it a beautiful campus?" Denise asked. "I thought you might enjoy it here because it's so peaceful. I often drop by to read or walk on the common."

I sure did take to the looks of the place, and the sound of it, too. Words such as 'common' make me think of neat old schools I've read about where the gentry say, "Hey, old Sport!" and wear raccoon coats and saddle shoes and blow their oogah horns. Wabash is one of those goldfish-swallowing schools that smells like leather. And money.

I noticed a couple kissing on a bench on campus. They were really getting hot. As I watched, suddenly the scene started to feel all wrong. There was something familiar about the guy on the bench, who by then was stuck to the girl like a slug on a drainpipe. The girl seemed familiar, too. When they came up for air, they got up and strolled (very chummy-like) to a car parked on the side street, at which point I could see them better.

The guy laughed as the girl scraped what appeared to be dog poop off her shoe with a stick. When they got into a green Chevy BelAir, my stomach sank faster than the Titanic. It was Rick Bills, alright, but the girl was not Laura but JoAnn Stevens, Patty Lynn's sister—the fish fry tart.

JoAnn snuggled up real close to Rick in the car as they sucked face some more. I didn't need Annie Sullivan to describe to me what Rick's hands were doing. He and JoAnn looked as if they'd been a team

GWEN BANTA

longer than Bogie and Bacall. I wasn't sure whether to yell or puke, I was so angry about the entire situation.

"Aren't they from our neck of the woods?" Denise asked.

"Yep. He works over in Greencastle, so they must be out for a drive." I didn't want to elaborate because I felt so humiliated for Laura. And now I was tormented about whether or not I should tell Laura that the man she planned to marry was a slime-sucking bastard. I was so peeved that I wanted to run Rick down with his own BelAir. Backing over him again seemed like a good idea, too. I was imagining the pleasurable sound of Rick's bones snapping like bread sticks when Denise laid another zinger on me.

"My boyfriend goes to school here," she said. "I can't wait for you to meet Robert. He's pledging a fraternity, so he couldn't get away to join us today, but he says to say hello."

I have to admit, I felt myself deflating. It's not as if my erotic fantasies haven't included Denise. The truth is though, I was also relieved. Denise's involvement with Robert takes all the pressure off me to always be so cool. It's a relief of sorts.

When we got back to Hattie's place for lunch, a delicious aroma greeted my nose. We gathered in the kitchen, a festive room where everything has a blue and white checkered pattern. I didn't feel like eating much, even though Hattie had made grilled fish and mounds of mashed potatoes. The Laura and Rick situation had my guts in too much of a heap to pile anything else in there.

Over lunch, Hattie got Ols talking about Ollie's days with the carnival. They were both VERY animated. There was a half-empty liquor bottle on the shelf, so it didn't take Einstein to figure out the old gals had been tippling. I was silently begging God not to let Ollie sing. All six ears of the Trinity are apparently stone deaf because suddenly Ollie let loose with a doozy. Ollie not only burst into tune, but she also whipped into a hold-onto-your-hats shimmy like she was squeezing her way out of a garden hose.

I was ready to fall on the floor, feigning death as a reason to leave, when Denise whispered, "Ollie is great, Weed! I haven't had this much fun in ages. And Hattie is having a ball. I'm so glad she came."

At first I thought Denise's kindness was to keep me from sticking my tongue into the toaster. However, when I saw how sincere she was, I began to see my grandmother in a different light. Ollie may be incapable of controlling that spirit of hers, not to mention her lethal hips, but she sure is fun. And she's got some very slick moves. She could have been a June Taylor dancer. Or two.

Suddenly I felt terrible for being ashamed of her and I decided to throw all my support behind Ollie just to make up for my harsh thoughts. Ollie was singing something about a little grass shack in Hawaii when I abruptly jumped up and started doing the hula, wiggling better than Elvis. Soon everyone was on their feet. Hattie had some cool moves herself, including something called a "cake-walk." Our big number was "Rum and Coca-Cola" which spurred Hattie into pouring more liquor into some jelly glasses. I still hadn't figured out what a mojo is, but it was working all over the kitchen.

When we were too pooped to pucker, Hattie offered to open up the antique shop, and Ollie and I got pretty fired up about that. The shop, which looks out on scenic Wabash Avenue, is chockablock with knickknacks, furniture, fabrics, records, and lots of old photos.

While Ollie browsed through records, Denise and I rummaged about. I was trying on a monocle when I spotted a tiny china rose. It was pink and so detailed it looked real. I remembered Laura's yearbook photo caption, 'Loves Frank Sinatra & Pink Roses,' so I decided to buy the rose. I wanted to do something to ease Laura's sadness. I figure a little gift makes more sense than the words a person mangles when trying to express himself.

Denise didn't ask any questions. She even wrapped the rose in paper and put a ribbon around it. I paid with the money Murray's dad forced on me when I left Scranton, then I tucked the package in my jacket pocket before anyone else noticed.

I also found a Kewpie doll, which I thought would remind Ollie of her great times with the carnival, and a bright pink and green fringed scarf that was the kind of thing Jackie Kennedy would wear. I purchased those, too, because Ols deserves some nice things.

All in all, the day was going pretty swell when suddenly God pulled a "Liam" on me. God seems to operate exactly the way Liam-The-Load-O'Gara does. Just when things are going fine, God sends a mutant frog.

There I was having a good time with Denise in Hattie's antique shop when I saw a small pair of wooden Dutch shoes. That's all it took, then the doom train pulled in. I suddenly felt so much pain I had to sit down on the floor. All the pain just poured out of me and I began to cry like a girl. I couldn't stop myself because I was too tired from holding it in for so long.

Denise waved Hattie and Ollie away as she sat down next to me on the floor. "I hate to see you so sad," she whispered.

I tried to get a hold of myself, but it was real hard. "I'm okay," I lied. "I just miss my brother and my folks so damn much!"

"What happened to them, Weed?"

"They were killed in a goddamn car accident! All of them. Even my little brother. Dead. All of them dead!" I had never told her, but once I started, it just kept coming. "I never got to fly my brother around the world like I promised. I said we'd stop in France to do the Can-Can, and ride in a gondola in Venice, and go to Holland to see the windmills.

"And Leland said he'd love to have a pair of those wooden shoes the Dutch kids wear when they walk through the tulips. That's all he ever asked me for, Denise, so I promised I'd get him a real nice pair. Now I find these great Dutch shoes, and he's not even here. Jesus, it's not fair, Denise! He was just a kid when he died. How could God be such a sonofabitch that He never let a little guy like Leland have a chance to grow up? God should have taken me instead, and then Leland could wear wooden shoes and dance around the kitchen with my folks instead of being stuck in a cold box in the dark ground when he's afraid of the dark in the first place! How could God do such an evil thing?"

My tirade ended when I couldn't get any more breath. Denise held me and kissed my forehead, and I cried so hard there was snot running out of my nose, but I was too upset to care. Hattie and Ollie were beside themselves, and I feared I had ruined a darn good day for everyone.

"I used to think God was mean, too," Denise whispered. "When I was eleven, my father had been gone for a year. I thought he was in Detroit building cars to make money to send back home.

"Our neighbor, Jackson McGhee, knew I used to listen to the Indy 500 race on the radio with my dad every Memorial Day weekend and drink lemonade and cheer for whoever Dad had bet on. It was always Johnnie Parsons or Mauri Rose or Bill Vukovich. That's why the year after my dad left, Mr. McGhee took me to the speedway so I could see the race.

"The day of the race, right in the middle of that huge crowd, I spotted my father standing with his arm around a strange woman. He looked right at me, then he turned and ran away as fast as he could through the crowd. I chased after him until I thought my chest would burst, but he disappeared beyond the stands.

"By the time Mr. McGhee caught up with me, I was hysterical. He looked at me with the kindest eyes I've ever seen and said, 'Chile, I jus' know dere's got to be the happiest life awaitin' for ya cuz dis pain is proof of dat.' When I looked at him as if he was loony, he smiled gently and said, 'It's a scientific fact, hon.'

"After he bought me a snow cone, he led me to the grassy infield. Although the race cars were pulling out onto the track, Mr. McGhee paid no attention to anything except me. 'Chile, have ya never heard of Newton's Law of Motion?' he asked. 'It tells how when a force hits a body and pushes it hard in a certain direction, then that ol' body has no choice but to swing right back just as hard as it's done been pushed. So ya see, if life pushes a body to the point where the pain is so bad you think you gonna break, dat's a guarantee yo' life is gonna swing back so hard it ain't stoppin' till you see Heaven right on dis here earth.'"

Denise nodded knowingly. "I think Mr. McGhee knew what he was talking about, Weed. We just need to see the rest of God's plan. My daddy never returned, and it still hurts... but a little less each day. I'm slowly swinging the other way just like McGhee promised. And I plan to 'experience Heaven right on dis here earth,'" she said, mimicking McGhee. "Or at least a beer. How about a beer and a game of Checkers?"

I was damn glad she offered me a beer. I don't have a taste for it, but at least she wasn't treating me like a whimpering little paste eater. I drank two to make a point.

We sat there a long time as Ollie and Hattie pretended to browse. Those two liquored-up gals worked so hard at being nonchalant that the situation became perversely funny. "Oh, Hattie," Ollie fake-whispered, "look at this lovely fox wrap." She was holding a stole that must have been run through a combine. Denise and I paused a moment and then fell all over each other like howling coyotes. By the time Denise took us to the station, my head felt huge, but my nerves were finally calm and my stomach was no longer trying to eat itself.

We were all saying our good-byes at the depot when none other than Rick Bills pulled into the station right behind us. I kept my eyes down, but I managed to watch his every move.

Ollie and I boarded the bus as Rick kissed JoAnn good-bye. They ground hips for so long I thought we'd have to hose them down. Rick looked around sheepishly, probably worried that someone might recognize him as the diseased boner that he is. After JoAnn finally retrieved her tongue from Rick's lung, she boarded the bus and sat right in front of Ollie. I tried to fake a nap, but it was impossible not to stare at the back of her horned head.

Before the bus pulled out, Denise jumped on long enough to hand me my gifts for Laura and Ollie. I tried to focus on her smile as we pulled out, but all I could see was JoAnn. She was scowling at Ollie and me and then back at Denise as if we were a mob of Philistines.

Thank goodness Ollie was so pleased with her gifts that she didn't notice JoAnn's sour mug. When Ollie impetuously stood up in the aisle to model her new scarf, JoAnn rolled her eyes in disgust. I figure if JoAnn's going to be blind about good people, she might as well donate her peepers to shell-shocked Andy. He could use them more.

I was exhausted and worked up again by the time we arrived home. Just before I turned in, I saw something on the floor outside my bedroom door. It was the pair of wooden Dutch shoes with a note from Ollie attached:

Weed Dear,

I had such a lovely time. Thank you, darlins. I bought these shoes for you to save for another day. Someday I hope you'll be able to look at them and think of Leland dancing in Heaven with all the happy little Dutch children. I know you're in pain, darlins, but please don't do anything that would break my heart.

Your loving Ollie, Queen of the Carnival

P.S. You could paint them poppy red. It's so cheerful, don't you think?

CHAPTER NINE
OCTOBER 28, 1960

WE HAD AN HONEST-TO-GOD DAY OFF FROM SCHOOL today, so I didn't have to create one. Russ picked me up just after noon in his dad's old Ford truck, a lumbering relic with a steering wheel as big as the trunk of a sequoia. Just bouncing around in that old cab makes you want to yell words like "yee-haw" out the window.

We decided to stop for a Coke at the sundry store. Russ and I slid into a booth, rubbing our butts along the vinyl just to create those rolling-fart sounds. When Snarls heard the rumble, he laughed and stepped out from behind the pharmacy counter. My mouth fell open when I saw his face. He had a shiner so bloody-looking it could have doubled as his liver. Even his puff of red hair was flat, which was unsettling in an odd way.

"Whoa!" I yelled. "How did you get that shiner?" Russ abruptly kicked me in the only good leg I've got left. I drilled my eyes into the back of his skull while I tried to assess the situation.

"Is your eye okay, Mr. Searles?" I inquired, ignoring Russ's furled brow.

"Oh, sure, it's fine, son. When I was unloading boxes, I dropped a jar on my head," Snarls explained, not looking me in the eye. "But I'm tougher than a toadstool," he added. "You just let me get you boys some sundaes. Feeding hungry teenagers is enough to make any man feel as fit as a flapjack."

I wasn't buying his cheerful act. As soon as he went to get our ice cream, Russ filled me in on the town gossip. Word is out that Snarls and the Fraulein Snarls haven't been getting along for some time. Supposedly she's meaner than a junkyard dog and clobbers him frequently, if you can imagine such a thing. The poor guy can't thump her back because a good guy doesn't hit a woman, not even a Nazi hag. The town talk is that Snarls has been sad and mistreated for years.

I was digesting the information along with a spoon of marshmallow topping when Janine's friend Patty Lynn Stevens walked into the joint with her mother. She headed toward us immediately, almost as if she'd been tracking us. "Hey you guys!" she said. "I saw your truck outside, Russ. Gee, your hair looks great!"

When Patty Lynn sat down next to Russ, I sensed he felt like he was finally something more to her than the vapor he had been prior to the Kamasutra incident. However, as she shifted her look toward me, I could hear the gates of Hell open up to suck me in. "My sister JoAnn tells me she saw you and your grandmother on the bus coming from Crawfordsville," she baited.

"Yep, your sister is quite the sleuth," I confirmed, trying to get the jump on her. "I never did ask JoAnn what she was doing in Crawfordsville." *Besides jumping all over Rick Bills like a jackal on fresh carcass.*

"Oh, she dates a Wabash student. JoAnn told me she saw you with Denise, that Negro girl you went to the Roundabout with."

"I know who 'that *Negro* girl' is, Patty Lynn," I retorted. Talking to Patty Lynn was like talking to Janine-same girl, different sweater. They must be part of a coven. It was shocking to me that my visit with Denise Williams was such a topic of interest to anyone. "Patty Lynn, if you're going to be the next Walter Winchell," I sneered, "then you better get yourself a jaunty little reporter hat!" I don't think my blow landed because she kept on smiling like the fool she is.

"Well, aren't you afraid people will think you're low-class by hanging out with colored people?" she pressed.

"Aren't you afraid people will think you're a laundry lady, the way you go to such trouble to separate colors from whites?"

"Don't be rude, Weed Clapper. I'm just looking out for you. If Janine's parents hear about this, they might not let her date you. But don't worry, I won't say anything."

As I was formulating a retort, she got up to leave. "Thanks, Patty Lynn," I grunted to her back, "and tell JoAnn to say hello to her Wabash stud from Laura's friend, Weed Clapper." Patty Lynn shot me a curious look before hustling out after her mother.

When I turned back to Russ, I saw that dark look he gets when he's worried. "Weed, about Denise—"

I cut him off faster than an Indy race driver. "Not you, too," I snapped. "Denise Williams and I are friends, Russ. Like you and me."

"Take it easy, man," he said. "You won't hear any of that crap outta me. I just don't want you to have any trouble. There are some idiots around who can make life miserable for you if they get a notion."

"You mean I might find myself swinging from a tree if I continue to be friends with Denise?"

"I hope not. But it's not advisable to piss off the wrong people. There was a bad incident here two years ago. It happened to a guy named Ray Duncan. He's not much older than us. He now lives in a convalescent home in Indianapolis.

"The official story is that Ray hit his head on a rock while diving into the lake. The true story is that some guys held Ray under water too long just to punish him for defending a Negro in a bar fight in Spencer the night before. Apparently, Ray had tried to pull the troublemakers off the guy, but the instigators beat the Negro to a pulp for being in a white man's bar. They got Ray the next day."

"A 'white man's bar'? Isn't that against the law?"

"So is beating a Negro, but it happens." Russ shook his head. "Anyway, the Negro eventually recovered, but Ray was severely brain-damaged. By the way, the Negro was Cotton McKamey's son."

"Holy shit!" Cotton's fear finally made sense to me, and I was starting to feel the fear myself. I certainly don't relish the thought of getting my brain crushed for being friends with Denise. "How did you find out Ray's 'accident' was intentional?" I asked.

"Because Ken Rollins, my neighbor, overheard the assholes who did it. They were laughing about it in a bowling alley in Spencer."

"Why didn't Ken tell the police?"

"He did. But it was his word against theirs. Then all that summer, the animals on Ken's farm kept turning up dead. Now Ken won't talk about it to anyone. Nobody in his family will either."

"That's outrageous!"

"I know. Most people around here don't behave that way, but I'm afraid you could run into some grief if you continue to pal around with Denise. Russ then shot me one of his dopey grins. "Aw, hell, I've got your back, pal," he assured me, "as long as no one messes with my hair." He polished off his sundae and wiped his mouth with the back of his hand. Then he wiped his hand on a napkin, which struck me as backasswards.

Because I can trust Russ, I decided to ask some questions of a more personal nature. "While we're at it, how 'bout telling me why people turn a cold shoulder to Ollie, Russ? I've seen it for myself—at church, and everywhere. By all appearances, she's not a 'N-E-E-GRO,' so what's up with her being so ostracized?"

"Aw, jeez, Weed, why did you have to go and ask me that?"

"Give it to me straight, Russ."

"All I can tell you is that I've heard people say she's, well, sort of eccentric."

"So? Spit it out, man!"

"Aw, crap, Weed! Okay, okay. To be honest, I once heard someone say Ollie was a stripper, so I think some snotty types won't associate with her because of her past."

"Ollie wasn't a stripper, Russ! She was in a sophisticated dance review. She wore high-class, fancy costumes and did elegant French dances, and she was well-known as an exotic—" When my brain finally kicked in, my mouth suddenly ground to a complete halt.

Then the horrifying images came at me with more firing power than an attack of Russian MiGs. All I could conjure in my head were scenes of Jolly Ollie and her mounds of pink flesh gyrating in front of a crowd of drooling, inbred hicks in a moth-eaten tent in some backwater town. I could picture those gargantuan breasts of hers flapping like two deflated wind socks, and her puckered haunches, like a bleu cheese moon, shaking under the lights as toothless half-wits called out for more. My imagination was so revved up I was about to puke.

"Aw, Jesus," I groaned. Okay, so maybe I should have known it all along, but a guy believes what he needs to believe to get by. After all, Ollie *is* my grandmother. After I finally put it all together, I got up and rushed out before I could lose control and hit something.

Russ caught up with me. "Aw, man, I should never have said anything," he whined. "Ollie's a good ol' gal.

GWEN BANTA

My dad says she's a wonderful lady. I was even supposed to tell you to say hello for him. He really respects her."

"Yeah, right!" I moaned.

"For God's sake, Weed, Ollie was a stripper, not a hooker!"

"Same difference," I retorted as I crossed the street without even looking to see if old monument-ramming Mrs. Byrd was anywhere in sight. I knew even she couldn't plow down my mountain of misery.

"At least let me drop you home," Russ yelled.

"No, thanks. I need to unwind. I'll catch up with you later," I mumbled. I knew I had to find some way back to my old life.

———

Ten minutes later I was staring at Laura's front door. I was so relieved to find her home that I almost wrapped my arms around her. She must have sensed it because she just stood there and quietly stroked my shoulder. After I pulled myself together, I walked past her and plopped down on her sofa without any invitation at all.

"I'll make us some coffee," was all she said. When she returned, she put an old Glenn Miller record on the HiFi and sat down next to me. "What's wrong, Weed?" she asked.

I was too ashamed of Ollie to even discuss it. I just wanted to look at Laura before saying good-bye to this place forever. I didn't know what I wanted. "If I had the money that's coming to me, I'd beat it out of here so fast I wouldn't even be a memory," I suddenly blurted. "Maybe I'll just hop a train anyway." *Or throw myself in front of one.*

"If you decide to go, Weed, please let me give you some money. I couldn't sleep at the thought of you going hungry."

The irony killed me. Here I wanted to end my miserable life, but Laura was hell-bent on keeping me well-fed.

"Are you still planning to marry Rick?" I asked. Frankly, I don't know where the question came from, but it was stuck there in the middle of the moment like a tit on a forehead.

Laura answered so softly I could hardly hear her. "Is that what's bothering you?"

"No, not at all. I was just changing the subject," I lied.

"To answer your question, Rick wants to save more money."

"How much does he need? You won't be difficult to support. I've seen plants eat more than you do."

She smiled at that one. "He wants to be able to buy a house, and he needs to pay off some loans."

"Well, he drives a real fancy car," I said a bit too snidely.

She smiled again, thank goodness. "Yes, that's true... but the people who are truly well-to-do around here are not always the showy ones."

"Give me a 'for instance,'" I said, relieved to be diverted.

"Well, Barley Edinburgh, for one. He invested well, and he owns the Roustabout. He even has his own helicopter that he keeps in a field near Kinney's farm. Then there's Roy Kinney, Russ's dad. He's a very wealthy rancher."

"Russ is rich?"

"Most people would say that. The Kinneys own the greater part of the west side of town, and they raise a fine breed of stud horses. Many other farmers, like Jimmy Dale's father, rent their land from Roy Kinney. That's probably why Jimmy Dale is not very friendly toward Russ. I suspect JD feels a bit inferior."

"I don't know why JD, the class stud, would feel that

way. Russ never acts snooty at all...at least not like Janine or Patty Lynn," I said.

"Janine and Patty Lynn come from average-income families, Weed, but perhaps they act arrogant because they're beautiful. For young girls that's a type of wealth and power."

"I guess everyone wants some kind of power," I nodded.

"You're right, Weed. But power comes from many things other than money and beauty. I think there's power in loving another person, don't you?"

"Yes," I answered. "Did you ever love anyone besides Rick?" I asked. "Like that, I mean?"

"I don't know..." she hesitated.

"What about Joey Burris?"

Laura turned around so fast you'd think I'd asked if I could shave her back with hedge clippers. "How do you know about Joey?"

"The yearbook. Were you the Laura he was in love with?"

At first, Laura didn't respond. I was sure I had stepped over the line, a move I've perfected. But finally, she answered.

"I'm that Laura, but I wasn't in love with Joey Burris. I loved him as a friend. We dated for a few months, and I promised him I'd go to the movies with him when he came back from Korea, but we never got a chance. One year later, Joey's body was sent to San Francisco in a coffin then shipped here for burial."

"Joey and Andy Johnson were good friends, weren't they?"

"Yes, they were. Joey wasn't much of a correspondent, but Andy wrote to me regularly. They were in the same battalion, so we all were worried sick when the letters from Andy stopped coming around the same time Joey was killed. For ten months Andy was missing in action, but eventually he was located and sent back to San Diego. His parents heard that Andy stepped on a mine going back to save Joey from the North Koreans. When Andy returned to Indiana, everyone was shocked and heartbroken to see what had happened to him.

"Andy wouldn't talk or let anyone help him. As bad as Andy's physical injuries were, his emotional state was even worse. Now he's just a shell." Laura stared at some place far in the distance, like she was no longer talking just to me.

"Laura, I think Andy is quite a bit more capable than people give him credit for. On my way here, I saw him at the Coke machine in front of the I.G.A. grocery store. He put in the right amount of change to get a drink. That must mean something."

I could tell Laura was thinking about that because her brows dipped over her eyes. "I suppose that's good," she nodded. "I've never seen him do that...but the doctors told Andy's parents that Andy's mind is gone. He still thinks he's in Korea."

"Then why does he read newspapers?"

I watched as Laura's thoughtful expression changed to one of complete surprise. "Yes, Laura," I elaborated to make my point, "More than once I've seen him sitting behind the school reading the paper to catch up on the news."

Laura sat in silence for a long time. I knew she was troubled. Then suddenly she switched gears the way I do when I don't want to talk about something anymore. I wasn't sure why she couldn't deal with the subject of Andy, but I let her change the topic. That was a mistake on my part because it led us back to the subject I was avoiding.

"I forgot to pour our coffee," she apologized. "And I baked some macaroons. I'll wrap some up for you to take home to Ollie."

GWEN BANTA

"No, don't bother, Laura," I snapped. "I don't intend to go back to Ollie's,"

"Why not, Weed?" she asked, as if I was just going to open up and blab to her about my low-class, carnival, stripper, Queen-of-the-Carnal grandmother.

"Because she's a low-class, carnival-stripping, Queen-of-the-Carnal grandmother," I retorted--like the dope that I am.

"Ummm. Who told you such rubbish? Janine?"

"No. I made Russ tell me. It's not as if I haven't noticed how everyone shuns Ollie. She's a tart, Laura, and everyone around here knew it except me. That's why they avoid her. They're no doubt convinced she has gonorrhea, like some sort of human petri dish."

"Stop it, Weed. You're blowing this out of proportion. Ollie has one of the biggest hearts I've ever known. If others want to judge, that's a sign of their own ignorance and narrow-mindedness!"

"Ollie took her clothes off for money," I exclaimed. "Most folks don't need a priest to know that's a goddamn cheap thing to do!" I didn't mean to cuss in front of Laura, but by then I was so wound-up that if I didn't cuss, I would've burst my prostate.

"Have you ever heard of Sally Rand?" Laura demanded. Her hands were on her hips in that teacher sort of way, but by now I know her too well to cower when she tries to pull rank on me. Therefore, my mouth just kept right on going.

"No, why, was she a gonorrhea carrier, too?" I asked with a fake smile. Sure, I was being a mouthy, but it had to run its course.

"Sally Rand is an exotic dancer."

"Jesus, they're everywhere."

Laura ignored my ranting. "Sally Rand is the best there is," she told me. "When she performs, she uses fans in such a way as to be erotic and at the same time, very classy. Her dances are more of a suggestion than a

108

delivery. She has entertained more dignitaries than the famous dancers of the Moulin Rouge in Paris. Ollie was just ahead of her time like so many other artists."

"You're saying Ollie was an artist?"

"Yes, and a lady. Ollie has never been anything less than honest about who she is. She celebrates life, and we could all learn from her. You should be proud she's your grandmother."

She let me mull that over in silence while we listened to "Moonglow." It gave me a chance to put some things in perspective. I guess it's not Ollie's fault that people who haven't lived the high life are shocked because she has. Sometimes I think judging others is a way for the disappointed ones to forgive themselves for never having had the courage to take chances in their own lives.

I felt lousy for being so judgmental myself. "Thanks, Laura," I said as I stood up to leave before I wore out my welcome. "I want to apologize for the gonorrhea outburst. I was just lashing out. I didn't know Ollie when I was growing up, and I don't want to leave here without knowing her at least a little."

After I grabbed my coat and opened the door, I remembered what was in my jacket pocket. "Here," I said, as I took out the gift from Hattie's shop, "I heard you like pink roses."

Laura had the strangest reaction to that. After she unwrapped her gift, she smiled. Then she reached up, took my face in her hands, and pulled me down to her. I didn't know what to expect. She looked at me long and hard, then she pressed her soft lips against my face for a brief moment before she turned around and walked out of the room.

After I stood for a moment with her kiss still warm on my cheek, I quietly closed the door. What I did after that is unclear to me. I remember I had to sit down by her tree before I was able to walk home. My thoughts

were so jumbled I was only able to focus on small
things, like the curls of birch bark on the ground in front
of me. Everything else was too big.

Now the whole world feels as if it has tipped to one
side. My life has suddenly changed, but I'm spinning
too fast to try to understand it all.

CHAPTER TEN
NOVEMBER 7, 1960

LAST NIGHT WHEN I WAS IN BED, I HEARD VOICES. NO, NOT the kind of voices that order you to put on lipstick and go rearrange your neighbor's face with a hatchet. There were muffled voices coming from Ollie's bedroom, and some occasional giggling, too. I finally heard the back door close around six o'clock this morning.

When I got up, Ollie was buzzing around, singing, and laughing at God knows what.

"You're mighty chipper this morning," I said.

"Cheerfulness is a thank you to the world for its blessings," she replied like a twittering fool. "That's what Reverend Harper says."

I promptly decided I needed some coffee, and an Alka-Seltzer to go with it. "That preacher guy has something to say about everything," I muttered as I filled my cup.

"Yes, and I've always liked a man who is sure of himself."

The hair on my neck suddenly mushroomed. There was something in Ollie's voice when she mentioned Bible-thumping Harper that made me stop what I was doing.

"You like that guy, Ollie?" I asked. "He wears white-tipped shoes, for criminey-sake. That is so hick!"

"I think he's rather sexy," Ollie giggled.

Then it hit me. Ollie was being saucy! And before breakfast! It was all I could do to keep from lighting the oven and broiling my head. I want Ols to be happy; she deserves it. But what if her bedroom antics involve our local man of the cloth? Nobody wants a bald minister with slimy hands slinking around like an Unholy Ghost offering his sacraments to an aging, overweight stripper. Russ's father would be a better choice. However, they're *both* married, so it ALL seems damn immoral if you ask me. I'm still just trying to deal with all the 'exotic dancer' information—I'm hardly ready for anything adulterous!

I was so busy thinking about the whole business that it took me awhile to notice the vase of flowers on the table.

"Nice flowers, Ols," I commented. "Who are they from?"

"Oh, I picked them," she smiled.

Now that's an amazing feat, I thought. Roses in the middle of a colder-than-a-witch's-tit November, and with a tiny card attached! The old gal sure is resourceful. I got a peek at the message which said, "I love you, a barrel."

I was shocked that anyone would call Ollie a barrel, hefty though she is. When she wasn't looking, I flipped the card over to see if there was a signature. (I decided it was the honorable thing to do in case someone out there is taking cheap shots at Ollie and needs a harsh talking-to.) The message continued, "...and a heap." No signature. Then it dawned on me that those are the words from some old, sappy song, and Ollie's caller was just trying to be as cute as the ever-lovin' dickens.

I was about to comment when a disturbing radio report got my attention. Ollie and I listened as the news reporter described how four guys in Terre Haute beat a Negro for using a restroom at a department store.

THE REMARKABLE JOURNEY OF WEED CLAPPER

According to reports, he was hurt real bad. Now the Negroes are demonstrating at the store. Ollie says the world is a pressure cooker, and the steam is building.

After breakfast, I kept thinking about her words as I headed out to mail a card to Denise. She has invited Ollie and me to join her and Aunt Hattie and Robert-the-boyfriend for Thanksgiving here in town at her mother's house. Ollie was thrilled; she says it will be a nice change of pace for us.

When I got to the post office, which is the size of Leland's tree house, I saw Andy sitting on a bench, so I sat down next to him. It was hard not to stare at his caved-in skull. I admit I'm kind of obsessed with studying his cranium. Somehow, I think if I can memorize every gruesome detail, I'll be able to get past the horror of his injuries and find what's left of the guy who's in there.

It just seems so fake to me the way folks act polite and turn away as if he's invisible. If I were him, I'd yell, "Oh, right, like you didn't notice I left half my brain and body in Korea fighting for you and your stinkin' corn fields! You're all more brainless than I am. So what do you have to say to that, you rude asswipes?"

When I sat next to Andy, he moved away from me. "Andy," I explained, "I know you're in there. But please don't start calling me Joey, because my name is Weed, Weed Clapper. And please don't look at me like I'm a freak, because I'm trying real damn hard to belong somewhere."

He didn't say anything. He just nodded slightly before he lit up a cigarette. I was blabbering on about Castro and how we might someday have to go down there and kick his butt when Andy offered me a Lucky. As I mentioned, I'm not as fond of smoking the things as I am of the look of them, but I accepted one just to be social. Then I told Andy about the graveyard I visited.

I don't know why, but I've always enjoyed a good

graveyard. That's one of the reasons I can't wait to see New Orleans. There are usually some clever epitaphs in a graveyard, so you can pick up some wisdom. But the graveyard in this town stinks.

Several days ago, I checked it out because I wanted to see Joey Burris's grave out of respect for him dying for us in the war. It really got to me when I saw that Joey was only twenty years old when he got blown up. I bet he never got to see many great places, and it kills me to imagine he probably died thinking about home.

I didn't want to bring up a sad subject with Andy, but I thought we could talk man-to-man, with me doing all the talking of course. "I saw Joey Burris's grave, and I want to thank you both for fighting for our country," I told Andy. "That's real brave what you did. I would have crapped my pants every day and all night long. And I'm real sorry for the awful stuff that happened to you. Your face and body are pretty messed up, but I know you can still think about things because you always know where to find Luckies, and you had the manners to offer me one. Good brand, too. I just wanted to tell you if you ever want a Dusty Road, I'll be happy to buy you one."

When I got up to leave, he scared the bejeezus out of me. "How is Joey?" he mumbled. The words seemed to be oozing from a melted wax head. But I was sure that's what he said.

I felt so uncomfortable I wanted to pretend I didn't hear him, but my dad always told me a man doesn't run away from something he started. "Joey didn't make it back, Andy," I finally answered.

Andy nodded slowly, as if he already knew the answer. Then I saw something I don't ever want to see again. He started crying. The damnedest thing was that there was a tear coming out of the duct in the knot of scar tissue where his missing eye once was. His scar was crying! I was so shocked I gasped, which is probably a great deal more impolite than ignoring him in the first place. I started walking as fast as I could. I wanted to get away from there before I became irrational, being the jerkwad that I am.

Suddenly Andy said to my back, "Laura?"

I stopped dead in my tracks and turned around to face him. "Laura who? Laura Saslow? Is that who you're calling to, Andy? The girl Joey was in love with?" Andy nodded then looked at his feet, so of course I had to go back.

When I approached, I was unsure about what to do next. One of his tears was stuck in a crevice of scar tissue like a tiny puddle. "Here," I said, as I brushed his face with my sleeve, "no need to cry." I was shaking, but I tried to be as gentle as I could. I was afraid his face would come apart if I rubbed too hard.

"Laura knows Joey," he mumbled. As his mouth rotated around the missing jaw clumps of scar tissue yanked at Andy's lip exposing his mangled gums. "Laura knows Joey," he whimpered again. "Tell her Joey lives in my heart." He shook from the effort to make me understand what he was saying.

"I promise I'll tell her, man," I nodded. "You just take it easy, okay? And you remember that you're a real hero in my book."

I wanted to get away from there, yet I walked very slowly. I had an irrational fear that if I moved too fast, something would catch me, but if I kept moving slowly, whatever was chasing me would stay a few steps behind.

———

Laura was hanging clothes out on the line when my feet found their way to her house. She said hello, although I'm not so sure I answered. I started hanging clothes because I had a burning desire to keep busy.

115

She waited quietly until I got up the momentum to talk.

"You look real swell in Levi jeans," I finally said. "I mean, real relaxed."

She just smiled. By now she knows that when I get no response, I continue making nervous conversation until I spill my guts. "How am I doing?" I asked, nodding at the clothes on the line.

"You're very good at this," she said in that soft way of hers that means she's enjoying my company.

"My mother taught me."

"She did?"

"Uh huh, she taught me a lot of things. She seemed to enjoy everything she did. Mom always told me that as long as a person is stuck on this planet, he should 'commit to really living every minute to its fullest.'"

"I need to remember that," Laura said quietly.

"Yeah. I think my mom knew more about the world than my father, even though he was the talkative one. I inherited his tongue-wagging gene."

Laura shot me a big smile. "Well, it seems your father had good genes, Weed," she said, "and your mother sounds wonderful, too."

"She sure was." I didn't plan to say much more about my mother than that. It's too difficult. One time I tried to discuss her with a doctor in Scranton who kept prodding me to break my self-imposed silence. When I tried to use the words my mom deserves, my voice crawled out of my throat wrapped in a huge ball of ear-assaulting pain. I'm not sure a person can tell someone else what his mom was like anyway. Or how everything in the whole world seems as if it's floating when your mom is dead. And sounds become fuzzy and very far away. And colors are thick around the edges like the colors of an old Life Magazine shoved aside in an empty attic.

"What else do you remember about your mom, Weed?" Laura asked.

Laura was so gentle about asking the question that to my surprise, I answered. "Lots of nice things," I told her. "My mom loved music—any kind at all. She said music is like water because it sustains life. She's the one who taught me how to dance. The radio was always on, so we'd all take turns dancing around the kitchen. Even Leland could cut a rug."

As I continued talking, Laura gestured for me to follow her inside. "Anyway," I continued as she brewed coffee, "Mom had a knack for explaining things that Dad couldn't. Like the time my friend Murray and I asked Mom why we should believe in God if people such as Hitler were allowed to live, while Mrs. Fiorelli, who was super-nice, had to die of cancer. Mom explained how sometimes it's hard for a person to see the whole picture. 'The world can seem much too big and far away,' she said, 'even when you're standing right in the middle of it. If you can't see the forest, try to focus on one small, lovely tree. When you focus on the small things in life, you'll discover God isn't just out *there*, like a dim memory of something from long ago. You'll find Him in the little things, such as your daddy's smile or Leland's toes or the smell of lilacs. Or music... God is always in music.'

"My dad, who was listening, just smiled at her the way he always did when he wanted to tell my mother how much he loved her but couldn't find the words. He looked at me and said, 'Mom's right about focusing on the little things, son. Whenever I see cherries, I think of that little pin with two cherries your mom often wears on her collar. And I always smile. Cherries remind me that God made your beautiful mother.' Then my dad turned and left the room."

After telling Laura about that incident, all I could picture was my father walking away with his shoulders held high. And I saw my mother touching the cherry pin on her collar and smiling at something that I knew was very private. I shouldn't have been talking about such stuff. I tried to force the image of the two of them out of my mind, but my brain was trying to hold onto it. Suddenly I felt as if someone was squeezing my neck. There was no air left in Laura's kitchen, so I had to take deep breaths to keep from suffocating.

Laura reached out and took my hand. "I don't have the words to tell you how sad I feel about what you've been through, Weed. I'm so sorry you lost your parents….and dear Leland."

Something happened to me then. I didn't see the black hole in front of me, but it had no boundaries, so I couldn't step around it. Before I could stop myself, I jumped up, knocking the chair to the floor. "Why do people use words like 'lost,' Laura? Those phony words can't cover up the truth!"

Maybe I was yelling, I'm not sure, but I saw Laura pull back from me. That didn't stop what was coming.

"I didn't 'lose' my parents and my brother, Laura. They didn't 'pass away,' and they didn't 'succumb,' or 'expire,' or 'kick the damn bucket,' or any other euphemism! They were killed in the ugliest way you could ever imagine. They were SMASHED and MANGLED and TORN until they were deader than dry rot!

"The day it happened I had the Asian flu. My mom had made me baked apples, and she had baked Leland a cake because it was Leland's eighth birthday. While I stayed home, they went to pick up Leland's new puppy. Leland was going to name his dog Fala, like F.D.R.'s dog, but he swore he'd never leave his dog behind the way F.D.R. once did.

"My family was in the car when they got stuck on the Lackawanna Railroad tracks in that stinking Ford Galaxy. They managed to get out when they saw the train coming, but my Mom's foot got caught. My father got around to her side of the car in time to save her just like the hero he had always been. Then my mother let go of Leland's hand, which makes me sometimes hate her for not being strong enough to hold on. The moment she let go, Leland went back for his new puppy. And that's my father's fault, because he once said, 'What kind of a hero wouldn't save a puppy?' And Leland heard him say it.

"Mom and Dad ran back to the car after Leland. The train didn't stop...it just kept coming, because God is a miserable fool who can't even stop a stinkin' train on a track!

"And at the funeral I overheard Liam O'Gara's father describe in a low voice how my parents were thrown a hundred yards, and how my mother suffered. She died in agony while she was wearing those little cherries on her lapel—those cherries my father said to focus on if I wanted to understand God. Well, Laura, you tell me how to understand a God who crushes a dad and makes a mother suffer and traps a little kid in a wrecked car!

"Mr. O'Gara said when they found my brother, his head was torn completely off. And Leland had the puppy with him because the little guy wanted to be a hero just like Dad. All the caskets had to be closed to hide all the horror, which made the horror even bigger. I didn't even get to say 'Good-bye, Dad,' or 'The apples were great, Mom,' or 'You were damn brave, Leland,' or 'Kiss my ass, world!'

"And Mr. O'Gara can eat shit for lying because I KNOW Leland's head is still attached. Even God wouldn't do that to a little kid on his eighth birthday before he even got to see his cake, which I threw all over the walls. I'll tell you what I see when I focus, Laura. I see a useless, Nazi sonofabitch called God, who isn't worth my pissing on!"

There's no way of saying how long it took me to notice Laura was crying. My insides were so jammed up that I wanted to keep yelling, but I was too tired to go on. I picked the chair up off the floor and threw myself into it with so much force I heard the wood crack, which felt good. I tried to catch my breath while I grabbed a napkin off the table to blow my nose. That's when I realized my hand was bleeding. It was a small cut, but I had smeared blood on my clothes and on the chair. I tied a napkin around my cut and tried to pull myself together.

Laura's face was hidden behind her hands. Although her shoulders were heaving, she wasn't making any sound. It was if her sorrow was too big to have a voice. I know the feeling because it moves through me like a ghost. I stared at her tears, which escaped through her fingers and flowed down her hands.

Suddenly it hit me that I had yelled at Laura because I was tired of carrying the pain all by myself, and I just wanted to die. I wished I could take it all back and make her smile again. I wanted to be strong enough to carry my own hurt, and all the hurt life has ever inflicted on Laura, too. I had lashed out at the one person I care about and trust the most in this town. Or maybe anywhere.

I leaned into Laura and took her hands. Somewhere under all my confusion, I believed if I could get rid of her tears, her pain would disappear. I kissed her hands all over, wiping away her tears with my lips. I was trying so hard to make things right that I held her and rocked her back and forth. "I'm so sorry, Laura," I moaned. "I'm so darn sorry. I never meant to hurt you."

"Shhh, Weed," she breathed into my hair, "shhh, I'm

okay. I'm not crying for myself," she assured me as her tears kept coming.

I kissed her eyes as tenderly as I could, trying to sop up all the sorrow so the ache in her voice would go away. I held onto her so tight that we were breathing together. I needed her more than air, but the closer I got to her, the more pain I felt. Our chests lifted up and down, pushing against an invisible weight. I didn't know what exact personal loss Laura had suffered, but somehow, I knew it was as great as mine. Laura kissed my face and said, "Shhh," over and over again until the sobs stopped crawling out of me.

My body felt a different kind of loss when Laura finally pulled away from me. She stood up and turned on the radio. "Come here, Weed," she said, "we need to hear music...just the way your mother heard it. Come dance with me the way you used to dance in your kitchen back home."

When she came near me, I stood up and took her into my arms. Perhaps she sensed my leg was no longer effective because she didn't move much. At that moment I tried very hard to see life the way my mother taught me. I knew I had to focus on the small things, because the rest of the world was way too big for me to handle.

When I closed my eyes, I realized how small Laura is in my arms. Her hair was soft on my chin, and it had that Prell fragrance, just like my mother's always did. I heard every word of the song on the radio. It was "In the Still of the Night" by The Five Satins.

Finally I truly understood what my mother meant when she said music was like water because it sustains life. Laura and I stood there holding onto each other and swaying in one place for a very long time. I know in our minds we were dancing all around the kitchen. But at that moment it was enough just to hold on.

I have a feeling those moments with Laura, and that

tune, and the way she smelled, and the way she fit into my arms are things that I will remember all my life... even long after I leave here. I'll be honest, I've been trying real hard to find a reason to stick around this world. Until I can find some motivation to live, I'm going to try to concentrate on the small things. I don't want to focus on anything else. Or I might lose Laura, too.

CHAPTER ELEVEN
NOVEMBER 9, 1960

WELL, MY DELAY HERE, BESIDES LAURA, IS BASED ON MY need to save money and get my leg better before traveling. The dang thing aches a lot, and it's the color of moldy marble cake. I picked up some more antibiotics just to be safe. But I refuse to go back to those morose purveyors of medical malfeasance who prescribed them. It's a matter of principle... MINE!

Friday night I saw a new TV show called "Route 66," and the idea of hitting the road got me charged up, so yesterday I picked up a map. The Route 66 possibilities look very adventurous. I've thought about this route many times before. I even told my little brother that when I got my license, we'd "get our kicks on Route 66," which I first read about in *The Grapes of Wrath*.

One day I put Leland on my back to do a practice run down the "Mother Road," which was under the lilacs in our back yard and made pretend visits to various Route 66 pit stops I had read about. We ate tons of greasy food at the Pig Hip Restaurant in Illinois (Leland oinked the entire time, and I faked a heart attack). Then we bought a two-headed snake at the Riverside Reptile Ranch in Stanton, Missouri. Leland planted the snake on the seat of a fat lady named

"Wanda" at the Coleman Theater in Miami, Oklahoma. After Wanda screamed and burst out of her girdle in a four-alarm fat explosion (a great performance on my part), we burned rubber to Tulsa to eat burritos at the Rancho Grande. We spent ten minutes trying to make bean farts, which got Leland laughing so hard he needed a pee break.

We finally "drove" on to a rowdy motorcycle hang-out in Arizona and got ink tattoos before heading to Hollywood, California, where we got Charlton Heston's autograph at the Formosa Grill. This is what Heston wrote (in writing which looked suspiciously like mine):

Dear Leland Clapper,

Tell Kenny Warner he's going to get butt boils for telling everyone the gaping hole in your front teeth is a result of your mother marrying her cousin. You can also tell him I said he's a nose-picking idiot with a halitosis problem.
Yours very truly,

Charlton Heston (Ben-Hur Himself)

It was a great practice trip, but I'm not sure how I feel about going without Leland now. I can't imagine it being the same without him. Anyway, I'm going to have to think about it some more.

While I've been planning my next move, I attended a school dance. I know it's hard to imagine a chronic ditcher going to school when it wasn't mandatory, but Janine asked me if I would ask her to the Autumn Dance on October 29. I said, why bother asking since I already know the answer to my own question? That's how it all happened.

The Autumn Dance is a big deal in this whistle stop. It takes the place of a "homecoming" dance because there's no real football team. The football team introduced at the rally was an intramural team I'm now told. Anyway, I admit I wanted to go because I knew Laura would be there. But I didn't want to show up dateless and stand out like a pubic hair on a plate. What's a guy to do? I took Queen Janine.

We all met up at the gym, which had been changed into a fantasy palace for the shindig with the ironic theme, "Shangri-La." I was wearing my usual black, and Janine said I resembled Paladin on "Have Gun - Will Travel." I did look good.

When Mr. Kennealy greeted us, he was so sloshed his breath needed a fire extinguisher. He was peering down Janine's dress as we walked by, so I accidentally trounced on his foot. It happens.

I have to admit, Janine looked very pretty in a pale blue dress that dipped at the neckline. Her heart-shaped necklace was dangling down between her hooters, so my eyes kept getting stuck in her cleavage each time she adjusted the chain. She got so much attention that I was feeling somewhat proud of myself, considering how she picked me to pick her to go with me.

Russ brought Carol Beth Harper, the minister's daughter ... not a good choice for a horndog like Russ. And I hate to say it, but Carol Beth could have passed for a pink Minotaur.

When Jimmy Dale arrived with Patty Lynn, we all started dancing. In this area, they're still doing the Stroll, which is a dance I learned two years ago. I have to boast a little—I was very smooth as Janine and I strolled between the two lines. In spite of my leg problem, I spun around and did a little hesitation side-step movement which was a crowd pleaser.

Janine asked me where I learned to dance like that. When I told her I had gone to Philly a few times with Murray and Kenton to be on "American Bandstand," you would have thought I told her Buddy Holly was back and wanted her phone number. She got so wound up she couldn't stop asking questions like, "Did you talk to Dick Clark?"

"Sure," I shrugged. (I figured a little bragging was in order. I didn't want to disappoint anyone.) "And I met Bobby Darin, who was there to sing 'Splish Splash.'"

"BOBBY DARIN?" For a moment I thought Janine was going to grab the microphone to announce the news. "Oh my God," she squealed, "I've always wanted to be on Bandstand!"

"Shhh, keep it down, Janine," I urged. But by then, I had a small group around me, and I was feeling powerful. It seemed as appropriate a time as any to let go with some selective metaphors about the girls on Bandstand. I owed it to the guys. "I even danced with Frani Giordano," I announced.

"Frani is so beautiful!" Carol Beth gushed.

"No kidding!" I agreed. "We had a blast. My friend Murray was chosen to rate a record. He took it so seriously, you'd think he was judging the Dead Sea Scrolls. Murray told Dick Clark, 'After careful consideration, I'll give the record a '99,' Dick. It's got a good beat, and you could cha-cha real good to it if you had on a good pair of shoes.' Kenton and I busted a gut, but it turned out that Murray had hidden genius because the song was a huge hit. It was 'Hushabye' by the Mystics."

They were quite impressed. After a few more Bandstand stories, I suggested we get some punch. My leg wasn't feeling so good, so I needed to sit awhile.

We were all on the bleachers drinking sherbet-7UP punch and eating cake when Laura walked in. She was wearing a black dress and pearls, and she looked so beautiful I couldn't swallow my cake. Her dress was so simple that all you could see was *her*. Laura's body moved under that dress so gracefully that I could practically feel it rubbing up against the linen. Even her sexy T-strap heels were cut low enough to show toe cleavage. I had to cover my mouth to keep from gasping. She was a three-dimensional fold-out of a lascivious mountain range.

When the music was paused so the dance committee could crown the king and queen of each class, Janine got very excited about the whole event. She did look cute standing there in her crown next to Jimmy Dale, king of everything this side of the Missouri River. Kingship must be JD's major. During the speech part of the adulation scenario, I couldn't focus on anyone but Laura, who was crowning the heads of state.

After the royal rigmarole, the principal introduced this year's basketball team. Can you believe a hick institution of less than 150 high school students has a team that made it to the state semi-finals last year? They probably had to recruit a few tall third graders to make up the team, but these agrarians can obviously kick the butts of the bigger schools. They're nuts about basketball in these parts.

Just as I turned to check out all the pennants from past years, Laura tapped me on the shoulder. "You look very handsome, Weed," she said as I struggled to get my lungs pumping again.

"Thank you, Laura...uh, I mean Miss Saslow," I managed to croak, "and you look very nice yourself. Really very beautiful."

Laura laid a smile on me that was so bright it made everyone else vanish into the background... until Rick Bells sauntered into the gym. Laura glanced at her watch, and it was obvious she was peeved. I was hoping nobody except me noticed that Rick's shirt was crumpled and hanging out of his pants as if he had gotten dressed in his car. When he fawned over Laura, I wanted to deck him so badly I bit my cheek.

Before I could think of a reason to excuse myself, Jimmy Dale came back over and announced to our group that he needed to go somewhere to feed his royal face. I was relieved to have a reason to exit, even if it meant leaving Laura. Everyone stood up to leave except Russ. When Jimmy Dale nodded at Russ as a way of invitation, I decided JD was finally earning that crown of his.

We all jumped into JD's old Bonneville and took off to U.S. 40 to the Roadway Restaurant for fried tenderloins. That's when the fun really began.

Jimmy Dale entertained us with a report about a ruckus he had heard just before he left for the dance. According to JD, his neighbor, Bob Burnett, was standing on his porch in his boxers and undershirt, holding a can of beer while getting a tongue-lashing from Pete Acres. JD reckoned he was only being neighborly by listening, and we all agreed.

Nobody was too surprised to learn that it was Bob's son, known for having the intelligence of a prehistoric rock, who had gotten Pete's daughter, Barbara, quite pregnant. Barbara is a senior who always has goop in her eyes. JD said Pete insisted Bob's son do right and marry his ruined, crusty-eyed daughter who's about to burst.

"Bob said it 'weren't his problem' and that he had to go in to 'take a BU-R-R-R-R-NING WHIZ,'" JD told us. "Pete wasn't too happy about that, so he stomped his foot, pulled out a Bible, and blurted, 'I, sir, am a proud Lutheran, and I am demanding righteous action for the sins committed by your wayward son!'

"All that religious talk got Bob's goat," JD continued. "The next thing ya' know, Bob shook his fist and got right up in Pete's face and yelled, 'A Lutheran?

THE REMARKABLE JOURNEY OF WEED CLAPPER

That's no better than a Catholic in a sheep-skin suit! And you're a lousy dancer to boot.'

"That last bit sure got Pete's shorts in a twist," JD hooted. "Pete sputtered, 'I ought to dance on your face, you stupid horse's ass! I am a God-fearing--'

"But Bob cut him right off. 'I'll tell you who you should be fearing,' he yelled, 'the person you should fear is ME, you puckered-ass fornicator!'"

(That got a rousing chorus of applause from our group.)

"But Pete held his own," JD said as he puffed up his chest to imitate Pete: "'And you, sir, are nothing more than a slobbering drunk!'"

JD was laughing so hard at what was coming that we had to wait for him to catch his breath. "Well, Bob was so ticked off he ripped off a wicked belch right in Pete's mug and yelled, 'You're friggin' right I'm a drunk, and this drunk needs to piss like a race horse. So listen here, fool, you better get the hell offa my porch or I'll pull out my pecker and piss all over your shiny Lutheran shoes!'

"Pete blocked Bob's door and yelled, 'You'll stay right here and settle this, you stinkin' alkie!'"

"What happened next?" Janine squealed.

"Bob yanked out his whizzer and aimed a stream right at Pete's shoes. I'm serious! And he soaked Pete's Lutheran trousers in the process! I swear there was more steam rising off Pete's shoes than off a tuna casserole," JD howled.

"Holy shit! What did Pete do?" Russ asked.

"He raised his Bible like he was gonna give a benediction, and then he brought it smack down on Bob's whizzer. No lie, man—I *heard* it! Bob just sort of crumpled up and screamed, 'You broke my friggin pecker, you sumbitch! You broke my pecker!' Then he grabbed Pete by the throat and shook the crap outta him. I nearly pissed myself. Bob's willy was spinning around like a weather vane in every direction. And what a sad willy that guy's got! I've seen better on a goldfish!"

(We all were dying by then, especially when JD held up a pickle and spun it around like Bob's assaulted willy.)

"When Pete finally broke away," JD continued, "he threw down the Bible, which I bet had pee on it, and then he jumped into his car and peeled out right past me. There was gravel flying all over the place. That's when Bob flagged me down to hitch a lift to Dr. Hawkins's house to check for pecker damage. I could hardly focus on the road because Bob rubbed his dinky willy the whole way there and moaned like a two-dollar whore. I feared maybe he was relieving a woody right there in the seat of my Bonneville."

By the time JD launched into another imitation, everyone in the booths around us was in on the story. His broken pecker pose got him a standing ovation—even from Carol Beth, and she's a minister's Minotaur.

When Janine suggested we pitch in to buy Peeing Bob a "cock sock," nobody knew what that was, but we laughed like hyenas at the sound of it.

"It's something the ladies knitted to protect the privates of their men on the Russian front in war times," she informed us. Then she turned to me and whispered, "I learned that from some library books I got so I could talk about stuff with you, Weed."

I suddenly stopped laughing. Janine was looking up at me as if she was desperate for my approval. I can't explain why, but her need for my approval repelled me as much as it touched me. And that made me feel even more messed up than usual. My fun night went right into the crapper.

After we finished eating, Janine invited me back to her house. For a girl with the mental capacity of a doorknob, she sure knows how to rile a guy up. She put her hand on my leg and stroked my thigh under the table, which rendered me senseless. Although I never think about anyone but Laura anymore, my lower region sometimes thinks for me. I was horny and sad all at once. These things girls do to a guy can be tortuous. Unfortunately, the hormonal part of me had no respect for my other emotions that night.

CHAPTER TWELVE

No Date – Time Stands Still in Corn Town

All Hail Your Murrayness!

*Thanks for your last enlightening epistle. A stagecoach
delivered it to my campsite. The driver's ass was full of
arrows, if that's any indication of how civilized this
settlement is.*

Yes, my leg is fine, so stop fretting, mom.
*Congrats on getting into U. of P. With your grades, you'll
have no trouble landing a scholarship, especially if you're still
cribbing off Maury Kirschbaum's math tests in exchange for
letting him touch your cousin Dani's panties. Think third
grade.*

*Michelle sounds legendary among Murray babes. I want the
details. I haven't exactly been a monk myself. These small-
town girls have big-town hormones. Janine can be nice, in a
sad-and-sorry way, but I'm not comfortable with this sense of
obligation to feel something for her that I'm not up to feeling.
And the less I pay attention to her, the more she likes me.
What a screw-up!*

132

Last week we went to a dance and ended up back at her house. After one minute of necking, she grabbed my manhood, big-as-you-please. (Note my play on words.) I suddenly got the guilts because of my mixed feelings toward her, so I started acting completely obnoxious, being critical and stuff. I realize now I was trying to cool her off by being repulsive. That's easy for me. I felt terrible, but it was the only defense mechanism I could muster up at the time.

Then I noticed her eyes were watery. Jeez, Murds, Janine is so desperate for attention, and all I did was hurt her, which wasn't my intention. She's like a goofy kid sister. Here's my dilemma, man: What do you do when a kid like that fires your jets? It's like some sort of existential incest. I'd be a pervert if I let it continue. I'm resisting from now on, although my willpower is notoriously low. But, quoth the raving: "NEVERMORE!"

In spite of all that, there IS someone I do care about a lot. But I can't talk about her until I figure some stuff out. She's different from anyone I've ever met. She defies words. So, I'm ready for the next installment and some advice. Tell Kenton and your folks hello. And tell Michelle I look forward to checking her out. Thoroughly. In Depth. Haha!

Best Regurgitation,
Weed, The Prairie Wiener Wrangler

P.S. I heard someone with Ollie AGAIN last night. She said Dora the hair hack dropped by. No way. And get this—Russ's father has been sending a lot of "hellos" to Ollie through me. I wonder…?

PPS Our man is in! J.F.K. is just what this country needs.

CHAPTER THIRTEEN

Murray's Palace of Quivers
Scranton, Pa

Hey Porker,

*I got your smoke signal and I'm sending ammo and supplies.
I have to make this short because I have two tests tomorrow.
But I have three things to tell you which won't wait for
academia:*

*1. Kenton says you can kiss his ass for not writing to him yet,
but hi anyway. Liam also sends his doom-filled best, a
contradiction in itself. He fears the town you're being held
captive in is suspicious, like the one in Invasion of the Body
Snatchers. He says to check Ollie's garden for pods.*

*2. I GOT THE SCHOLARSHIP!!! Yep; they're paying me to
grace their fair campus with my wit and wisdom (not to
mention my collection of dirty magazines). Mom is so excited
she's throwing me a big party. (You know how ol' Rachael
always goes completely out of her way to show her friends
how humble she is.)*

3. Michelle and I are, shall I say, carnally close! I can't believe

*it. It's indescribable! It's like sinking into a warm cocoon. I'm
telling you, man, you won't believe how great it is. I should
also add that I've never felt this way for a girl before. Yup,
Malcolm, I'm really whipped. And I recommend it. I also
recommend that you forget the "sister" attitude about Janine
and accommodate her, uh, needs. It's the least you can do
for her.*

*About Ollie... well the night noises are certainly str-a-a-nge. I
assume you've ruled out Marley's ghost. Maybe Ollie just
roams the plains and talks aloud in peculiar voices.
Remember how my grandmother used to do that? Well things
are even worse now. Recently the Big Bubby Bopper has been
stripping in the most unlikely places-like the A&P. Last
Saturday Bubby started out for temple in nothing but her hat.
I swear it on Murray-Senior's moldy hairpiece! (The sight of
Bubby in the buff will leave a permanent scar.) Now they
want to put her in a nursing home, which is as inhumane as a
Tabasco enema. But I swear, Weed, I won't let anyone near
her unless it's to admire her damn hat!*

*I'm dying to know about your mystery woman, even though I
know not to press you until you mull it all over a thousand
times. But I'M STILL HEERRRE, hear?
Keep going to Greencastle for medical matters, buddy. That's
all I'll say about that. BUT I SAID IT REAL FRIGGIN
LOUD!! Gotta go. I remain the one and only—
Murray the Great*

*P.S. Indiana can't be all bad if James Dean Himself hailed
from there. (Kenton's drummer swears James Dean and Sal
Mineo were lovers. Is he high, or what?)*

CHAPTER FOURTEEN
NOVEMBER 20, 1960

I CAN'T STOP THINKING ABOUT LAURA. WITHOUT HER, LIFE would be terminally dull here. Even the cows are so bored they just stand in one spot like cow-print wallpaper. If livestock could climb, they'd be throwing themselves off barns all over Indiana right now.

My grades aren't exactly noteworthy these days. (I'm smashing records in the impressive 'C' category.) But I can't see any reason to worry about it. I'll be gone before graduation. My new plan is to head to Stockbridge, Massachusetts, where Norman Rockwell lived. From what I read, it's a really peaceful town. And I doubt if the Report Card Magistrate will check my grades at the town border. Imagine the inquisition:

"Weed Clapper, huh? Let's see that report card, son. Hmmm, you're a helluva dunce, aren't you, kid? You don't even remember who wrote The Diary of Anne Frank??? Step out of the car, dumbo. I betcha you're even concealing Cliff's Notes."

You can see how I'm trying to corral my overwhelming concern about my grades. I only mention town borders because an event took place here that was so pathetic, I had to write Murray about it. There's a sign on the edge of town that says POPULATION 953. I was out there one day when I saw an old Negro guy named Dexter painstakingly painting over the '3.' When I asked about it, he informed me that Lutheran Pete's daughter had given Peeing Bob a peeing grandson. I told him I was surprised the Blue Angels weren't flying overhead in formation in honor of such an auspicious occasion.

"Yep," he chuckled, "good thing Bob had a grandkid cuz it seems like all I ever do is lower this here number. This town has been dying longer than Miz Cutler... who used to be 953."

As Dexter painted, we discussed job opportunities. "You should get yourself over to meet Barley Edinburgh," he advised. "Barley owns the Roundabout Hamburger Stand... great onion rings. Sometimes he needs help fixin' his helicopter."

I was darn excited to hear that. "Yeah? Do ya' think he'd let me fly with him?" I asked.

"Might. My cousin Abe did. Abe used to help Mr. Barley out till Abe went and got himself laid up. 'Got into some trouble out near the lake. 'Won't be going back to work no time soon. No sir. No more."

Something about Dexter's expression got my attention. "Well, Dexter," I said, "I couldn't help but noticing you're a Negro. That fact wasn't the cause of Abe's trouble, was it?" I asked.

"I don't know nothin', son. But Barley weren't no part of it. He's a good old salt—a bit unusual is all. There's no need to discuss anymore than that. Let things be, is what I always say."

"But the attitude around here stinks," I protested. "I was told folks don't mix, and I think that's dumb, don't you?"

"No siree, son. Mixin's not healthy, so I sure don't need me no white folks as friends. No offense of course. Don't mean no insult. Jus' the way 'tis in dis life."

"No problem," I shrugged. "But I bet you know my friend, Denise Williams. My grandmother and I are going to join Denise's family at her house for Thanksgiving. No harm in that, is there?

"Well, Mr. Weed, I wouldn't broadcast the news around here. People don't like change. Like I said, mixin' is not healthy. Now you go on and find Mr. Barley."

I knew there was no sense pushing it, so I decided it was time to make my departure. I found out where Barley lives and hitched a ride out there with a fellow called Bubbylee Brant. He pronounced "Bubbylee" like a belch. He's a nice guy, so we shot the breeze awhile before Bubbylee pulled over. In a huge pasture, an Army chopper was glowing like a beacon under the late autumn sun. I knew the guy near the chopper had to be Barley Edinburgh, because Bubbylee had warned me about Barley's eccentricity. I just wasn't prepared for *how* strange the man really is.

Barley was sporting the mangiest hat I've ever seen. It looked like he had shot a coon then affixed the remains to his skull with two tail feathers. The old coot didn't say hello as I approached, he just began talking as if we were resuming conversation after a pause. If it seems my mouth gets ahead of me, you should hear that guy.

"She's a beauty, huh?" he grinned. "There's something holy about a chopper, the way it lifts and hovers like a spirit over the land. This 'un was a heroine in Korea. She did insertion and extraction missions for recon teams. I picked her up last year. I call her Marlena 'cause she sings to me real low and sexy. What's your name, son?" As he addressed me, Barley abruptly slapped his ear with a blow so dang loud and unexpected that I spit out my name as fast as I could make my tongue move.

"I'm Weed Clapper, sir," I barked.

"Yeah, you're new in these parts. I'm Jack Edinburgh. But folks call me Barley. You can, too, son."

"That's an interesting nickname."

"Talk into my left ear if you can. The right one got snafued. The dang thing rings till my eyes spin. It happened in the Big One."

It was a relief to have an explanation for his habit of clobbering his head like a spastic lunatic. I moved to his left side, but he hopped around so much when he talked that I had to bob to stay with him. It was quite a workout. "I was commenting on your nickname, sir," I repeated as he smacked his gourd again.

"It's short for Barleycorn, a Jack London character who was always as tipsy as a one-legged sailor. Hell, I was a better guzzler than Ulysses S. Grant! They shoulda given me a medal for seeing sideways and shooting straight! Hence, my nickname."

"You said you fought in World War II, Mr. uh, Barley? My dad was in that war."

"Hells-bells, son, the whole world was in that war, hence the name. I'm a retired Colonel. Fought in both World Wars. I was an amphibious landing genius, but I also trained as a paratrooper. Now that's a fun activity... if you don't slam into the side of the plane on the way down. That'll getcha a bum ear like mine."

"That's too bad, sir."

"Hell, Reed—"

"Weed. Weed Clapper."

"Sounds like a garden tool. Anyway, Weed, as I was about to say, I never took more than a nasty cut and a slew of skin holes. And I was a Dalby's Ranger for Chrissake! I fought at Sened Station in Tunisia in the last one. Hand-to-hand combat, with knives, bayonets, and balls of steel!"

Suddenly Barley grabbed his crotch then thrust a clenched fist into the air and yelled at the top of his lungs, "SEIZE AND DESTROY, YOU MAGGOTS!" I instinctively ducked. After his momentary mental lapse subsided, I had to slap my own ear just to stop the echo.

"Hey, Barley," I said in an attempt to bring him back from the sands of Tunisia, "what caused your skin holes?" I had noticed the pocks all over his face and hands, but I wouldn't have brought it up if he hadn't mentioned it. I'm sensitive to that kind of stuff.

The question sent him into fits of laughter. "Well, son, it happened in the first war," he said. "My outfit was about to be pulled out of Belleau Wood after kicking Kraut ass. Two of us secured some canteens of hooch from the medic in order to relieve him of his tiresome load. Boy, I got so hammered I couldn't find the ground I was crawlin' on!

"When I woke up the next day, I was on fire. It turns out I had passed out next to an enemy anthill. I had upchucked all over myself, so the ants were crawling up my ass like a von Hindenburg enema. I got a hell of a skin infection, hence the polka dot skin." Barley whacked his ear again, which brought him back to the present. "'You ever been up in one of these babies?"

When I said no and added that "hence" it was my hope to earn extra money and maybe get some flying lessons to boot, Barley slapped his thigh, waved his roadkill hat, and yelled, "Then let's get Marlena here a'perkin'!"

I was so excited I yelled and slapped my own thigh just in case it was some odd ritual of rural communication. Then I jumped in the chopper before Barley could change his mind. I hadn't yet discovered that the old coot had no mind left to change.

When he started the engine and got those rotor blades turning, it was a boner-rouser. We lifted slightly, hovered for a moment, then rocked forward. Because Marlena was shorn of her doors, I was afraid I might tumble out, so I braced myself as we picked up speed and lifted higher. Barley yelled the whole time, feeding me information about equipment and controls. "We pull pitch by yanking on this lever. Give her a yank, boy," he ordered. "It's like pullin' your pud. I'm sure you can do that!"

I pulled the lever and grinned as we lifted higher. It was an unbelievable feeling to be above the world yet close enough to almost touch it. Suddenly the world was no longer bearing down on me like it usually does.

As we flew over a mustard field, Barley demonstrated a flare. "Let's say that's our landing zone there at nine o'clock to the barn ahead," he yelled pointing at a dilapidated barn with a neat old Mail Pouch advertisement painted on one side. "We're going in, maggot," he bellowed above the roar. To slow down, the chopper lifted its big belly in the direction we were heading. We nearly came to a stop by the barn, hovering just twenty feet above the crops before the chopper rocked forward and picked up speed again as we lifted out of the area. It was thrilling!

"What's it like to jump out of a plane, Barley?" I shouted.

The expression on Barley's face was as near to complete bliss as any I've ever seen. "It's powerful," he said so quietly I could barely hear him. "More powerful than lovin' a woman."

At about the time I was wondering if the old codger had any basis for comparison, he warned: "Stay away from women, son. They'll kill ya if you're not tough. My last gal, Uki, was a complainer That gal even groused that the daisies I gave her weren't fit for someone as 'high-class' as her. So I told her to bend over and shove 'em up her behind so at least she'd have a high-class vase!"

I was trying to picture Uki as a vase when Barley made a sharp turn, dropped about a hundred feet, and zoomed over the lake. Marlena came so close to the water that we were soaked by the icy spray. It was like being pelted with snow cones. Barley whooped it up adding to the party atmosphere. When I yelled, "Let's cruise the lake again!" he turned that bird on a dime.

"Marlena's better than any wife," he yelled as we dipped toward the lake again. "She does what I ask. And I don't have to give up my other girlfriends to keep her happy!" (He got a charge out of that.)

We were traveling fast and low over the road that runs along the lake when I spotted Bubbylee cruising in his truck. "Hey, Bubbylee," I screamed as we hovered above, "duck!" When he stuck his head out of the driver's window, his eyes hatched. I'm sure Bubbylee thought he was a goner, and he had good reason. The chopper was threatening to land on Bubbylee's truck, a slick trick perhaps, but not too good for the truck... or for Bubbylee.

"Maybe we should back off a little, Barley!" I yelled as I watched Bubbylee swerve close to the lake to escape us. The chopper was dropping lower, and I was afraid we might drive Bubbylee into the lake. "Barley!" I yelled again. My eyes were on the road below, so all I saw was a wall of green trees coming to claim me like a green Grim Reaper.

"Barley!" I screamed again. As I reeled around to face him, my heart went deader than the late Mrs. Cutler's. Either Barley was operating the controls with his ant-eaten face, or he was dead at the wheel. Someone was screaming like a downright hysterical girl, which I'll go ahead, and venture was me, seeing as how I was the only conscious person in the helicopter.

I tried to pull pitch, but Barley's body was dead weight on top of the lever. Before I could shove him aside, the chopper abruptly pitched to the right. I tumbled backwards and had to use all my limbs to keep from being hurled from Marlena's heaving bosom.

I looked over at Barley and realized I couldn't even push him out of the chopper if I wanted to because the lever was rammed up his sleeve. He was stuck tighter than an all-day sucker. Seeing as how his left leg was now dangling out of the chopper like a loose turd, the lever was the only thing holding him in his seat.

We dipped at such a sharp angle I saw everything sideways. I closed my eyes and held on, the whole while wishing I had taken up drinking in my short youth, because a good alcohol-induced black out was urgently called for. After I gathered my wits, I shoved Barley's arm with my foot, which momentarily held us at altitude. But Barley's weight on the lever hindered our lift.

I won't say my life flashed in front of me, but Bubbylee sure did. His truck spewed gravel as he zigzagged from shoulder to shoulder. He must have felt like Cary Grant in "North by Northwest." His truck dropped into a ditch, bucking like a bronco for thirty yards. Somehow, he got the truck back onto the road, but it fish-tailed before veering sharply to the left. The last I saw of poor Bubbylee was a flash of blue heading into a strip of land between the trees, but at least *he* had made *his* escape.

In an instant, Barley came back to life. He grabbed the controls and piloted the chopper up over the trees smoother than you could imagine. He let out a yelp before turning to grin at me as though nothing out of the ordinary had transpired. Then the bastard lit up a smoke as though he had just had six hours of sweaty sex with Brigette Bardot.

"What were you doing back there?" I screamed after I checked all my body parts, including my shrunken tooter.

"What's the matter, boy?" Barley grinned. "Your face couldn't be greener if your brain pissed in your skull!"

I couldn't decide if he was the world's biggest prick, or if he was mad as a hatter. "Back there," I screamed, "what were you doing with your head down? You better tell me you had a stroke, or I'll give you a reason to lose consciousness, you crazy old buzzard!" Being courteous was no longer an option in my book.

"Oh, did I go to sleep for a minute back there?" he inquired nonchalantly.

"'Sleep'?" I sputtered. "Is that what you call it? You just said to your irrational self, 'I think I'll take a nap right here over Bubbylee's truck'?"

"Don't worry, kid. It's just a little tick I have called narcolepsy. I sleep sometimes when it's, uh, 'inconvenient.' That's why I couldn't renew my pilot license. Dozed off during the exam."

"Are you daft?" I yelled.

"Oh, settle down, squirt. As a rule, I fly low, so how far could we possibly fall? At most we would have taken a little dip in the lake. You can swim, can't ya?"

"Not with a broken neck, I can't."

"Well... can you float?" He laughed raucously at his own wit. "I haven't crashed yet," he assured me. "The sleep episodes are usually pretty brief. Had quite a thrill, huh?"

"Put me down now," I demanded.

"Huh?"

"Land this crate and let me out, unless you're craving the really Big Sleep. I know Tony 'the Meat Hook' Mancini, so don't even try to mess with me, you jackass. Put me down now."

"Jesus, you're emotional! You're going to have ulcers before you're twenty, son. Okay, I'm landing, okay?"

"Keep talking to me so I know you're awake," I ordered.

"Hells Bells, you're worse than my last wife! Then again, she fell out of the crop duster, so I guess she had some cause for complaint." He laughed again then whacked his snafued ear. "Relax, kiddo, I'm just pulling your leg. But I suppose you're no longer interested in them lessons?"

"I'm no longer interested in anything that's not attached to the ground. Not even air!" I jumped out while we were still four feet above ground. I can truthfully say the pain in my trembling legs was a good thing because it reminded me of how solid the earth can feel under a guy's feet.

As I weakly hobbled toward the road, Barley guided Marlena into the clouds , his coon tail and feathers blowing wildly in the breeze. He circled several times before taking off into the unsuspecting sky.

———

I was too shaken up to go home. I knew Ollie would be home late because she'd gone into Greencastle for yarn and a new dress to wear on Thanksgiving. And Laura, the person I really wanted to see, was with Slick Rick. Russ was out with his dad, Roy, so Janine was my only option. I've been avoiding her because she bores me to death if we're not necking, but after the flying fiasco, my only requirement for conversation was someone who could stay awake.

When I got to Janine's, she was just putting her brother Timmy to bed. I noticed that he had a sticky paper fly strip attached to his pajama bottoms like a nasty growth. There was one maimed fly trapped on the paper strip, so the kid kept turning in circles to find out where all the buzzing was coming from. It was very entertaining.

I disposed of the disgusting thing (not the brother, the fly strip) after I administered euthanasia to the fly. I didn't want to think about the fly busting loose inside the trash can only to discover it was about to die from lack of oxygen. I could just imagine its little fly-cries for mercy as it called to me by name from atop a pile of coffee grounds. I admit, my imagination is often a burden.

Janine's parents were down at Coonsie's Tavern as usual. I suspect Janine gets very lonely, so you can imagine how I felt about making her cry again. Yep, I did. I've developed an uncanny knack for messing up. If I majored in it, I'd be scholarship material.

The troubles began when I told Janine I didn't feel up to making out. Sure, it's tempting, but I hate myself afterward and I go home racked with guilt. Quite frankly, the struggle with my libido wears me out, which is why I suggested we watch "The Ed Sullivan Show" and dig into the Sealtest Cherry Vanilla ice cream in her freezer.

When she got real pouty, I made the fatal mistake of asking what was wrong. I've noticed that girls are very good at getting a guy to pin a bull's-eye on his chest while they're busy loading ammunition into their little pink automatic rifles.

Janine informed me that I hardly ever pay attention to her, and that I act as though I don't like her. When I assured her I felt she was a good kid, which I thought was a friendly thing to say, you would have thought I said she had a nice moustache. She became very indignant and informed me that King Jimmy Dale wanted to dump Patty Lynn and go steady with her again, and what did I think of that?

I said I thought Jimmy Dale was a decent guy for someone who's fairly dense, and the idea was certainly a good one because I know Russ would love to get a chance with Patty Lynn. I stopped short of saying Janine and Jimmy Dale could get married and have kids with two names each and only a half a brain between them, but apparently what I had already said was enough to set her pants on fire.

"Then I'll tell Jimmy Dale yes!" Janine huffed. "He wants me to go with him up to Indianapolis next weekend. We might tell our parents the car broke down and then spend the night in a motel."

I'm not so dense I couldn't see she was trying to make me jealous. It worked a little, so I decided to jump into the fray. After all, I never was a relationship expert. "It sounds fun, Janine," I said. "I heard there's an Indian museum up there, so could you pick me up a Potawatomi arrowhead at the museum store? Oh, and while you're gone, I'll drop in on Patty Lynn to make sure she's not heartbroken." I felt darn good about landing a solid blow like that. Even if I didn't want Janine, I had a male obligation to defend Weed's Forty Acres and a Mule.

I give Janine credit for hanging in there until the finish. She jutted her chin and said, "Have you heard of a new thing called 'the pill'? Well, I plan to get some from a doctor there so I can have lots of sex and not get pregnant. Jimmy Dale is very excited about it."

"Gee, I don't blame him. He'll be gaining another starting linebacker for the intramural team," I said as pleasantly as an undertaker in an out-of-left-field shot to her kisser.

"Linebacker? What are you talking about, Weed?"

"Those pills work by changing your hormones, Janine. My friend, Liam O'Gara, told me he read that when a woman takes the pill, she becomes half-man and sort of freezes that way. You'll grow facial hair, then pretty soon you'll be shaving and wearing boxers. You'll get a lot of bad gas…and huge pimples on your ass, Janine. But I'll be glad to teach you how to throw a football. It'll come in handy."

With that, I picked up the sofa pillow, formed it into a football, and threw Janine a pass. You can imagine how I felt when she just sat there and let it bong her in the kisser. When I looked at her to make sure she was okay, I saw tears in her eyes again. I have that effect on everyone. I'm a human onion.

I couldn't believe what was happening. When the tears started to fall silently down Janine's face, I was so

GWEN BANTA

shocked and upset that I wanted to run. But I couldn't. I knew that wherever my mother was, she would be very disappointed with me if I left, because she always told me that tears were a woman's silent plea to be held. Once again, I had to finish what I started. I walked over, put my arms around Janine, and pulled her close to me.

"Shhh," I said, "I made that up about the pill. Don't go throwing away your bras or anything. Besides, I only went along with what you said because I want you to do whatever makes you happy, Janine. I like you a lot."

That made her calm down a bit, so I kissed her just to make her smile. When I tried to pull away, Janine was breathing real hard and clinging to me so tightly that my trusted lower half suddenly sprang to attention. I completely forgot my previous resolve to cease and desist. I should have left right then and there, but my libido was in the driver's seat. And Janine's tongue was in my ear so far, I could hear the ocean. I can't believe what happened next.

I reached under her sweater to release her bra strap, a move I've perfected. I was surprised when I got a handful of cotton, because I hadn't noticed before that she stuffs her bra. She probably does that because her breasts aren't much bigger than her brother's. But I wouldn't have cared at that point if she had cloven hooves.

After she whispered about how this was a safe time of the month for her and that she wasn't a virgin, I knew what she wanted. Faster than a trained dog, I jumped right in there with my part of the warm-up. Five minutes of lip-lock led me to a point of no return. Being a gentleman was the farthest thing from my mind. And my mind was the farthest thing from my body. And my good sense had left the room completely.

Janine and I did it right there on her couch. Yep. We did! For anyone who has never tried it, I highly recommend it. By the time we were done, I was

148

shaking, sweating, and turned inside out. Never, ever, have I experienced anything so amazing in my life. It was a workout because the girl is a contortionist. Janine said I was GREAT. Not just good—GREAT. I definitely was impressive.

Unfortunately, I was thinking about Laura the entire time, so I was tempted to put a pillow over Janine's face so she wouldn't interfere with my fantasies. However, I suspected she might object to death by suffocation.

Afterward, Janine looked at me as though I was Marlon Brando. No fooling, I was GREAT... and darn proud of a championship performance. I just wish my evening with Janine had ended right after the Marlon Brando moment, because as I was sitting on her couch trying to catch my breath, she began to get jumpy. She looked out the window periodically, giving me the impression she was expecting someone. "You better leave now, Weed," she urged, "before my parents get home."

"Why?" I asked her. "It's still early." When I saw the odd look on her face, I should have just stuffed my socks in my mouth. But no, I had to rush in... and without a helmet. "Spit it out, Janine," I demanded. "Am I not supposed to be here or something?" She wouldn't look at me, which made me very uneasy.

"It's nothing, Weed," she reassured me. "It's just that my parents heard some rumors down at Coonsie's Tavern."

"Rumors about me? I hope you're not referring to those murders I committed back in Scranton," I said sarcastically, "because it was just a troop of blind Girl Scouts who needed to be put down."

"Stop it, Weed. It's not a big deal, just some stupid stuff."

"Stupid? What a surprise! Spill it, Janine."

"Well... my folks heard you've been seen around

149

town with Denise Williams, and they think it's inappropriate."

"That's it? Because Denise is my friend and she's a Negro, I'm no longer good enough for the Queen of the junior class?"

"Sort of. They're concerned you'll stir up anger by hanging out with Denise and her people. My dad said there might be trouble brewing already. Besides, it's bad taste to mix races," she sniffed.

"Jeez-Louise, how can you go along with such ignorant crap?"

"Oh, simmer down, Weed. The Negro stuff doesn't concern us."

"Are you dense? Of course it does! Especially if 'trouble is brewing.' Where's your backbone, Janine? My father always said if a person doesn't stand for something, he'll fall for anything."

"You are being very antagonistic, Weed Clapper. At least I stood up for Ollie."

"Ollie? She's not a Negro! What's the matter, is she so colorful that she ALSO offends your parents' delicate sensibilities?"

"Settle down, Weed. My folks aren't prejudiced. And they don't hate Ollie. They just want me to date someone from better stock."

"Better *stock*? Did you say better *stock*?" At that point, I let forth with a remarkable imitation of a horse. "Is that horse shit I smell? You should pick your dates from a farming catalogue," I spewed. "Your parents are bigoted, boozing freaks, Janine, and they're poisoning the half-a-mind you've got left!"

"Don't you dare talk that way about my parents! And it just so happens I did defend you. I said it's not your fault Denise Williams hangs all over you, or that Ollie is, well, rather low-class."

"Ollie? Low-class? And this comes from the parents

who told you Hyannis Port is a liquor? Your parents are confused bigots, Janine."

"At least they never dated coloreds the way Ollie did. My parents said you might even have some Negro blood in you because of Ollie's past... but I still like you even if you do."

"Well thank you, Queen Janine! Are you all nuts? Don't you think I'd know if I was a Negro? I can't even tan! I get sunburned when I open the refrigerator. Who makes up this hogwash anyway?"

"Well why are you so sympathetic to their cause?"

"Because Negroes are people just like us. And because I have a good friend back home named Kenton, who was a Negro the last time I checked. And he deserves better than he gets, and so does Denise. Nevertheless, Ollie didn't date Negroes. They were her friends, which is more than we're ever going to be, Janine!"

Janine couldn't have jerked back faster if I had slapped her face, but I was too wound up to take back my words. I headed for the door without looking back. I wanted to be anywhere but there.

"Weed," she said softly, "please don't be mad. I love you."

I stopped in my tracks, then I turned and saw her crumpled face, and my heart sank. I lowered my eyes, trying not to notice that she was crying again. The stuffing from her bra was stuck to her sweater, and I was so embarrassed for her I had to look away.

"I shouldn't have come here tonight. I am so sorry. Let's just be friends. Okay, Janine?" I mumbled. Before she could answer, I opened the door and walked out. I felt such a sense of relief when the door slammed behind me that I wanted to run. But my leg was as heavy as my spirit.

I suddenly realized I'm stuck in something I can't see,

GWEN BANTA

like that fly on the fly strip. And it's slowly killing me.
Poor Janine is stuck, too. We're all struggling like helpless
insects. We'd be better off if God would just put us out of
our misery with one hefty swat. At least it would be
merciful. Maybe a guy has to do everything himself.

CHAPTER FIFTEEN
NOVEMBER 21, 1960

THE JANINE'S-SCHOOL-OF-PAIN INCIDENT LEFT ME VERY
distraught. After returning home last night, I wrote to
Denise just to say how much I was looking forward to
Thanksgiving. Then I was lying in bed thinking about
Laura when I heard Ollie return. I turned off my light
and pretended to be asleep. I had too many
conversations going on inside my head to involve
another person.

A few minutes later, I heard a giggle, followed by a
thud and TWO distinct laughs. I admit to moments
when I question my sanity, but last night wasn't one of
them.

My only question was who was crashing around like
a buffalo in an outhouse. I know it's none of my
beeswax, but I was in an ornery mood to begin with. I
wanted to blow something up, and Ollie's secret life
seemed as good as anything else. Without even thinking
it through, I jumped up, ran out into the hallway, and
flipped on the light. When I glanced downstairs, I saw
Ollie at the bottom doing a fine impersonation of a deer
in the headlights.

Ollie was in a Tijuana Tart get-up, and her hair
looked like something a cat spit up. Her lips were
streaked all over the lower half of her face. When she

saw me, she tried to pull her blouse back down over her gargantuan hooters, but it would have been easier to stuff an inflated raft into a shoe.

"Weed, what a surprise!" she exclaimed.

"You were expecting J. Edgar Hoover?"

She laughed as she made a big deal about coming up the stairs to greet me. However, I quickly picked up on the little hand gesture she gave to someone out of my viewing range.

"Do we have company?" I asked innocently as I peered over the railing.

"Oh no, darlins. I was just talking to myself."

I didn't take the time to tell her that all the lip-flapping had smeared her lips half-way to Pittsburgh. I was too intent on getting past her wall of flesh and cleavage to see who was lurking in the shadows. When I tried to slip between Ollie and the railing, she thwarted my attempt with a skirt wide enough to house a Texaco station. We did a dance right there on the stairs, with her bobbing to the left and me weaving right then faking left again. The ol' girl was darn good at keeping up with me. I could see she was tipsy, so I kept bobbing. When she got dizzy, the advantage was mine.

I heaved myself over the railing and dropped onto the loveseat below just in time to see a man disappear into the kitchen, buckling his belt as he fled. As I pulled myself up to follow, I heard Ollie call, "Weed!" It was more of a plea than an exclamation. There was such an expression of concern on her face that I hesitated, a blunder which allowed her visitor to escape. I last saw the mystery man yanking on his jacket as he headed out through the dark kitchen door into the night.

After a brief and embarrassing silence, Ollie finally spoke. "Weed, darlins," she said softly from the stair, "please don't think badly of your silly old grandmother."

By then the sport of catching someone red-handed

was gone, and I was feeling like a politician for being so sneaky. After all, it is Ollie's house. And she's an unmarried woman who has a right to see any man she wants without answering to her sleuthing grandson.

"It's none of my business, Ols," I replied. "I only wish you didn't feel you had to hide your friends from me." As soon as I said it, I realized that I've been feeling resentful because she hasn't trusted me enough to confide in me.

"Oh, someday you'll meet him, darlins," she grinned, "... if he ever stops running." As she smiled wide, I had to laugh. It was just like Ollie not to hate me or call me a prying nitwit.

"I'm sorry I acted like such a jerk," I said contritely.

"Oh, hon, it just added to the fun! Now, if you'll excuse me," she said, "I have to give the signal, or my gentleman friend will wait out there until his corn dog freezes." Ollie then flipped the light switch two times before stepping to the window in the upstairs hallway and blowing a kiss.

I admit, I was struck by what a sweet gesture it was. It's nice to know there's a man who thinks my grandmother is so special that he'll stand out in the cold until she gives him the signal that all is well. And I'm glad to know that unlike some folks around here, Ollie's boyfriend sees what a big heart she has. And apparently, he would give the shirt off his back for her. Literally. I found it lying on the floor beneath the couch.

———

The shirt I retrieved looks too large to fit Reverend Harper's bird chest, but I can't be sure. On the other hand, Russ's father Roy is still a suspect. Roy sends his regards every time I'm with Russ, and he's nicer to Ollie than anyone. Therefore, I decided to ask Russ if his dad has been disappearing at odd times, or if he's missing a shirt.

I stopped by Snarls's store before meeting Russ so I could look over the old yearbooks. Harper is from another town, so I couldn't investigate His Holiness, and the book that contained Roy Kinney's senior picture was missing. However, I did find him in the sophomore class photo in Ollie's senior yearbook. (Roy Kinney married someone much younger, which explains how Russ popped out).

Russ's dad was a goofy-looking kid. His hair jutted every which way, and he had a chipped tooth. Ollie, however, was real cute. She wasn't as bountiful as she is now, but even those odd clothes couldn't disguise the signs of an impending fat-attack. I must say, she has a great smile. It's one of those arms-wide-open smiles. The caption under her photo was a good one:

Choir. Home Ec. Honors. Reading Club. Cincy Reds Fan. Suffragette. Loves "Cider"& Driving & Dancing. Cake Baker. Roland's Gal-Pal

I was staring at the photo when Snarls shoved a banana split under my nose. "We need to get a little meat on those bones of yours," he said as he came around the counter and plopped his round body down on the stool next to mine. "You're losing weight, Weed. I could knock you over with a feather duster."

"I'm fine, sir," I protested.

"Pooh. You resemble a skinned cat. Weed, I couldn't help but notice you still have some serious problems walking, what with that injury of yours and all. I'd be happy to drop you off at school in the mornings. I could use the company."

"Thanks, Mr. Searles, but the walking is probably good for me. My leg is okay. It's just the cold that gets to me sometimes."

"Sure, son," he said, shaking his head doubtfully. "But you'll call if you need a lift?"

"Sure thing. Thank you, sir." I pointed at Ollie's yearbook photo and attempted to detour him from me as a subject. "Wasn't Ollie a cute young girl?" I asked.

"She sure was."

"Did you know the person mentioned in the caption under her photo—this Roland guy?"

"Sure." Snarls flipped to a photo of Roland Jennings, a rakish-looking sort with a moustache. "They went out quite often," Snarls explained, "but they were just buddies. Ollie loved to dance, and Roland was a good-time Charlie. Poor guy died real young."

As I stared at the photo, I took an instant liking to Roland, mainly because he wasn't a Negro. I know that sounds bad, but I felt good about Janine being wrong regarding Ollie's choice in men. "What happened to the guy?" I asked Snarls.

"Roland got shot while hightailing it out of a Chicago speakeasy during prohibition. Alcohol is a killer, son," he quipped as he flipped the page and pointed to a guy who had lots of red hair parted down the middle.

"Hey, that's you, Mr. Searles!" I exclaimed.

"I was a silly looking bugger, wasn't I? But at least I had a full head of hair instead of this landing strip right in the middle like I've got now. And I sure could show the ladies around a dance floor. Me and Ollie used to have a grand time kicking up our heels. She sure is a good tomato. She has always been real nice to me, even though I've never been much to look at. Once she said I resembled that old time actor Rudy Vallee, but she was just being sweet. And she has always pretended never to notice my awkwardness. Or my peculiarities."

That struck me as a painfully honest statement. Snarls seemed so vulnerable I decided I could trust the old guy enough to bring up some delicate things—

things a guy can't discuss with just anyone. "Mr. Searles, do you think if a white person has Negro friends or dates a Negro, they're low-class for mixing races, like some people say?" I asked.

"A lot of folks around here think that," he answered, "but I can't see the harm, if you want the truth. To me, good souls are all the same color. 'Class' is how you behave toward humans, not which humans you do your behavin' with."

"Well, what would you think about a person's 'class' if perhaps she's been getting too personal with someone who might be married? Wouldn't you say that person, and the married guy, had no morals?"

He sat there a moment before answering. "In most cases I would, son. But it's dangerous to judge because each case is different. I once knew a guy who was diddling the married gal next door. He claimed it was a Christian thing to do because Jesus said to 'love thy neighbor.' Isn't that a kick in the pants? But it's a good example of how folks apply moral rules any way they see fit. It seems a moral is only as good as the people involved and the situation at hand. I call it 'situational morality.' What's really important is forgiving others for their own humanity."

"I'll try to remember that, sir," I said as I dug into my banana split. "Thanks."

As Snarls hustled about, I mulled over our conversation and swore to myself that I'd try not to judge Ollie because I don't know the situation. Even if her nocturnal visitor turns out to be a Negro or Russ's philandering father or a smarmy married minister with a Minotaur for a daughter, I can handle anything... except maybe Monkey Boy.

After I finished my ice cream, I headed over to the church to meet Russ. When I arrived, the parking lot was full due to a combined event: Food for the Needy and Fallout Shelter Preparation. What a head scratcher!

It seems the rationale is that when each doomed person is herded into the nearest well-stocked fallout shelter, he can better face a prolonged, ghastly, twisted death on a full stomach.

After I tossed Ollie's donation of canned goods into a collection box, I was looking around for Laura when I spotted Janine. She hasn't spoken to me since the night we fought about her parents' demand that she date better stock. She glanced my way but pretended not to see me, so I mooed. I couldn't resist. It was an effort to prove I'm from a respectable herd.

If the fake laugh on Janine's face had been any bigger, someone would have had to peel her lips off her forehead. But when I saw the hurt under her plastic smile, I immediately regretted my barnyard sounds. In spite of my anger and shame over Janine's comments about Ollie and me, I felt guilty. I suppose I should have tried to talk to her, but I just mingled around until I found Russ.

Russ was on the steps boxing blankets for the fallout shelter. Apparently, it's also important to be toasty while being broiled alive by radioactive particles. Russ was talking to Norma Marie Donner, a real friendly senior I've met only twice. I sense Russ is much more comfortable with Norma Marie than he is with Patty Lynn. The only reason he wants Patty Lynn, I'm sure, is because pretty girls like her never looked at him until I coached him on how to be cool. But Patty Lynn isn't nearly as fun as Norma Marie.

Norma Marie is one of those girls who has a real easy laugh. She doesn't worry about getting messed up when the wind blows, and her eyes are beautiful. The problem is her skin. Imagine flying over London after the Blitz and looking down at all the holes and mounds—that's poor Norma Marie's face. If I get to know her better, I might mention how my face cleared up when I was on antibiotics last year, so she might

GWEN BANTA

want to try them. But how do you bring that up with any finesse?

After Norma Marie went off to sort canned goods, Russ and I sealed cartons. I wasn't sure how to find out about his father's nighttime activities, but I took a shot. "Is your father around?" I asked nonchalantly.

"No, he's collecting stuff from folks who can't drive."

"Oh." That was enough prelude for me, being diplomatically deficient as I am. In my next breath, I blurted out what really was on my mind. "Do you ever wonder if your dad fools around?"

Unfortunately, Russ's detours are as bad as mine. "No, why? Did you hear something about Jimmy Dale's dad? He's always running around with his hose hanging out. Who's that dog after now?"

"I dunno, Russ. I was asking if you wonder about *your* dad diddling around, not JD's. Isn't it natural for kids to wonder where their dads go sometimes?"

"Who cares, Weed? And why are you asking this stuff?"

"I was just wondering if he ever goes to Greencastle," I prodded, knowing that's where Ollie was last night before I caught her little clandestine act.

"Yes, all the time. He was there last night. Why?"

"Last night? Did he come home with his shirt on? Because I found one, uh, on the road today, and I'm sure it's one I've seen him in before." (It was a piss-poor fishing expedition, I admit.)

Russ shot me an are-you-liquored-up look. "You mean you think my dad's shirt flew off his back as he drove past your house?"

"Of course not. Keep up here, Russ," I said defensively. "Maybe he had taken it off and it fell out of the truck."

"Hell, Weed, how would I know? He got in late. Just bring the shirt by if you think it's his."

160

I sensed Russ was getting a little hot under the collar, and I didn't want him to think I'm the new Joseph McCarthy. "I was just asking about where he goes because I thought I might hitch a ride with him sometime," I covered.

Russ defuses quickly. His mouth suddenly sprang into that goofy smile he sports when he's his usual happy-go-lucky self. "Sure, call him anytime, Weed. Hey, how about going to the drive-in movie with me tonight?"

"I dunno... are you a good kisser?" I teased. "And what's with the drive-in? I thought it closed on Labor Day."

"Yeah, but Mr. Carroll opens it up every Thanksgiving weekend and screens Christmas movies. I know it's corny, but it's meant to get everyone into the spirit of the coming holidays. He offers the same double billing every year: *Miracle on 34th Street* and *It's a Wonderful Life*. It's a tradition, and it's free. Everyone goes. We even decorate our cars. So how 'bout it?"

"Okay, I'll be your date. I'll wear something low-cut."

I said good-bye to Russ and was heading home when Laura and Rick passed by in his BelAir. I tried to act nonchalant, but my gut did a few flips when Rick made a U-turn to come back my way. They pulled to a stop right next to me.

"Hey, Weed, get in. It's cold out there!" Laura called out to me. Her voice is like warm pie.

I walked to the car and leaned in the window. Rick looked VERY annoyed, so I kept my body away from the door in case he decided to peel out, rendering me senseless. "Thanks for the offer," I said, "but the walk will do me good. It's not cold."

"Weed, it's warmer in Antarctica."

"It feels good," I lied. I really could have used a lift, but I didn't want to share Laura with Rick. "Don't worry, Laura," I added, as I pointed to the mortuary nearby, "if I get stiff, I'll just lie down on that porch." Laura laughed, but Rick stared at me as if I had just announced that I have syphilis.

As Rick eyeballed me, my brain was trying to mount a good offense. I was afraid if I lingered much longer, I might ask him if he ever retrieved his tongue from JoAnn Stevens's esophagus. I would have gotten even more hostile if I hadn't gotten a whiff of Laura's Chanel No. 5, which makes me weak in the knees.

"Are you sure, Weed?" Laura smiled as she passed me a thermos of hot cocoa. "We're loaded up with canned goods for the collection," she said, "but you can sit up front, and I could sit on your lap."

Just the idea of having Laura on my lap warmed my Mr. Happy so much you would have thought I had dipped it in the cocoa. I was about to get in when Rick observed, "You don't look as if you can walk too far on that crippled leg, kid. I saw you limping."

Laura poked him hard in the ribs, which was even more humiliating. I didn't need her to defend me like a mother slapping her kid for staring at some freak drooling into his cup of nickels.

"No thanks," I mumbled. "When I was running back there, I turned my ankle. I just need to walk it out." As I shoved the thermos back through the car window, I made sure I chipped the car paint in the process.

"Okay, Weed," Laura said softly. When she reached out to touch my hand, I looked down at her fingers and noticed a ring I had never seen her wear before. I dreaded hearing the answer to the question my mouth was already asking: "Is that a new ring?"

"Yes," she smiled, "Rick gave me my Christmas present early so we can announce our engagement over the holidays. It's no surprise to anyone, but now it's official."

I took a series of deep breaths and then plastered my

best party expression across my kisser. "Congratulations!" I said with a heap of insincere enthusiasm, wondering how much of a surprise their engagement might be to JoAnn Stevens. *I hope the three of you will be very happy together*, was what I wanted to say, but I restrained myself for Laura's sake.

Rick nodded and guided the Chevy back onto the road as Laura waved and called out, "Come over tomorrow, Weed. I have another book for you."

After they drove off, I started running as fast as my leg would allow. My eyes were stinging, and my nose was dripping, but I kept going because my leg could never hurt as bad as the ache deep inside me.

———

After I got back to Ollie's, I soaked my spongy leg in a hot tub then got ready for the drive-in. I didn't feel like being social at all, but there was no way I was going to let Russ down. Russ called to tell me to bring a supply of beers because his dad won't let him drink. I also grabbed some old blankets because one of the windows on Russ's truck is broken.

When Russ pulled up, Ollie and I screamed with laughter. Russ had affixed a big plastic Santa to the cab of his truck. No ordinary Santa, *this* Santa sported a Playtex bra and a garter belt pasted to his trousers. Two elves and a reindeer were cavorting in the bed of the truck. Russ had somehow managed to mount an elf onto the reindeer's hindquarters, so when the truck bounced over the ruts in Ollie's driveway, the elf repeatedly humped the bored reindeer with glee. The second elf had a wry look on his wee plastic face, obviously delighted with the action. It was a hoot.

By the time Russ and I got to the drive-in, which is just off Route 40, a line of cars was waiting to get in. A series of old Burma Shave ads on sign posts lined the road, and each was decorated with a Pilgrim or a wreath. (I love how they blend holidays here on the prairie.) Everyone was honking and waving to each other, so I was in a festive mood, despite my sadness about Laura.

Janine was only two cars ahead of us in Patty Lynn's Fairlane. While traffic was stopped, Patty Lynn jumped out to say hello, but Janine stayed in the car. "How're y'all doing?" Patty Lynn asked.

Russ told her we'd be a lot better if the elf in the back would stop moaning. That got us all laughing. "Tell Janine I said hello," I said, thinking maybe it was time to call a truce. Patty Lynn just raised her brows to show her disapproval, so I tossed her a beer and told her to forget I ever said it.

It took us forever to get up to the entrance because a truck had broken down ahead, but we finally made it past the abandoned vehicle, which I immediately recognized as Bubbylee's truck. Although the truck had survived Barley's chopper assault, it was now covered with fake snow, half-eaten sandwiches, and a few unmentionables that had all been contributed by the passing revelers. Russ and I felt obligated to do our part, so we contributed one demented-looking elf holding a beer bottle.

By the time we got through the gate, Jimmy Stewart and Donna Reed were already cavorting in front of the old Granville house in Bedford Falls. "Damn, we can't miss 'Buffalo Gals'!" Russ groaned, giving the truck a shot of gas. Santa suddenly made a head-first suicide jump down the windshield. During the leap, Santa's bra slipped up around his head and caught on the radio antenna, so the fat fellow was bouncing alongside the truck like Isadora Duncan as we pulled up to the speaker mount.

Our parking spot was only one car away from Patty Lynn and Janine. We were given a car heater at the entrance, so we got it pumping as fast as we could. The only options were freeze or burn, so we alternated. I was fiddling with the heater when the drive-in crowd broke into a rousing chorus of "Buffalo Gals." Russ was singing at the top of his lungs, so I joined right in. Everyone laid on their horns afterward. It was a raucous event.

In spite of the cold, people were milling around, so it was very social. Jimmy Dale dropped by long enough to jump in the back of the truck and make out with the elf as bystanders applauded. JD slapped the elf on the butt and said, "Be sure to call me sometime," just before starting up a game of toss-the-elf. I last saw the hapless elf heading north with no head and only one leg as Jimmy Dale yelled promises never to forget him.

Patty Lynn came by again with a bucket of popcorn. She didn't seem as interested in Jimmy Dale as she usually is, and I don't think it was because JD was humping Santa. Actually, she was all over Russ, who was too dense to notice. But as a result, he didn't clutch for once. He just went on breaking everyone up with his imitation of Jimmy Stewart. When I jumped in as Donna Reed, we got rave reviews.

We were well into *Miracle on 34th Street* when I saw Rick Bills's Bel Air parked a few rows ahead of us. I was dying to see Laura, but I decided that a word with Laura wasn't worth Rick's condescending attitude.

I was straining my neck to see if Rick's car windows were foggy when Janine finally strolled over. She stood smack dab in front of Russ's truck to talk to Jimmy Dale, who by then was so drunk he could hardly talk at all. Janine leaned into him and whispered something.

"I suspect she's testing his ability to stay upright," Russ chuckled.

"Yeah, JD has an amazing ability to talk and keep barf down at the same time," I nodded.

Suddenly Janine kissed JD right in front of us in

what I thought was a very sad attempt to make me jealous. There was so much slurping we needed raincoats and boots. Russ hit the horn, and I threw popcorn.

"Hey, Janine," Russ yelled, "how 'bout dragging your roadkill athlete off our viewing highway!"

We were about to hose them down with soda when all hell broke loose outside the drive-in. The ground suddenly started to vibrate, and then a hollow, echoing sound drowned out Natalie Wood and everyone else on 34th Street. Above the road, an eerie cloud of dust was rising, illuminated by the neon light of the marquis. Despite the cold weather, the air smelled worse than rotten eggs.

A high-pitched squealing filled the night, and then a wall of enormous pigs emerged from the darkness into view. They looked rabid in the neon light, and maybe they were. All I know is they were running faster than I knew a hog could move. We all whooped and shouted as the bacon brigade herded past, crapping everywhere. I swear they were shooting it out horizontally!

When Patty Lynn screamed, "Look, a fire!" we all turned in the direction the pigs had come from. On the hill, flames licked the dark sky. "That's Barley's place!" she yelled.

The fire truck and the sheriff's car suddenly came speeding down the road blocking the pigs in, causing the crapping to reach record levels. (A mass of pigs backing up is a surreal sight, let me tell you. These things just don't happen in Scranton.) Finally the pig wall moved sharply to the left, mowing over a wooden fence across the road from the drive-in entrance.

As the frantic pigs overtook the field, the horses who resided there became understandably miffed and decided to escape from their unsanitary guests via the road. As luck would have it, the horses headed straight for the drive-in.

"Oh-oh," JD groaned in the most colossal understatement I have ever heard.

We all came to life and scattered faster than buckshot. That's when Russ jumped into action like a true rodeo stud. "Get back!" he yelled as he shimmied up the fence that surrounds the drive-in. We all ran inside and gathered in a group near the entrance where we could have a view of the action.

When the lead horse came by, Russ jumped off the fence. For a moment he appeared to hang in mid-air, then he landed square on the horse's back. There was more testosterone in that feat than in a John Wayne double feature. He literally rode the animal bareback through a pig shit slick, and we all screamed and cheered as he disappeared into the night. Within seconds, Russ circled back into the light again to herd the other horses away from the theater. Even the pigs were impressed.

After Russ got the last of the horses back into the pasture, a bunch of us propped the fence back up, using whatever we could find to secure it. We used Carol Beth Harper's pink girdle to clamp two posts together, which is probably what her mom had in mind when she bought it for her little Minotaur in the first place. It was quite entertaining. In fact, the whole affair was the most fun I've had since my life got so sidetracked.

As Russ hopped back over the fence, we all clapped and hollered and leaned on our horns to show our appreciation for his bravery in the line of shit-fire.

Russ wasn't even back in the truck long enough to warm up before Patty Lynn slinked over and took his hand. "You were soooo amazing," she sighed. Russ just shrugged and sucked it up.

He was still basking in the attention when all the cars began to exit. (It was during Edmund Gwenn's final attempt to prove he's Kris Kringle. I notice these things.) Naturally, everyone migrated to Barley

Edinburgh's place to see if the old duffer had survived the blaze.

By the time we arrived at Barley's, the flames were out, but the smoke was heavy against the night. There wasn't much left of the ranch house, but the neighbors had managed to save the bunkhouses. Through the haze, I spotted Barley sitting on the fire truck enjoying a flask. We heard a fire fighter tell the sheriff that Barley's narcolepsy had kicked in around the time Barley was lighting a fire in the fireplace, so it seems he lit the rug instead.

"No wonder the Fire Marshall has nicknamed him 'Sparky,'" Russ whispered.

"Well, he doesn't seem too fazed by all this."

I had no sooner said the words when suddenly Barley yelled, "SEIZE AND DESTROY!" at the top of his barbecued lungs. Then he stood up, weaved, and fell off the fire truck onto his gourd. He just lay there like a smoked turtle calling people "maggots" and "troops" and saying he wanted to go back to a whore house in Okinawa for something called a "steam and cream." When he finally broke into a chorus of "There Is Nothin' Like a Dame," Russ and I had seen enough, so we pulled out before what was no doubt a raucous finale.

As we backed down the road, we spotted old Cotton McKamey leaning against a tree with four white guys. I knew by their blackened clothes that they had been among the group who had helped put out the fire, so we stopped to tell them what a great job they did. They all seemed real beat but darn pleased as they passed around a jug of water. What got my goat though was the way they refused to share it with Cotton. No kidding, they wouldn't pass him the jug! When I saw what was going on, I immediately jumped out of the truck to offer Cotton a beer.

You can imagine how dumbfounded I was when

Cotton looked at his feet and said, "No thank you, sir. I don't rightly think I'll be needin' that."

His demeanor made me feel prickly all over. "Hey, it's me—Weed Clapper," I told him. "Dontcha remember me, Cotton?"

"Yes, sir," he said, "and I be thankin' you. But you jus' get back in dat dere truck and get yo'self outta here." When he lifted his face slightly to look at me, his eyes were darker than the night around us. "Goon now, son," he urged.

I took the hint and jumped back in the truck. When I told Russ what Cotton had said, Russ peeled out of there fast. It all seemed like a big overreaction to me, and I told Russ so as I tried to persuade him to slow down. I no sooner had my say when we spotted a dark car tailgating us with its high beams on. Russ sped up, but the car stayed with us.

The car came darn close numerous times, which rattled us both. Suddenly the punks who were tailing us rammed Russ's bumper so hard Russ had to fight to keep control of the truck. I nearly went through the windshield. We couldn't make out who the driver was, but the jerks stayed with us until some stray pigs rushed the road. The pig confusion gave us enough distance to ditch the troublemakers, but by then Russ and I were both shaking. The last thing we heard over the squealing of pigs and our own heavy breathing was someone yelling, "Watch your backs, you filthy nigger lovers!" My guts were churning by the time Russ dropped me off, and I'm sure Russ didn't feel any calmer than I did.

I didn't get much sleep that night because I couldn't quiet my mind. I'd really like to believe there's a Bedford Falls somewhere out there, but every time I work up a little bit of hope, something horrible comes speeding along faster than a damn Lackawanna train, and I just can't seem to get out of its path.

CHAPTER SIXTEEN
NOVEMBER 22, 1960

ONLY TWO DAYS TILL THANKSGIVING. OLLIE IS BAKING PIES to take to Denise's house, and I made a centerpiece out of pine cones, branches, and candles because Ollie informed me, "A centerpiece would be proper, darlins." The centerpiece looks darn good, I think.

I got a letter from Murray today. It included a photo of him and Michelle in front of my old school, which sure makes me miss home. I admit, Murray's letter has me worried:

November, Something-or-other

Weedamemnon,

I can hardly write because my head is spinning. Michelle missed her 'time of the month.' Can you believe it? We tried to be careful, but something went wrong, and I don't know what to do.

She says she heard about a doctor in Philly who can take care of things, but I'm scared shitless something will happen to her. And I don't think I can handle the idea of being a baby killer. I'm trying not to panic, but I don't know what to do. I can't mention this to the Family Goldberg because all they talk about is my scholarship and what a great lawyer I'm going to be.

I went out to the home to talk to Bubby. (They've locked her up like a naked little bird with no wings, just a hat. I can't stand to see it.) I did all the talking 'cause Bubs often doesn't know who I am. I told her everything, and then she sang, "Till There Was You." I haven't cried that hard since... well, you know.

I think if Bubby could understand, she'd tell me to marry Michelle. What do you think? Next week I'm supposed to send money to reserve a dorm room at Penn, so I've got to make a decision fast. I'm so nerve-racked I feel like someone peeled off my skin.

On a lighter note, Liam-The-Load is going to New York to act. He now quotes Shakespeare and says shit like, "Forsooth, methinks I see a ghost" in a prissy accent. It's real "Twilight Zone" stuff. I told him he'd end up a fag. Kenton told him he already IS a fag.

Gotta go man. I need to concentrate on my studies. Hang tough, and take it from me—keep your tuna tucked in your trou'.

Breast Regards,
Murray the G-man

P.S. I enclosed Michelle's photo. Nice, huh? I really love her, Weed. And by the way, a couple moved into your house last week. No kids, just one mutt named Jerry Lee. The dog is cool, but strangers living in your house just ain't kosher!

After I read Murray's letter, I called him, but no one was home. I kept mulling it over because I want to give him the right advice. Murray has worked so hard for a scholarship and a good career, which will all go up in smoke if he has to support a family. I used to think I'd want a girl to get things "taken care of" if I ever got a girl in trouble, but since my kid brother died, I can't handle the idea of killing a kid. I guess that's what Snarls was talking about with the 'situational morality' stuff. Any way you slice it, this is bad.

I figured Laura might have some good advice for Murray, but I wasn't sure I really wanted to see her. I've been embarrassed since her fiancé treated me as if I was gimpy Chester from "Gunsmoke," and I'm troubled that Laura would even want to marry a jackass like him. But I decided to talk to her anyway, for Murray's sake.

I had to make my way over there in a wicked windstorm. When I got to her house, she was setting out a horn-of-plenty on the dining room table. "That looks real nice, Laura," I said. As I handed her the Frost book she had lent me, I couldn't help but notice the light flash of her diamond ring.

"Thank you, Weed. There's a Whitman book here I wanted you to look at," she said. "One of the poems reminded me of you when I read it again recently."

"Which one is that?"

"Read the book first, then I'll tell you."

"Ah, a subversive way to get me to read more sissy stuff!"

"You're on to me," she laughed. "By the way, would you and Ollie like to drop by for some pie on Thanksgiving?"

"We're going to Denise Williams's house for dinner," I said, wondering what her reaction might be.

"That sounds fun. Why don't you all come on by afterward? I'd like to get to know Denise and her family better."

"You're not worried about what people will think?"

"Anyone who'd think something bad is of no concern to me."

I was greatly relieved that she didn't have Janine's mentality. "Is Rick going to be here?" I asked nonchalantly.

"Something tells me you don't care for Rick too much, Weed," she observed.

I didn't want to lie, and I didn't want to hurt her. I decided it was best to dodge the question. "Is this the guy you really want to marry?"

"Rick and I have been discussing marriage for a long time, but we've been in limbo. Actually, you're the one who made me think about it—you know, your mom's advice to commit to living every minute. It made a lot of sense to me, so I admit, I forced Rick's hand. He didn't want me seeing other men, so he decided to make it official.

Can you believe the irony? I had convinced the most wonderful person in my life to run off and marry her cheating lover! When it comes to scaring off women, I couldn't do worse if I went through life dangling a load from my hind cheeks.

"And Rick is the person you want to spend your life with?" I asked again. "You're absolutely sure?"

"Gee... does anyone ever know for sure?"

"I don't know. It's a big decision, but I hope you'll be happy," I said half-heartedly. "My friend Murray is thinking about getting married, too. He got himself into a predicament." I let her read his letter, and I was happy when she said he sounds like a great guy.

"What would you advise him, Laura?" I asked.

"I'd tell him to wait until he has all the facts," she replied softly. Then she leaned against the table and asked, "What would you advise me to do, Weed?"

"The same thing."

She looked at me curiously, as though she had a

thought but dismissed it. After she sat for a moment she said, "I want to apologize on behalf of Rick for embarrassing you yesterday I think he was just concerned. However, I felt terrible about it."

"You don't have to apologize for him, Laura."

"Okay. But I have been very concerned about you, too, Weed."

"Thanks, but there's no need to be."

"I know your leg gives you a lot of trouble. And you don't put weight on it much anymore. Is it healing correctly?"

I could feel my agitation building. All the discussion about my deformities made me feel like a specimen in Frankenstein's laboratory. "I'm okay, Laura," I sighed. "The doctors said I'll probably have pain all my life."

"But I've noticed you've been having more trouble with it. Much more. Have you been getting the treatment you need?"

"I don't need any more medical treatment," I retorted.

"I read your school records, remember? You're supposed to be getting treatment in Greencastle. Have you been going?"

I instinctively stood up to leave. My face was burning, and my mouth was dry. "I can't discuss this," I protested, "because I'm afraid I'll get mad, and I don't want to offend you. I have to go."

"Weed—"

"Laura, I'll always limp the way I do!" I snapped. "I'm a gimp, okay? That's just the way it is! You don't need to worry about me."

Laura reached out a hand to stop me. "Do you know how much I care about you?" she asked. I listened, but I had to close my eyes to keep out a bad feeling that was trying to get in.

"Weed, you can be angry with me if you want," she

said, "that's part of friendship. And though I'm a few years older than you, I consider you my peer. You're the most real friend I have, so I'm not going to stop worrying about you. Please give me reason to feel relieved."

"Okay, okay," I answered as I tried to stop my body from running around inside my skin. "I'll try to see the doctors more often. But dang it, I hate those hospitals! And it's hard for me to get up to Greencastle," I said, already throwing out reasons to break a promise I should never have made.

How could I tell her they fill me with an overwhelming sense of doom? Even the living are walking around half-dead. And I can't bear the sounds. Echoes of everyone ripped from a guy's life are trapped in those antiseptic corridors that smell sadder than an attic. You can't run from them. They're like voices calling from the grave. There are times when I recognize the voices, and I just can't handle it.

"I'll be happy to take you to Greencastle," she said. "I always enjoy your company. Tell me you'll consider it, Weed."

The plea in her voice made her sound smaller than she is. I memorized her face because my gut told me I wouldn't be seeing her much more. I nodded in agreement, but then I withdrew so fast I almost lost my balance. "Thanks, Laura, I'll consider it," I said.

"Okay," she whispered. "Will you all drop by tomorrow after the Thanksgiving meal at Denise's?"

"If it's not too late," I answered cordially. Our talk had sucked the air out of the room, and no change of subject could lighten the atmosphere. But I tried. "Incidentally," I said, "last time I was here I forgot to tell you Andy Johnson sent a message. He said to tell you, 'Joey lives in my heart.'"

Laura's expression changed so fast I was startled. She put her hand to her chest as though she was hearing the words with her heart. "What, Weed? Tell me again, exactly as Andy said it."

"He said, 'Tell Laura Joey lives in my heart.' It seemed quite important to him."

Laura stared straight through me as if I wasn't there anymore. Sometimes even a thick guy like me can read a moment correctly. I had no idea what she was thinking, but I knew she wanted to be alone. "Happy Thanksgiving, Laura," I whispered. Then I picked up the Whitman book and walked out with a head full of confusion.

CHAPTER SEVENTEEN
NOVEMBER 24, 1960

TODAY WAS THANKSGIVING, AND WHAT A DAY! AFTER coffee and milk toast, I was cleaning up dishes when Ollie asked me to put down the dishcloth, close my eyes, and count to ten before taking a gander at a gift she had made for me. When I opened my eyes, I was visually assaulted by a yellow sweater so bright it nearly singed my corneas.

"Cheerful, huh?" Ollie grinned. "Try it on over your shirt, dear." Before I could even muster up a defense, Ollie yanked the thing over my head, tugging and pulling so hard my ears would have been bleeding if my blood supply had been able to get past my throat. "Ollie, the neck is too small," I squeaked.

"Don't worry, Weed," she assured me, "the yarn stretches."

By the time my head popped through the neckline, I was dizzy from lack of oxygen. After Ollie shoved my flailing arms into the sleeves, she stepped back to admire the effect. "Malcolm Clapper, you are more handsome than Elvis Presley! Look at yourself in the dining room mirror, dear," she beamed.

I did. The effect was blinding. The neon yellow sweater was squeezing my Adam's apple so tight my head looked like a pimple on a jaundiced ass. Worse yet, the dang sweater came down to my knees. "Uh, Ols, don't you think it's too long?" I asked.

"Oh, no, darlins. I made it that way because I wanted it to protect your leg as much as possible. You'll wear it to dinner today, won't you, Weed?"

Only if we're having dinner at the School for the Blind, I thought. "I, um, I'm afraid I'll get too hot and sweaty," was my audible response. "There will be lots of oven heat in Denise's house. I could fry like a chicken!"

As I sat on a chair waiting, I looked like a deformed duck. I swear I was a foot higher than usual because I was perched on half a sheep.

I was sweating so much I was well-basted by the time Ollie pranced in wearing a straight brown skirt (an unusually subdued color for Ollie) and a much-too-snug brown sweater set. It would have been quite sophisticated on a woman half her size, but Ollie is big enough to sport a Mail Pouch ad. It was the shoes that really killed me. You know those sexy shoes with high heels and no backs that make a guy think dirty thoughts? Well, Ollie's clodhoppers were wedged into a pair of those, her meaty hooves rupturing over the edges so that she resembled a giant roast beef served up on two Yorkshire pudding popovers. I was speechless.

"I thought this outfit was classy," she twittered. "What do you think, darlins? I want to make a good impression."

That ripped me up. Ollie is such a sweet lady she'd wear a spear through her head if she thought it would please her host. I gritted my teeth and tried to curb my bad attitude, then I stammered, "You're a vision, Ols, but I'm afraid your feet will freeze. You should wear warmer shoes."

"Oh, I *have* to wear these, dear. The sales woman said this sleek shoe style compliments my look."

"Okay, Ols," I gulped, "but if your legs get cold, you can borrow my sweater. You're so short that on you it would be a ball gown!" It made me happy to see her giggle. I assured her she had done such an excellent job I wouldn't need any more sweaters this winter. Or next winter. Or ever.

When we heard Denise honk the horn, Ollie put on her coat and gloves while I grabbed the centerpiece. Ollie couldn't resist donning a red hat with a pilgrim pin on it before we headed for the car. We were a frightful sight. Ollie was carrying a pie while balancing on those shoes so precariously I half-expected her to whip into a spinning pie plate stunt. I, on the other hand, had to fight to keep myself from doing a Dorothy-and-Toto act as my fifty-pound sweater billowed in the wind.

Denise seemed a little taken aback, but she had the sense just to say, "Happy Thanksgiving" instead of, "What the hell just happened here?" She also subtly turned down the heater, but by the time we got to her place I was sweating so much I needed an I.V.

As we pulled up in front of Denise's house, I grew a little uneasy thinking about the racial attitudes in this area and recalling Russ's story about the guy who was brain-damaged for defending a Negro. After we parked, I got Ollie to the porch as quickly as her popovers could maneuver through the snow.

Martha Jane and Mrs. Williams both met us at the door. "Mrs. Williams, Martha, this is my grandmother, Ollie Clapper," I said by way of introduction.

Ollie held out her hand and almost bowed. "I'm so happy to be here, Mrs. Williams," Ollie said. "Thank you for inviting us."

"Lordy me, it sure is an honor to have y'all, Ollie," Mrs. Williams smiled, "and I'd like it mighty fine if you'd jus' call me Jessie."

"Why, you're from Biloxi!" Ollie exclaimed. "I'd know that accent anywhere!"

"Lawdy, Weed, your grandmother is as smart as she is fine," Jessie smiled as she led Ollie off to sip eggnog and poke at the turkey. Meanwhile, Martha and Denise and I caught up on the news. Martha was hula-hooping for us when Aunt Hattie pulled up and rushed in out of the cold wearing a fragrance of green beans and bacon. I assume that had something to do with the dish she was carrying. Right behind her was Denise's boyfriend, Robert, who had hitched a ride from Crawfordsville with Hattie.

Everybody kissed hello while I floated around like a yellow raft. To be honest, I was surprised to see that Robert is as white as I am. In fact, he's even whiter with that red-head complexion of his. He's got one of those special grins that's all teeth, and he's a very sharp dresser. Best of all, he didn't stare at my leg even once. I give him a lot of points for that. He's a darn nice guy.

I slipped off my sweater after we all sat down so everyone could see my cool black (and very wet) shirt. Robert suppressed a laugh when I told Ollie I was removing the sweater only because I thought some other people might want to try it on. There were no volunteers, so Robert skillfully changed the subject even faster than I can. He must be getting a good education at Wabash.

Robert is from Long Island, and he's a lot of fun. He told us that although New Yorkers have the reputation of being a bunch of unfriendly grouches, they're really very social and always show up in large numbers when there's a group shoot-out. That killed us.

He then got Jessie talking about how she and Mr. Williams came to Indiana. Jessie said they were Mississippi sharecroppers until Mr. Williams cut off four fingers in an old piece of machinery. After that, he drove trucks until he eventually found steady work for a company in Greencastle. "Now he's workin' in Detroit," she added.

"He's coming back to us when he makes some more money," Martha Jane chimed in.

"Yeah, if he wins a floating crap game," Hattie mumbled.

"Hush," Jessie admonished Hattie, and then she turned to Martha and said, "Chile, how 'bout you fetchin' us all some eggnog?"

While Martha Jane was out of the room, Jessie told us how Mr. Williams had taken up gambling. "He still calls once in a spell when he needs money," she added, "though nobody's done seen him since he up and left." (Denise stared at her hands and never said a word about her day at the Indianapolis 500.)

Jessie then went on to describe how she had always had a difficult time reading and never finished school the way Hattie did, so she cleaned houses and took in wash to support the family. She was quite surprised to hear Ollie's house was the big white one on Old Greencastle Road. "Why I'll be, I used ta pick up washin' for Miz Aubrey when she lived there some decades back," Jessie told Ollie.

"That must be another house you're thinking of, Jessie," I explained. "The big white house has always been Ollie's."

"No, darlins," Ollie corrected me. "Jessie's right. My mama didn't leave the house to me. I had to buy it back some years later when I returned to town."

"I thought it wuz so," Jessie nodded. "A colored man owned it awhiles. And he rented it to Miz Aubrey."

"And he was as nice a man as a man can be," Hattie added. "I felt real bad when he left town. Real bad."

"Why, yes," Jessie nodded to Hattie. "Caint say as I blame 'im for thinkin' it best to go somewheres else. He couldn't even stay in 'is own home 'count of him not being able to live in a white neighborhood."

That information launched Robert faster than even I can get flying. He's an earnest sort, and I respected what he had to say. "That's exactly why Denise and I are heading down South to join S.N.C.C." he said. "It's intolerable that a man scraped enough cash together to buy a home then couldn't even live in it because he was the wrong color!"

"What's the S.N.C.C.?" Jessie inquired for the rest of us.

"The Student Non-Violent Coordinating Committee, Mama," Denise explained. "They promote integration without violence."

Aunt Hattie sat up in her chair. "Well good for you. I just may come down there and join you. Only I might want to kick some behinds, so I hope that ain't considered violent."

I was watching Denise across the room. Her smile was so warm I didn't want it to go anywhere South, especially with her attached to it. Therefore, I didn't receive the news well at all. "You never mentioned that in your letter, Denise," I said.

"Oh, we just decided, Weed. One of Robert's professors at Wabash was expelled from the faculty for giving up his seat to a Negro lady at the Wabash Eatery. It resulted in a sit-in, and lots of people were arrested. Many of them were roughed up by the cops. Now Dr. Marsh is organizing a group to join up with some others down in Mississippi. He says we'll accomplish more with larger numbers."

"That's a real good idea," Ollie chimed in. "I've been thinking a lot recently about an experience I had down in New Orleans one Mardi Gras."

I was suddenly on humiliation alert. I didn't remember Ollie ever mentioning Mardi Gras. And with Ollie, you never know where these little memories are going. I was just praying the story wouldn't include Monkey Boy's nude audition for King Kong. Or Mr. Beano's after-dinner performance farting the "Star Spangled Banner."

"It was back in 1947," Ollie was saying. "The Mardi Gras crowds were huge and rowdy. I was on a side street when some folks in the back started shoving to get through. They weren't pushing all that much I later heard, yet we were all propelled forward. We couldn't hold them back. Within minutes I was flat up against a building and I couldn't breathe. I was scared half to death. If the owner of the building hadn't opened the door I was pressed against, I would have dropped dead right there. That's a true story. I thought Martha might get something out of it."

The silence was stunning. While we all sat trying to figure out the connection between Mardi Gras and Civil Rights in Mississippi, Ollie smiled serenely and let the moment hang there like a discarded colon. Jessie and Hattie were puzzled, and Martha Jane was downright befuddled. I bet Jessie was wondering if she should move sharp objects away from Ollie before any other peculiar behavior reared its ugly head.

"I get it, Ollie," Robert suddenly exclaimed, flashing Ollie a huge grin, "the total of the mass increased the force! That's genius!" he said slapping his knee. "Those few people in the back moved some others, who in turn, moved a HUGE MASS!" Suddenly Robert stopped short and gulped. "Uh, I didn't mean the 'huge mass' was you, Ollie," he added. We all choked, but Ollie kept smiling and didn't bat an eye. Robert was a hero to me for saving the moment... in spite of the gaff.

"I know what you meant, darlins," Ollie laughed heartily as she patted his hand, "and I'm glad you understood what I meant. I've always remembered what a powerful force that was. I guess it's my way of saying that even though you can't force anyone to change, a slow and steady push in the right direction can change the outcome of many things."

"Why, that's real good thinkin'!" Jessie exclaimed.

"Oh, Mama," Martha Jane whined, "do we have to talk about civil rights junk? That's all anybody is talking about these days, and I'm bored enough to drop dead on my head."

"We gotta discuss it till there ain't no more reason ta be discussin' it, little one. But not today. I'm thinkin' we better protect that hard head o' yers, so we all better get ta eatin' on that turkey in there."

"Yeah," we said in unison as we headed for the table and settled down for a feast to remember. Martha Jane said grace, and then Jessie dished out huge slabs of juicy turkey as the crowd commented on my centerpiece. Jessie had whipped up a vat of potatoes which was so creamy and rich that I mentioned how I'd be tempted to roll around in them after dinner. That started the conversation with a bang.

Eventually Robert contributed a sampling of funny stories about fraternity life. He really got us choking when he described how someone dropped a "loaf" in the group shower one day as a joke, so they all had to rotate their shower heads like gunners to hold back the offensive slider. He shouted "Incoming!" and "Call in artillery!" as part of the demonstration. It may not have been dinner talk, but it sure got the party rolling.

We laughed so hard Martha Jane snorted milk out her nose just the way Leland used to do. When Robert used an imaginary showerhead to shoot invisible boogers away from him, we all joined in with showerheads and artillery coordinates of our own.

Ollie, Jessie, and Hattie were tossing back cups of spiked eggnog, so even though they pretended their senses were offended, they laughed as hard as the rest of us. By the time we got to coffee and Ollie's pies, we felt like best friends for life.

Following our meal, we played cards awhile, but the turkey was having an effect. Soon we wound down slower than a 45 record on 33 speed. When we all got rubber-lips syndrome, Ollie and I departed.

After Denise dropped us off, I headed back out into the cold. I felt guilty about not mentioning Laura's invitation to Ollie, but as much as I enjoy the way Ollie is a jolly ol' grandmother, I don't want to be treated like a boy around Laura. There were other reasons I wanted to get on with my day. Jessie had packed tin foil pouches full of leftovers. It only seemed right to share the booty with Andy Johnson, and I knew where to find him.

Recently I've seen him sleeping behind the old civic building which now houses a small library and a two-room museum. (A tour of the museum is a ten-minute event. It's full of oddities from these parts, such as unusual mushrooms, arrowheads, and even a spent casing from a John Dillinger bank heist.)I've been going by there daily to start a fire for Andy because it's been so cold lately. I also took him a scarf and hat to keep him warm. And to be honest, I thought he might feel better with his head covered.

Sure enough, when I arrived Andy was struggling to shove sticks into a trash barrel, so I gave him a hand. Although he didn't say hello, I knew he recognized me. He wasn't wearing the hat, so he was hard to look at because his mangled face was purple from the cold, and debris had settled in the crevice in his skull. After we piled the wood into the barrel, Andy held out his hands to warm them, even though there was no fire. It was sad to see how much he fades in and out of reality.

"Andy, maybe you should take one of your matches and toss it in there on top of those newspapers," I suggested. He looked at me with some confusion, but he followed my directions. When the fire started, he warmed his hands again.

"I've been meaning to tell you," I said, "I gave your message to Laura Saslow... the message about Joey."

Andy's face showed instant recognition. "Laura?" he said. One corner of his mouth hiked up in a smile while the other half of his face betrayed him and simply collapsed inward. Even though it was very unsettling, I was happy to see he could still feel some pleasure despite his bleak circumstances.

"H-h-appy Thans-giving," he said, struggling to pronounce each syllable as clearly as he could.

"Same to you, man," I smiled.

"I m-meant...to Laura. Tell Laura."

"Oh, okay, Andy," I nodded. "Well, here, I brought some real good food for you to eat," I said as I handed him the leftovers. Andy nodded in appreciation then lumbered off with the food. I didn't follow because I figured he might want to eat in private, considering how his mouth is out of commission.

I was turning to leave when I ran into Margie White, the elderly librarian who loves books and reeks of mothballs. "Malcolm," she said, "Happy Thanksgiving! I wondered if I'd find you here again."

"Hi, Margie, Happy Turkey Day. What are you doing here on a holiday?"

"I dropped by to make sure I had turned off the electric heater. Sometimes I'm quite forgetful. Would you like to come in for a moment?"

It was a perfect opportunity for me to check on something I was darn curious about. "Sure, I'll come in and warm up a bit," I nodded. "By the way, Margie, are there any town records I can look at, like property deeds and that sort of thing?"

"By all means, Malcolm. Come on in," she said with a dramatic gesture.

While Margie puttered around talking to her books (her train is a bit off-track), I flipped through the grant deeds beginning in 1940 and found some interesting information. On January 23, 1941, a Mr. C.R. Turner took title of the house Ollie lives in from the estate of Beatrice Clapper, a deceased person, who was my great grandmother. Turner rented the house to Miss Loretta Aubrey, the lady Jessie did wash for. Then on October 19, 1942, (just after Ollie left the carnival) Mr. Turner sold the property to Olivia Clapper, my grandmother, for the token sum of two hundred dollars... a suspiciously low price, even in those ancient times.

"Can you find out anything else about Mr. C. R. Turner?" I asked Margie.

"Sure. I'll check the old real estate contracts in the files," she offered.

As soon as Margie located the file, I glanced over the document, and I was shocked at what I discovered. The name on the contract identified Mr. C. R. Turner as Caleb Turner, forwarding address: Binghamton, New York. Wow - Ollie's Caleb was the Negro who once owned the home we were living in before he was forced to leave! And that's how my grandmother got it so cheap. I couldn't help but think it was a darn suspicious coincidence that Caleb bought the house. I can't help wondering what Caleb really meant to Ollie.

———

When I returned home, Ollie was moving around the kitchen faster than a whirling dervish. I've noticed a pattern with her. Either she Ajaxes the sink until the enamel bleeds or she makes sandwiches. Mounds of sandwiches. It usually means she's mulling something over, but it's hard to pin her down because her mouth clacks like a loose shutter about everything except what's gnawing at her. The first words she fired at me as I walked in were: "Pickles are peculiar little vegetables." The meaning escaped me entirely.

"Ollie, did you have a nice time today?"

"Oh, real nice, darlins. They're all so lovely. And that Robert is a pistol. Martha Jane is going to come over and teach me how to hula hoop. Do you think she eats pickles on her sandwiches?" At least that explained how the pickles fit in.

"Sure, Ollie. Your sandwiches are the best. And Martha will love to root around in this old house. I wonder if that lady—that Miss Aubrey who rented this place—appreciated the house as much as you do." (It was a remarkable segue for someone about as subtle as a peeping Tom on a pogo stick.)

"Ummm." It was more of a grunt than a comment as Ollie continued to pile her inventive ingredients into the sandwiches like a fat Mr. Wizard.

"So how come your mother didn't leave you this house, Ols? Did she think you weren't coming back this way?"

"No, darlins, that wasn't it at all." Ollie let out a long sigh, and her hands finally stopped moving. "You see, Weed, dear, after my mama disowned me, I found out the house was for sale, and I wanted it real bad. As I mentioned, it was important to me that your dad always be able to find me. I didn't have enough money to buy this place myself, which was very upsetting. But someone I knew bought it, so it all worked out."

"I know the man who bought it was Caleb," I said quietly. "I had a hunch, so I looked it up. I hope you're not mad, Ols."

"No, I don't mind none, dear."

"So why would Caleb want to buy a house in Indiana?" I asked. I had heard enough rumors about my grandmother's past, so I felt it was about time I knew the truth.

"Caleb had saved some money, so he wanted to help me find a place where I'd be able to settle once the war was over," she answered while pulling up a chair and gesturing for me to sit. "After he bought this place, he rented it to Miss Aubrey awhile until him and me could return to these parts. Caleb was from this area, Weed, from what was known as 'Nigger Town.' That's what they called the area where Jessie lives. Some still do, I guess.

"I first met Caleb at a dance hall I used to visit with my friend Roland. The place was Fatty's Joint. It was out by the lake, although very few whites ever went out there. But Roland and me and our friends used to drop in because we liked folks of all colors, and we could dance up a storm there. Caleb played piano and sang like nobody I'd ever heard.

"You've probably figured out I never married your daddy's father."

"Really?" I asked innocently.

"No, Weed. When I got pregnant, he deserted me. As a result, I was snubbed by all the 'proper folk.' A lot of un-neighborly neighbors knew I frequented Fatty's, so there were rumors that the baby's daddy was a Negro. I wanted to run away because no one would talk to me, not even Mama. It was Caleb who said I could go away with him to join up with the carnival and see the U.S. of A. He was the only one who would help me out, Weed," she sighed.

"I hope the man who deserted you died of something hideous," I blurted out in her defense.

"He did," she smiled, "he was shot in the behind in a speakeasy a few years later."

That made my neck snap! Finally, it all made sense. I remembered the photo of Roland Jennings, the cocky-looking mustachioed guy in Ollie's yearbook, and I realized how much my father resembled him. "That means I'm the grandson of a two-bit rogue with an extra butt-hole," I grinned.

"That's right, darlins," she smiled. "So, when Caleb was ready to hit the road, he borrowed an old car. I had to ride in the back so it would appear that he was my chauffeur. A white lady couldn't travel with a colored man back then. I delivered your father in Kentucky, right in the back seat with Caleb glued to my side. He needed a highball after that ordeal," she laughed.

"Caleb and I brought your daddy right back here. My mama agreed to raise him proper, but she ordered me to never come back. She swore if I ever brought a colored man on her property again, she'd call the sheriff on both of us. I had no money and nowhere to live, so I knew your daddy's only chance in life was to stay put. Walking out that door was one of the four saddest days of my life. But Caleb and me moved on. And we were best friends all those years."

"Then how come Caleb left here, Ollie?"

"Well, darlins, the white folks around here weren't too welcoming. We had to make sure never to be seen together because it was dangerous. Why, I remember hearing about a colored man over near Terre Haute who ended up with his private parts shoved down his throat just for being friendly with a white woman. Therefore, we were careful. But folks found out about us in spite of our caution, which didn't leave Caleb much choice but to move on. The dear soul sold me the house for next to nothing—just enough to make it legal. Then he moved to Binghamton, and we made plans to see each other in the New Year."

"Was Caleb really just your friend, or was he in love with you, Ollie?" I asked.

Ollie stood up and turned her back to me. She hesitated for a moment, and then she spoke in a voice so gentle I had to lean in to hear her. "I do believe he loved me to pieces," she nodded.

When Ollie turned back around, a glimmer of something moved across her face like a great old movie, and I could see glimpses of the young girl she had once been.

In that moment Ollie became different to me. I

realized that we always see people the way they are in the present—old or mangled or gimpy or eccentric—but we don't take the time to see a person for where they've been in their long-ago past. And Ollie sure has been someplace special. I'm determined to learn more before I say good-bye.

CHAPTER EIGHTEEN
NOVEMBER 25, 1960

TODAY I GOT A LETTER FROM MY FRIEND KENTON, WHO'S
been on my mind a lot lately because of all the racial
strife that's going in the country. Negroes and
sympathizers are getting injured everywhere, so I told
Murray to warn Kenton that being a Negro is a
dangerous predicament right now. We're all hoping
Kennedy can help matters some. Murray said he'll
watch Kenton's back if anything starts brewing back in
Scranton, but I wish I could be there, too. I liked
Kenton's letter:

Kenton Washington Smith
14 Pomona St, Scranton, Pa.
November? Beats me!

Dear Weed,

*I was happy to finally get my own letter from you, man. I was
tired of getting all your news second-hand from Murray. I've
got info for you that's nauseating!*

*Liam-the-Ghost-of-Morose is going to N.Y. to Juilliard acting
school, so he dropped out of T. J. High! He had to audition, so*

*he did some bit from A Streetcar Named Desire. Knowing
Liam, he probably changed the part and gave Stanley leprosy.
He's now calling himself "Houston Skies." Do you believe
that shit? Houston, my ass! He's never been to no Texas.
He's never even been west of Altoona. He's such an asshole.
And that doom monger got a scholarship, pardon my pink
putter!*

*I think you should know that Master Murray hasn't been his
old self lately. He's down in the chops about something. If you
ask me, the Murds Man could use some of his Bubby's
chicken soup. Remember how ol' Bubster always put money
under the bowls for us? And remember when Houston Skies
asked her if she had washed her hands first. ASSHOLE! I
don't like to think about that nice old lady being in a home.*

*More news: Miss Scarpella married Mr. Tarr, so we've been
catching him copping feels around school. Who wouldn't?
(Remember Scarpella's rack?)*

*You know Epworth, the snot-eater in my grade? Well, he got
himself suspended for asking Miss Scarpella if she was going
to have a tar baby. He told me he meant a "Tarr baby,"
because she married Tarr. Anyway, old Brearly heard about it,
and he decided to make an example out of Epworth for
insulting us people with African roots. Ep didn't mean
anything by it. (Ep's cool when his finger's not up his snot
hole.)*

*I told Frankie James I thought it was harsh to make a guy a
goat for something so stupid, and that I was gonna set
Brearly straight. But Frankie says it's time us African
brothers speak up. He said I was talking like a Steppenfetchit,
and if I don't stand up I'm as bad as the whites who keep us
down. He wants to organize protests. For Chrissake man, I
just want to pass history and make music. Frankie's on my
butt all the time 'cause I ain't angry enough. HE'S the one*

193

*pissing me off! Frankie's an asshole, too. It's an asshole world
out there.*

*Here's my big news, man. The cousin of our drummer
(remember Squeaks?) owns a recording studio in N.Y., so the
band is gonna drive up there over Christmas to make a
quality tape to send around. I'll send you a copy, Clap Man.*

*Murray says you're getting some action from some corn-
shuckin' honey. Let's hear the dirt, man. I'm trying to get
Sally Levon to go out with me. She's a senior, and she's sooo
fine.*

*Are you going to the doctor like you're supposed to, man?
You better be. I ain't foolin' about that shit. And don't tell me
to stay off your case, 'cause that ain't gonna happen. So
sue me.*

Yours truly,
Kenton Smith

*P.S. My Almanac says the fattest guy in history was buried
in Bremen, Indiana in a casket bigger than a grand piano!
The fat cat weighed more than a thousand pounds! That's a
lot of corn dogs. That's all I know about Indiana, but it's
good, huh?*

It's the middle of the night, and I can't go back to sleep.
Earlier tonight I took some pain pills I had stored away
for emergency situations. To be truthful, all this walking
in the cold has been affecting my balance.
Unfortunately, the pills cause horrible nightmares. I just
had one about Leland. It was the same nightmare I've
been having a lot lately. It leaves me with a hole so
enormous inside I feel I might cave in, but the pain

inside the hole is so huge my body can't even collapse to end the misery.

The dream always starts out nice. Leland and I are in an airplane, and I'm the pilot. He's wearing a little helmet, and he can hardly see up over the control panel, so I give him a box to sit on that says Post Toasties Cereal on the side. We fly over Route 66 then on to the Grand Canyon where the bright colors of the canyon walls radiate upward like heat waves. Leland gets so excited that he stands up in his seat, and I have to tell him to please sit back down and drink his milk.

I let him out to see the canyon while I shut down the plane. Suddenly there's a roar, and I look up and see a bunch of guys riding motorcycles. My eyes are off Leland for only one godawful second before a look of horror flashes across the face of the motorcycle leader. As I turn to see what he's looking at, a train rises out of the canyon like a giant tarantula. It's heading right for Leland, who is smiling and waving at me from the edge of the canyon.

I yell, but Leland keeps waving. When I try to get out of the plane, the door won't budge. I hear Leland call my name just before I hear the train's piercing whistle.

Suddenly the motorcycle guy's mouth falls open revealing a dark hole in his face. His scream comes out as a train whistle.

I look back toward Leland, but I can't see through all the blood that is running down the windshield of the plane. I shove and shove against the door of the plane until I feel my bones breaking. The whole time I'm shouting, "I'm coming, little guy! I'm coming!" until my throat hurts so much, I can't yell anymore.

When I finally get the plane door open, I tumble out onto something soft and wet. It's Leland's head. Just his head. He's looking up at me with those big eyes and his

GWEN BANTA

silly gap-toothed mouth, and he's crying. He's in terrible pain, so I know I have to do something for him.

"Hold on, Leland," I try to say calmly, but it comes out as a scream, so my little brother cries even harder. Then I pick up his head and carry it around in my arms as I search for his body, but I know the train splattered the rest of Leland all over the canyon. Still, I keep searching, and Leland keeps crying until I want to throw his head into the damn canyon.

I tell Leland I can fix him up just fine, but can he please stop crying? I promise I'll take him to Disneyland if he'll just calm down. He asks me will I go back and find his puppy first, because he doesn't want to leave his dog behind the way F.D.R. did. Then he tells me he's cold, and he sobs so much his eyes bleed. No matter what I do, I can't stop the bleeding. He cries so loud I feel like my heart is going to rupture.

Leland asks when can we go home to Mommy and Daddy. That's when I get so worked up that I do something to his head that's so bad I know my mind is rotten. But by the time I realize how depraved I am, I'm awake, like I am now, and I sincerely wish I was dead.

CHAPTER NINETEEN
NOVEMBER 26, 1960

WHEN I GOT UP TODAY, I FELT AS IF WARD BOND AND HIS whole damn Wagon Train had trampled me in my sleep, so I broke down and called the doctor. I expected him to give me the big lecture about not showing up for appointments, but he was *very* pleasant, the way folks are when they speak to dangerous mental patients. I got a laugh out of it.

He seemed to understand when I told him those pills that are supposed to keep me as cheerful as a village idiot are actually depressing the hell out of me. They make my tongue flap until my mouth gets dry and my lips cling to my teeth tighter than a cat stuck to a screen. My hands shake, and I can't sleep. I have no appetite, so my clothes are hanging off me like Spanish moss. The pills I take to go to sleep make me dream those horrible things about my little brother, and I just can't stand it anymore. Doc said if I'd just come in for some X-rays, she'd fix me up with something better, so I decided to give the medical approach one more shot.

My day got a heap more exciting when I was hitching a ride up to Greencastle to see the doctor. I was about to give up and take the bus when Laura Saslow zipped by me in her Buick, made a U-turn, then came back and pulled over.

I had just enough time to smooth my hair and pull up my sagging jeans before she rolled down her window and called out, "Weed, where are you going?"

"Hi, Laura. Uh, Greencastle. Where are you off to?"

"Well, I was going up to Indianapolis to look at wedding dresses at Ayres, but I'm having second thoughts. The stores are always packed on Thanksgiving weekend."

"Sounds about as exciting as Latin class," I groaned.

"You're right," she laughed. "Can you use some company in Greencastle? I've been wanting to drop by the DePauw Library."

"Sure," I answered, and then I jumped in the car before she could decide a wedding dress was more interesting than me. "You can drop me off at the hospital, then maybe we can meet up afterward," I suggested.

"Oh, I'm so glad you're going there, Weed. You've been looking so thin lately." She reached over and touched my hand when she said it, which made me pretty darn glad about going.

Laura reminds me of a photo, hand-tinted with such warm delicate pastels that the image is so alive you want to touch it. She was wearing a blue coat with a fur collar that brushed up against her face. It was enough to make me want to grow fur just to be sewn to her coat.

When we got to the hospital, Laura insisted on waiting while I saw the doctor. In my opinion, the doc was unnecessarily grim. I told him all I wanted was some different medication, and I 'metaphor-ized' about how I'd return if he'd just scribble down something for the pharmacist to decipher using the handy pocket version of The Rosetta Stone for Physicians' Handwriting. Without even cracking a smile, the doc just let out a big sigh. Electrocution would have been more fun.

I cheered up when I got back in the car with Laura. Before grabbing some lunch, we decided to hit the library, but that's when the day turned weird. It made me realize how even a day that starts out routinely can be a day that changes your perspective on life. Or, as in Laura's case, changes your life forever.

I decided to check out Caleb's obituary while Laura looked for the books she wanted. Obituaries can be very nice because they tell you how the deceased person's life affected others. I kept the obituaries about my family because at times my folks and Leland seem so far away, I wonder if I imagined them. I've learned something strange about Time. It dulls images faster than it dulls the pain.

Ollie told me Caleb died in January 1944, in Binghamton, New York, but I was hoping his death had been reported locally because he was born here. It was fun rustling through the old newspapers, and I got distracted quite often by articles on the H-bomb, the Rosenberg trial, and Jackie Robinson signing with the Brooklyn Dodgers, but eventually I found what I was looking for.

Caleb's obituary was a good one, although there was no photo. It reported how he'd been shot up in Binghamton in a street altercation. The obituary said he had been born in this area and had been a "road show performing artist." I liked that, and I planned to tell Ollie that's what she should call herself. According to the obituary, Caleb dropped out of school in the eighth grade, but he was a self-taught musician who had played with Joseph "King" Oliver and Louis Armstrong in a jazz band up in Chicago. (Kenton will like hearing that.)

I was about to close the paper when I noticed an article on the opposite page. The headline caught my eye: LOCAL MAN SHOT IN RACIAL DISPUTE. I knew it had to be referring to Caleb, but I was dumbfounded when I read it.

BINGHAMTON, N.Y:

Local restaurant owner, Richmond L. Parkins, has pleaded innocent to aggravated assault charges stemming from a fatal shooting that occurred outside the Rivoli Theater at 10:00 P.M., Saturday evening. The victim, identified by police as Caleb R. Turner, 51, was an Indiana native.
Friends of the accused told police the victim perpetrated the altercation with Parkins. They claim Turner threatened Parkins as they were buying tickets for the theater. However, a second witness gave a conflicting statement to police.
The man, who asked not to be identified, claimed Parkins' group had been seen harassing the victim. The witness reported seeing Parkins and his companions beat and kick Turner repeatedly. According to the report, when Turner refused to stay down, Parkins pulled a gun and fired.
The victim was taken to Binghamton City Hospital where he died of a gunshot wound and multiple injuries at 11:34 P.M. Mr. Turner was a traveling musician and a veteran. He is survived by his wife, the former Olivia Clapper of Indiana, who was with him at the time the incident occurred.

I was stunned, and so sad for Ollie. She has lost so many loved ones, and in such violent ways. My mind saw her bent over Caleb watching the life pass out of him the way it passes out of Leland's eyes in my nightmares. I wanted to tell her I was terribly sorry she had suffered so much.

But as sorry as I was, I was also ashamed to discover she had married a Negro. I know that sounds really bad, but I can't help it. I believe Negroes are as good as me, but I've always heard whites and Negroes shouldn't *marry*—that it's taboo because of mixed kids and all the other stuff adults warn you about. It's a controversial subject. Just ask actor Sammy Davis, Jr. I thought about how much I've always liked my friend Kenton and never thought of him as any less a person than me and Murray. Of course, I never had any intentions of marrying him either! But does that mean I don't *really* think we're the same? It's damn confusing.

I then considered worse possibilities. What if Ollie lied about who my grandfather was? And what if I'm really Caleb's grandson? Maybe that's why Ollie's mother disowned her. It made sense. My head was reeling. I started to wonder again if maybe Ollie really is as unrespectable as Janine's parents said. But what rule book on life is a person supposed to follow?

I was sitting in the library feeling ashamed of myself for my critical attitude when suddenly I had to shove my festering pile of thoughts out of my head because Laura was talking, and I wasn't hearing a thing she was saying. "Are you all right, Weed?" she whispered.

"Yeah... sure. I'm fine. Did you find what you needed?"

"Yes, how about you?"

I turned the newspaper over and left it face down on the table. "Yes, I did. Now, how 'bout if we get something to eat? I saw a nice coffee shop over near Walnut."

"Sure. But I picked up a book Rick has been waiting

for," she told me. "Do you mind if we drop it by his apartment before we eat? He's home, grading mid-terms."

The last person I wanted to see was Rick Bills. I would have preferred a funeral wake with Liam O'Gara... or *for* Liam O'Gara. But Laura gave me such a nice smile that I decided to be a good sport.

Rick lives in a big house on Poplar Street, just off campus. When we saw his car, we parked and went in. Someone in the building was cooking roast beef, so I was drooling more than a St. Bernard as we climbed the stairs to Rick's apartment on the second floor.

We were discussing what to have for lunch when Rick stuck his head out his door. He seemed shocked to see us. "Laura," he stammered, "I thought you were in Indianapolis!"

"Change of plans, hon. Aren't you going to say hello to Weed?"

"Sure, hi, Weed," he said like the effort was giving him a hernia. He was wearing only a pair of corduroys and no shoes, and I thought it was odd the way he kept blocking the door with his body. Little Anthony and the Imperials were singing "Tears on My Pillow" from somewhere inside, so I at least had to give him credit for good taste in music, if not in manners.

"I was at the library, so I picked up the book you've been waiting for," Laura said as she handed it to him. She made a move toward the door, but Rick stepped out into the hall instead.

"I'd ask you in," he said, "but I've got to get those mid-terms finished. I'm afraid that if I stop for five minutes to be social, I'll never get back to them."

I never heard Rick talk so fast, so I knew the bastard was hiding something. Laura continued to smile, but I sensed she was nervous and wanted to get out of there fast. When she backed toward the railing, I stopped her with my hand.

Meanwhile, Rick's innocent expression stayed welded to his smug puss, and the charade was making me nuts. Sometimes in life a guy just doesn't have a choice and needs to force someone's hand. "Rick, man," I said, "I've got a pain in my leg. Can I come in and sit down for just a second?" Laura didn't look at me, but I could hear her trying to regulate her breathing.

In a remarkable imitation of a lobster in boiling water, Rick squirmed around awhile before becoming dead-still. Finally, he looked down at his feet and mumbled, "You don't want to come in, Laura. I'm so sorry."

For a moment I feared Laura might cry, but she retained her amazing sense of dignity. She held her head high and said, "Tell me who she is. I don't want to be surprised when people talk. And they certainly will talk, Rick. I want to know."

"She's just a co-ed," he answered sheepishly. "Susan Grimes. She doesn't mean anything to me."

I couldn't believe it. I was expecting him to say JoAnn Stevens, but apparently Rick has a selection of dishes—it's as if he's a Horn and Hardart Automat for women.

Laura removed her engagement ring, but she didn't shove it up his nostril as I would have suggested. She just handed it to him, and then she turned and descended the stairs more regally than Queen Elizabeth. I was so proud of her I almost cheered.

———

We drove in silence a short distance before Laura pulled the car over near an old bridge. The narrow river underneath was rushing over the rocks in a hurry to be somewhere else. Through the trees, I could see the remains of a railroad overpass. The dead ivy on the overpass coated the bricks like old brown veins. Faded letters identified the structure as the Monon Railroad. A light snow had begun to fall, softening the edges of everything around us... except maybe what Laura was feeling.

"Rick and I used to come here," she said quietly. "It's beautiful in the summer. When we were younger, we used to jump off the bridge into the river below. One time I landed wrong and injured my eardrum. I can't come here anymore without being reminded of that. Isn't it odd how one incident can completely change the landscape of your memories?"

All I could do was nod because I wasn't ready to think about the weight of all that.

"Greencastle, for instance," Laura continued, "it's such a beautiful town, but now I'll probably always see it as a place I need to get away from. And I'll never think of Rick again without hearing Little Anthony singing and seeing the guilt on Rick's face. I knew what was going on the moment he opened the door, Weed." Laura shook her head and shuddered at the memory.

"He's such an asshole!" I exclaimed. "I can't believe he would do that. He's so stupid."

"You knew he was cheating on me, didn't you, Weed?"

I didn't know what to say. I didn't want to lie to her like Rick did, but I didn't know how much to tell her or how to defend myself for keeping so much from her for so long. She let me off the hook in a way I hadn't expected.

"I knew it, too, Weed."

"You knew?"

"In a way. Did you ever get yourself into a situation that wasn't good enough to feel joy, but it wasn't bad enough to change? That's the worst place to be because it keeps you stuck in the middle. Maybe people stir things up in order to tip the situation in one direction or another. I realize I did that when I told Rick I wanted to get married or move on. I pushed for a decision. He did the same thing... in his own way. He's not bad, Weed. He's just a coward...but no more than I am, I suppose. Neither one of us had the guts to let our relationship die of natural causes, so we destroyed it instead."

"Maybe you can start to live now."

"Yes, maybe. But he was my whole life for so long." Laura's lip was trembling. I wanted to tell her that I know how hard it is to face a future after your past has vanished. You don't even know who you are anymore, so the loneliness gets even bigger. It's something I've learned from experience.

"Come here," I said. As I held her in my arms, we sat there for a long time, the snow falling quietly around us. Her tears streamed down her cheeks, although she hardly made a sound. Somehow, I knew her pain went to a much deeper place than a guy like Rick could ever touch. There's a pain inside her she can't yet talk about. I recognized it by her silence. It's as loud as mine.

———

When I got home, I didn't talk to Ollie about Caleb because I wanted time to think. I really had no desire to go to the game after my afternoon with Laura, but I had promised Russ. Everyone was revved because the basketball team would make the play-offs if they beat Shelbyville, so I couldn't back out of the sacred event without causing pestilence and plague.

Going to the game turned out to be just what I needed though. These Hoosiers are fanatics, which makes for a rousing event. I even got into the spirit myself. Russ and I slammed into each other and slapped each other's back with gusto. If the game had been any closer, we would have beaten each other to a pulp. Russ says you can always tell a great game by the amount of carnage.

Jimmy Dale was the star of the game. I had no idea what a genius he is on the court, especially for a guy who, according to Russ, thinks animal husbandry and bestiality are the same thing. I hope he's not planning a career in farming.

Ever since Russ's feat at the drive-in, Patty Lynn has been infatuated. At the game she sat next to him, then Janine plopped down alongside her wearing Jimmy Dale's class ring with enough angora wrapped around it for Ollie to knit a sweater. She was waving her hand as though she was John Philip Sousa, so I got the idea she wanted me to notice her ring.

"Hey, Janine," I said, "I hear you're going with Jimmy Dale. That's cool." Boy, you'd have thought I said, "Holy mackerel, Janine, your butt looks like two unbaked loaves of bread." She turned her back to me and wouldn't speak. Patty Lynn gave me one of those "shut up" looks, so I gladly did.

In the last minute of the game, Jimmy Dale pulled off a fake pass followed by a real smooth layup shot. The crowd went nuts. We beat Shelbyville by two points, an amazing feat for being the smallest guy on the basketball block. I was glad when the game was over though because the air was getting mighty cold around Janine. Afterward I told Russ I thought I should scram, and then promised I'd drop by the next day for a progress report on him and Patty Lynn.

When I got back to Ollie's, the lights were still on. As I stepped onto the porch, I heard Ollie singing "Whatever Lola Wants, Lola Gets" in a low, seductive manner. A voice in my empty head told me not to enter. However, I was so darn cold I couldn't stay outside any longer without losing my manhood, so I opened the front door a crack to see if the situation would allow for interruption. What I saw was enough to make a teenage guy join a monastery in the Yukon.

Ollie was in the living room dancing up a storm.

Here's the retching part—the woman was naked, hidden by only a large, pink feather fan. She was wearing nothing except a boa and pair of Marilyn Monroe shoes that were impaled into her fleshy feet like cocktail toothpicks. I was so shocked my lungs shut down. She was stroking her thighs and posing Garbo-style, complete with pouty lips and dramatic gestures.

The horror kept me riveted. As she turned around, she whipped into a shimmy, her ample butt undulating like monsoon waves. She paused, held up a finger in a come-hither pose, then belted out, "'Little man, Lola wants you.'"

I had my last glimpse of my own sanity when I heard the accordion music. The worst of my nightmares was confirmed when I heard the song change into "Makin' Whoopee." Ollie sang, but her accompaniment changed.

From out of the shadows popped Snarls in all his glory, naked except for his socks and shoes. Without any forethought as to how his geriatric parts were flapping around in the breeze, he made his way across the room carrying a brightly colored squeeze-box and tapping all the way! His woodpecker hairdo was hanging over his forehead, so his bald spot glowed brighter than a spanked ass.

Ollie giggled and slinked up to him like an estrogen assault weapon. She wrapped her boa around Snarls's neck, and then they danced their way up the stairs stopping once to smooch. I could hear those old, thin lips smacking together like a flat tire on dry pavement.

After they ducked into Ollie's room, I ran for the safety of my bed. I could still hear giggling, so I pulled my pillow over my head, but there was no way to block out the strains of "Lady of Spain."

I can't tell you what else I heard, because of the decency laws. But I can tell you this much: I will never, ever be able to have sex again, not even same-sex. I

GWEN BANTA

won't be able to eat a Dusty Road or even talk to a woman named Lola. I'll choke an accordion player AND his monkey if I ever run into one. And now I even hate Spain. I'm damaged forever. If I don't get out of this hamlet soon, I'll be carried out in a straitjacket.

CHAPTER TWENTY
NOVEMBER 27, 1960

I SPENT HALF THE NIGHT IN MY CLOSET DUE TO THE bumping and grinding of fossils in the next room. After Snarls tapped his little pink buttocks on out the door, I finally got some shut-eye.

I got up early and tried to call Denise, but Hattie said she was out with Robert. After that I decided to head over to Laura's house because I wasn't ready to face Ollie. Besides, it seemed like a good idea to check in on Laura after what Rick did yesterday.

I don't know how I would survive in this place without Laura. I suspect that she in some way needs me, too, because she's also hiding a devastating loss and an unspeakable loneliness. That scares the stuffing out of me because it's a responsibility I want to be strong enough to handle. I'd never want to let her down.

As I was walking toward Laura's, I was a little more relaxed than usual. The new pain pills I got have had a good effect so far. My leg is pretty numb, but that beats the pain.

When I stopped in front of the I.G.A. grocery store to warm up, I ran into a Salvation Army Santa who was ringing a bell over a money pot. After I tossed in a handful of coins, I lingered to warm myself by a fire he had started in a tin barrel. It was still too early for church, but the streets were showing signs of activity. Soon some other early risers joined us, and I was surprised when a few of them spontaneously broke into a rollicking version of "Jingle Bells." I didn't want to act too snobby to participate in small-town activities, so I piped right in.

By the time I got to the library, I was feeling pretty chipper. Andy Johnson wasn't around, but I decided to build a fire for when he returned. When I reached into my pocket for a match, I found a letter from Murray that arrived yesterday. Due to my ordeal with the tap-dancing relics of last night, I had forgotten all about it. As I stood by the fire, I had to read it more than once just to try to absorb the news. Here's what Murray had to say:

712 Elm St., Scrotum, Pa.

Weed man,

Sorry I keep missing your calls. Mom said you've been trying to reach me. I've been staying away from home as much as possible because the atmosphere around here has been severely strained due to my "shocking irresponsibility." (There's no shalom in this corral I'm saying.)

It's been confirmed that Michelle is carrying my tainted seed, buddy. The rabbit bought the farm. When the senior Goldbergs heard the news, they launched into so much hand wringing and chest pounding I wouldn't be surprised if you heard them out there on the tundra.

After endless discussions, Michelle and I have decided not to go the abortion route after all. I can't do it, man. It just feels WRONG. Thus, the parents are insisting she put the baby up for adoption, but Michelle says she can't give our baby away.

She's losing weight because she can't eat, and I can't either.
We both look like the shit stew we seem to be drowning in.

I've taken a part-time job at Gross Hardware as box boy and
salesman-in-training. I am now the idiot savant of key
grinding. Much to the wailing accompaniment of my parents,
I turned down U. of Penn. There's no way I can now afford
any costs not covered by my scholarship. I'm contacting other
colleges for alternatives, but most scholarships won't cover
married housing.

Yes, you read that right, Weedster--Michelle and I are taking
the Big Step. It seems to be a small step after creating a new
life form, but my parents and Michelle's folks are dead set
against it. Not because of our age mind you, but because she's
a bead-praying Catholic, and I'm a bagel-noshing Jew.
Horrors! No one will stop kvetching long enough to think of
our feelings... OR our child. I can't take this narrow-minded
crap.

I told Kenton everything last night. Incidentally, do you
know what he did? He took soup to Bubby! An old geezer at
the home who keeps an eye out for Bubs (probably because she
still strips every chance she gets) told me Kenton sat with her
for an hour and sang her some tunes he wrote. Kenton's a
good guy, man.

I'm afraid our plans for the summer are out. Sorry, W. I hope
you understand that my first priority has to be Michelle. But
Kenton says you can stay with him if you come home. Don't
worry, I'll find you, man, no matter where Michelle and I end
up. My life is changing faster than I can keep up. I'll call once
I know what's happening. Have a prairie-nice Holiday.

Yours drooley,
The Murd Meister

P.S. Michelle says if the baby is a boy, we can use Leland as a middle name. I hope that's okay with you. She's great, man. I'm real lucky to have her.

———

After I put Murray's letter back in my pocket, I added more sticks to the fire, but when Andy didn't show up, I headed for Laura's. By the time I got there, it was almost 10:00 A.M. She was still in her housecoat, so I handed her the Whitman book she had loaned me and turned to leave. "Wait, Weed," she called as I stepped off the porch. "Did you enjoy any of Whitman's poems?"

"Yes, but he's a long-winded guy, isn't he?" She smiled at that. "I couldn't figure out which poem made you think of me," I continued. "I didn't see anything in there about lunatics."

"You must have missed that one," she teased. "Read 'I Sing the Body Electric.' There's a message in it for you. But right now, get yourself in here, because I'm starving."

I can never resist a free flapjack because I know my priorities where food is involved. Hence, while Laura made breakfast, I put on a pot of coffee and tried to keep my eyes in their sockets. I couldn't get over how young and pretty Laura looked in her pink robe. Her hair was partially fastened with a gadget, allowing the remainder to fall to her shoulders.

She put on a record by Nat King Cole, who's a bit dated for my taste, but it seemed just right. With the winter sun shining in the window and the electric space heater glowing, the room felt as warm and familiar as an ad in The Saturday Evening Post.

"I'm sorry you witnessed my break-up with Rick yesterday, Weed," she sighed, "but I want to thank you for everything."

"Are you okay?" I asked as I peered over her shoulder to watch her make pancakes.

"Yes, and maybe I'm even a little relieved. I always knew Rick wasn't the love of my life, and I'm angry with myself for being willing to settle for less. What does that say about me?"

"That you lost hope?"

Laura laughed, which threw me a little. "That was intended as a rhetorical question, Weed," she explained, still giggling.

"You must have taught rhetorical questions on one of the days I cut class," I smiled back. "Have you ever met the love of your life?"

Laura was quiet for a moment, so I wondered if she had heard my question. Finally, she answered. "Yes, Weed."

"And...?"

"Life changed us both, and then he no longer wanted me. The reasons are too painful to explain."

"I'm sorry, Laura." I wanted to ask a lot of questions, but my good sense thermostat was working for once, so I temporarily dropped the subject.

"I feel a strange sense of freedom," Laura admitted. "With Rick gone, there's a world of possibilities out there for me."

"Yeah, maybe you can become a short-order cook," I laughed gesturing to her flapjacks. Laura was making the oddest pancake designs I've ever seen. They were squares and triangles, and something that could pass for a fish. "What *are* those?" I teased.

"Well, that one is Santa."

"Of course, Santa. Yesiree Bob!"

"It's not obvious?" she asked with a fake pout.

"Give me a moment to formulate a safe response, Laura."

"Well?" she grinned.

"Uh, I'm sure it's a work of art to the pancake-informed."

"And it looks delicious?"

"Something tells me I better say yes if I want to eat."

"You better say yes if you want to *live*."

"Wow, what an incredible likeness of a Santa!" I shouted. "And who is this lumpy guy with two heads and a goiter?"

"That's you."

"Thanks, I'm flattered. Now give me the spatula before someone gets hurt." The next thing I knew I was tossing her creations up in the air like a flapjack-flipping pro. One landed on a plant, but I kept flipping and whistling to "The Banana Boat Song." My moves were spectacular. Eventually we gathered enough body parts from all her pancake people to sit down to eat. With syrup and butter, they were quite tasty, as long as you didn't have to identify the limbs. We laughed and ate and poured cup after cup of coffee.

We were talking about Murray when Laura stopped mid-sentence. I followed her stare out the window where I saw a slight movement. Someone was lurking in the shadow just beyond the corner of the house. "Stay here," I ordered, jumping to my feet.

Laura placed her hand on my arm and tried to pull me back down. "It's okay," she hesitated. "I'm sure it was nothing."

When I looked again, I saw something overlapping the window frame. Instinctively I knew it was a man's arm. I gestured to Laura to stay put while I sneaked around to the back door and opened it slowly.

As quietly as possible, I crept along the porch, hugging the wall of the house. When I got to the corner, I leaned out for a clear view and was startled by what I saw. Pressed up against the wall was Andy Johnson, and he was wielding a knife.

Before I could hurdle the railing to go after him, Laura sidled up next to me. Instinctively, I covered her mouth to silence her, but she shook her head violently and pushed my hand away. That's when I spotted the plate of food in her hand. My heart was pounding pretty hard at that point, so I tried to make her understand. I gestured to her that Andy had a knife, and to get back inside, but Laura refused.

"I think Andy uses his Army knife as a fork," she whispered. "He has very few teeth, and he's missing most of his jaw."

"'You've been feeding him?" I inquired, relaxing only slightly.

"Only recently. I have to leave the food outside for him. He won't come near anyone. Except you, Weed."

"Do you think we can get him to come in?"

"No, he won't look at me. He's ashamed of the way he looks."

"But he was staring at you through the window," I reasoned.

"That's different, somehow. He needs that distance. He won't hurt me, Weed. He has never come closer than he is now. Let's just leave the food here. Trust me, Weed."

We turned to go back inside, but before Laura closed the door, she dragged the space heater out onto the porch for Andy. I set out a cup of coffee, and then we made a big show of cleaning up dishes inside. By the time we finished, Andy was gone.

I'm glad Laura feeds Andy, but I still have an unsettling feeling that something isn't right. When I glanced out there to check on him, Andy was eating with his fingers. He never used the knife, so I could see no reason for him to have a knife in his hand in the first place.

I think there's more confusion and anger left inside Andy than anyone suspects. Who knows how crazy the war has left him? And I don't want to gamble Laura's safety to find out.

I'VE HAD A LETTER BONANZA RECENTLY BECAUSE I'VE BEEN writing more often myself. Today I heard from Denise, which was great, but her letter was troublesome:

1000 W. Wabash Ave.
Crawfordsville, Ind.
November 27, 1960

Dear Weed,

Hattie said you called when I was out today and you two had a nice chat. She and I were discussing how much fun we all had on Thanksgiving. You and Ollie are so much fun. You'll come for Christmas, too, won't you?

I'll have to be brief because Hattie needs help in the kitchen. We have two boarders this week. One guest is a judge from Gary who dresses like a woman at night because women's clothes soothe his "jangled nerves." Can you imagine?

Last night he came to dinner in a dress and bent over in front of Robert, causing Robert to drop a big stack of plates. Robert was so embarrassed all he could do was stammer, "Mr., uh,

216

Miss, uh, Your Magistrate, could you pick a team and stay
put so other people know where they stand. Or maybe where
NOT to stand?" I nearly died!
I know you requested a photo of Robert's frat house, but I
wanted to tell you (just between us) that the fraternity
dropped him from pledging for dating a Negro. No one came
right out and said it, but it was obvious they disapprove
of me.

Last week after he attended a rush party, he returned to his
dorm room and found fried chicken and watermelon strewn
all about. Some very nasty things were written on the mirror,
but Robert wouldn't elaborate.

I was terribly upset when I heard, but Robert handled it with
his usual humor. He said the fried chicken was lousy, so it
was fortunate he was turned down by a fraternity with such
bad taste, because although rampant ignorance won't kill us,
bad chicken might. However, I know the incident really
hurt him.

We had a long talk yesterday and I told him I thought it
would be wise if we quit seeing each other, but Robert
wouldn't hear of it. He says he loves me, Weed! I can't
believe what a lucky girl I am. He's such a decent, honest
person.

I think Newton's Law is working for me. Good is a powerful
force coming my way. I just pray it won't be too difficult a
road for a sensitive guy like Robert. But he's tough. He
reminds me so much of you.

Please give my love to Ollie and write back soon. Robert sends
a hello. Almost forgot—he said he wants to challenge you to
an insect race. The object is to use one nostril to blow your
own dead insect across a table faster than anyone else. Robert
says it produces interesting results amongst the highly

competitive, so he knew you'd love it. I think you're both sick. See you soon!

Love,
Denise

Although I was happy to hear from Denise, I got so angry about the dorm incident that I wadded up her letter and threw it across the room. What in the hell is going on in this world? College educated guys are behaving like bigoted pricks, and judges are wearing dresses. HAS ANYONE OUT THERE NOTICED SOMETHING IS VERY WRONG HERE?

CHAPTER TWENTY-TWO
DECEMBER 4, 1960

WOW, IT'S DECEMBER, AND MY EIGHTEENTH BIRTHDAY ISN'T far off (December 20). There's fresh snow on the ground, which is nice to look at, but it would be nicer if there were mountains. I bet the Appalachian Mountains are beautiful right now. My dad and Leland and I used to drive up there for some great adventures. Those memories sure make me miss my life back in Scranton.

Ollie and I have maintained our usual cheery rapport because I had the good sense to keep my mouth shut about the dance recital I witnessed. Snarls has been by only twice since the revolting incident, and I try to go deaf during his visits.

School is so boring I sleep between yawns. My grades need a respirator, and I think the teachers realize I don't give a flying fart about academia. I've got other things on my mind.

I'm worried about Murray. Kenton wrote to tell me Murray hasn't been at school for days and he hasn't shown up for his job at the hardware store. His mom, Rachael, has been calling everyone. Kenton said Murray left a note in his locker asking him to check on Bubby. It's not like Murray to disappear and not be in touch with us guys or his grandma Bubby.

I can think of only two places Murray might be. He's

GWEN BANTA

either at Bubby's cottage near Asbury Park or someplace down south where he can marry Michelle without their parents' permission. Murray's the type to do the right thing no matter how hard it is.

In order to keep my mind off Murray's dilemma, I'm staying busy. After my success with the Thanksgiving centerpiece, I decided to pick up some Christmas decorations so I could make some centerpieces as gifts. (I'm not a dork. I'm just financially depleted at the moment, so I need to be resourceful.)

Ollie has a forest of trees out back, so I cut a pile of branches and painted some pinecones. After separating them into four arrangements, I tied each with ribbon and decorated one with fake pearls for Ollie because she's always talking about Jackie Kennedy's "dramatic, yet simple pearls." What the heck.

I made centerpieces for Laura and Denise also. Believe it or not, I also threw one together for Janine. I've been feeling bad about us going all the way then not even speaking to each other, so I decided to do something to let her know I consider her a nice girl...when she's not thinking too hard.

After I gave Ollie her gift, she got teary-eyed, which made me swallow all my critical feelings about her "Lola" spectacle. "No one has ever done such nice things for me, darlins," she sniffled. "Except maybe Caleb." Her comment opened a door real wide for me, and I'm a good one for rushing right in.

"I'm sorry you never got to see Caleb again after he left here," I said as innocently as a district attorney.

"Oh, but I did, Weed," she confessed as she handed me a cup of hot cider and then sat down at the kitchen table. "I remember clear as a bell," she said. "Caleb came down from Binghamton around this time of year in 1943 to drive me back up North. Truth be told, I was being run out of town."

"Oh God, why, Ols?" I asked, not truly sure I wanted to know.

"We got married, darlins."

You should have seen my face. I feigned surprise better than Laurence Olivier could have.

"It's a fact, Weed," she nodded. "We had talked about it for years, but times were different then. It just wasn't done. But that summer before Caleb went east, we drove over to Terre Haute and got hitched by a J.P. We only had a one-day honeymoon, but it was lovely. We stayed in a tent out at the lake where Fatty's Joint used to be, and we sang songs and roasted marshmallows.

"That night Caleb wrote a song for me called 'Ollie By Golly.' It was quite comical." Ollie snapped her fingers and started singing with gusto.

She's my Ollie by golly
A salty hunk o' bacon
'n' a doggone wonder
when her porch starts shakin'!

She's my Ollie by golly
You should see her shimmy
She ain't too fat'
But she sure ain't skinny."

Ollie laughed until her eyes misted up. "Yeah, that man sure was something," she said.

"Anyway, it didn't take long for word to get around about us being hitched. The war was going on, and Hitler had stirred up a lot of hate all over again. Caleb lived here with me for exactly seventeen days, but we didn't make any show about it. He always came in the back door, and we were seldom seen together. Then one day we came home to broken windows and some real nasty words painted on the house.

"The next night we heard a noise on the porch. After Caleb stepped out for a look, I heard a terrible cry. When I looked out, I saw him kneeling over a bloody heap, sobbing his eyes out. Those bastards had skinned his dog Tater. I don't even want to say the inhuman things they did to that innocent animal.

"I saw Caleb take a note off what was left of Tater. He shoved the note in his pocket, came in, packed his things, and said he was going. He wouldn't tell me what the note said, but I know it was a threat toward me or he never would have left here.

"Caleb promised he'd send for me, and he signed the house over to me for two hundred dollars. I tried to sell it so I could join him, but it's hard to unload a house in war times. We missed each other real bad, so he returned to take me back to Binghamton for a visit. When we got there, we rented a cheap motel because Caleb's sister wouldn't have us at her place."

"Why not?"

"Margaret said I was white trash for marrying her brother, 'cause a 'good' white woman wouldn't do that. It was tough all around, dear. But Caleb and I got to ring in the New Year together. It was 1944. What a swell time! We went to a club where Caleb got to jam with his old pals, including Muddy Waters himself. What a time we had!

"The next night we went to see a picture at the Rivoli Theater. I'll never forget which one. It was *Shadow of a Doubt*. Caleb took me to see it because I always had a crush on that actor, Joseph Cotten.

"We were waiting in line when some men started mouthing off about 'niggers' and 'white nigger whores.' They'd been on a bender, so we tried to ignore them, but one guy kept knocking into us. When Caleb didn't respond, the man shoved Caleb into the building. We tried to leave, but they were having too much fun.

"The big one, a guy called Parkins, threw Caleb to the ground. He put his foot on Caleb's head and told Caleb to beg. Caleb threw the guy off, stood up, and then backed away with his hands held up in peace. We were walking away when two of them jumped Caleb from behind and threw him to the ground again. At that point, most of the bystanders scattered real fast.

"The men held on to me so tight I couldn't run for help, and one of them stuck his glove in my mouth so I couldn't scream. The attackers made me stand there and watch as they kicked Caleb over and over again. I heard his bones break, and I saw his skin split, leaving pieces of flesh on the sidewalk. Then one by one those animals peed all over him. But Caleb had more dignity than Jack Kennedy, Weed. He picked himself up, wiped the blood and urine off his face, put on his hat, and said, 'My wife and I will be leaving now.' He could barely stand, but he held his head so high. I was so darn proud of that man..

"Then Parkins, angry as a coon cat because he couldn't drag Caleb down as low into the gutter as he was, pulled a gun and shot Caleb right in the chest. Parkins dropped the gun and ran like a coward. He got hit by a car, which stunned him just long enough for the cops to nab him.

"Caleb was losing blood fast, and I was trying to stop the bleeding. But Caleb wouldn't sit down. He leaned against the wall until they put him in the ambulance. Right to the last minute, he stayed erect, a good, proud man. He died in my arms at the hospital. The last thing he ever said to me was, 'You're my Ollie, by golly.' He was quite a man, Weed."

When Ollie was done telling her story, she sat for a long time staring into her cider. I made her a piece of toast and asked if she'd prefer to be alone.

"Oh, no, darlins. You know, in a way it felt good to tell Caleb's story. I never had no one to tell it to before."

"Ollie, I think I should confess I came across his obituary at the library. It was a real nice write-up."

"Thank you, Weed. I remember it. The newspaper listed me as the only kin because his sister had disowned him. She later said he'd still be alive if he hadn't messed with white man's garbage."

"Jeez, doesn't *anybody* believe we're all alike?"

"Oh, but we aren't, darlins! We're all different. And as I see it, we're all attracted by our differences as much as our similarities. But we need to see the differences as something special... something *good*. Part of what I loved about Caleb was how his color, in every sense of the word, expanded my world."

"I started by loving just one. And I loved him all my life."

"You never loved anyone but Caleb, Ollie?"

"I can't say that, hon. There are all types of love. Are you asking me about Bart Searles?" she smiled.

I was not prepared for that meteorite to land. I'm sure I turned redder than jock itch.

"It's okay, Weed, I don't mind at all. I've been waiting for you to figure out that all you have to do is ask me what you want to know. I admit I fudged about a few things when you first got here, but I wanted you to get to know me first so you wouldn't judge me too harshly. You're mighty special to me, Weed. And yes, so is Bart Searles."

"I'm happy you have someone to love, Ollie." I took a long pause before blurting out my concerns with the verbal idiocy I seem to have perfected. "But if you'll excuse my asking, Ols, can't you find a guy who's not married?"

"At my age and at my size I'm lucky to find a girdle that fits, darlins! Bart's wife is real mean to him, hon. I guess she has been for forty years. But she won't give him a divorce, even though he's been honest with her about me."

"She *knows* about you?"

"Uh-huh. And she says she doesn't care a bit as long as he supports her and doesn't see me in public or spend a penny on me. People talk, Weed. And most of 'em never wanted much to do with me 'cause of Caleb. But Bart never judged me for that. We've been friends since we were school kids. Awhile back it turned to something more, probably 'cause we were both so lonely. He loves me, and he's real good to me, just the way Caleb was. You know, I've always lived life on my own terms, Weed. When I kick the bucket, I want my tombstone to say, 'She Lived and Let Live, and She Gived and Got Gived.' Caleb used to say that," she chuckled.

"Well, Ols, I once saw a tombstone in Scranton that said, 'Here I lie in a cold dirt bed, 'cause the tongues kept a'waggin' till they killed me plum-dead.' That might work, too!" I suggested.

Ollie's smile was so full of light that I could never imagine her dying. I don't think there's enough earth to keep her under.

CHAPTER TWENTY-THREE
DECEMBER 6, 1960

GOOD NEWS! MURRAY HAS FINALLY SURFACED!

Fredericksburg, Va.
12/02/60

Hey Weed,

I wanted you to be the first to know that Michelle and I were married by a J.P. Monday at 2:00 P.M. The guy was a weasel, and his wife looked like a Marine in a dress. But it was a nice dress I'd say. Michelle looked great for someone green in the gills.

I'm trying to do the right thing by her, but sometimes I feel as though I'm living somebody else's life. Nothing has turned out like we planned, huh, buddy? But at least I have Michelle. And you now have three of us, pal.

The J.P. mentioned job openings at a shoe factory. Michelle and I had no place to go, so I checked it out. Due to my superior knowledge of good shoes (think "American Bandstand"), I got the job. I reek of glue when I come home,

so I have to shower outside so Michelle won't puke.
Everything nowadays makes her gag.

I bet you're wondering how I wash the Murray schlong in
public without being surrounded by cops or mobs of sex-
hungry women. Well, I'm using my college fund to rent a
mobile home with an outside shower where I can de-stinkify.
Our house is made of tin, and it's the size of a tuna can. A
good fart would blow out the door.

Yesterday I enrolled in the local high school to finish the year.
I'll probably apply to community college here next year. Don't
laugh. It's a Mecca for education. I believe it's called The
College of Conjugal Cousins. They won't let Michelle enroll
because they view her as a knocked-up, despicable life-form. I
wish she didn't cry so much.

I'm considering calling the folks when I'm done with this
letter, so if the Earth implodes, you'll know the senior G's
have received the news. Dad was beside himself when he
found out Michelle's a shiksa. You know how traditional my
father is. I've dishonored everything they stand for, so I'm
worried he'll cut all ties with me when he hears we're
married. That would kill me, but I have to think about my
own kid now, not everybody else.

Michelle doesn't plan to call her folks at all because they said
she's going to Hell with her bastard child. Can you believe it?
But she's a great girl, Weed. You'll love her. (And you'll do it
from at least a six-foot distance, you will.)

So how are you, Weedster, honestly? And why the shitty
grades? You were always the neighborhood genius. Talk to
me, pal. I'm still your black sheep friend known as
Murray the Shoe

P.S. Call Kenton for me, ok? All I have available is a pay phone.

Now it feels like Murray has lost his future, just as I've lost my past. When I get my parents' insurance money, I plan to send most of it to Murray so he can enroll in a good school. He deserves it, and he needs to do well enough to take care of Michelle and the baby. Besides, I only have me to take care of.

I can't help but feel down in the chops though because I sense I've lost Murray. He's closer to somebody else now, and I honestly just never thought about anyone being closer to him than me. With Murray, I was holding the last piece of the puzzle of who I am. But then I opened up my hand and it was gone.

————

After reading Murray's letter, I decided to ditch school. My leg has a few oozing sores, so I doused them with Mercurochrome and wrapped my calf. Ollie was in Greencastle at the dentist, so I was able to lounge around most of the day reading and sleeping.

After my second nap, I took some antibiotics and then called Kenton. Due to the time difference, he was just returning home from school. Kenton's a down-to-earth guy, so I was happy to talk to him. He was quite surprised to hear that Murray got married. "Wow, man, that sounds serious," he said, which got me laughing. He's the master of the understatement.

After we talked, Kenton sang me a new tune him and the guys wrote, which I think could make the charts. I rated it for him using my best Murray-American-Bandstand voice, "Well, Dick, I'd give it a 99.

It's got a great beat... one you could really whack off to."
Kenton split a gut.

He and his group plan to go on the road this
summer with another doo-wop group called the
Marcels, who, according to Kenton, just did a smashing
re-make of "Blue Moon" that I'm looking forward to
hearing. Maybe I'll meet up with Kenton somewhere on
the road when I leave this place.

After we hung up, I managed to drag my bones
down to the learning asylum to wait for Russ to escape.
As soon as he saw me, he told me I looked like a string
bean and insisted on buying me a Dusty Road over at
the sundry store.

Today was the first time I've been there since the
night I saw Snarls shaking his pokey at Ollie. To be
truthful, I've been avoiding him, but once I saw him
again, I was reminded of what a likeable sort the old
duffer really is.

Snarls was behind the pharmacy counter when Russ
and I walked in. None of the other education hostages
had arrived yet, so the place was empty. Not long after
Russ and I settled into a booth, he confided that he
doesn't plan to give his ring to Patty Lynn because he
has the hots for Norma Marie, the girl with the, uh,
irregular skin. Russ claims her skin has been getting
better recently.

"Russ," I said, "Even though I applaud your choice,
as your coach on what's cool, it's my duty to remind
you that Patty Lynn is real popular, so you're risking
being the town turnip again, instead of the Frankie
Avalon of the frontier you currently are."

"A lone man is an unencumbered one, Weed," he
intoned.

"That's a good one, Russ! I'll remember that when
I'm on the road."

We continued shooting the breeze and drumming on
the table to Chuck Berry's "Sweet Little Sixteen" until

Snarls lumbered over. His arm was in a sling, which was quite a shocker to see.

"What in the heck did you do to your arm?" I blurted. I was darn tired of pretending not to notice his injuries, which is apparently what folks have been doing for years. Russ hammered me with a warning look. "Hey, man, it's obvious he's hurt," I protested. "I'm not blind OR stupid! What happened, Mr. Searles?"

When Snarls sat down at our booth, I noticed a change in him. I've seen it before, but it didn't register until today. He looked less beaten down. And more teed off. He sat up straighter than MacArthur addressing his troops, took a breath, and boldly pronounced, "Well, boys, all I can tell you is, never marry a scrappy gal, because she'll just get meaner."

"Your wife did that to you?" I sputtered.

"Yes, she did, son. I was on my way out the door for good. I've wanted to go for a long time now. But the missus was having none of that. She pulled me back and slammed the door on my arm so hard she broke a bone. I even heard the dang thing crack. The thing blew up faster than a rabbit's uterus."

"Does she do that stuff very often?" I asked in horror. (My horror was as much about the image of an inflated rabbit's uterus as it was about his plight.)

"Lordy, yes!" Snarls said, "I've been so dang ashamed of a woman beating on me that I've never been able to talk about it. But now I don't give a fiddler's turd who knows. The missus hits me because a man can't hit a woman back."

"Why do you stay with her, Mr. Searles?" Russ asked.

"Sense of duty, I guess. I made a vow to take care of her. But you know what? I'm gonna leave this time. I really am. I want to be with someone who loves life as much as I do," he said, jutting his chin for emphasis.

Snarls got up and walked away with his head held higher than I've ever seen.

When I saw how powerful a person can feel just by making decisions, I realized I have some darn important decisions to make myself. But my train of thought was derailed when Russ whispered, "My money says he's plunking someone else."

"No way, Russ!" A discussion about Snarls committing adultery with my own wayward grandmother was not something I felt like taking on just yet. I decided to save the truth for another day. Or maybe tell him in a letter after I'm gone.

———

Before heading back to Ollie's, I needed to make one more stop to deliver the centerpiece I made for Denise. She and Robert were scheduled to arrive from Crawfordsville by dinner time and stay through the weekend, so she had asked me to drop by. It was getting close to dark, which is why Russ offered me a lift.

"I've never visited a Negro's house before," he said, "it might be educational."

"Yeah, Russ," I laughed, "you can learn their ancient traditions... like human sacrifice."

He grinned kind of sheepishly. "I just meant it's time for me to experience other kinds of people."

"I know," I nodded, "it's cool."

When we got there, Martha was eating an early supper so she could watch "Wagon Train" at seven o'clock. Jessie loved the centerpiece so much she cleared all her Christmas decorations off the table and plunked my gift right down in the middle. She has a real way of making someone feel appreciated.

She was fixing a great-smelling meat loaf, so she insisted Russ and I stick around for dinner. After we helped set the table, we chased Martha Jane around the house with a dart gun that shoots suction darts. Russ stuck a dart on the middle of his forehead and hung a Christmas ornament on it just for kicks.

We waited a long time, but Denise and Robert didn't show. Finally, Jessie fixed us each a plate of food, and we ate in front of the TV. By eight o'clock Denise still hadn't arrived, and we were all starting to worry.

Martha Jane insisted on standing by the window to look for any sign of her sister, so Russ and I set up a campsite in the living room to distract her. On the coffee table, we made a Lincoln Logs 'fire' with a candle in the middle. When Russ hid behind the sofa, I wasn't sure what he was up to until I saw three fingers jut up from behind the sofa and then bob in a westerly direction.

"I see trouble, little one," I warned Martha Jane in a remarkable rendition of TV wagon master, Ward Bond. I pointed to Russ's bobbing fingers, "Don't worry, Missy. I reckon if we can't tame 'em, then we can cook 'em up!"

From behind the sofa Russ whispered, "Don't tell the kid you can cook up an Indian, you idiot!"

"An INDIAN?" I exclaimed, "I thought you were attacking us with a herd of elk! Indians don't have antlers, you moron!"

"They're feathers," Russ shouted, "and because of your own stupidity, your entire encampment will now be wiped out!" Russ pounced, but Martha and I were able to fend off his attack with a few good shots from her cap gun, gravely 'wounding' Russ. He flopped around like a mackerel and died. Four times. It was a side-splitter.

We were roasting marshmallows over the candle when Jessie returned. I could see by the look on her face that she was still very concerned. "Hattie says they left Crawfordsville at 4:30. They shoulda been here within an hour or so. It's near nine o'clock now. Those roads out there are gettin' bad."

"They must have stopped somewhere, Jessie," I said.

"I don't think so. I jus' know Denise woulda called, Weed. That girl's a thoughtful one."

"She sure is. But everyone forgets things, Jessie." I knew I wasn't very convincing. I didn't even believe my own words. By now Jessie was wringing her hands and Martha Jane's smile had turned upside down. "How 'bout if Russ and I drive along the road to see if they had car trouble?" I offered as a solution.

"Why thank you, hon. I'd be so grateful."

"I'll call you when we get back to Ollie's," I promised as I threw on my jacket. I kissed Martha Jane on her cheek and said, "Mighty obliged for the eats, li'l lady." Russ stuck a marshmallow on his nose just to make her smile again before we rushed out to look for Denise and Robert.

I know Denise always stays on the main road in case she has car trouble, so Russ and I drove all the way to Greencastle. We were hoping Robert and Denise had stopped at a motel and had some fun for themselves, and then maybe fallen asleep.

After several hours, I had a sick feeling inside. When Russ finally dropped me off, I called Jessie, who informed me she had already called Sheriff Cooper and been told there had been no accidents reported. I suggested she get some sleep, but I knew she'd be up until Denise got home.

After I informed Ollie, I also put in a call to Laura just to hear a reassuring voice. "Please call me as soon as you know something, Weed," she insisted.

As I climbed the stairs to my room, I could hear Ollie talking to herself as she paced the hallway. "I have to talk to Hattie and Jessie, darlins," she said more to herself than to me. I had never heard Ollie's voice so full of concern.

CHAPTER TWENTY-FOUR
DECEMBER 7, 1960

TODAY WAS THE ANNIVERSARY OF PEARL HARBOR, AND LIFE here was a reenactment. After only four hours of sleep, I woke up at six o'clock and called Jessie right away. There had been no word from Denise, and the hospitals had no record of admittance. I told her to stay put, and then I called Russ to come get me.

Once again, Russ and I searched along the road between here and Crawfordsville, but we didn't see Denise's old Studebaker anywhere. Then, on our way back to Jessie's, I spotted fresh car tracks in the snow on an old road that leads to the lake. "Is there a short-cut to Jessie's place off that road?" I asked.

"Yeah, there's a turn-off," Russ nodded. "But why would anyone take the old road, especially in the snow?"

"Looks as if somebody did. Let's check it out."

Although the road surface was rutted and slick, we kept driving. The sun had risen enough to allow us to see evidence of two cars, and both seemed to have had some trouble staying on the road. By all indications, one vehicle had slipped into the ditch and gone thirty yards or so before pulling back out. When we reached a bend, we saw something odd. One set of tire tracks continued up the road ahead, but the other set vanished into thin air.

"Oh, shit," Russ groaned as he slowed to a stop near an old cement culvert that was barely visible in the snow. It was apparent that it had been rammed by something. Above the snow line, I saw the streaks of maroon paint.

Before Russ could shove the truck into park, I leaped out, ran for the ravine, and then hopped over the culvert. There on the ground below me was debris from where an airborne car had crashed through the trees.

As I started down the snowy embankment, I could hear Russ behind me. My breath was coming out in short bursts while I struggled to get my footing. I glanced to my left and stopped dead in my tracks. Russ slid into me, then looked up and let out a gasp. There, at the bottom of the ravine, was the twisted wreckage of Denise's car.

Everything that happened after that registered in my brain like a film clip, one frame at a time. I heard myself yelling, "Go for help, Russ," as I mechanically moved on. Minutes later I could hear his tires on the road above spinning in the snow before finally taking hold. The cold and deathly silence around me got bigger as the sound of the truck vanished on the wind.

I lost my footing and slid straight down the embankment so fast I couldn't stop until my injured leg slammed into a large rock. My cries of pain echoed around me until they were swallowed up by the emptiness. As I rolled over to pull myself to my knees, it took all my will not to scream again.

On the other side of a row of trees was a huge blood slick that looked like an angry red gash in the hillside. It appeared that someone had tried to crawl up from the ravine to the road, but I didn't see anyone. All I could see was blood. I've never seen so damn much blood in my life. I had to lean over and vomit before I could pull myself together.

I was moaning involuntarily as I hobbled over the uneven ground toward the wreckage. When I reached the car, I stared, trying to make some sense of its form. It was only half its normal size, and the metal was twisted so badly there was no door to open, and most of the frame was wedged under a huge tree limb.

In order to get to the car, I had to climb over the tree limb. Blood was all over the hood, an indication that someone had been thrown from the vehicle. I forced the upper half of my body into the wreckage through a hole which had once held the windshield.

What I saw was ghastly and unnatural. The smell of blood and feces was so awful it had sound, and the sound cut through my head until it erupted in a scream.

I saw Robert first. His crushed body was affixed by the broken steering wheel to what was left of the front seat. It had pierced his chest and was protruding from his back. When I lifted his head to feel for a pulse, I gasped at the sight of his face. Hundreds of splinters of glass jutted from his skin like cactus needles in raw meat. His mouth was open, as if Robert the human had crawled out through the mouth hole leaving his twisted carcass behind. There was no indication that the shell I was staring at had ever been alive. He was wet-cold, and his eyes were frozen open in horror, impaled with shards of glass.

I wanted to run, but I kept on going. My mind was moving in slow-motion, but I suspect my body was moving very quickly. The back door of the wreckage was open on the downhill side of the ravine. By all appearances, someone had crawled out of there. Or maybe into there. "Denise?" I screamed. The fear in my voice taunted me as it echoed off the twisted metal.

I peered into the remains of the back seat. The crushed roof and the tree blocked the light, and there was very little room to move, but I thought I detected a crumpled object in the corner on the uphill side of the wreck. The car listed so sharply I had to pull myself upward along the seat as my hands slipped through puddles of half-frozen blood.

I saw Denise's legs at the same instant I touched her. I tried to be gentle, but when I grabbed her, I slipped backwards due to the sharp incline. She virtually lurched out of the dark corner and fell onto me. I had to brace my feet in the snow outside the car to keep from sliding farther down the hill into the creek with Denise on top of me.

When I shoved Denise back against the seat, her head fell backward as if unhinged. Her neck was open, and the right side of her face was slashed into hunks of flesh and bone. She had wedged her sweater into a huge neck wound that had partially closed around the fabric. It was obvious she had lost a tremendous amount of blood. Debris was embedded in her legs from her fruitless efforts to crawl for help.

As I held Denise in my arms, my tears fell on her face creating tiny red rivers. I felt trapped in that casket-sized space, and I was shaking uncontrollably. It wasn't the fear of death that scared me, but what death leaves behind.

Suddenly I heard a moan that sounded as if it had come out of Denise's neck. I lifted her face toward me and yelled, "Denise, it's Weed! Denise? I'm here. Can you hear me, Denise?"

The moan came again from somewhere so far away that I feared she was leaving me before I could even get her back. In my mind I screamed: *Oh God, don't let her die out here in the cold with blood matted in her hair and part of her lip torn off and her eye all messed up. Oh please, please don't let her leave her mom and Martha Jane and her friends behind to suffer. I can't take this! Don't do this, you rotten sonofabitch! You can't do this!*

237

I decided that if I had to die right there with Denise, I was not going to leave her alone. "If there's any God who gives a shit about all of us down here struggling to get through just one stinking day without hurting, then why in the name of Jesus is this happening?" I screamed. Then I heard another moan.

"Denise," I yelled, "sit up! Tilt your head toward me to close the wound. I've got you, Denise." She moaned again, which scared me as much as it relieved me. "It's me, Weed. Russ went for help. I'm right here, and I won't leave you," I promised.

Denise had so many wounds I didn't know where to apply pressure first. When I saw fresh blood, I pressed my hand against her neck wound, but my hand sunk in so deep I didn't dare remove it even for a second to get my coat off to cover her, so I used my body as a blanket. And I started singing. I don't know why, I just did. I sang "Amazing Grace." And then I think I might have even sung "Silver Bells."

"Look, Denise," I whispered, "It's snowing again. It's really beautiful." Her eyes were closed, so I described how crisp the air was and how I hoped the cold would slow the blood flow. Then I praised her for being smart enough to press her sweater into her wound and stay upright, because lying down would have caused her to bleed more. As I tried to warm her with my body, I told her I didn't know anyone else brave enough to try to crawl up that hill for help with so many wounds.

Then I told her about the beautiful Christmas tree I saw right there next to the car. I said it had great decorations such as ham sandwiches, and Coca-Cola, pink angora, and Dusty Roads, colorful little Dutch shoes, and great records, and a big heater blowing hot air on us. I described the ruby lights, and strings of Jackie Kennedy pearls, and even the diamond star at the top.

My body hurt from the cold, and the trees rustled with noisy ghosts. I wondered if the sounds were a dark thing, as if Denise was blowing away on the wind. I talked about anything I could think of, except my fear, which I kept swallowing. When Denise squeezed my finger, I spoke louder. I talked about Murray and Kenton, and then I told her Russ had played wagon train with Martha Jane and that Jessie was saving her some excellent meat loaf.

It seemed like hours before I heard voices on the road above. I don't remember the siren. I can't recall much beyond the struggle to get Denise on a stretcher and up the hill. Before I climbed back up the embankment, I do remember looking at Robert and wishing I had tipped his head forward on the wheel so he wouldn't see us leaving him there alone. "Don't worry," I told him, "someone's going to get you out of here soon." It didn't matter that he couldn't hear me. I just had to tell him.

Russ and I followed the ambulance to Greencastle Hospital, but we didn't speak the entire way. Russ had called his dad from the sheriff's station, so Roy Kinney was waiting with Jessie in the emergency room, then Bart Searles and Ollie rushed in. Ollie looked so white I had to make her sit down and drink some water.

As they were wheeling Denise into the emergency room, she briefly regained consciousness. She opened her eyes and moaned, "They were after us, Mama... called me 'uppity coon'." As the doctor rushed her into the operating room, Jessie collapsed against Roy Kinney. Nobody could say much of anything after that.

Twenty minutes after I called Laura from the waiting room, she arrived also. After hugging Jessie and squeezing Ollie's hand, she put her arms around me and held me tight. She didn't care that I was covered with Denise's blood, or that I had to lean on her just to stay upright.

Denise was in surgery for seven hours. She is still alive, but barely. And if she survives, she'll be scarred for life. It took more than two hours to pull Robert out of the wreck. I wish I had been there to tell him it was okay to let go...okay to leave the darkness behind.

If Denise can live long enough to describe the car that followed them, I'm going to find the bastards who did this to her and Robert. I'm not a violent person, but I have so much anger inside me, I want to strike out at something real bad.

CHAPTER TWENTY-FIVE

DECEMBER 8, 1960

DENISE IS ALIVE AND STABLE. ONLY FAMILY CAN SEE HER, but Jessie updates us every few hours. Although I overslept, I went to school today to keep my mind occupied. And I needed to talk to Laura. Word was out about yesterday's events, and Laura had already taken up a collection for flowers. When Janine expressed her concern about Denise to Russ and me, I was pleasantly surprised.

Roy Kinney said the sheriff had heard from a witness that a car with three guys inside was tailgating a Studebaker around seven o'clock the night of the accident. They appeared to be drunk, and they were hurling bottles at the Studebaker, but the witness thought everything was fine after the Studebaker pulled into a motel. I asked if the three guys were in a De Soto, but Roy didn't know.

The sheriff had determined that the motel owner wouldn't let Denise and Robert, a mixed couple, rent a room or use the phone. But he did let them wait in the parking lot. The owner, a guy named Largent, said he didn't call the cops as Robert requested because he didn't want any trouble. Largent also swore he never saw the other car. Sheriff Cooper thinks Denise and Robert spent several hours hiding in the motel parking lot, but the troublemakers were obviously lying in wait. According to the sheriff, the incident had all the markings of the K.K.K.

Russ told me that Snarls, Roy Kinney, and a number of others are offering a reward for information. Russ and I talked for quite awhile because he's in a mood to hit someone, just like me.

We both decided to go home after fourth period. I was still exhausted and hurting. My antibiotics don't seem to be helping the sores on my leg, and those other pills the doc wants me to take set my stomach on fire.

As I neared Ollie's Palace-of-Portly-Pleasures, I could hear Christmas music coming from the HiFi. When I opened the front door, I prayed Snarls wasn't lurking around in lederhosen or some other fancy-ass attire. God finally threw me a small bone.

Ollie greeted me in a get-up that must have been made in a tinsel factory. She was decked out in silver from head to toe, and the effect was blinding. As rotund as she is, she looked like the Liberty Bell. And it was only four o'clock in the afternoon! As she swept across the room like Miss America on silver slip-on shoes she calls 'mules,' she actually jingled. Literally. A string of garland with little silver bells and holly was affixed to her head by two Santa pins. It was a struggle for me to close my gaping mouth.

"Darlins, how do you like my holiday attire?" she asked.

"Uh, are you going somewhere?" I stammered.

"No, Weed, dear, we're having a party here. Just you and me."

"But Ols, don't you think that's inappropriate with Denise lying in a hospital, and Jessie going through so much right now?"

"Nonsense. We're celebrating because Denise is alive."

"But what if she dies?" I asked.

I wasn't sure if she heard me, but with Ollie there's no way of telling unless she decides to answer. She fetched a bag and hummed as she danced her way over to me. "Then we'll celebrate our joy in knowing her. But she is NOT going to get worse," Ollie insisted. "Jessie says the doctors are amazed at how much of a fighter Denise is. She is going to make it, dear. Now, no more negative talk. Do you know what today is?"

"Nooo," I said slowly while eyeing her silver headgear, "but what I do know is that you better not have wet feet if you plan to plug anything into a socket. Does that thing light up?"

Ollie laughed as she adjusted her balls (so to speak). "No, dear. And for your information, today is the day CBS is broadcasting my favorite Christmas movie, *Holiday Inn*... you know, the one with Fred Astaire and Bing Crosby, where Bing sings that lovely Irving Berlin song, 'White Christmas'?"

Ollie then whipped into song and signaled for me to follow her into the living room. I was humming and following the silver Sputnik when I stopped in my tracks. There in front of me was a big Christmas tree decorated completely in silver. "Ols, that's super!" I exclaimed. "I knew I smelled pine. And maybe some rum."

"Maybe," she giggled. "Every year I dress up as an ornament to watch my favorite movie. I've been doing it since 1942. Here, have some eggnog," she said as she handed me a cup of spiked brew. I thought it would be rude to protest just because my parents didn't let me drink booze. Why ruin a good moment?

"Now tell me how I look," she prodded.

"Well, you certainly look, well, very shiny!"

"Well, dear, you have something new to wear, too," she smiled. Then she pulled a dark object out of her bag and held it up for me to see. It was hand-knit from black wool, but as God is my witness, I had no idea what I was looking at.

Ollie laughed at my perplexed expression. "Please note it's made of that morbid color you insist on wearing," she said as she held it aloft. "It's a hat, darlins!"

Never in my life have I seen a hat so misshapen. Or so large. I mean L-A-R-G-E. It was made for a head the size of the Capitol Dome. Worse yet, Ollie had attached a pompon (more like a hairball) to the top of her nightmare creation.

I mechanically reached out and placed the thing on my head. I didn't know front from back or up from down. The dang thing slid down to my neckline in the back and roosted at brow level on my face. With my peripheral vision, I noticed that the hat that had inhaled my head had appendages. Each time I moved, my hat chased its own tail. All the action was making me dizzy.

"It's slightly large," I squeaked. I was weak from the weight of the dang thing. I looked in the mirror and saw the most pathetic sight I've ever seen staring back at me. Beneath the huge black hat, my blanched face looked like a golf ball protruding from a bear's butt.

"You look so handsome, Weed! Please promise me you'll wear your new hat to church on Christmas," Ollie pleaded.

I know I choked. I chugged down a whole cup of eggnog then poured another. After Ollie hung a Christmas ball on my pompon, she broke into peals of laughter. She was laughing so hard her balls were jingling. Mine were hiding. "Smile," she howled, "the joke's on you! I just made the hat to keep you warm while you're shoveling snow. It started out as a tam-o'-shanter, then I added the ball on top, then the earmuffs, and I got carried away after that. I thought I'd get a chuckle out of you."

"You're a very sick woman," I laughed. Then I

strutted through the room and pirouetted to let her enjoy her handiwork. Ollie clapped at the effect. "I'll need a whip to tame it," I chuckled as I tipped it to a jaunty angle. "But I can't wear it for shoveling, Ols."

"No? But you look divine!"

"It's hunting season. I'll end up with a gunshot in my ass, strapped to the hood of a Ford."

"Well, we don't want that to happen, now do we dear?" she laughed. "Come and sit down now. I've made Christmas sandwiches, and the movie will be starting soon."

There was a platter of chicken and bologna sandwiches on the coffee table. They were made of white bread cut in the shape of Christmas trees. Pickle 'pine branches' stuck out from the sides, and a cherry tomato adorned the top of each tree. The 'trunks' of the trees were cut from black olives. I was surprised the trees didn't light up. "You know, Ollie," I said, "you're off your rocker, but you sure know how to cheer a guy up."

"That's what Bart Searles says," she grinned devilishly. "That's why we're going to get married."

I had to sit down at the news. My hat slipped over my eyes, but I wasn't any more disoriented than I was when I had vision. I shoved the hat back and replied, "Are you counting on another Allied invasion to dispose of his charming Nazi wife?"

"Not really, dear. After all these years, the Nazi agreed to give Bart a quickie Mexican divorce."

"Why would she do that? I would think she'd prefer to go ten rounds. I've seen evidence of her work."

"Because if she doesn't, Bart's going to tell the judge about his injuries. And Doc Haber said he'd back Bart up. Bart says no judge in the land would believe a wife would abuse her husband, but a good threat is all he needs to get his wife to agree," Ollie explained. "Besides, he's giving her everything."

"Surely not his accordion?" I cracked.

"How did you know he has an accordion?"

"Aw, he mentioned it once," I covered. "So why bother to make it legal now, Ollie? Why not just keep things as they are?" (I know I was being selfish. But I wanted the circumstances of my life to remain the same for at least five minutes.)

"It was you that got me thinking, Weed. You know how you said you wanted to take a trip down Route 66 to feel part of something that had a past? Well, I realized that all my links to my past are gone, too. And it's been forever since I've lived with anyone I love. Except you, dear."

I was surprised by what she said. I never thought about Ollie loving me because I'm so new in her life. But I didn't have time to mull it over because Ollie went right on talking. "You once said you were tired of feeling death all around you, and you wanted to feel life. I like the way you expressed it, Weed. And I know you won't be staying long... mostly on account of my knitting," she teased. "But because I've already lost Caleb, I want to have a few years of fun with Bart while I can."

Who would believe that, once again, I had encouraged someone I care about to run off into the sunset? I would have taken a gun to my head if a bullet could have penetrated my hat. Maybe Ollie wasn't literally going away, but it felt that way.

In spite of it all, after a few more eggnogs, I felt downright generous about the subject. "Well, that's real nice, Miss Olivia," I said in my best Clark Gable voice. "You can use my hat as a knapsack if you decide to elope." I was so touched to see her so happy that I jumped right into the festivities. "Let's have some more of those great sandwiches," I suggested.

"Wonderful, darlins!"

While Ollie went to the kitchen for more food, I

ducked outside. Actually, I serpentined down the front walk into the night with an eggnog-induced lurch to my gait. My head was bobbing in the air as if it was attached with a Slinky. After a few minutes of gazing at the moon, I tried to recall why in tarnation I was standing in the snow with a bear squatting on my head. After I slipped and fell into a bank of snow, I suddenly remembered. I located a stick, shoved it up the back of my shirt into the rim of the monster hat, and I sneaked back inside the house.

A few minutes later Ollie returned with more food. As I munched and moaned with appreciation, I moved my torso just enough to cause the hidden stick to make my hat jump. Ollie looked befuddled. She blinked to clear her eyes, and then she took a cookie and turned on the television. When she sat back down, I prodded my hat again. I left my hands exposed and plastered an innocent expression to my mug.

Ollie reached for her eggnog, thought twice, then shoved it aside. I saw her watching me out of the corner of her eye, so occasionally I nudged my hat. After a few warm-ups, I sent it scurrying from one side of my head to the other. Ollie screamed and spit out a deviled egg. By the time she finally caught on, she was laughing so hard she got the hiccups.

By seven o'clock there was more rollicking than at an Elks' Club convention. After a duet of "White Christmas," we cleaned up and made get well cards for Denise. Ollie had art materials already set out, which made me suspect the whole evening was an elaborate plan to take my mind off yesterday's nightmare, although she never needs an excuse to dress as an ornament.

I had never understood the idea of people laughing at a wake, but I do now. Although I was still very sad about Denise, I felt much better after the film. I think it's okay to be happy about our own temporary survival.

With the world going to hell on a Harley, maybe brief moments of relief are all we ever get.

———

I was still in a darn good mood when Ollie said she was pooped and needed to call it a night, even though it was only 9:00 P.M. She had been knitting a sweater for Denise throughout the entire movie. I suggested she quit after four sleeves, but she advised me not to interfere with an artist. She was still chuckling about my hat when she stopped on her way upstairs. "Oh, darlins, I forgot to give you a letter which arrived for you today. It's on the mantle."

712 Elm Street
Scranton, Pa

Malcolm Dear,

I hope this letter finds you well and adjusted to your new home. Is it nice out there? We were relieved when Murray told us you're receiving medical attention in another town. Please let us know if we can help, Malcolm.

This place seems so quiet and sad with you and Murray gone. I feel as if I have lost two sons. Life can be so painful, can't it, dear? I want you to know we love you very much. Please remember that even if Murray is not here this summer, our home is yours. I haven't had a good laugh since you left.

As you must have heard, Murray left home. Murray's father has threatened to disown him for betraying our faith. Please don't be too harsh in judging Mr. Goldberg, dear. Tradition is very important to us. But between you and me, I don't always understand how some of the older traditions apply to modern

life. I'm torn between husband and son, and I'm frantic with
worry.

I must talk with Murray, Malcolm. I will find a way to help
him and Michelle and their baby, no matter what. Please tell
me how and where I can reach him. I must reach him. But Mr.
Goldberg must never know I am defying him.
Forgive me for putting you on the spot, but I know Murray
must be in contact with you, as you two have always been
closer than brothers.

It's cold here, and snow is falling. When it lets up, I plan to
take Bubby some of those macaroons she enjoys so much. I
assume Murray told you we had to put her in a rest home. It
broke our hearts, but it was for her own protection. I have to
trust God knows what He's doing with our lives.
Thank you for listening. Please call me collect as soon as you
receive this, no matter what time of day it is. I miss you very
much, and I anxiously await your call.

With much love always,
Rachael Goldberg

I read Mrs. Goldberg's letter again just to hear her voice.
Murray's mom is the worrying type, so she must be
frantic now. When I think about Mr. Goldberg being so
stubborn, I want to cream him. But Michelle's folks
aren't any better for condemning her for being pregnant
by a Jew. Where's God in all that?

I don't want to leave the impression that Mr.
Goldberg is a bad guy. Not at all. He's a good man.
When I was in the hospital, he gave me a ball from the
fiftieth World Series he got in '53. That was the year of
the Yanks' fifth consecutive Series win. It was his prized

possession. The ball is on my night table here at Ollie's. It helps me keep my grip on reality.

Mr. Goldberg really loves Murray, so I just can't understand him now. Perhaps us religiously confused types just can't understand tradition. But I want to smack him just the same.

After reading Mrs. G's letter one more time, I decided I'd better get Murray's permission to give out his address. I didn't call his mom. I knew she'd cry, and that would slay me. Instead, I wrote her this note that I plan to send airmail:

Greetings from the Midwest
December 8, 1960

Dear Mrs. G.,

I was very happy to hear from you today, although I'm sad to think about you being so upset. I'm writing to tell you Murray is safe, I promise. I'll write to him and tell him to call you immediately. No ifs, ands or buts.

I suspect Murray is just worried about what you and Mr. G. might say if he calls. He's very upset about all this. Couldn't you all just sit down and talk this over? I don't mean any offense, but what good is your tradition if it hurts your family?

Thanks for your invitation to stay at your home this summer, but I don't know if I can handle being back there without Murray. But I sure miss you, too. I miss home all the time.

Could you please send me Bubby's address so I can send her something to cheer her up? It's a real nice thing that you take her cookies. Your macaroons are the best.

Please try to talk some sense into Mr. G. If your family breaks

up, then a guy wouldn't have anything left to believe in,
which would stink. Please don't be sad anymore. It will all
work out. Love to all and have good holidays.

Yours always,
Malcolm Clapper, a.k.a. Switzerland

After I wrote that letter, I wrote to Murray, too. I can't
call him because he doesn't have a phone. I think I
made my point though:

Tundra, USA 12/08/1960

Dear Murray,

Congratulations! But first things first. I just heard from ol'
Rachael, and she's frantic. CALL HER NOW! You can't get
anymore disowned. And things just might work out. You
have to let her know you're okay, Murds. Don't be a coward.
She's hurting, man. Promise me you'll call her.

I hope you and Michelle are okay. When will the mini-
Murray arrive? I'm glad to know you're a stand-up guy who
did the right thing, no matter what the sacrifice. I'll help you
any way I can. And I'm really proud to be your friend. I'll
write more later. I've got lots to tell, but I want to get this
mailed. Hap-a-havy-Hanukkah.

Clap Man

P.S. I'm enclosing a few bucks so you can take Michelle
somewhere for a nice dinner. Hopefully, she'll keep the food
down. It's a wedding present, so you can't send it back.

By the time I finished, it was almost ten o'clock, but I needed to get some advice, so I decided to go see Laura. She stays up late reading, so I didn't think she'd mind a late visitor in the form of yours truly.

I had to fight a cold wind as I made my way to her house. It gets tortuously cold here on the tundra with nothing much to buffer the elements. I dragged my bum leg along with the rest of my frozen corpse. After a while, the cold numbed the pain somewhat, but the effort required for each step exhausted me.

As I rounded the bend, Laura's house welcomed me from a distance, and I realized it felt as close to home as anything I've known since my family died. (Besides Ollie's house.) A light was on in Laura's downstairs bedroom, and I could hear soft music.

Before knocking on her door, I leaned against the oak tree across from her house to catch my breath and clear my nose of any potentially offensive matter. Suddenly I got one of those prickly feelings that occur when threat is lurking about in a black cloak carrying an ax. As I looked around, nothing seemed out of the ordinary, so I tried to shake off my uneasiness.

As I was about to cross the road, I detected a movement near Laura's house. Although the image was faint in the moonlight, I could see someone hiding on the side of the house near her bedroom window. I pinned myself against the tree and watched. Through Laura's bedroom window, I could see her silhouette.

When the shadow by her window moved again, I wasn't sure what to do. The prowler reached into his pocket. Before I could react, I saw the flame from a lighter as he lit up a cigarette. In the brief flicker of light, I recognized Andy Johnson. I couldn't be sure if he was holding only his lighter, or if he was also wielding his knife.

As quietly as possible, I crept across the road to a thicket of trees for a better view. When Andy moved closer to Laura's window, I moved in, too, until I had a clear view of Laura. There was nothing between us but a pane of glass. And Andy Johnson.

Laura was standing near the window, swaying to the music. She was dressed in a blue sweater and a slim gray skirt. I could see her brushing her hair as she looked out into the moonlight.

While Andy watched Laura, he boldly continued to drag on his cigarette, apparently unconcerned about being detected. I still couldn't make out what he had in his hand. I took a deep breath, then I closed in even closer until I was only twenty feet behind him. As Andy watched Laura, I watched Andy.

While we stood there in the freezing night, we were each focused on something different. Then I heard a noise I'll never forget. It was a howl—almost an animal cry. Then Andy moved. He reached out and groaned, "Joey… Joey."

I was sure Laura must have heard, but when I looked in the window, she seemed unaware. She was slipping her sweater over her head, and as she undressed, the bedroom light illuminated her creamy skin. For a moment I was as transfixed as Andy was, because she looked so soft and vulnerable.

Laura stepped out of her skirt and stood near the window in her lace bra and slip, her hair skimming her shoulders in all the places I've always wanted to touch. She was just so damn beautiful I couldn't move.

Laura then removed her bra exposing the most beautiful body I could ever imagine. She swayed slowly, as if she were thinking of something long ago and far away. I imagined her face against my cheek, and although I was aroused, I also felt a sense of peace I can't describe.

A footstep in the snow brought my attention back to

my immediate surroundings. When I realized what the two of us were doing, I was repulsed. I couldn't believe I was lurking around, invading Laura's privacy with Andy, a guy with only half a brain. It felt as if I had violated her, and that made me more ashamed than I've ever been in my life. My instincts told me I needed to get away from there as fast as I could. I was so furious with Andy for dragging me into his perverted activities I was afraid of what I might do to him if I hesitated.

Then he groaned again. When I whipped around, I could see Andy stroking himself and moaning like a madman. He cried out, "Joey! Joey!" His disfigured head bobbed up and down while he choked back his own drool. The sight was unbearable.

Suddenly I lost all control. I ran at Andy and jumped him from behind throwing him against the house. He was still moaning as he reached around and got me in a headlock. I knew he could break my neck with his one inhumanly powerful arm, but I was too angry to care. I lifted my body and twisted, getting the better of him. As I flipped him over my shoulder, I was aware he was still aroused.

"You disgusting pervert!" I screamed as I jumped on top of him. When I grabbed his head, his shattered skull felt like a craggy rock in my hand. I looked for some semblance of a person inside his mangled face, someone I could punish for visually assaulting Laura. But all I saw was skin and scar tissue. And all I heard was something so primal and so detached it terrified me.

"Shut up!" I yelled. "Shut up!" His face was wet, as if he'd been crying, and he was choking on his own saliva.

After I yanked him upright, I shoved him away from me, but my feet went out from under me, and I fell back into a snow bank. I frantically rubbed snow all over my face in an attempt to feel clean, then I tried to stand, but my legs wouldn't support me, and I went back down.

I was humiliated, but Andy was looking beyond my own pathetic physical wreckage. He whispered, "Joey!" and started to sob as he stared up at something behind me.

When I reeled around, I saw Laura. She was trembling as she stood over us, her face distorted with pain. Her body was bent, as if her stomach hurt, and she was crying so hard she barely made a sound. Her lips were forming words she couldn't say. I pulled myself upright again as she kneeled in the snow near Andy.

"Joey," Andy moaned again, "Joey."

Laura cradled him in her arms. She kissed him on his scarred face, which shocked and repulsed me. "It's okay, Andy," Laura cried as he tried to pull away, "shhh, everything is okay."

"Laura," I blurted, "he was watching you undress. He's a pervert. Andy was..."

"Shhh," she said, this time to me, "Andy's not a pervert, Weed. He's a man who has been badly injured." She reached down to tuck him in, which was shocking to watch.

"But Laura, what he was doing was disgusting!"

"Stop it, Weed--please!" she yelled. "Stop! I know he watches me!"

"You know?" I blurted. "You mean you *let* him?" As I looked at her, I saw someone I had never seen before. I couldn't listen. I reeled around to leave, but she stopped me.

"Weed, he's not disgusting. I love Andy," she whispered.

I couldn't believe what I was hearing. She seemed so desperate and lonely that I felt sorry for her.

"You dance for him?" I said through clenched teeth. "You let him watch you in some sort of twisted sex ritual?"

"Yes," she whispered. "Maybe you're too young to understand."

That angered me more than almost anything she could have said. I wanted to drive my fist into the ground, but I saw something that stopped me cold. Laura had a look of deep sadness on her face. It was the same look that greeted me over and over again after my parents and Leland were killed. It was on the faces of those well-meaning visitors who came by the house with clichéd condolences. It was on the faces of the doctors who operated on me after my own accident, and it was on the face of my girlfriend, Annie Peterson, when she said we had to break up because I was no longer the same.

It was the look of pity. Pity for those of us who have rotten, oozing bodies that won't heal. Pity for the freaks who can only get love from those martyrs who will wade through the stench for the sake of our hopeless lot. But even us freaks know it's really all for the sake of the martyrs, who think their sympathy will earn them a spot in heaven.

But the joke is on them because heaven doesn't exist. There's just this lonely Earth, where broken corpses keep on twitching long after they're dead. As I looked at Andy and Laura crouched in the snow, I realized she saw Andy and me the same way... as two broken people.

"You're the needy one!" I screamed at her. "You knew I was out here, too, didn't you? Did you think you were being generous, selling yourself through a window to two freaks who can't have normal lives?"

"Weed, you don't know what you're saying—"

"Don't condescend to me! I'm not Andy. I love you! But you just go around gathering injured sparrows because you're too lost to live your own life. You offer your kindness to us as if we should be grateful for your crumbs, and you think you can fill some hole inside yourself by sacrificing yourself to us monsters. You're the monster, Laura! I pity *you!*"

I was crying so hard I couldn't stop. Although I tried to run, I fell several times, but I kept going. Anything was better than having to look at those two crumpled bodies in the snow.

When I got to the oak tree, I heard Laura call out my name. I wanted to go back to her and fall into her arms and hold onto her so I wouldn't disappear. Then I heard Andy. He yelled Joey's name out into the night. And the cold night yelled it right back at him as some kind of ironic reminder that Joey is the luckiest bastard of all. Because Joey is dead.

CHAPTER TWENTY-SIX

DECEMBER 11, 1960

I DON'T KNOW HOW LONG IT TOOK ME TO GET HOME FROM Laura's that night. I can't even remember what I've done since then. When I'm alone, my mind is so loud I can't drown it out. But I'm the only one who hears me. The good news is I'll be eighteen in nine days, and then I can leave all this madness behind me.

After I returned from Laura's, I couldn't sleep, so I took some pain pills. I even took a shot of Ollie's rum hoping it might kill the pain in my leg and knock me out cold. I ended up having a terrible sleep. It was the kind where you feel the crushing weight of sleep as you dream.

I think my dream had something to do with what I did just after I took the pills. I threw my books and my journal and some clothes into a suitcase. Then I took the Dutch shoes off my closet shelf. Inside one is my favorite snapshot of Leland.

Leland was as happy as a flea in a mitten the day it was taken because Dad had treated us to a local carnival. We played every game we could and went on tons of rides including the Sputnik and the Tilt-a-Whirl. Leland got dizzy, but that was okay because he loved to be dizzy. It was pretty funny to watch him stagger afterward. When he got the hiccups, Dad said in a very loud voice, "I told you five beers was too many, son." Lots of people laughed at that.

Dad let us sample any food we wanted. Leland had two cotton candies, so his cheeks were so sticky that by the time we got around to the hot dogs, the bun stuck to his face. He even had a chunk of bread up his nostril. At that point Dad dragged Leland into a photo booth, shoved in a quarter, and yelled, "Say, 'Hi, Mom!'" Instead, Leland yelled, "Weed's a turnip head." That's what he was saying in the photo. He was the cutest kid you ever saw.

Seeing his photo is what caused the nightmare. In my dream, Leland was lying in an open casket, and his head was sewn on with big black stitches. When I reached down to adjust his shirt, flies swarmed out of his jacket, and I knew he was covered with maggots.

I panicked and started running around the room asking people what to do. Everyone was there except Laura: Murray's folks and my folks, even Barley and Janine. Although I didn't see Denise, I knew she was in the room. And Robert, too.

All the guests were eating pie and shaking their heads back and forth. No one would tell me what to do for Leland, not even my dad. Murray and Michelle were sitting alone in the back row facing a wall.

As I yelled for help, the air grew thicker with flies. I was angry with everyone because they ignored the flies that annoyed Leland as he tried to sleep. I told them all to leave if they weren't going to help me, so they did. Even my folks. And Murray. They literally marched out, which was damn disrespectful because they made entirely too much racket.

When I was finally alone with Leland, I came up with a good idea. I pulled out a fly strip that I knew belonged to Janine's brother Timmy. "This will do the trick, little buddy," I reassured him. As I unrolled the fly strip, one small fly landed in the sticky sludge. "I got one," I shouted.

I studied the fly as it struggled. It was hanging there, but it wouldn't die. The fly struggled until it became so tired it stopped moving. The other flies watched from above as the captured fly suffered alone. They knew if they got too close, they'd get trapped, too.

I tried to free the captured insect, but my hands got stuck. Within seconds I was coated with the glue, and I couldn't move. I gasped for air. Finally, I slumped forward, falling on top of Leland. We were both overtaken by flies. But they weren't moving or buzzing. That was the worst part of the dream, because I knew *we were all dying*.

By the time my flailing awakened me, I was on the floor next to my bed with the blankets tangled around my legs. For the rest of the night, I stayed huddled on the floor because I was too terrified of sleep to get back in bed.

The dream is following me everywhere. It's stuck to me as tight as that fly strip was stuck to the back of Janine's little brother. I can't free myself of it.

———

After the sun came up, I called Jessie. She said Denise has made some slight improvement and might get out of intensive care tomorrow, so I can go visit her then. She also told me Sheriff Cooper has no information on who forced Denise and Robert off the road, but there's rumor of more trouble brewing. Frankly, I can't imagine anything worse than what has already happened.

When I said a quick hello to Martha Jane, she sounded sad, so I decided to get her a gift at the sundry store to cheer her up.

As I headed into town, I was thinking about Laura. I was feeling so sick and confused and ashamed about the things I said to her the other night, I actually found myself looking forward to talking to Snarls.

Today is Sunday, so Snarls didn't open the store until noon. He was entering as I arrived, and no one else was around, which was a big relief because I didn't want anyone to see how much my leg was twitching. It's been feeling pretty miserable, which I expect is due to the cold, but I decided to pick up some more pain medication for when I hit the road.

"Sorry I'm out of breath," Snarls said as he greeted me. "I've been running around like a chicken with my feet cut off."

I was laughing to myself about the mangled cliché as I followed him inside. Snarls turned on some Christmas twinkle lights, which made the store look very festive. Everywhere I looked there were ropes of tinsel garland and clusters of glass Christmas balls. Snarls sure has a way of arranging things, right down to the large plastic Santa propped up in front of a Coke and a half-eaten piece of pie. I got a bang out of that.

While Snarls filled my prescriptions, I browsed through the Christmas merchandise until I found a square of clear soap with a cute plastic duck inside. I picked that up for Martha Jane, along with a bottle of nail polish called Blushing Bride. As I set them on the counter, I said, "Throw in a Sugar Daddy, too, Mr. Searles."

"These things will pull your teeth out," Snarls warned as he handed me a sucker.

"No, they'll pull Martha William's teeth out," I corrected him. "This is for her. I plan to visit her later this week."

"Glad to hear it, because the nail polish is way too bright for you, kid."

"Yeah, hardy-har-har," I laughed. "Now how 'bout whipping up a Dusty Road," I said. "A big one," I added, figuring it might be the last one I ever have. "And one for Santa, too. I'm buying."

Snarls grinned and shook his pompadoured head as he headed for the ice cream freezer. He has taken on a springs-in-the-shoes gait, which was darn nice to see. "You're sure looking chipper, sir," I said as he dug ice cream out of the bin.

"I'm feeling real good, Weed. My wife up and left me last night. Damn shame."

When I saw his eyes roll toward heaven, I burst into laughter. As Snarls brought the sundae over to me, he did a fancy little dance step.

"Thanks, Mr. Searles. I'm glad things are working out. You've been real nice to me."

"Why did that have a 'good-bye' sound to it, son?" he asked, plopping himself down on the stool next to me.

"Because I'm planning on leaving here in a week."

"Does your grandmother know this?"

"She's always known I wouldn't be staying long, sir. I'm a wanderer. I take after her."

"She thought you'd be staying at least until summer, son."

"Things have changed. My birthday is coming up, and it's time to go."

"You should get your diploma. You could even go on to college with that brain of yours."

"I've lost too much time, and I'm too far behind to ever catch up. I don't want to be twenty-five and still be a senior."

"Chicks go for older guys," he deadpanned. "Seriously, Weed, if you stopped ditching school you could graduate before you're twenty-five. And what's Russ going to do if you leave? He told me you're the guy who turned him into a 'cool cat.'"

"He said that?" I laughed. "Russ is a good guy. He

just needed style. But I've got personal reasons why I've gotta go."

"I understand. But Ollie sure will be sad. She was alone until you came along. She's never been as happy as she is now."

"You have a lot to do with that, Mr. Searles. Now that you're a bachelor, she won't be needing me."

"Don't you be discounting yourself so fast, Weed Clapper. You brought something special to her."

"I did?"

"Yes, acceptance. You never judged her the way some of the others around here do."

I felt guilty when he said that because I've hidden a lot of shame about Ollie being such a fruitcake. I didn't want Snarls to think of me as a better guy than I truly am. I needed him to see the real Weed Clapper, or it would be like I was never here at all. So I came clean. "I haven't always been so accepting in my head," I confessed. "I've been embarrassed... and critical."

"Oh, hell, son. Everyone feels that way about their family at one time or another. All that matters is that you keep hanging in there in spite of the nasty things other people might think or say. Blood is thicker than mud."

"You know, sir, you sure have a way of pummeling clichés, but that one sorta made sense."

"It's a talent. I developed it just to keep people on their toes," he laughed. "And maybe to torture the wife a little."

"I'm gonna miss you," I said, and I realized I meant it. Other than the hideous vision of him dancing across Ollie's floor in tap shoes, my experiences with Snarls have been nice. "You've been real good to me," I told him, "and I want to thank you."

"No need, son. When do you plan on leaving exactly?"

"December 20. I haven't told Ollie the details yet, so

please let me take care of it before you mention anything."

"Sure thing." He got up and went behind the counter. I thought he was going to get me my pills, but he returned with something else. "You said you were leaving the day of your birthday," Snarls beamed, "so I'd like you to accept this as a birthday gift. It will bring you luck on the road. I always wanted to drive 'cross country myself. But now I want to stay around and take care of Ollie. You take this. That way I'll be traveling along with you in a sense."

Snarls handed me an old-fashioned teak 'suicide knob.' It was the kind that attaches to a steering wheel. "It's fourteen-karat gold inlay," he told me proudly, pointing to the replica of Elvis Presley's face. " 'Be worth big money someday. It's yours, son."

"Holy cow, Mr. Searles, this is great! Thanks a lot. Are you sure you don't want to keep it?"

"Nope, I want you to have it. I picked it up in Memphis some years ago. Maybe you can go there and meet 'The King' one day."

"That would be cool. This'll look great on my car," I said.

"What kind do you have?"

"I don't exactly have one yet. I plan to buy one when I get some money on my birthday. I wanted a Thunderbird, but my friend Murray needs money for college, and I want to help him out. That won't leave much, so I'll just look for a junker."

"How would you like a '55 Bel Air Sport Coupe? It belonged to the wife, but she won't be needing it now that she's flown the coop. 'Car's a beaut'—she hardly ever drove it. It'll be a good car to get you to California or wherever you end up. Ollie won't be wanting it; she doesn't take to driving. How 'bout it?"

"How much?"

"Nothing. She's yours for the taking."

"I couldn't accept that, sir. It wouldn't be right."

"Oh, hell's bells! When I marry Ollie, you'll practically be my grandson. And that knob belongs on your steering wheel. It'd look real nice, don't you think?"

"But—"

"But nothing. How 'bout you pay me a hundred bucks? Will that suit you? And promise me you'll try to gain back some of that weight you've been losing so your bones won't go poking through that fine upholstery."

"Sure. That would be great. Wow, thanks!"

"Settled. No hurry paying. The garage is unlocked so you can go on over to my place and have a look at the car anytime. Let me know when you'll be needing it. But you might want to wait until after you've had your talk with Ollie to pick the car up."

"Okay. That's great, Mr. Searles."

"Call me, Bart."

"Thanks, Bart!" I was so excited I actually forgot about Laura and Denise and Leland and my folks for a short while. Of course, they were clanking around my mind like ghosts in chains, but I just smiled and ate ice cream and ignored them all while I polished the Elvis knob. As I was propping it up on the napkin holder, I caught my reflection. I have to brag a little and admit I resemble Elvis quite a lot.

Who knows—perhaps Bart's good deed is God's way of saying He really *is* listening. Geez, maybe He's talking to me through Elvis! Wait till Murray hears this. He'll give it a '100' even if he can't dance to it!

CHAPTER TWENTY-SEVEN
DECEMBER 12, 1960

I THOUGHT MY RECENT DESPAIR WAS DUE TO A PERSONALITY defect that makes me even more cynical than great philosophers like Nietzsche and Lenny Bruce. But it's not me who's off-center. It's the whole planet! Ollie is right. As long as people hate, they'll hurt others. And ignorance brews hatred. I witnessed it with my own eyes during one of the most unforgettable moments of my life.

It all started with a report in last night's paper. It was an update about what happened to Denise and Robert. The editor of the newspaper has been receiving criticism for not mentioning the racial factor that led to Denise's accident, so he finally touched upon it in last night's paper. His editorial said, "Certain members in our society place their own hatred above social responsibility and respect for humanity." His comments led to a horrifying incident that occurred in the Negro section of town. It wasn't expected by anyone... except maybe the folks who live there.

Russ called me at about 9:00 P.M. to tell me his dad was almost run off the road by a caravan heading toward Jessie's neighborhood. Apparently, Roy expected the worst. Russ said his dad immediately rallied as many responsible citizens as he could to try to protect the Negroes from any possible harm.

"What kind of harm?" I asked Russ.

"The K.K.K. The guys in the caravan were wearing white hoods," Russ explained. "Dad recognized Leonard Sitz. He's a cop over in Greencastle, and he's the local leader."

"Holy crap! Come and get me, Russ!"

Ollie begged me not to go, but I knew I could never be the guy my parents raised me to be if I just sat there and did nothing. Before I had enough time to chicken out, Russ pulled up out front and laid on the horn. Jimmy Dale was with him, and they both looked as worked up as I was.

"Does this kind of thing happen here often?" I asked as I jumped into the truck.

"Nothing this bad has happened in years," JD answered.

"So why now?"

"Dad heard that the Klan is riled up because of all the heat on them since Denise's accident," Russ said. "They say Denise and Robert were asking for trouble, so they're gathering just to make a point."

"Yeah," JD added, "and with all the sit-ins going on, like the one over in Crawfordsville, they're saying it's time to put Negroes in their place 'cause they're getting too 'uppity.'"

I couldn't even respond. As we veered off onto a dirt road, my gut was burning, and my mouth was dry. My mind couldn't make sense of it. I had no idea things were this bad. Maybe the only people completely awake in life are the ones who are on the receiving end of badness.

Before we reached the strip of houses where Jessie lives, we saw the glow of headlights through the pines. The area was very quiet, and so were we. But as we turned the bend, the three of us gasped aloud at the blur of white hoods in the road before us. The Klan was out in force, and there were vehicles everywhere. The K.K.K. had blocked the road, leaving a strip of gravel just big enough for one car to pass. By the time I spotted the De Soto with the Spencer Gun Club sticker, my heart was pounding.

Russ drove as near as he could before pulling off the road to park. We jumped out of the truck and ran over to Roy and the other citizens he had hastily gathered. But there must have been close to one hundred of the Klan present, more than twice our number. And no law enforcement had yet arrived. I have seen some frightening things in my life, but nothing comparable to that line of men in white robes with freakish hoods. It was horrifying. I could *feel* their malice.

As Roy's group moved in closer to the houses, I was momentarily relieved to see that the homes were dark. Not one light was on. Then when I saw Cotton's station wagon and Jessie's old car, I realized people were hiding inside.

The K.K.K. gathered around a cross lying on the ground. It was wrapped in rags, which one Klansman doused with gasoline. One of Roy's group strode over to reason with them, but several Klansmen pointed shotguns at his chest keeping him back. Nobody seemed to know what to do next.

Suddenly I heard a click in my ear, so I instinctively spun around in the direction of the sound. Roy Kinney had his rifle leveled at the head of the Grand Dragon. Then I heard other guns being cocked. When I looked up, I saw at least ten Klansmen with their weapons aimed at Roy Kinney. One of them had white-tipped shoes, just like the ones the righteous Reverend Harper wears.

Russ yelled, "Dad!" But Roy didn't look his way.

"Move away from me very slowly," Roy cautioned everyone around him in a quiet voice. 'You, too, Russ."

Then he shouted at Leonard Sitz, "I've got my sights right on you, Leonard. So does Cooper and Sam and Draper."

"There's twice as many guns pointed at your head, Kinney," a Klansman shouted from somewhere.

Roy stood tall and didn't flinch. "Is that so?" he said calmly. "Then we better all stay calm or there's gonna be a lot of funerals tomorrow." Then he shouted at Leonard, "And yours will be one of 'em, Leonard, 'cause I'll get you before I go down. I'm not afraid of the likes of you. You can have your right to free speech, but you better talk quick 'cause the sheriff is on his way. And don't go agitating trouble, or my fingers might get jumpy."

"This here is what I have to say," Leonard shouted. Suddenly the cross was yanked upright by two ropes, and Leonard tossed a lit match. There was an audible whoosh as the flames exploded and the cross shot up upright. It loomed over us like a tower of evil. We were all pushed back by the heat, but throughout it all, Roy held his weapon steady.

Leonard yelled above the blaze, "Stay back! Our fight isn't with white folk, but we ain't lettin' no white man cross this road to the nigger side. We won't tolerate liberals who will destroy us as sure as the mixin' of races will. We're here to do the work God intended," he yelled. "His plan was to keep the races separate, just like this here road separates us from them coons. No one better cross if he knows what's good for him! The great white race will not be tainted with nigger blood!"

As I stared at the burning cross, the contrasts were too overwhelming to absorb. Hurting others in God's name only seemed to make sense to those with white hoods. And black souls. The whole ominous event unfolded like a movie. There was an invisible screen that separated me from what I was watching, and I didn't know how to break through it.

Seconds later, the leader signaled someone, and then a truck suddenly took off at break-neck speed down the narrow strip of road. Tied to the back bumper was a dummy made of pillows spray-painted black. As the truck careened in the snow, the dummy slid back and forth over the jutted road. The car stopped, abruptly reversed, and ran over the black effigy.

As we all watched, two hooded agitators soaked the mangled likeness of the Negro with flammable liquid. "Let this be a warning to all you niggers hiding inside," the ringleader yelled, "you ain't gonna taint white blood. This is what happens to those who defile the white race." He then set the symbolic black man ablaze. The pillow curled up like a human suffering at the hands of a demon. It was ghastly.

I thought I'd seen the worst until Leonard signaled again. This time the truck door opened, then two people were forced out at gunpoint. To my shock, it was Jessie and Martha Jane. They tried to back away, but a Klansman made them stand beneath the cross. In the firelight I saw that Jessie had been covered in whitewash.

"These little gals have been warned. Next time will be worse, so you darkies in there better listen up!" the leader yelled toward the dark houses.

Martha buried her head against Jessie, but Jessie stared dead ahead as if she was looking straight at me.

"Jessie!" I screamed. When I started toward them, Russ and Jimmy Dale held me back. I struggled to break free, but then Roy Kinney placed his hand on my shoulder and spoke into my ear.

"Wait, Weed, we're outnumbered!" he warned. "Don't do it. Don't force Leonard's hand!"

I could hear the words Leonard was vomiting. "Hear this, all you nigger cowards hiding in there like scared black sheep. You stay on your side of the road. Know your place, or the next ride any of you takes will be a longer trip than these gals had."

Leonard nodded. Then the ringleaders abruptly got in their cars and left in a procession that was as solemn as a holy ritual, which made it even more frightening and unforgettable.

A group of Jessie's neighbors suddenly burst from their houses and ran to assist Jessie and Martha Jane. I tried to go, too, but strong arms still held me in place.

We all watched as the remaining Klansmen formed a sinister line down the middle of the road and stared us down.

"What's going on?" Russ whispered to his father.

Roy lowered his gun slowly then took a deep breath.

"They're waiting for us to leave first," he explained. "It's all for a show of power. This was meant as a warning."

"Why doesn't someone just shoot them?" JD mumbled.

Roy put his rifle back in his truck. "We'll use peaceful measures," he answered, "... as long as we can." Roy clenched his jaw as he wiped the sweat off his forehead with the back of his hand. "If we weren't men of peace, that bastard Leonard would be six feet south of here by now," he growled.

That wasn't good enough for me. I wanted to peel off my color. I knew Denise and Robert hadn't tainted my race any more than Ollie and Caleb had. It was the men in hoods who made me ashamed to be white.

Roy's words were still ringing in my ears as the cross came down with an ear-shattering thud. When two Negroes ran out to smother the raging flames with blankets, the Klansmen seemed to enjoy watching the desperate attempts to keep the fire away from the wooden houses. The smoke cloud from the cross billowed up into the night and dissipated into the darkness.

Roy put a hand on my back. "Com'on, son," he said, "let's go. The Klan is watching. They know who us sympathizers are, and they can make life real bad for you. You must protect yourself."

My mind told me to get the hell out of there. But my conscience told me something else. I'm no hero type like my dad, but I knew that if I didn't do something, my soul would be deader than the souls of the hooded monsters, so I might as well be, too. I figured if I had to die at the hands of those evil men, it should be while doing something worth living for in the first place. I took a deep breath, then I abruptly turned and ran straight toward the line of Klansmen.

"Weed, no!" I heard Roy yell as I shoved my way into the line of Klansmen.

Just as I glanced back at Roy, I saw Ollie and Snarls pull up. Ollie jumped out of Snarls's car before it had even come to a halt. I heard her scream out to me, but I kept on heading straight for that ominous line.

The Klansmen jabbed and poked their guns into my ribs, but I kept pushing. When my bum leg buckled under me, I went down. As I hit the packed snow I cried out in pain, but somehow, my legs got me back up.

At that moment, Ollie seemed to come out of nowhere. She ran right up to one of the Klansmen and poked him in the chest. "You keep your hands off my grandson!" she warned.

I couldn't believe my eyes. The Klansman stood there as if he wasn't sure what to do next. Ollie didn't back down. "Now get out of my way," she ordered. Although the Klansman continued to stare her down, he instinctively took a step back.

"We've got your back, son," I heard another voice say. I knew without looking that Snarls had moved in on the other side of me.

My hands were trembling, and there was spit on my

face. But I pushed my way through the wall of white robes.

I heard a commotion behind me. Over my shoulder I saw Ollie, Snarls, Roy, Russ, and JD also pushing their way through the line. Soon others followed. Then more. The line of Klansmen gradually broke up as small groups rushed the line. Within minutes, our entire group was on the other side of the road. The Negro side.

At first no one knew what to do. As the Klansmen watched, Ollie and I knocked on the door of the neighbor who had taken Jessie in. Several moments of heavy silence passed before the porch light finally came on. On the other side of the door stood a Negro man, obviously shaken. I was rattled, but I eventually found my voice. "I'm, I'm really so sorry, sir," I stammered.

"What can we do to help?" Ollie asked.

As the man stood there, I heard frightened whispers from inside the house. I thought he was going to slam the door in our faces. Instead, he reached out and put a hand on my shoulder and said, "Step inside, y'all... that's mighty brave of you."

We all turned back to look at the monsters in hoods. To make their point, they fired several warning shots into the sky before the night fell silent. Finally, one by one, they got into their cars and left. We watched as the last car turned the bend and disappeared into the night.

Our group then filed into the house. After some time passed, other Negroes came over from their homes to join us. Soon there were so many of us we had to open the doors despite the cold.

Cotton McKamey came, too. He nodded to his neighbors, but he didn't say much. His face remained motionless as he lowered his tired body onto the sofa. "I'm so ashamed to be white, Cotton," I said as I took a seat next to him. I sat by him awhile, but I made my mouth keep still.

Cotton finally leaned in to me and rasped, "Bad

hearts don't have no color, son." I was amazed that he could be so nice after all that happened.

"I heard about your son, Cotton," I told him, "and I am just so darn sorry."

Cotton patted my knee. "God bless you, Mr. Weed," he whispered.

While Ollie and the ladies tended to Jessie and Martha, other folks discussed how to make changes around here, and maybe even run the likes of Leonard out of town.

Finally, the sheriff and his crew arrived. They explained how a number of their vehicles had been vandalized in an obvious and planned attempt to delay their response. "Don't y'all worry, we'll be makin' some arrests," the sheriff promised everyone.

"How 'bout making it more than just talk this time, Joe?" Roy challenged.

There was more talk, and before the impromptu meeting ended, I kissed Martha and Jessie. I couldn't say much because my emotions were backing up on me. When we finally stepped onto the porch, it was nice to see a lot of handshaking going on. They were lingering handshakes—the kind that says a person is feeling more than just the other person's skin.

When we stepped off the porch to leave, I could still see pieces of the burned effigy dotting the snow near the remains of the cross. Ollie and I stared at each other with unspoken grief. I could hear Caleb's words to Ollie echo through my mind, "In God's time, Olivia. In God's time."

CHAPTER TWENTY-EIGHT
DECEMBER 13, 1960

I STILL HAVEN'T SLEPT MUCH. I HAVE TOO MUCH TO THINK about, like how I can do my part to change this messed-up world. I went by to see Jessie and Martha, but no one was there. A neighbor says now they're staying up in Crawfordsville with Hattie because they're afraid to come home.

I left there and headed to Snarls's house to see the car he's selling me. By the time I got there, my anticipation was out of control, but I wasn't disappointed. The Bel Air is cherry all right, even the paint. The seats match the exterior, which is black and sky blue. It's real classy.

I sat in my new car awhile and turned the knobs and checked out my image in the mirror. If I can get my hands on some fuzzy dice or a set of dog tags, I might hang them from the mirror. I saw some in a car once, and I really admired the effect.

When I got back to Ollie's, I was real jazzed to learn that the mailman had delivered a package from Kenton that said: HANDS OFF TILL CHRISTMAS, MAN! I couldn't imagine what it was, so naturally I had to rip it open. Inside was a round tin that contained a flaky, suspicious-looking lump with a plastic puke-pile in the middle. I nearly split a gut when I realized what it was: the famous chain-letter fruitcake.

It's crazy how this fruit cake caper first got started. When I was fourteen, we got into a discussion about why people send each other fruitcakes that always end up in the trash. Kenton said it was because humanity is made up of dishonest scum who won't admit they hate fruitcake. Liam-the-Load swore it was because fruitcakes signify bounty, and without them we'd be doomed to a year of starvation and eight-foot tapeworms. Murray figured people sent fruitcakes to remind each other of how poor folks have to eat gross food while the rest of us stuff our faces with really good cakes. But *I* speculated that there was really only one fruitcake in the world, and it had been passed around for centuries because no one wanted to eat the darn thing.

Before you know it, Murray received a fruitcake in the mail. We suspected Kenton, but Kenton would never admit to the prank. The next Christmas the same fruitcake showed up at my door with a fake finger on top. We all added "flavor" to it and passed it around on every occasion we could think of until a year ago when it vanished. Murray accused Kenton of hoarding it, and Kenton accused me. But it has finally surfaced again.

Glued to the lid is a picture of Kenton in the middle of Times Square holding the fruitcake. He's grinning and wearing a hat that makes him look like a high school Sinatra. Well, a dark Sinatra. It's a good photo, and his note was a beaut':

New York, New York, New York, etc.

Hey Man,

I'm on Broadway, as in BROAD-way. My group is trying

out for a recording contract with RCA tomorrow. Cool, huh? We met some cat today who wants to help refine our image. I agreed, but only if I can keep wearing my hat. I get hot chicks with this hat.

I took Murray's advice and tried to excuse Liam for being born an asshole. (Pardon my pud-I mean, 'Houston.' Soooo... I looked him up at his N.Y. digs. It's a dump with roaches as big as Chevys. And there's an old guy next door who stinks all the way into the hallway. The pipes leak orange ooze, so I told the Doom Monger that I read that the ooze makes your noodle limp.

Houston is strangely peppy nowadays. He didn't mention disease once. He has fallen for a Swedish actress named Ann-Margret. She doesn't use a last name, so she may be in a witness protection program. Her figure is amazing. She'll be famous for sure. Ann-Margret has a breathy voice that drips with desire...but probably just around me. She's trying to talk Liam into dropping "Houston Skies" She could talk me into cutting my head off and using it as an ashtray. I suggested he call himself "Pennsylvania Pestilence." It suits him.

How do you like the fruitcake? Rank, huh? Well, guess what... Liam's the one who's been hiding it all this time! He planted it in my suitcase. There's hope for him yet. I bet you nearly crapped when you opened it, man. Why don't you send the fruitcake to Murds? I know you know where he is. And tell him to write or he's Jew-goo. You too, asshole.

Fondle yours,
Kenton Cool-Daddy

I looked at the photo again and laughed aloud. Then I packed up the fruitcake and headed for the post office before it closed. When I got there, Janine's dad, our "friendly" postmaster, was behind the counter. He handed me a letter from Murray that had just arrived. When he asked me why I wasn't in school, I told him about my plan to drop out next week on my birthday and hit the road. He seemed relieved to know the town was losing a bad seed.

Outside the post office I saw Andy Johnson...well, I saw the shadow of his misshapen head.) I was ducking behind the building to avoid him when I heard him call my name. Suddenly I felt angry about the whole Laura incident all over again. I can't bear to see him. I feel bad for him, but I don't want him to think I'm his friend. I got away from there as fast as my bum leg could carry me. I read Murray's letter as I walked home:

December 7, 1960 En Route

Dear Weed,

How's home on 'de-range'? Are you keeping your ammo dry and your wiener wet? I'm writing from a motel in Hershey. Michelle wanted to visit the chocolate factory. We're on our way back home to Scrotum, pal.

Two days ago, I called Rachael to let her know I was alive because I knew she'd be having a cow. When she started crying, I wanted to fall on a cyanide-tipped sword, but all I had was a ballpoint pen. After a bit of melodrama, the old girl announced that Dad really needed to speak to me. I wanted to hang up before I was cursed from Canaan, because Dad has been so inflexible about the tradition thing.

But get this! Before Kenton left for New York, he went to my house to report a "miracle." You know how he's been visiting Bubby? Well, he told my dad how Bubs, who can't even remember who Dad is or why she flushed her dentures down the john, "spoke" one day during a lucid moment. Kenton swore she said, "The hell with the old ways! Kenton, tell my son I said to keep the family together NO MATTER WHAT. Make damn sure he listens, or I'll suffer for all eternity."

Can you believe it, man? Kenton probably even added an echo and some thunder for effect. Anyway, my father told Kenton he couldn't help but be suspicious because Bubs never cursed. But Kenton suggested Bubby's cursing was the bad influence of one of the old men there who plays with his tooter all day.

My dad dragged Kenton to the home to confirm his story. Bubs, who was wearing her little black hat and housecoat recognized Kenton and smiled. But she ignored my dad! That was a sure sign Kenton had been to the Mountain. It was all my old man needed to take me back into the fold. He's really a softie, as you know. When it gets down to it, I think he was looking for an excuse to relent. But I plan to carve Kenton's face on Mt. Sinai.

Dad eventually promised Bubs he'd respect her wishes and provide a place for Michelle and me and the baby. He swore he'd get us both through college even if he had to sell the house to do it. When I talked to him, Dad cried and asked us to forgive him.

As I write this, I'm a little drippy-eyed myself. I'm going home, man. The senior Goldbergs are hanging in there for us. It's a lot easier when someone's there for you. So listen pal, you can come home, too. YOU HEAR WHAT I'M SAYING, BUDDY?

Gotta run. Michelle just got back from the store, and she's dying to eat, which is a nice change from the prior pukerama.

I hope you are doing great and that I'll see your ugly mug soon. Miche says hello. I, on the other hand, forced out some ass-gas in your honor. Ahhhh. See ya!

Best fishes,
Murray, Sower of Sacred Seed

I was stoked to read Murray's letter. I'm glad he's doing okay, but I can't go back there. Murds and I had a real good time growing up together, and I still see us all the way we were before my family died and Murds got married and the whole world changed. I need to remember it that way. And I need to leave before something else leaves me.

CHAPTER TWENTY-NINE
DECEMBER 18, 1960

SCHOOL LET OUT FOR CHRISTMAS ON FRIDAY. OF COURSE, I wasn't there. Today is Sunday, and I haven't done much since last Monday except walk around trying real hard not to sleep so the dreams don't come. I check the post office every day to see if the insurance company sent my parents' beneficiary check. Still no sign of it, which is frustrating. This is an exceptionally boring town to be killing time in. Another monument ramming is long overdue if you ask me.

I did go to Greencastle Hospital a few times to see Denise, but she was sleeping. Her face and head were wrapped in so many bandages I couldn't even see her. I left her a card from Ollie and me and a little plaster cat I picked up in the gift shop.

At dinner, I had the big talk with Ollie about me leaving. She was real sad, but she said it was important for me to see the world, and she hoped I'd consider finishing school after I travel around some. I didn't mention that I just don't see any need to.

"Where do you plan to go, darlins?" she asked.

"I've pretty much decided to go to Mississippi and help out with some of the freedom marches Denise and Robert talked about."

"Oh, what a good idea! Maybe when you get settled

somewhere, I can come down and march, too. I want to do my part."

"That would be great!" I said with genuine enthusiasm.

"Weed, do you think you could at least wait until after Christmas day to leave? I've gotten so used to having you here."

"You won't be alone, Ols. Bart Searles is free, so he can come around this year."

"Even Bart can't replace you and all the fun we've had. Remember when I told you how leaving your daddy with my mother was one of the four saddest days of my life? Can you guess what the other three were?"

"The day Caleb died had to be one of them."

"Yes, a part of me died that day, too."

"Fortunately, you have enough life for two people, Ols," I smiled. "The third day had to be when my dad got killed," I surmised, "and the fourth day... well I'm not sure—"

"It hasn't happened yet," she said sadly. "It will be the day you leave."

When I looked at her sweet, round face, I had a strong urge to hug her, so that's exactly what I did. I admit, I liked the feeling of those big floppy arms wrapped around me. It was a nice moment.

A minute later, the doorbell rang, so Ols retreated into the hall to answer. She ushered in a saleslady who was gussied up like a hooker-on-hooch. It came as no surprise to me that Miss Violet Laudig was peddling cosmetics. Apparently she had failed to relieve her corpulent self before her trip from Greencastle, a fact not difficult to deduce from the moment her beefy buttocks suctioned themselves to the kitchen chair.

Violet began her presentation by opening a bag of makeup products. When Ollie asked in her whispery Jackie Kennedy party voice if she had a lipstick similar to her old favorite, 'Cherries In The Snow,' Violet offered up a concoction called 'Strawberry Explosion.'

"What other fruits are in season?" I asked just to be clever.

Ollie laughed heartily and shot back with, "Do you carry 'Pardon My Papayas'?" That sent Violet into peals of laughter, which was the beginning of a complete olfactory assault.

I don't mean to be sophomoric in my description of the events, but Violet started tooting like a one-woman symphony, and she wasn't even embarrassed! An apparent hearing problem allowed her to think her gas torpedoes were silent. As she leaned forward to test her wares on the compliant Ollie-Kennedy-Clapper, Violet let a killer one rip. Ollie didn't even bat an eye... but mine were rolled all the way back in my head. (I think with all the attention she was receiving, Ollie had left reality and entered Jackie Kennedy's world where salesladies don't expel deadly gas.)

Ollie simply lifted her pinky finger and pasted on more bright lipstick. She nearly curtsied before getting up to pour tea and serve vanilla wafer "biscuits"—a tactical error on Ollie's part because Violet didn't need anything else in her septic system.

Violet was still chewing when she let out a series of blasts that skipped across the vinyl chair like rats scurrying through a drainpipe. I was surprised the toxic vapors didn't detonate the stove. Ollie, the First Lady of Nonchalance, sat there patting her bouffant, completely unfazed.

When Ollie *finally* caught on, she cleverly requested a perfume demonstration. As Violet bent to retrieve her wares, she raised her evil haunches in my direction. Her lower region produced such a woeful sound, anyone within fifty yards would assume a moose had detoured up her intestinal track and was sending out an SOS.

What beats all is that those two old gals acted as

though nothing was out of the ordinary! You know those carnival games where you throw balls at the eternal smile of a painted clown That was Ollie. And Violet was smiling like an insane person, probably from gastric relief.

I was stupefied, but not nearly as much as I was when Violet whipped into her finale. It was masterful the way she actually covered the musical scales by shifting back and forth on the vinyl chair. It was truly symphonic. I'm surprised the vinyl didn't melt. I had to retreat before I lost consciousness, so I left jolly Ollie to enjoy her guest, as only a great lady like Ollie could.

After I got outside, I decided to head over to Janine's to give her the centerpiece I had made for her. It seemed wise to smooth things over before Christmas. And truthfully, I wanted her to remember me as a decent guy.

I've spent some time thinking about my night of carnal pleasure with Janine. I know Janine was no virgin when we went all the way. She probably even invented sex. However, despite her advanced training, I wouldn't want her to think she gave herself to someone unworthy of her considerable talents.

Janine seemed very surprised to see me at her door. Her parents were in the basement, probably getting sloshed. Jimmy Dale had just left because His Royalness is in basketball training and needed to hit the sack early.

When Janine saw the centerpiece, she flipped out. I had even glued a Santa and some tiny elves on it for her brother Timmy because I figured the loony little squirt might get a kick out of it. I also brought along a Roy Rogers gun for him. I suggested he shoot his fly foes off the wall of his corral because it would beat breathing in all those insecticide fumes that were impeding his development.

After Timmy 'shot' his way to bed, Janine and I sidestepped our way through some uncomfortable moments. She confessed Jimmy Dale didn't know about the evening we got carried away. She seemed embarrassed. In an effort to reassure her, I said I was sorry things had turned out so bad, and that it was probably all my fault because I'm new here and don't know prairie etiquette.

Janine was *very* quick to agree. She allowed me to beat myself up until I was just short of hanging myself by the neck from the curtain rod for her entertainment. After I promised I wasn't about to shoot off my mouth to JD about what we did, things got better. For about five minutes.

Everything was going real smooth until Janine confessed she really wasn't in love with Jimmy Dale and that she always wanted to go steady with me. She went on about how I must like her, too, because I had gone to all the effort to make her such a nice centerpiece. When she concluded by asking me if I wanted to make out after her parents went to bed, I knew I was in trouble.

Don't get me wrong, it was tempting, but I know the term "emotional release" with Janine is a contradiction. She takes even the slightest thing as a rejection. If my johnson were to fall off during a romp on the sofa, she'd consider the event a personal affront and beat me over the head with it. Knowing I'd have to be careful in handling the ongoing negotiations, I had a back-up plan ready.

"Let's go ice-skating," I blurted.

My suggestion wasn't completely random. Russ had called me earlier to harass me about ditching and to inform me that a group of locals would be skating out on the lake after dark. I had begged off, explaining how I haven't been able to skate since I got hurt, but Russ assured me it was more of a party than anything else. I figured Janine wouldn't want to miss it, and to my relief, I was right. After she threw on some warm

GWEN BANTA

clothes, we both piled into her car and headed to the skating party.

By the time we got there, the fire was blazing, and quite a few people were out on the ice. It was a great sight. The trees stood out against the clear night, and the ice was so shiny it looked wet.

As we pulled into the clearing between the pines, I spotted Russ sliding across the ice in his shoes. Norma Marie was skating circles around him, and there were dragon-puffs of vapor coming from their mouths. They skated over as soon as they saw us. "Hey man!" Russ called."Glad you changed your mind. I wish you'd been here sooner. You missed some of my best moves."

"Yeah, I can tell," I grinned as I checked out the holes in the knees of his pants. "Nice work. Hi, Norma Marie."

"Hey, there," she said cheerfully. "Where have you been hiding yourself, Weed? Have you been up to see Denise?"

"Yes, but she was asleep and didn't know I was there."

"Well, you'll be happy to hear the latest scoop," Russ interjected. "Not too long ago my father got a call from the sheriff who told him a car was involved in a crash down around Madison on the same night Denise and Robert were run off the road. There were three guys, and the driver was drunk and speeding like a maniac. The sheriff said the car went under a semi and was crushed. The motel owner confirmed the car matched the description of the car that chased Denise. Everyone in the car was killed."

"Well, that's tragic, but I can't say I'm overly sorry," I admitted. And that won't give Denise her face back. Did your dad talk to the Lions Club about starting a fund for her plastic surgery?"

"Yeah, but it's a no-go. I'm not sure why."

"I think I know why," I said, shaking my head.

"It may not be what you're thinking, Weed," Norma Marie piped up. "There are good folks here. Really. No town is all bad, here or elsewhere."

"Yeah," Russ agreed, "In spite of the rumors I've heard, I'm sure that not every tourist who visits New York ends up in a trunk in New Jersey."

I had to laugh. Even Janine cracked a smile.

"Anyway, no need to worry," Norma Marie smiled. "Russ's dad and mine and some other families are going to pay her medical expenses themselves."

"That's great," I nodded. I knew the news would thrill Jessie. And it made me feel a lot better about my own species.

Norma Marie gestured toward the campfire. "You guys better grab some hot dogs before they're gone," she urged.

That sounded darn good to me. I knew Janine wouldn't want to make out as long as there was food in my pie-hole. While we roasted dogs and marshmallows, we all sat around talking. I was having a real good time until I heard a sudden, ghastly noise that made me gag on my wiener.

Out of the blue, the sound of demonic chopper blades cut through the night air. The hair stood up on my neck when lights suddenly appeared over the lake as if to signal the End of Days.

The plane dipped low and held at a steady pace as it headed directly toward where we were gathered. Everyone grew silent. When the chopper got closer, Norma Marie was the first to speak up. "Should we take cover?" she asked. Her voice was so calm it sounded eerie; it was as if she had already accepted her cursed fate at the hands of Barley Edinburgh.

My feet couldn't move. No place was any safer than the next out there in the open. I had a brief thought about last rites just to cover myself, but I was sure if there were any priests around, they were hanging themselves with their rosary beads.

As the chopper circled the lake, we were frozen in place, staring up at the sky. Barley came in even lower on his next pass, kicking up an icy breeze. While the chopper hovered, I saw Barley's leg hanging out of the craft. I feared Barley had dozed off again and was about to do a nosedive. Or maybe he had wisely decided to jump out of his own way.

We were all surprised when a slew of small objects suddenly rained down from the plane. The more sensible skaters hit the deck. (It seems the school air raid drills had achieved a lingering effect.) As the chopper picked up altitude once more and flew toward the tree line, most of the skaters remained immobilized. Then one by one we all gradually took on life and moved in to check out the objects.

"What are they?" someone yelled from land.

"Bags of potato chips!" one of the skaters laughed, "and Hershey bars!"

While the girls ran out to help gather up the food, Russ and I sat down by the fire, keeping our gaze riveted on Barley. He barely cleared the trees before disappearing into the dark. Even the trees ducked.

As Norma Marie and Janine returned with their hands full of Barley-rations, I scratched my head in bafflement. "Doesn't anyone except me know that guy shouldn't be allowed in a plane?"

"Oh sure," Russ grinned. "Old man Haley is suing Barley because he flies so low over Haley's pastures his cows are having nervous breakdowns. Haley found two of his cows belly-up after a Barley fly-by."

"Probably suicide," I mumbled. "Thank God Barley's condition isn't contagious."

With that, Norma Marie jumped up and started whacking her ear in a perfect imitation of Barley. We were all laughing hysterically when Janine whispered to me that she wanted to sit in the car where we could talk alone. I told her I was having a good time and suggested we stick around with the others awhile, but she kept pulling my sleeve to get me to go.

"Can you please wait just a few minutes?" I pleaded.

Janine stood up and yanked my arm again. "C'mon, Weed," she whined in one of those annoying voices which is supposed to be cute but really sounds stupid. I truly was embarrassed for her. I politely told her that if she couldn't wait, to go on, and I'd be happy to catch a ride back with Russ.

I'm not sure I even have the words to explain what happened next. As I turned to speak to Russ, there was a sharp kick in my ribs. When I twisted around, Janine was standing directly over me. There was a dark look on her face, and her eyes were slits. Janine remained extremely still, but her breath was coming hard and fast. Before I could respond, she clenched her hand into a fist and hit me in the chest as hard as she could. Everyone else was as shocked as I was. As I struggled to catch my breath, she let out a strange sound. It was like a yell that got caught in her throat.

"Who are you to ignore me, Weed Clapper?" she screamed. "You think you're so dang important, don't you? You think you're a big-city big shot. But I know all about you. Did you believe I'd ever really be interested in a crazy freak like you? I know what happened back in Scranton. When I was working in the principal's office, I read your transfer records."

All at once I sensed a danger big enough to swallow me whole. I felt myself falling into a black pit. Falling and falling and falling. "Easy, Janine," I said, easing my voice out as calmly as I could. I held up my hand in a vain attempt to stop the train I could see heading straight towards me. "Don't do this Janine. Please don't do this."

But Janine was out of control, and she wanted to

hurt me. The expression on her face told me nothing was going to stop her. "Tell them!" she taunted. "Tell them about the hospital you were in and why you were there. You never had a track injury, you cripple! You lied!" She yelled to keep the tears from coming. I know that's why because I yelled back for the same reason.

"Stop it," I shouted. "You better shut your mouth, Janine!"

"Why? Don't you want everyone to know you were sent to a mental hospital after your family got killed?" Her words reverberated through the cold night air like a death rattle.

When Russ grabbed her arm to try to head off her attack, Janine shoved him as hard as she could. "Get your hands off me, Russ Kinney!" she ordered as she came right back at me. I tried to walk away, but she wouldn't step aside. By now everyone was watching. Many of the skaters had gathered near the bank to see what the shouting was about. Then Janine moved in closer.

"Tell them what you did," Janine persisted. "Tell them how you climbed to the top of a building."

"No, Janine," I pleaded, "no!"

"Tell them, Weed! Tell them how you jumped off! That's why you limp. You crushed your legs and smashed your face. And now you're supposed to take medication because you're so unstable." She turned to face Russ. "Did you know that Russ? Did you know your 'cool' friend is a mental case?"

"Don't do this, Janine!" I cried. No matter which way I turned, I couldn't get away from her voice. It was cutting the night into shreds. The eyes all around me were staring, and I was trapped like an injured animal. "Get me out of here, Russ," I rasped.

As Russ fumbled in his pocket for his keys, all my mind could focus on was Janine's stabbing voice. "Weed was in a hospital for nine months," she announced. "A booby hatch. He wouldn't speak to anyone. He just sat in a corner and stared out the window. And he attacked a doctor who tried to get him to talk about the accident. Then the lunatic escaped. Tell them where you went, Weed," she taunted.

I was so humiliated I began to turn in circles. There was a terrible noise in my ears. It was a train, and it was getting louder and louder. I turned to Janine and moved in on her to block the sound pouring out of her mouth.

Russ stepped between us. "Shut up Janine!" he warned. "Leave him alone. You're the one who's acting nuts!"

"Don't you dare put me in the same category as Weed Clapper!" she snapped. "He's insane!"

"Janine," I pleaded, "don't do this. You don't know what you're saying. Please stop." I held out my hands in a prayer-like gesture, which was senseless because there was no God there to help me. "Please," I begged again.

"No! These kids all look up to you because you act so mature, but they don't know what you're really like. Tell them what you did the night you escaped from the booby hatch, Weed. I'm sure they'd love to hear that."

"Shut up! Shut the hell up!"

Janine turned her back to me, and only Russ stood between us as she landed her final blow. "It says in his file that Weed went to the cemetery and dug his little brother up. They found him sleeping on top of his brother the next morning, right there in the graveyard. And his brother had been dead for nine months!"

My mind snapped. In one move I shoved Russ aside and tackled Janine. I sat on her back and shoved her face into the snow until I couldn't hear her voice anymore. I had to shut her up. The others struggled to pull me off her, but I held her down with all my strength, pressing her face into the snow to suck up the sound and stop the onslaught.

"You're suffocating her!" a voice screamed. I didn't care. I had to make Janine stop. It took several people to pull me off her, but my hands held on. The memory of that night with Leland was all I could see in my mind as my fingers grasped her neck. I wanted to crush her along with the gruesome memories. I needed to block out her bone-scraping voice. But the noises I heard were now coming out of me. I was sobbing so hard I couldn't control myself.

Russ pried my hands off her while the other guys held me down. After Janine got up and brushed the snow out of her mouth and eyes, she looked down at me with more hatred than I've ever felt in my life. When I saw the large rock she had picked up, I silently begged her to kill me. Unfortunately, Norma Marie wrenched the rock from her hand before Janine could put me out of my misery.

Janine got in one last shot before she stalked off. "Ollie was the only relative who would take him in, he's so crazy."

I was in a sort of daze when I grabbed the keys from Russ, and then jumped into his truck and took off. I don't remember much after that beyond the deafening noise in my ears that would not let up.

I don't know what I'm going to do now. There's no hole big enough to crawl into. I don't want to see anyone from here ever again for as long as I live. Never have I felt so embarrassed and ashamed. I just want everyone to leave me alone and let me disappear.

CHAPTER THIRTY
DECEMBER 20, 1960

AFTER THE HORRIBLE INCIDENT AT THE LAKE, I WAS UP ALL night. Norma Marie and Russ arrived in the morning to pick up his truck and check up on me, but I didn't go downstairs. I tossed the keys out my bedroom door to Ollie and said I was too sick to get up.

After they left, I sat in the closet a long time until I had to get up and take a handful of painkillers for my leg. I don't know how many I took—half a bottle, I think. Now I'm having difficulty focusing. I passed out for some time, but then I rallied long enough to finish packing the last of my belongings.

While emptying my closet, I discovered I still had Laura's Walt Whitman book. Out of curiosity, I read the poem she said reminded her of me, "I Sing the Body Electric." One of the lines really jumped off the page at me: *If life and the soul are sacred, the human body is sacred...*

It never dawned on me until I read the poem that Laura also knows how I got injured, because she read my school file, too. It seems my transfer records have been circulated more than the Gutenberg Bible. Maybe her reference to Whitman was an effort to assure me that even bodies of gimps like me are whole and good. I admire Whitman's optimism... but he's a wishful idiot.

Just as I was closing the book, I spotted an

inscription written to Laura. It was on the back leaf, which is why I had never noticed it before. The discovery was startling, and it filled me with guilt and sadness:

To Laura Josephine Saslow-

Joey, I love you with words I cannot express. I will come back for you, and we'll never have to hide our love again. Wait for me, Joey. Be mine forever?

Your ever-adoring
Andy Johnson, USMC 12/25/50

I was dumbfounded. Finally, it all made sense. Joey Burris was in love with Laura, but she was in love with his best friend, Andy Johnson. Andy and Laura, "Joey," probably decided to keep their love a secret until he returned from the war. However, Andy was permanently injured, and Joe Burris never returned. The Joey who Andy keeps calling for is Laura. Now I understand their bond. And I understand the pain Laura has been hiding for so long.

I had some things I needed to say to Laura, so I decided to stop by her house before leaving town. I wasn't even sure I could make it that far. My leg can no longer support me very well, and it's oozing constantly. I wrapped it again and poured peroxide all over it, but I can't stand to look at it anymore. I took a bunch more painkillers to numb it enough to get me to Laura's house.

It seemed to take hours to reach her house because I had to sit down in the snow so many times along the way. When I finally made it, I propped myself against the door jamb and knocked. After Laura took one look at me, she pulled me inside. There was no anger in her voice, and I could tell she didn't hate me. She's always so full of love. I really wish I could be that way.

"Are you okay, Weed?" she asked. "What's wrong? You look terrible."

"I haven't had much sleep. I came to give you your book back and tell you I'm leaving town." Laura was very quiet. While waiting for her to speak, I had to struggle to stay upright. I got dizzy just trying to focus.

"I heard what happened out at the lake," she whispered. "I'm so sorry, Weed."

I couldn't believe how fast word spreads in a one-horse town. In spite of my stupor, or maybe because of it, I started ranting like the lunatic Queen Janine says I am. "Oh, was my mishap the subject of the 'Lizzie Borden Television Hour,' Laura? I hope they used the shot of me in a straitjacket with the flag of Indiana flying proudly out of my farter!"

Laura tried to shush me, but I was just winding up. "Do you think Jack Kennedy will mention me in his inaugural address next month? *My foul Americans, we need to address the Weed Clapper threat to the future of America. In the meantime, lock your doors and keep your innocent children inside.*"

"Hush. I didn't mean to upset you, Weed."

"Why should I be upset?" I interrupted. "Hitchcock is offering me tons of money for my life story: *Lunatic on a Slab*. It'll be filmed at a morgue. That way they don't have to pay the extras."

"That's enough, Weed, you're rambling. Quiet!" Laura ordered as she pulled me inside and shoved me down onto the couch. "Norma Marie called me because she was extremely upset."

"Norma Marie?"

"She's my cousin."

"Your cousin? Holy mackerel, how many times did the same gene split to create this one-horse town? And I have to ask, what happens when the one horse dies in a one-horse town? Does the town evaporate?" I tried to stand up, but my body wasn't moving as well as my mouth was.

"Weed, lie back and put your legs up. And for God's sake, stop your incessant talking."

"'For God's sake'? Why should I do anything for *His* sake, Laura? God never does anything for *my* sake. He hates me. I'll probably get coal in my stocking for Christmas."

"I think you're confusing God with Santa."

I pondered that one for as long as my attention span would allow. One second later I was done. "Same difference. They're both sadistic impostors."

"Don't you find it ironic that you're being persecuted by a God whom you don't think exists?"

"Good point, Watson," I mumbled. "You're smarter than a silk suit."

Laura was smiling. I couldn't really see her smile through my haze, but I felt it. I can always feel her smiles.

"Now while you're busy wallowing in self-pity," she said, "I'm going to make us some cocoa."

"Don't bother. I have to get over to Bart Searles's house to pick up a car he's selling me. Tonight, I'm riding on to another campsite. Me and my horse, Electroshock... he's a real live wire." I laughed at my cleverness for what felt like six weeks.

"You've had more than a few pain pills, haven't you, Weed? Where are you going anyway?"

"It doesn't matter anymore."

"It matters to me. When will I see you again?"

"You won't."

Laura sat down next to me. The sofa gave slightly, causing me to moan aloud. When I looked at her, she appeared to be floating. "You can't go anywhere like this," she said. "Stay awhile. You can leave when you feel better."

I was too tired to keep ranting. "Okay. Maybe for a short while, '*Joey*,'" I nodded.

Laura suddenly became very still. "I see you finally read the inscription," she said quietly.

"Why didn't you just tell me?"

"Because when you first told me what Andy said, I wasn't sure he was referring to me... and because it still hurts so much."

"I'm sorry, Laura. But if you were so in love with Andy before he went to Korea, then what happened when he returned? Was he just too unbearable to accept because he's a freak like I am? It seems we're both just gimps to be discarded on the cripple-heap." I closed my eyes and let my head, which was too heavy to carry any longer, fall back onto the pillow.

Suddenly Laura jerked me by the shirt until I was sitting back up again. "Look at me, Weed Clapper!" she demanded. I tried, but I was so woozy I couldn't really see her clearly. "If you were in any better shape, I'd slap you for that," she snapped.

"Go ahead. I deserve it. Please do it."

"You're too medicated to feel it." She let me fall back onto the couch before she continued. "I waited for Andy, Weed. I would have waited forever. But when he returned, *he* didn't want *me*. He ran whenever I tried to go near him. He's never had anything to do with me or with anyone else since he got back. Each time I tried to see him it upset him so much I finally gave up. I thought it was best to leave him alone. Then *you*, a total stranger, treated him as if he were whole. That's more than anyone else around here ever does. They only see the carcass, but you saw a war hero. And you had respect and empathy. I'm convinced that's what gave him the courage to finally come near me."

"Well why doesn't he come inside if he wants to see you?"

"His parents told me that the part of his brain that

was damaged controls his social responses. He can't allow himself to be close to anyone. But his memory knows what we once were to each other, Weed."

"And that's why you did what you did the other night... allowed him to look at you?"

Laura sat up straight and proud, a reaction I wasn't expecting. "I'm not ashamed, Weed. It wasn't charity or pity as you concluded. I was in love with Andy Johnson from the time I was in junior high school. We were so close, but he never actually dated me because I was younger. Then one day during his senior year, we were walking home together as we had so many times before. When he told me he was going to Korea, I became very upset. I grabbed him and held him as tightly as I could. Then he kissed me for a very long time."

"He's no fool," I smiled.

"Thank you. We both knew then and there that we would be together forever...or at least we thought so. Everyone expected him to marry Jeannie Beth, but before he left, he told her it was over. Then he came to me and brought me the collection of poems by Walt Whitman. And he asked me if I'd marry him when he came home.

"When he went to Korea, I missed him so much I couldn't stand it. I wrote him every day, even long after he stopped responding. No one ever knew about our relationship, but I've never felt that kind of love for anyone."

"Not even Rick?"

Laura shook her head. "Rick was just a substitute after being alone for so long. I wanted to love someone. Andy and I never even made love, Weed. We had decided to wait until he came home, but a different Andy came back. The other night I undressed for him just to let him know that no matter how much our lives have changed, I still think of him as a man. Even if he can't be one to me. It wasn't out of pity, it was out of respect."

"I'm sorry for judging you, Laura. I didn't understand."

"I know. I also know that Andy's injuries scare you. Yes, they do, Weed. Every time you look at Andy, you're repulsed. And your biggest fear is that others will see you and have the same reaction."

"Like Janine does?"

"She didn't always react that way. She wanted to date you, remember? It's you who sees yourself as damaged, and others see us the way we see ourselves. You let Janine see your weak spot, and when she got angry, she went after it."

"I tried to treat Andy as if he was normal, Laura," I protested, "but he's not."

"No, he's not normal. He's different. But he's not less of a person than you or me. He's injured, that's all. I'm injured, too. Two lives were altered irreparably when he stepped on that land mine, not just Andy's. And you've been injured, too. We're all the same."

Laura reached out and took my hand, and I could feel the hole inside me start to close. "Then you don't see me as a twisted freak?" I asked.

"I don't see you as anything but a person I deeply care about. And I can't bear to think about what you've been through." There was so much sorrow in her voice I wondered how I had ever doubted her in the first place.

"You're too good to be going through all this turmoil with me," I said. "I'm so sorry you lost Andy."

"So am I. And now look at you. I know you're in pain and you haven't been getting any help. How many damn times do I have to go through this with someone I care about so much?"

"I can't believe you still care after all the nasty things I said."

"Oh, Weed, I ignore most of the things you say," she

teased. Laura shoved my damp hair back off my forehead. "I need you in my life," she said quietly. "You are more to me than just another student. You touch my soul."

"You didn't just take pity on me?"

"No, I felt sad for you. There's a difference."

"Then you know about the things I did back in Scranton?"

"Yes. That's why I suggested the journal the first day of class. I knew you went nine months without talking. I didn't want you to hold all that inside you. I know what you did after you were told about your parents' accident, how you—" Laura stopped to clear her throat.

"You can say it. I jumped off a three-story building and splattered myself all over the parking lot like a watermelon."

Laura shuddered. Suddenly she put her head on my chest and wrapped her arms around me. I could smell her hair. And I could feel her breath against my neck. We were so close I finally felt calm inside. And for the first time, I wanted to talk about that night I jumped. I wanted her to know exactly what happened. It was important to me that she understood.

"After the police came to the house to tell me about the accident, I didn't sleep. Not for four days. I just walked and walked until I couldn't walk anymore. The day of the funeral I overhead Liam's father say that Leland had been decapitated and that my mother had suffered terribly. No matter where I went, the pain kept following me. I couldn't shake those awful images of my mother screaming. Or the images of my father's body with no dad inside. But the worst image was the one of my brother with no head.

"The night I jumped, I had taken too many pills, Laura. I just wanted the pain to stop. I remembered how I had always promised Leland I'd take him flying. The little guy was afraid of heights, so I assured him I'd be right there with him. I described how we would fly together the way birds do and look down on the whole country and stop whenever we saw something special, like a circus or a roller coaster or an ice cream truck. I had *promised*, Laura.

"I couldn't bear it, so I just started running. But no matter where I ran, all I could see was my brother's head. I kept on running. Somehow, I found myself on top of Mr. Goldberg's warehouse. I shouted to Leland that he was flying to Heaven to see God, and that his head was just fine.

"That's when I realized I'd broken my promise to my brother. He was flying alone, and I knew he'd be scared. I yelled, 'Don't be afraid, little pal, you can do it. Just stay with Mom and Dad.' But I thought I heard him crying. The cries seemed so real. I couldn't let him go alone... not without me.

"I loved him so much, Laura. Leland and Mom and Dad were the only things in this world I would have died for. And when you no longer have anything you'd die for, then you don't have anything you can live for. I knew Mom and Dad had each other, but I just couldn't let Leland go. 'I'm right here beside you, little buddy!' I yelled, but I wasn't sure if my words were reaching him. I was frantic because I needed to reach Leland. I just had to go after him..so I jumped off the building.

"When I woke up, I was in a nuthouse. They wouldn't let anyone visit me, so I stopped talking altogether. Besides, there was nothing worth saying. Everything was dead to me.

"One doctor used to yell in my face, trying to provoke some earth-moving breakthrough. He carried on that way for months. Finally, I had my own kind of breakthrough... I hit him in the face and broke his nose. I knew I had to get out of there before I killed someone. That's why I decided to leave that night."

"You went to the cemetery?"

GWEN BANTA

"Yes," I winced, "but I'm not nuts, Laura. Honest to God, I'm not. I understood my parents and Leland were dead. But I remembered Leland was always cold. The caskets were closed at the funeral, so I didn't get to see how warm they dressed him. And while I was in the hospital, I had dreamed he was lying in his casket with his teeth chattering. That's why I tried to dig him up.

"I took him some blankets from the hospital to cover him. I knew he couldn't actually feel the cold and that he wasn't really there in that little body. I just had to cover him because I couldn't bear the thought of him down in that dark damp ground. I had always looked out for him, but I had failed to even keep him alive. The least I could do was keep him warm. It was symbolic.

"See, I didn't really do it for him. I always knew I wasn't doing it for him. I'm not crazy like they thought. I did it for me. So I could stop worrying. For *me*, Laura!

"I wanted to lie on top of Leland's coffin just because I never got to hug him good-bye," I explained. "When a person doesn't have the chance to say good-bye, the pain never goes away, Laura. You can't accept the death part. You can never get past imagining them lying there in their human forms with human needs and feelings. All I wanted is just for Leland to be warm IN MY MIND, but no one understood that. I needed to say good-bye.

"When they found me, they dragged me away in some sort of a medieval straitjacket. They kept me until Ollie sent for me. But I'm not insane, Laura," I cried. "Please tell me I'm not crazy."

"Shhh, you're not crazy, Weed. You're just carrying around too much hurt for one person to handle alone. Shhh," she soothed as she slipped a pillow under my head and made me lie back down. I was so dizzy I was sick. I don't remember her leaving the room, but shortly afterward I felt a cool cloth on my head.

"Laura," I whispered, "did my transfer records say I broke open the coffin?"

"Never mind, Weed. It doesn't matter."

"It matters to me! That's really sick. And in my shape, how would I be able to do that anyway? I dug for hours, and I barely uncovered a corner of his casket. My leg had pins in it, one foot was in a cast, my teeth were broken, and my nose was a blob."

"Well... I have always heard crazy people have superhuman strength," Laura said.

At that, my eyes flew open. Thank God Laura was smiling. It's odd how a gentle tease can make you believe someone else understands why you acted irrationally. I was relieved because I was too darn tired to keep explaining.

Before I could thank Laura for listening, I felt my body start to float off the sofa. I grasped her hand for safety, and then I got a bone-rattling chill.

"Drink some hot cocoa," Laura urged. "Your clothes are sopping wet, Weed. And you're burning up with fever. Come with me. You're taking those clothes off."

She slipped her arms under mine while I got to my feet. I was so wobbly the room became a reflection in a fun house mirror. "Laura is the most beautiful name I've ever heard," I mumbled as I struggled for balance.

"And Weed is the most peculiar name I've ever heard," she said as she led me to the bedroom.

"I think I took too many painkillers."

"I'd say so. Are you in pain now?"

"Somewhere. But I hurt less when I'm with you."

When she sat me down on her bed, I tried to take in my surroundings. I had never been in her room, but I felt comfortable, because in my mind I had been there a million times before. There were stacks of books and a big over-stuffed chair with a stuffed bear leaning against a pillow. Everything looked soft, like Laura.

"That's nice," I said.

"What, Weed?"

For a moment, I thought the bear was talking. "He's damn clever," I mumbled. "But one more word out of him and he gets it between the eyes."

"Who?"

"That short hairy person with the bow tie."

"Weed, you're making me nervous. You're very sick."

I tried to shrug, but even that was an effort. When she put a robe on the bed next to me, I took her hand. "Laura, I have to know something. When you look at me, do you see a boy?"

"No, Weed. At times I see the boy, but most of the time I see a man."

I forced my eyes open because I needed so much to see her. I leaned into her as she brushed the hair off my forehead. "Talk to me," I pleaded.

"I see a wonderful man," she said, "... someone I don't want to lose. Someone who touches me in a way no man has since Andy. But I also see someone who is my student. Now take off your clothes and get into my robe." She draped a robe over my shoulders and waited.

"Laura, I look terrible in pink."

"You look terrible, period. Then take off your clothes and get under the covers." She turned around and walked out.

I did as she said, but it was a struggle. My leg bandages were stuck to the inside of my jeans, so it hurt like hell to pull my pants off. After I was under the covers, Laura knocked and came in.

"Weed, I heard you moaning. I know you're in pain. Please let me take you to the doctor."

"No, Laura, no more doctors!" I sat up and tried to get back out of bed, but my weight had settled in all the wrong places.

"Weed—"

"Promise me, Laura, or I'm leaving right now."

"Okay, okay, you have my word."

"Promise?"

"I promise, Weed, now please lie back down."

Lying down was easier than trying to sit up, so I did as she said. "I just want you to sit here with me awhile," I told her. "I'm feeling very strange."

After Laura sat down and felt my forehead again, I took her hand. "Laura, I'm not your student anymore. I dropped out."

"Weed, I did recently hear you withdrew. Listen, your education is—"

"I'm not talking about my education," I interrupted. "I'm saying you have no obligation to be professional just because you were once my teacher. That's over. I'm now just another guy. What time is it anyway?"

"It's 12:39 A.M. Why?"

"Because today is my eighteenth birthday. Seeing you one last time was my present to myself."

"Happy Birthday, Weed!" she said.

"I'm officially a man, li'l lady." I drawled in a failed attempt at a John Wayne voice. "And I'm damn lovable, too, wouldn't you say? Well, for someone who's semi-conscious."

"Yes, I'd have to say that," she laughed. Her smile was so soft my heart felt as if she were holding it in her hand. I suddenly remembered something my dad once told me: Life is wonderful if you only let it break your heart a little bit at a time. I had finally found the 'wonderful' part.

When Laura leaned in to kiss me on the cheek, I took her face in my hands. She looked so perfect and delicate, and so incredibly beautiful. All of a sudden, my life was still, even though my heart was pounding. And my mind slowly told me what was about to happen.

I pulled Laura into me and kissed her on the mouth.

She hesitated for a moment, and then she responded. I kissed her again and again, all over her face and neck. I breathed her into me, and I tasted her skin and her hair and her ears.

It was difficult to move my fingers because they were numb and thick, but I could still feel her soft skin in my mind, and my body stopped hurting. Then Laura slowly undressed. I kept my hand on some part of her body the entire time because I couldn't bear to let go of her.

Laura lifted the covers and crawled into the bed next to me. "Wrap yourself around me so I can keep you warm, Weed," she whispered. "You're shivering."

As I pressed my body against her small frame, I willed my heavy eyes to watch her face. She smiled, and in that moment, she became part of me. Her body gave me more comfort than I have ever known. Whatever I had experienced before had only been physical, but this was so deep and pure it touched me even through my drugged darkness.

I never wanted those moments to be over. I needed to hold onto the only sense of wholeness I've felt since I lost my family. Laura was my lover, and my love, my friend, and my family. She was my body before it was damaged, and she was my heart the way it used to be. I couldn't hold my emotions in because I was too alive. I cried with the sense of relief I felt. I think she did, too. We were two injured souls clinging to each other for life. She held me until I finally fell asleep.

————

My eyes opened to a piercing light. It took me some time to remember that I was in Laura's bedroom. Strange people were standing near the bed observing me like a specimen in a jar. Then I was in an ambulance, which was making a helluva lot of noise.

Laura also was there. She stroked my face and cautioned a man I didn't know not to jostle me. I remember thinking how absurd her warning was as the ambulance bounced over roads rutted with snow and ice. The lights from the ambulance flooded the inside of the vehicle with a warm red glow, but the light was so warm it burned my skin. I tried to tell them, but no one listened. Perhaps my thoughts were simply ghosts inside my head.

We stopped in front of a hospital. I couldn't see it, but I knew it was there. "Don't take me in there!" I screamed. "Don't let them take me, Laura. I'll never get out of there!"

Laura tried to calm me, but she didn't stop them. She walked alongside me as they hauled me into an emergency room that was so bright it made me angry. I ordered the huge faces that loomed above me to get the lights out of my eyes and to close the door because it was so darn cold. But no one listened. After the faces made Laura step aside, they pulled a curtain so I couldn't see her face anymore, but I could hear her crying.

Suddenly I knew she was the one who had called the ambulance. She had betrayed me. Laura had given me her word, but apparently her word meant nothing. And that told me that I meant nothing to her either. The pain of that realization was worse than the relentless pain I could feel somewhere in my leg.

I closed my eyes and tried to think of something else. I heard loud voices and activity, but I shut it all out and went to sleep. Sleep was the only safe place, and I hoped I would never wake up again.

———

Leland stood at the foot of my bed. He was grinning, and I could see the gap in his front teeth.

"Hi, little buddy," I said.

"Hi, booger-head!" he laughed.

"Where have you been, pal?"

"I went to Mexico to get a gigantic piñata."

"Cool. What did it look like?"

"It was the hugest donkey!" Leland exclaimed. He held up his hands to show me how big it was, and he got so excited he waved his arms in every direction.

"Yeah, a donkey? Well, what did you do with it?"

"I hit it with a stick. That's what they do with piñatas, Weed. You hit it until it squishes, and all the candy falls out. And guess what else came out when I hit the donkey?"

"Gee, I dunno. A model car maybe? Or a baseball?"

"Nooo... a great big FART!"

Leland started laughing so hard he made my bed shake. I had to laugh, too, because the little guy was having such a good time. The more he laughed, the more the bed shook. But the more the bed shook, the fainter he became. He was leaving me again.

"Wait, buddy!" I yelled. "Don't go!" I called to him.

"I have to. I'm so cold, Weed," he said. Suddenly he started crying. Before I could give him my blanket, he vanished.

———

The bed continued to shake until suddenly a doctor in a white coat pried my eyes open. Some other guys in hospital coats poked me with needles like I was Leland's piñata. When they finally departed in a solemn procession, they left the curtain open a crack.

There was a sliver of bright light just beyond the curtain. Ollie stood in the light, and Bart Searles was holding her as she cried. Laura suddenly appeared next to them. She was wearing a lavender sweater, which was very vivid. It was the only color in the room. As

Laura spoke, I studied her mouth, but the sounds were coming from somewhere else. "He has advanced gangrene," her voice said from the light fixture, "and the infection is in the bone. His body rejected the wires and pins they repaired the leg with. The doctor said it's a miracle the other foot healed."

"Can't they save his leg?" Ollie's voice asked.

"No, Ollie, it has to come off. Weed's in bad shape, but they're doing everything they can. The doctors said there's no other way."

Somewhere in my head, I knew I was the Weed they were talking about, and if anyone was going to decide what to do with my body, it would be me. I wasn't going to go in pieces. Not with my leg cut off or my head decapitated or my eyeballs full of glass. I knew I couldn't exist like shell-shocked Andy with half a body. I'm not as brave as Andy. I decided to do things my own way.

———

They moved me to another room where everything looked hard, even the curtains. The voices said I needed more fluids before they could operate. I informed a crossed-eyed orderly and the world's largest nurse that I am now eighteen, and therefore, no one has the authority to give their maim-team permission to chop off my rotten leg. Again, no one heard me. It was as if my words had no sound.

When I was finally alone, I sat up. It took me some time to get my bearings, and even longer to get out of bed. It was difficult to get my balance, but I did, then I ripped the needles out of my arms and watched the fluids run onto the floor. After I located my clothes on a chair, I struggled to dress. There were thick bandages on my leg so I couldn't get my pants on. The nurse had left gauze and scissors on a bedside cart, so I cut my pants open and pushed my leg through. The effort exhausted me.

Every step I took made me dizzy. However, when I peeked through the curtain into the outer room, the bright light jolted me enough to focus. At the end of the hall, I could make out Ollie and Snarls and Laura, who were talking to the same sadists who wanted to dismember my body.

I slipped through the curtain but stayed out of view. The first thing I did was grab blankets to wrap myself in so my teeth would stop clacking together. The sound was painfully loud. My hands were like cotton, so I fumbled repeatedly.

When I spotted the exit just beyond the double doors at my end of the hall, I inched in that direction. After reaching the exit, I rested against the wall until the colors in my head stopped colliding, and then I limped out. The hospital smell walked with me into the cold night.

On the ground outside the building, there was a new snowfall that was so bright I had to squint. But it was peaceful. A ragged line marked my path as my bum leg followed my body faithfully through the snow. Once I had my bearings, I realized I was at Greencastle Hospital, the same hospital where Denise was. I know the area well, and I also know the local bus schedule.

Within minutes a bus came by. "Good-bye, Denise," I whispered up at the wall of windows just before I dragged myself onto the bus. While I fumbled inside my coat to retrieve a dollar bill, the bus driver eyed me curiously. I couldn't understand what his mouth was saying, and I couldn't be bothered to wait for change. Besides, he had two heads, and I didn't know which fellow to address.

The bus ride was terrible. It was so cold my nose hurt, and each time the bus hit a rut, my leg curled with pain. When I screamed at a face in the window, the face screamed back, so I crouched in my seat until the screams stopped. When the bus finally pulled up in front of the town monument, I somehow got out of my seat and off the lopsided bus.

"Are you okay, son?" the driver asked the back of my head. I think that's what he said. I nodded, but I was too tired to thank him for his concern.

My plan was to get my car, but suddenly I couldn't remember where Snarls lived. Or where Ollie lived. I had to sit under MacArthur's horse to think. Somewhere far away I heard my mother's voice singing "Que Sera, Sera," so I sang along with her.

I was thinking about a lot of unrelated things when I saw Laura's shell-shocked friend. By that time, I could no longer remember his name, but I didn't give a rat's ass. I was just too confused to figure it all out. He was across the street at the I.G.A. store, and I could tell by the angle of his deformed head that he was staring at me.

"Even a half-head should know that's not polite," I mumbled.

I lifted myself off the ledge of the monument and crossed the street toward the church to ditch him. But the freak followed me, and he was gaining on me because my leg held me back.

"Wait, it's, it's me. I'm Andy!" he called. His barbed-wire voice clawed my back. "I have a fire!" The words tumbled over each other as his mouth fought to form the sounds.

"Don't come near me," I yelled."Leave me alone!" My voice must not have been working any better than my leg, because the freak kept coming toward me.

Suddenly I felt snow all over my cheeks, and I was surprised to discover I was lying face down in the street. However, the footsteps closing in on me told me it was an inopportune time to rest, so I forced myself to get up and head for the church where I could be alone.

After the Masonic Lodge clock tolled twice, maybe three times, I looked back over my shoulder and saw Laura's friend again, but I was so disoriented I couldn't remember why he was following me. When he yelled at me to stop, his voice made me dizzy. Suddenly there were strangers with odd bodies and unrecognizable voices all around me. They were in the sky and in the trees and the snow. I had made it to the back of the church, but Andy was still following me. And all I wanted to do was go home. To Mom and Dad and Leland.

When I got to the staircase that leads to the second story of the church, I pulled my limbs up the steps to the upper door. It was unlocked, so I stumbled into the church balcony and locked the door behind me. I fell onto something hard, and then I had to crawl a few feet before I could get up off my knees. Below there was nothing but darkness sliced by streams of moonlight.

At one end of the balcony was a narrow spiral staircase that appeared to be an escape route. I managed to climb to the top only to discover that I was penned in, so I pushed against the wall of darkness.

The cold air hit me so hard I gasped. Eventually I realized I was on the church roof, so I crawled along the roof to a low wall that circles the bell. Below me was a peaceful village. At first, I thought it was one of those Christmas scenes in a glass ball, but then it dawned on me that I was looking down at the town square tucked away on a bright pillow of snow. The Christmas tree across from the monument looked like a star, and the Sundry Store twinkled with colored lights. As the tiny town beckoned me in the moonlight, I hoisted my body up onto the ledge for a better view. The scene below was warm and friendly, but I wasn't fooled. I knew the place was full of ghosts.

I wiped my nose, polished off the remaining pain pills in my pocket, and sat quietly. I was done talking.

Sometimes a person doesn't want to talk ever again, because they know the words will be sucked up into the silence before they're ever spoken. Just ask Andy.

———

From somewhere far away, Andy Johnson forced out more words. "Don't move, Weed!" It seemed damn ironic that for years the guy wouldn't talk, and then suddenly he wouldn't shut up. He was prowling below with a bunch of tiny, noisy people with large heads. They were all looking up and shining some very annoying lights in my face, which was just plain rude. There were so many fire trucks you would have thought it was Barley on the ledge instead of me.

After some time passed with me watching them watching me, my leg was numb and heavy. Leland had climbed up onto the ledge to tell me he was cold, too, so I took off my coat and gave it to him. He wanted me to sing a song, so I sang "I'll Be Home for Christmas." "Join in, buddy," I urged.

"I'll be ham for Christmas," he sang.

I cracked up. Then Leland got real quiet again.

———

For some reason, I remember the next moments very clearly: Laura appeared out of the moonlight. I heard her voice. She was standing behind me, but I told her not to come any closer because I didn't want her to frighten Leland.

"Weed," she whispered, "it's me, Laura."

"I didn't hear you knock."

"Very funny."

"Did you hear my impersonation of Bing Crosby? Swell, huh?"

"Excellent."

"You're supposed to say, 'I'd give it a '99,' Dick, because it has a great beat and it's easy to dance to. Well, for those with two kickers.' Did you climb up here to put in a request, Laura?"

"Yes, I'm requesting that you not lean forward and that you hold very still. May I come over there and sit by you, Weed?"

"No, Laura." I held up my hand to keep her back. "You might frighten Leland. He doesn't know you."

"You're not well, Weed," she said quietly. "You have a bad fever. And you took too many pills. I've been very worried."

"You climbed up here for me? Gee I love you, Laura."

Her smile brightened the night. "I love you, too, Weed."

"Well, don't, 'cause I'm leaving. And you've had enough pain."

"We all have. But you've made my life wonderful again."

"Then why did you betray me?"

"By calling the ambulance, is that what you mean?"

"Unless you also called the New York Yankees and the National Guard, that's exactly what I mean."

"I had to. I knew you were in serious trouble. You needed help."

"Not enough to cut off my damn leg, Laura!"

"I'm so sorry. But I want you to *live*. They can give you a new leg."

"Will they give me a new name to go with it? How 'bout 'Spin, The-Human-Weather-Vane'? How 'bout it, Laura? Huh? Would a new name make me whole again?" I stopped ranting as soon as I realized she was crying. I figured it was bad enough to have her picture me as a one-legged man; I didn't need to be a one-legged asshole. "I'm sorry," I apologized. "Please don't cry, Laura."

314

"Okay, I won't. I'm fine, Weed. I just care about you so much. And I'm terribly frightened."

"Tell me I didn't dream it, Laura. We made love, didn't we?"

"Well-- yes, Weed."

"See, I was fine! I didn't need doctors. I was great!"

"You are the most loving person I know, Weed," Laura nodded. "But you had a lot of drugs in your system, and you still do. You became delirious. When I took the bandages off your leg to change them, I could smell the infection."

"Oh God, don't tell me I stunk, or I'll jump off the ledge." As I glanced down, I almost toppled off.

"Sit still, Weed!" she gasped. "I only meant that I knew you had an infection. Please stop moving! You won't jump, will you? Please, Weed!"

"Of course not! I did that once and it hurt like hell."

"You mean you actually intended to jump that night back in Scranton... you weren't acting out of delirium?"

"Well, I'm not sure I can separate the two. I'm sorry I lied about that, Laura. I have a metaphor problem, but I'll work on it." I promised. "But now I have to take Leland flying. Honest." My words all ran together, but she seemed to understand me.

"I see. And you'll fly from here? From this ledge?"

"Yes, it's a damn good launch site for a one-legged pilot. I don't want to leave you, Laura, but I have no choice."

"I understand, Weed. But *I* won't leave *you*," she vowed. "Do you trust me enough to let me come closer?"

"I don't know."

"Why not?"

"You don't keep your promises," I groaned. By that point, my dizziness was turning to nausea.

"I made a promise I couldn't keep, Weed. That happens sometimes. We make promises with every intention of keeping them, but circumstances don't allow it. It's like when you swore to protect Leland. You did all you could, with all your human ability."

"I'm going to keep that promise now," I insisted.

When I turned away from Laura, Leland was sitting on the ledge waiting for me. He started to cry again. "Leland's afraid, Laura," I gestured, "I have to help him with his head, so he'll stop crying."

"He doesn't need his body anymore," she whispered. "His body was never important. His spirit is what you knew and loved. That's intact. Leland's flying now, the way he always wanted."

"I want to go with him," I murmured while still struggling to stay on the ledge.

"You could do that, but then you'll be leaving Ollie and me to hurt in the same way you've been hurt."

"I wouldn't want that. Maybe we should all go."

"I'm not ready, Weed. I still have hope."

"Hope for what?" I scoffed.

"For all the good things in life."

"*Good* things? Life stinks, Laura. God's a no-show!"

"You're wrong, Weed. He was always there. He was in your love for Leland. And when you made Ollie feel loved. And when you made me feel loved."

"That was the best moment of my life."

"Mine, too. I promise I won't stop you if you need to go, but I want to say one last thing, Weed. Do you remember what your mother told you? She said when life gets overwhelming, we should focus on the small things. That's why I need to hug you one more time. I'll need that to hold onto after you leave," she whispered.

I looked out at the dark night then down at the crowd of people gathered below. The church seemed to be swaying, and everyone appeared to be so far away. Except Laura. "I want to hold you one more time, too," I whispered, "but I can't get down from this ledge."

"Then I'll have to climb up there," she rasped. Laura

hesitated, and then she walked toward me, steady and determined. When she held out her hand, I pulled her up onto the bell tower wall. She never looked down; she just kept her eyes on mine while clutching the ledge.

From below, the bright lights pummeled us again. In the light, I could see her lips trembling and her face streaked with tears. Laura leaned against me and held on tightly.

"You are so beautiful," I whispered, "And maybe a little bit crazy for being up here."

As the spotlight swept over us again, I spotted a colored object on her coat collar. I had to squint to see it. It was made of paper and held in place by a safety pin. At first, I couldn't make out what it was because it was so childlike and bold. When I finally realized what I was looking at, I started to laugh. I laughed so hard we both had to hold onto the wall to keep from falling. Laura was crying, but she was laughing, too, and our voices rippled along the crisp air filling up the night.

I couldn't take my eyes off her artwork, despite my dizziness. On her makeshift paper pin, she had drawn two red cherries. Two big, beautiful red cherries just like the ones my mother used to wear on her collar—the ones my dad said helped him find God when the world got too big to handle.

"Focus," Laura whispered through trembling lips. "Focus on the small things."

I laughed until my face was wet. Through Laura's attempt to save me, I discovered what my mom really meant. When you focus on enough of the little things, like paper cherries, and music and peanut butter smiles, as well as all the love that's behind those things, then sooner or later the hope becomes bigger than the hurt. And that's enough to give a guy reason to live. Even a one-legged guy.

At that moment, in spite of my drug-induced haze, I also knew that Leland and my parents would be all right. And Andy, too. So would all the rest of us poor slobs who try to get through the day while still dragging around yesterday. Because somebody out there really does care.

It's a baffler, isn't it... that I never found God, but *He* found *me*? And it was through Laura Saslow. Of course, a wiseacre like me can't ignore the obvious metaphor: Laura's cherry saved me. As Ollie would say, isn't that a hoot-and-a-half?

EPILOGUE
FEBRUARY 4, 1961

My life is a lot different since that night on the ledge. It's good... real good. After I got my hope back and my head clear, Roy and Russ Kinney brought me down from the church belfry on a gurney. I was then airlifted to a hospital in Indianapolis by none other than Barley Edinburgh. He was more of a threat to my survival than my bum leg. After Barley nearly missed the hospital roof in his attempt to land, he came to a stop within inches of a power line. At least the old fart was awake when we landed.

The maim-team removed the lower part of my leg on December 22. There were complications due to infection and exposure, but hey, I'm here. And I'm still a great dancer. My biggest disappointment is that the docs wouldn't send my severed limb to Queen Janine to use as a doorstop. (But I *do* have a lovely fruitcake for her.)

Ollie and Bart Searles were married in the hospital chapel on New Year's Day. Ols looked like a rainbow, and Snarls played "Sixty Minute Man" on his squeezebox. At least they kept their clothes on. At the reception in my hospital room, Ollie served green cake that was a big hit.

Here's the best part: Murray came out to visit after

GWEN BANTA

Christmas, and he's still the same ol' Murds. We had a
great time hiding our fruitcake all over the orthopedic
wing. It even showed up in a bedpan or two. Murray
said Kenton is rooming with Liam O'Gara in New York
(wow, huh?). Ann-Margret dumped Liam, but Liam
swears he's relieved because she's bound to go insane
from mutant red hair dye. Oh, and I got to hear
Kenton's recording. It's so good even my stump was
dancing to it.

Russ and Norma Marie visit me all the time. Russ
carved me a small "wooden leg" that has a flask, a
comb, and a pack of Luckies attached. He presented it to
me in a vase, so I keep it on my bedside table next to my
photo of sticky-faced Leland. Even JD and Janine and
Patti Lynn have dropped by. Janine apologized for
being the antichrist, but I suspect she still carries a little
pink pitchfork in her purse.

Incidentally, folks can hardly believe Andy Johnson
was the one who went for help when I was in trouble. It
seems the demands of the situation forced him to come
out of his shell awhile. Andy still won't let anyone take
him in, but at least he's letting folks help him out more
nowadays. And he's still talking from time to time.

The doctors plan to fit me for my prosthesis as soon
as possible. That's great, because Laura and I are both
hoping to participate in the Freedom March this spring,
so I could use the extra leg. Otherwise, I would have to
do a Freedom Pivot.

Denise Williams is out of the hospital and
recuperating at home. Jessie says Denise will be having
plastic surgery this spring thanks to a collection taken
up by the locals. I plan to visit her as soon as I'm
released from this funhouse.

I almost forgot to mention an important thing: On
Christmas Eve there was a peace rally in town. Roy
Kinney spoke, and he acknowledged *me*. Laura told me
he said I was "a man with only one leg to walk on," but

that I "went the distance with my heart." I admit, I was proud of that. A man has to stand for something, no matter how many legs he has.

Ollie and Bart have planned a trip to "get their kicks on Route 66" in my Bel Air. I'll need gimp-care, so I'll be staying with Laura. Laura says if folks have a problem with it, they can write their congressman. We have a special relationship other folks may not understand. She told Ollie I brought her back to life... and she saved mine. Laura makes me whole. There's just no other way to say it.

I've accepted that my life can't ever be the way it was back in Scranton before the disaster, but just being alive feels swell again. Although I'm still stuck on the prairie, I'm happy to say that I finally broke free from the fly strip.

Weed Clapper
February 4, 1961

Dear reader,

We hope you enjoyed reading *The Remarkable Journey of Weed Clapper*. Please take a moment to leave a review, even if it's a short one. Your opinion is important to us.

Discover more books by Gwen Banta at https://www.nextchapter.pub/authors/gwen-banta

Want to know when one of our books is free or discounted? Join the newsletter at http://eepurl.com/bqqB3H

Best regards,
Gwen Banta and the Next Chapter Team

ACKNOWLEDGMENTS

The author wishes to thank Next Chapter Publishing for their belief in the merits of this book. It's a pleasure to take this journey with such a professional and committed support team. I will be forever grateful.

My journey into literature started with Elaine Scorsolini Tarr, who gave me the love of language and taught me that the written word would allow me to travel anywhere. She was right, and my journey has been exciting.

These characters are composites of folks I have met along the way, the people who comprise the fabric of my life. You probably know who you are. To mention a few: Millie, you were one special Jolly Ollie; Cotton and Leland, I remember so much; Donny and Buzzy, I am so thankful you survived; Beanie, you may be gone, but you still make me laugh; and Brian and Liam, you both are the heart of Weed. Thank you all for your light.

I had a great team throughout this adventure: Joanne Hoffman, my trusted attorney; Jeff Lester, who always believed in my book; and Dr. Dmitry Arbuck, whose encouragement made miracles happen. I would also like to thank Paul Connors, Bernie Bush, Lori Patterson and Jan Pastras, who have continued to encourage me and read my all drafts, probably for longer than they care to remember.

Special acknowledgment goes to my beloved friend Ann Connors, who typed, edited, and hung in there with me for so long. You and the P's are dearly missed, Annie.

It was Sophie and Buddy who made sure I always had company throughout this "birth of a notion." And it was a higher power who first gave me that notion. I am grateful and humbled.

I hope it goes without saying that I have endless gratitude for my siblings, Lisa, Brian, and Laurie, as well as for my precious family, Kristin, Antony, and Liam, for all their loud cheering from the literary bleachers. You know how much I depend on your love and support, and on the wine and dinners you so often provide. Okay, mostly the wine. I'm sure I'll be expected to pay the tab from now on.

Gwen Banta
From Somewhere on Route 66

ABOUT THE AUTHOR

 Gwen Banta was born in Binghamton, New York, and was educated in Indianapolis, Indiana, where she received B.A. and M.S. degrees from Butler University. She is a member of Kappa Delta Pi International Honorary Society in Education. Gwen also received a language certification from The Defense Language Institute in Monterey, California.

The author has received numerous awards for her fiction, including the Opus Magnum Discovery Award for New Literature (Honorable Mention). She has also won awards in many writing competitions: Great Northwest Book Festival, Los Angeles Book Festival, Pacific Rim Book Festival, San Francisco Book Festival, and Great Southeast Book Festival.

Gwen has written several screenplays. Her screenplay, *Skies A Fallin'*, is currently under option to an independent producer. Awards for her screenplays include: Writer's Project Semi-finalist, as well as: Columbine International Screenwriting Competition Finalist, Ohio Film Festival Semi-Finalist, and People's Pilot Semi-Finalist.

The stage play, *The Fly Strip*, based on *The Remarkable Journey of Weed Clapper* and co-written by Richard Kuhlman, is currently scheduled for publication

An award-winning actress of stage, screen, and television, Gwen is a member of SAG-AFTRA and Actors' Equity Association. She is a supporter of Global Green International, Project Angel Food, The Elizabeth Glaser Pediatric Aids Foundation, and St. Jude Children's Research Hospital. She resides in Los Angeles with her dog, Buddy, who is a major fan of her books... as long as there is food involved.

The Remarkable Journey Of Weed Clapper
ISBN: 978-4-86745-232-5
Mass Market

Published by
Next Chapter
1-60-20 Minami-Otsuka
170-0005 Toshima-Ku, Tokyo
+818035793528

3rd May 2021